The Baron of Clayhill

JOHN W. HUFFMAN

authorHOUSE®

AuthorHouse™
1663 Liberty Drive
Bloomington, IN 47403
www.authorhouse.com
Phone: 1-800-839-8640

This book is a work of fiction. People, places, events, and situations are the product of the author's imagination. Any resemblance to actual persons, living or dead, or historical events, is purely coincidental.

First published by AuthorHouse 10/23/2009

ISBN: 978-1-4490-3140-4 (e)
ISBN: 978-1-4490-3139-8 (sc)
ISBN: 978-1-4490-3138-1 (hc)

Library of Congress Control Number: 2009910001

Printed in the United States of America
Bloomington, Indiana

This book is printed on acid-free paper.

ACKNOWLEDGMENTS

My deepest gratitude to my devoted and hard working reader's circle, Jerry Neely, Judy Melson, Eleanor Deierlein, Tina Deierlein, Leonard Jordan and Susan Scoggins for their invaluable suggestions and feedback.

I would also like to thank my dear friend and fellow author Jennifer Patrick for her meticulous editing and constant encouragement, and Pat Coate for her precise proofing.

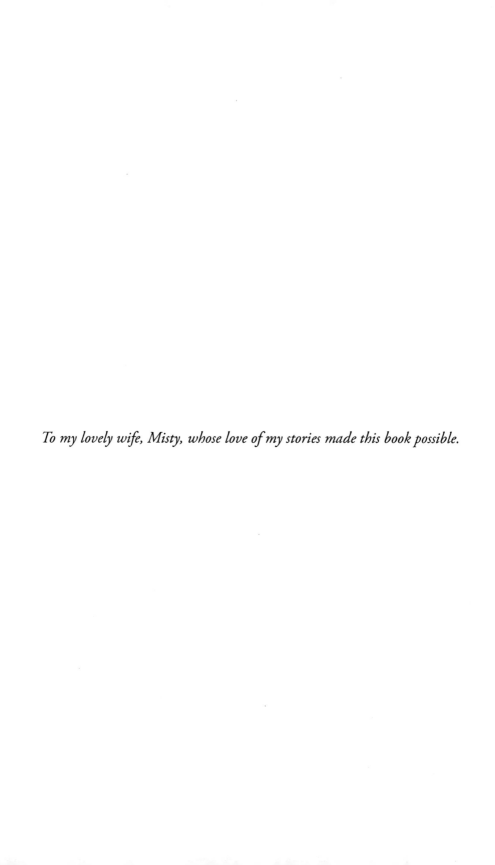

To my lovely wife, Misty, whose love of my stories made this book possible.

ONE

I never expected to return to this Godless void. The utter desolation of my plight on that previous occasion set me on a spiraling journey I never intended to take. Though love led me back to a plateau of eternal promise for a brief interval, I fear the price paid was my very soul. I've been stranded in this emotionally barren desert since, hidden away in this darkened room for endless months in a cocoon of intolerable pain while they rebuilt my wretched body. Now that their task is finished, I'm certain their tireless efforts are wasted, for it matters not what they crafted from my flesh with their magical scalpels and seamless sutures since mere surgical procedures alone are incapable of healing the vacuum of my depleted spiritual essence.

Today I must leave this hellish safe haven. I must rise above my callous fate by some incalculable means and strive to find my core persona again. I don't know where to begin my search for the path back … perhaps at the very beginning of the odyssey some two years distant from my current grievous dilemma.

I was an aged twenty years at the time, certain I had just experienced the worst humanity could offer, never imagining the true injustice fate could render …

* * *

"Paul!" a shrill, muffled voice jerked me into semiconsciousness. *"Paul, honey? Are you alright in there?"*

The hammering on the door grated on my nerves as I struggled out of the receding darkness billowing with orange-yellow explosions amid cries of wavering bodies locked in mortal combat. I breathed deeply to slow my pounding heart as my wits stabilized, relieved to find the images were only another bad dream. A flashback, the shrinks called it. A true experience lurking in my subconscious waiting to spring out at me without warning to drag me back into the living hell I had recently escaped from—or at least partially escaped from.

"*Paul?*"

I grimaced. "What do you want, Momma?"

"*Paul ... you were yelling ...*"

"I'm fine, Momma." Thankfully, the agonizing images came at me less often now, but were still as intense as ever when they did arise.

"*Are you sure, darling?*"

I sighed. "*Yes*, I'm *sure*, Momma!"

"*Breakfast is almost ready, dear.*"

I sensed her hesitation at the door before she turned back to the kitchen. She was almost a stranger to me now. Since my arrival the evening before I felt as if I were walking a tightrope, finding little to say and exhibiting even less patience when near her.

"*I'm setting the table now.*"

I lay in the tangled sheets searching for the energy to rise, smelling bacon frying and coffee perking as sunlight streamed through small gaps in the curtain-drawn window promising a hot, clear July day. I tried to adjust to the strange sensation of being here as I took in the once-familiar surroundings of the room, where I knew every item on the walls and shelves by heart, each a memento of my childhood lovingly preserved for the two years I had been gone. I studied my Most Valuable Player football trophy from the State Championship game, my first-baseman's glove lying on a shelf, my football jersey hanging in a glass case bordered by framed newspaper clippings boasting of past victories. A plethora of photos on the wall depicted me and my teammates throughout high school, some smiling, some with grim game-faces, eyes filled with youthful resolve. I rolled onto my side and picked up the picture on the nightstand of Linda, Allen, and me with our arms thrown around each other in joyful glee as we mugged for the camera. My mother had put it in the drawer beside my bed before my return. For no particular reason I could fully grasp, I had pulled it out and set it back in its former place. I fought the familiar deep quiver of loss as I studied the three of us together—my high school sweetheart, my best friend, and me.

I'd received Linda's tearful letter of apology breaking off our engagement near the end of my tour on a rain-swept day deep in triple-canopy jungle thousands of miles away. A short week later I learned from my mother that Linda and Allen had married. At the time I took their photographs out of my wallet and tore them to shreds, certain I was the biggest fool who ever lived.

I had anticipated returning here almost every day I was away, where everyone knew everybody in this slumbering lumber community of three thousand located in the great piney woods of East Texas. I now sensed there was nothing here for me. Most of my former friends were married, and a good number of them had kids. They had changed from freewheeling high school chums to young adults with mortgages, car payments, and dead-end jobs in the local sawmill. I didn't fit in anymore. Worse, I no longer wanted to fit in. I had seen a world they didn't know existed and fought in a war that was ripping our country apart while they, for the most part, ignored it. I could never go back to the naivete I possessed when I received my draft notice. A small part of me hated that, but a larger part was relieved that I had escaped their dismal fate.

I had undergone a dramatic change in my mindset since my induction into the Army, which I so eagerly anticipated with such patriotic pride on that faraway day when my country called. I never doubted it was my moral obligation to protect and defend our great nation. I also recognized it as a noble opportunity to escape the clutches of my diminutive hometown. An occasion to see the world, a chance to quench my insatiable thirst for adventure before settling down to the routine rat race of marriage, slaving long hours for inadequate pay, and raising a parcel of obligatory kids, which had been my overt fate upon graduating from high school.

When I entered the Army, I volunteered for the paratroopers, partly because they received almost twice the meager regular army wages, but mostly because I met a group of them en-route to my basic training station who displayed a swaggering sense of pride and passionate *esprit de corps* that set them far above the other, ordinary soldiers around them. I was always devoutly committed to being far better than average.

Near the end of my six months of grueling airborne training, our president announced he was committing troops to Southeast Asia to stop the communist infiltration of some half-baked nation called South Vietnam. From a global map, I determined the place was located due south of China and only slightly larger than some of our more moderate Texas ranches. No big deal. My foremost task at the time was convincing Linda to postpone our pending wedding until I returned.

I recalled my comrades on that long-ago day with dissolute sadness. We were an idealistic group of young warriors who answered that initial war toxin and flew into that besieged little land to dispose of a few pesky commies. Our enthusiasm diminished rapidly when we encountered a treacherous foe in a green jungle hell using tactics we were ill equipped for and poorly trained to face. We fought an opponent steeped in guerrilla warfare that we could not comprehend, an adversary who had fought for hundreds of years for causes that we could not understand. We chased a rival who knew and used every inch of the terrain that we more often than not found confusing and intimidating. We faced a brutal, cunning antagonist who employed every psychological ploy and physically incapacitating weapon known to man in a merciless, savage attempt to expel us from that pathetic little patch of mud and tangled foliage. We found as conventional soldiers we were vulnerable and naïve. We discovered as a nation we were not invincible. We learned as a country we were anything but united. We sowed only heartbreak and sorrow in that sad little land amongst those unfortunate people, and ultimately reaped a just harvest of bitter despair. I slowly slipped into a dark abyss during my tour as my comrades around me fell to both death and maiming injuries while the dissenters back home marched in protest and accused us of being war-mongering baby killers.

I placed the photograph back on the nightstand, pulled on my pants, and headed for the door, pausing when I caught my reflection in the mirror above the dresser to study the ugly scar tissue on my right chest and the three smaller patches of crinkled, disfigured skin surrounding it. I had sustained a light flesh wound to my left shoulder and right side from a sniper in an impenetrable jungle when my mind was so fuzzy from the stifling heat I missed a potentially lethal danger signal. A few months later, I took pieces of shrapnel in my right shoulder and cheek from an incoming mortar round as I sat hunched under my poncho in a rice paddy daydreaming of home in the cold, body-numbing monsoon rain. With two weeks left on my tour before my scheduled rotation back to the real world, a new point man walked our platoon into an ambush. I didn't recall much of the battle because I took an AK-47 round in the right chest in the opening mêlée. Afterwards, I lay in critical condition in a hospital in Saigon for two weeks, where they removed half of my right lung before shipping me to a hospital in Japan for five months of convalescence to eradicate the lingering internal infections. There I slipped from a robust 165 well-balanced muscular pounds on my five-foot nine-inch frame all the way down to 130 scraggly pounds during my recovery.

During those months I lay in a long ward filled with other mutants of the war effort and played poker, which I found I had a flair for, and watched the acrimonious news from back home as the antiwar protesters held rallies, burned their draft cards, and took over their college facilities while my buddies back in Nam were still getting their asses shot off. It was the most despondent period of my life.

In my half-crippled, weakened state I grew cold and withdrawn, cranky and resentful, and developed a sterling bad attitude toward anyone in a position of authority. Due to my growing antisocial behavior, I was, under duress, enrolled in behavioral adjustment classes as part of my rehabilitation to correct my warped attitude and cynical outlook. I despised all of the love-thy-brother programs they immersed me in, but in due course faked it well enough for them to judge my numb mind and therapy-caged emotions sufficiently balanced to return to polite society. At long last they gave me a medical discharge from that ménage of broken bodies, sick minds, and lost souls and shipped me ... *home?*

I accepted the fact that I was now a physical and mental wreck filled with self-loathing and consumed with what the head-doctors termed severe depression and apathy. Frankly, I desperately wanted to give a damn again, about *anything*, but couldn't seem to find a cause that much mattered. Furthermore, I didn't have a clue what I wanted to do with the rest of my life—except to get the hell out of this damned place—and even at that I couldn't decide on where else I wanted to be. As far as I could tell, the only socially redeeming quality I had left was that my mother still loved me, and I even found that annoying because I couldn't for the life of me figure out why.

I turned back for my shirt and then hurried out to the table as my mother poured orange juice and placed a heaping plate of scrambled eggs before me.

"You're so thin," she murmured, lingering to kiss the top of my head as she massaged the thick blond tangle of my hair with her fingers.

I found being touched and fondled irritating these days, but resisted the urge to pull away from her as I forked a mouthful of eggs and picked up a crisp strip of bacon.

"I'm not used to sleeping this late," I mumbled to break the silence.

She hugged my head to her waist. "You need lots of rest. I've got a surprise for you."

I buttered a piece of toast. "What surprise?"

She hurried out of the kitchen to return with a picture frame in her hand, pausing at the end of the table to stare at it in reverence before turning the recessed casing with a glass cover for my inspection, revealing all my medals and campaign ribbons from Vietnam arranged into a colorful display on a blue velvet background.

I bit into my toast. "I'd just as soon you put them in the trash."

"Don't say that! They represent all the sacrifices you've made for our country—"

"I'd just as soon never see them again."

Her pleased countenance slipped to one of dismay, sending a sliver of remorse through me. She was always so proud of my every accomplishment, treasuring each achievement as something sacred and displaying the evidence in prominent locations throughout the house for all to see. The damned place resembled a shrine to me now. It was even more disconcerting given that I had once actually enjoyed being the epicenter of her universe.

She studied the decorations wistfully. "Your father was a hero, too."

I almost choked on my orange juice. In all of my twenty years and some-odd months, she had never mentioned my father except on the one instance I had asked about him. She replied tersely that he had died before I was born and appeared so distraught I never brought the subject up again.

I stared after her as she hurried from the kitchen with the display case, and then poked at my breakfast, my thoughts in turmoil. My father was a hero? I had on occasion been curious, but he had never been a part of my life, or even a large part of my conscious thoughts. He had always been some distant, faceless stranger. There was not even a photograph of him in the house. I had a sudden, overwhelming desire to know more of him.

When my mother returned to busy herself with the breakfast dishes, I rose and picked up my plate. "Tell me about my father."

She paused, her back to me. "He died before you were born. I told you that."

"You told me that when I was eight years old, but you've never told me anything else about him."

"It would serve no purpose, Paul."

"How did he die?"

"Those were ... troubling times. Please, I'd rather not talk about it."

"How was he a hero?"

She fled from the kitchen, leaving the dishes in the sink.

* * *

I entered the Ford dealership showroom, where Charles Richardson, the owner's son and an old teammate from high school, hurried to greet me.

"Paul!" he thundered, towering over me eyeing my slim, emaciated frame, his gaze lingering on the slash on my cheek as he shook my hand. "I heard you were back! How you doing, old buddy? They say you got your ass shot off over there, but you don't look any worse for the wear and tear except for that scratch on your face that makes you look like a pirate!"

"I'm fine, Charlie, nothing serious. The little shits couldn't shoot straight worth a damn. How's the shoulder?" A former middle linebacker in high school, he'd tackled a bridge abutment in the drunken celebration following our state championship game to demonstrate how he had sacked the opposing quarterback, dislocating his shoulder and tearing some ligaments in the process, which he was now milking through a 4F classification to beat the draft.

He flapped his arm in a listless, exaggerated fashion and laughed as his eyes shifted in embarrassment. "Hell, I'm still near crippled! Hey, old buddy, sorry to hear about Linda and Allen. I know you had to take it hard. I heard you were lying in a hospital all shot up when you got her 'Dear John' letter."

I masked my annoyance with a wink. "Between you and me, I was in Saigon shacked up with a whore at the time. Look, I'm here to buy a new Mustang, and I don't want your crooked old daddy to make a dime off me. What've you got in stock that you can help me steal?"

"Paul Henry! What a pleasure!" Charles Senior's tall, broad form strode purposefully toward us. "Good to see you back home. You done us proud over there, son! Done us proud!"

I shook hands. "Thanks, Mr. Richardson, it's good to be back."

Charles Junior nudged his father. "Careful, Pop, he's trying to steal one of your Mustangs."

Charles Senior beamed. "Well, by God, he can have anything on the lot he wants at invoice price! I guarantee it! Hell, he's a bona fide hero! Not to mention the best damned quarterback we've ever had! I'd be proud to have him driving one of our cars around. It'll be good advertisement for us."

Charles Junior's eyes narrowed. "Say, why don't I show him that new Shelby Cobra GT 500 KR we just got in? It's the only car we've got that's good enough for him!"

Charles Senior's smile thinned. "At invoice? That's a special edition!"

"You *said* anything we had in inventory, Dad."

Charles Senior paled. "Bring him back to my office when he's made his selection."

Charles Junior smiled smugly and threw his arm around my shoulder as his father stalked off. "I ordered that car for me, Paul, but the asshole wouldn't let me have it when it came in. He won't sleep for a week over this. Come this way, my man, I'm going to show you the most beautiful machine you've ever seen. It's all brawn and muscle with 335 bad-assed horses that nothing else in the country can touch. A masterpiece of engineering and design perfection! If you can't get laid in this beast, there's no hope for you whatsoever!"

* * *

I drove my new Shelby GT out of the dealership an hour later with the King Cobra emblems inset in the gleaming silver-blue paint job looking deadly sinful. The admiring glances confirmed it was the sexiest car in the world and worth every cent of my poker winnings from the hospital and half my Army savings, even at invoice price.

I drove around town listlessly looking for something I feared no longer existed. At noon I pulled into the parking lot of the Forest Hill restaurant for lunch hoping to find a familiar face. Instead, I found Linda and Allen sitting in a booth. I'd given no thought to what I would do when I saw them again. I stood frozen in the doorway dismally cognizant of the fact that the betrayal of my girl with my best friend while I was off in a war zone still rankled. Before I could escape, Linda's eyes met mine and she stiffened. Allen stood slowly, anxiety marring his features, plainly unsure as to whether or how to greet me.

I turned to the door, as unsure as he.

"Paul?"

I turned back as he approached.

His eyes flickered over the rakish scar on my right cheek. "Paul … it's good to see you again …"

I fixed him with a hard stare. "Kiss my ass, you son of a bitch."

He face reddened. "I – *we* …"

I turned to the door, my calloused psyche deepening with anger.

"*Paul, wait!*" Linda slid out of the booth and hurried to us. "It's not all Allen's fault. You were gone so long and … and I wasn't as strong as I thought I was …"

I stared at her bulging midsection in shock, her words lost to me as the pent-up hostility seeped out. "Congratulations," I grated as I turned and pushed through the door.

* * *

Still hungry, I pulled into the Dairy Queen on the outskirts of town and revved up the Cobra jet engine to allow the mammoth Holley four-barrel carburetor to breathe before shutting it down, enjoying the throaty roar of the menacing power plant stuffed under the hood and every eye in the place staring at me with envy. I rolled down the window as a lissome, curly-haired blonde carhop hurried up ogling the Cobra.

Her come-hither honey-brown eyes met mine boldly. "Hi! I know you. You're Paul Henry, ain't you? Remember me, Tonia? Everybody's talking about you being back home now and about all the medals you won over there in *Vit-Num*. This sure is a pretty car you got here. You ought to give me a ride in it."

I checked out her long, golden-hued legs extending below her shorts and halter-top as she preened. In a couple of years she would be prime-time, but right now all I saw was jailbait.

I smiled engagingly. "Baby doll, I'd get in a heap of trouble hauling around something as young and pretty as you are."

Her lips pooched out in a sexy pout. "I'll be sixteen in five more months."

I sighed in mock disappointment. "Better give me a call on your birthday, sweetie. Right now, I'd like a strawberry malt and cheeseburger, all the way, please."

"Party pooper," she cast over her shoulder as she sulked off to place my order.

As I finished my cheeseburger, an old brown Pontiac pulled in beside me and two girls got out and strolled around the Cobra admiringly. I vaguely recalled they had been two years behind me in high school. The short, well-built blonde was something of a flirtatious tease back then, and the slim brunette was so pretty she'd made cheerleader for our varsity team in spite of her youth. The blonde propped her elbows against the top of my car and leaned down to peer in at me, ensuring her ample bodice was sufficiently displayed for my viewing pleasure.

"Hi, Paul, long time no see. Remember me? Barbara McDougal?"

I wiped my lips with a napkin. "Weren't you a sophomore when I graduated?"

"You *do* remember. How are you?"

"I'm fine. And you?"

"Well, I'm just all footloose and fancy-free these days, honey. I heard Linda took up with Allen while you was gone and got herself knocked up."

I appraised her breasts boldly to mask my irritation. "They're a great pair, aren't they?"

Barbara giggled as she rolled her shoulders back and thrust her twin peaks out. "I'm glad you think so."

The slim brunette peered around Barbara with shy, liquid brown eyes. "Hi, Paul! Do you remember me? Elaine Duckworth?"

"Weren't you a cheerleader back then?"

Barbara stood back to admire the dual white racing stripes and hood scoops on the Cobra, blocking my view of Elaine. "This sure is an awesome car. How about a quick spin in it?"

I shrugged. "Sure. Hop in."

She hurried around to the passenger side, slid in, and ran her hands over the dashboard and leather seats as I motioned for the little carhop to come get the window tray.

Barbara leaned across the console to stare up at Elaine, ensuring her torso rubbed against my arm. "I'll catch up with you later, girl!"

"Where to?" I asked as I backed out leaving Elaine and the carhop staring after us.

"It's so hot a cool dip would be nice," she suggested.

I had a mental image of the ugly scars on my body. "I'm not much into swimming these days."

"Don't be a spoilsport," she pressed, pouting.

To hell with the damned scars. "I'll need to buy a bathing suit on the way. Do you have yours with you?"

She eased into a seductive grin. "We don't need one if there ain't nobody else around, do we?"

When we reached Rocky Fjord there was nobody else around.

* * *

"Paul? Your breakfast is getting cold! This is the third time I've called you."

"Coming!" I groused as I reluctantly rolled out of bed and pulled on my pants and shirt.

"You were out late last night," my mother accused as she slid a plate before me and sat down across from me. "I waited up until after midnight."

I buttered a biscuit. "Don't wait up for me; I'm a big boy now."

"If you would let me know when to expect you home ..."

I paused. "Momma, I've been on my own and accountable only to myself for two years now."

"I just worry when I don't know where you are or when you'll be home."

"I don't always know where I'm going or when I'll be back."

She fidgeted. "Have you made any plans ... such as college or attending a trade school?"

"For now I plan to take things easy and see where the wind blows me."

"You should take advantage of your benefits under the G.I. bill ..."

"I *should* do a lot of things, Momma, but the fact is I *honestly* don't know what the hell I *want* to do just yet, okay?" I sighed when pain flickered in her eyes. "Look, I'll find a place of my own soon."

She twisted her napkin. "You've got a good home right here."

"I'd drive you crazy in no time, Momma, and you're already driving me crazy. I need my own space."

She blinked back her disappointment. "Was your new car expensive?"

"Charlie Richardson and his dad gave me a good deal on it."

"Your Aunt Kathy said she saw you driving up the North Highway with a girl."

I flinched. Aunt Kathy really wasn't my aunt at all. But she thought she was—and more. I had never known a time when my mother's best friend, aka my childhood nemesis, wasn't around. The two were a tag team when it came to raising me. While my mother was easy prey to my subtle childhood deceptions, Aunt Kathy was narrow-eyed, sharp-tongued, and could read me like a book. Large to the point of being obese, prim to the point of being taciturn, and proper to the point of being inflexible, with an irritating sixth sense for misinformation, she was a devout pessimist when it came to my contrived cover stories and half-truths. She would fix me with a disbelieving stare as I spun my tall tales and then pounce on the slightest inconsistencies, unraveling the threads of dishonesty with gusto and exposing them as pure fantasy. She also had quick hands and could thump an ear faster than a rattlesnake could strike, leaving me half deaf and stinging with remorseful pain. I suppose I loved her as one would a great-aunt who viewed it as her sacred mission in life to dispense necessary discipline to a wayward adolescent suffering under an overabundance of love administered by a widowed mother to an only child. But mostly I feared her and her intuition like the plague and thus attempted to avoid her at all costs when I had something to hide, which was almost always.

"Was that you, Paul? With a girl?"

There was a downside to having the flashiest car in town. "Yes, Momma."

"Who was she?"

"Just a friend."

Why I allowed myself to get involved with Barbara in the first place escaped me. She became insatiably tiresome as the night wore on. My standards had dropped considerably while in Vietnam.

"Kathy said she looked like that young McDougal girl. The one that has such a bad reputation? Paul, I hope you know what …"

"Tell me about my father, Momma." I'd learned in the Army that the best defense was a damned good offense.

She flushed. "Paul, I told you—"

When you've got the enemy off balance, press home the attack. "No, Momma, you haven't actually ever told me anything about him."

"You've never been curious about him before."

"How did he die?"

"It's … very difficult to talk about him. There are so many things …" She began clearing the table in nervous jerks. When she reached for my plate, I gripped it tightly, fixing her with a steely stare.

She froze, her eyes pleading. "Paul, please wait another time for this."

"I've waited more than twenty years. I want to know about him now."

She sank down onto her chair. "Talking about the Henrys is … distressing …"

A deep unease settled over me. "What about the Henrys? What's wrong with us? Do we have bad genes? Am I prone to epilepsy fits or something?" My blood ran cold when she lowered her head and began weeping. "Is it something even worse than that?"

She wiped at her eyes with a napkin. "Paul … your father … committed suicide. I was so distraught … you were born on the same day he …"

I sat immobile. On the one hand, I wanted to laugh like hell because I didn't have epilepsy or something. On the other, the knowledge that my father had killed himself at a young age on the day I was born sent chills racing through me.

"Was he depressed or something? Was he like, I don't know … sick? I mean, was he … *crazy* or something?"

She drew a deep, steadying breath. "I visited him just before it happened. I hardly got back home before the sheriff came to my door to tell me he had hung himself in his cell."

I stared at her, struck dumb. "My father was in *jail* when he *hung* himself? Why?"

"He got into a fight with J. R. and got arrested."

"Who is J. R.?"

"James Robert Henry, one of his distant cousins from Arkansas. There was bad blood between them."

The phone rang, and she hurried to answer it. "Hello? May I tell him who is calling, please?" She turned to me with thin lips. "Paul, it's Barbara McDougal."

I turned my back to her as she began clearing the table. "Hello?"

"Paul, you promised to call me!"

"It's still early yet."

"Did you have a good time with me last night?"

"Uh, sure …"

"I'll show you an even better time today. Come pick me up."

No way, José! "Uh, I've got to run a few errands for Momma—"

"Well hurry up then. I'll be waiting for you. And, Paul … I won't be wearing any panties." She giggled as the line went dead.

Momma turned to me as I hung up. "Paul, we need to talk about this McDougal girl …"

When an attack fails and you're faced with a determined counterattack, fall back and regroup. "Momma, I've got to go out for a while," I called as I rushed to my room. "We'll finish this discussion later, okay?"

"*Paul!*"

After I showered and dressed, I tiptoed out the front door before she had a chance to pin me down to any specifics concerning the McDougal girl, my mind still preoccupied with the gruesome image of my father hanging in some squalid jail cell.

TWO

I drove leisurely around town with no particular destination in mind or real desire to spend another day with Barbara, even without panties, though I freely admit I was wavering on this issue somewhat since there was little else to distract me. I glanced at the rearview mirror to find Elaine in her brown Pontiac behind me and impulsively waved as I swerved into the Piggly Wiggly parking lot.

She parked beside me and hurried over to the window on the passenger side. "Hi, Paul, what you doing?"

"Actually, I was cruising around looking for you, doll. Hop in, let's take a spin."

I appraised her sultry good looks and slim, tanned legs protruding from her shorts as she opened the door and slid in, thinking she had definitely evolved into a package that would turn a guy's head while I was away.

"I assumed you would be with Barbara."

I backed out, annoyed. "So why hasn't some lucky chap put his brand on you yet?"

"The right one hasn't come along. Barbara said you kept her out almost all night. She seems quite taken with you."

Clingy women turned me off, especially ones with a big mouth. "I can't imagine why."

She giggled. "She said you knew all kinds of Chinese love-making tricks."

I glanced at her. I'd only met Vietnamese whores overseas, and the only trick I'd learned from them was how fast they could separate me from my money. Still, if she was so overly curious about this Chinese thing, maybe I could play off it.

"Did she mention how many different ways there were?"

"Different ways for what?"

"Chinese lovemaking …"

She flushed. "Well … no …"

"One hundred and one, total," I advised with authority, figuring it was as good a guess as any, as long as I didn't have to pretend to know them all.

She turned her back to the door to face me as I drove, curling one leg under her in a casual, alluring fashion. "Do you remember when you won the state championship for us? At halftime I was the cheerleader who held your hand all the way to the locker room. Sheryl was on the other side holding your other hand as we led the whole team off the field. I've got a picture of it in my scrapbook."

"Yeah, I remember that," I lied, recalling only that there were so many people jumbled around us it was a mass of confusion. We were leading 14–10 at the time when nobody had given us a snowball's chance in hell of winning against Vidor, and everyone was in a near state of delirium, beginning to hope that we could actually pull off an upset victory. I jerked my thoughts back to the prospects at hand. "Do you want to go swimming?"

"Swimming?"

"It's so hot a cool dip would be nice, unless you have other plans?" It sounded better than riding around by myself—or spending the day with Barbara McDougal. Besides, Elaine had the longest, smoothest legs I'd ever seen and a certain element of class about her that I found appealing. I didn't dare pass up the opportunity.

She hesitated. "Sure, that would be nice."

"I need to buy a bathing suit on the way." I waited for her to insist we didn't need one, certain I could fake the Chinese thing.

She beamed. "Okay, let's go buy you a bathing suit then. Mine's in my car."

My heart sank. When we arrived at Rocky Fjord, it sank even lower when we found the popular swimming hole chock-full of families out trying to beat the weekend heat. I braced myself when Elaine's eyes widened as she took in my mottled torso after I stepped out of the bushes in my new bathing trunks, and then softened compassionately, which didn't appeal to me either, but what was, was.

"Do my scars bother you?"

"I … didn't realize you had been hurt so badly …" She hooked her arm in mine and led me to the swimming hole.

After a leisurely afternoon of splashing in the cool water and lying in the sun, I led her upstream for a ways in late afternoon and pinned her against a tree with my arms braced on each side of her.

"I feel a little guilty about all this, Paul," she whispered as I leaned in to her.

"Guilty about what?" I whispered against her warm lips.

"Barbara called earlier this morning and said you were picking her up later. I feel sort of morally wrong being here with you like this …"

"Like I said, I was driving around looking for you." Half lies count equally as half truths, I assuaged my irksome conscience as I devoured her ripe lips and cupped one of her small breasts in my palm.

She slid under my arms with a startled gasp. "Paul, there's people everywhere!"

"We can go further upstream," I offered helpfully.

"And I don't *really* believe you were out looking for me!" She took my hand and led me back to the main swimming hole.

* * *

I dropped the uninitiated-in-the-art-of-Chinese-lovemaking Elaine back at her car late that evening and headed for the Dairy Queen for a burger to rekindle my depleted morale.

A petite brunette glided up to my window admiring the Cobra. "Hi, I'm Gail. I heard you was back in town. Tonia said you was gonna give her a ride in your new car. I wouldn't mind it if you gave me a ride in it, too."

"I just might do that someday, Gail," I mumbled, my thoughts still on the elusive Elaine.

"I was at the game when you won the state championship for us. You had blood on your face afterward. I was standing near you when they took the picture they put in the newspaper. You know, the one with the scoreboard in the background and you holding your helmet over your head. You could see my face clear as day."

"I think we were all a little bloody afterwards. Those Vidor dudes were tough. You know, I think I *do* remember you." It was a listless effort on my part, but my mind was on a cheeseburger and strawberry malt. I needed nourishment after the previous night with Barbara and the long, drawn-out, fruitless afternoon in the sun with Elaine.

"Do you really remember me, or are you just saying that? When they lifted you up on their shoulders, I almost got trampled because everybody was shoving and pushing to get near you. Did you know that when you threw that last touchdown my mother started jumping up and down and screaming and fell down in between the bleachers?"

"I hope she didn't hurt herself."

"Oh, she didn't. She was just mad at Daddy because he was jumping around and yelling so much himself he didn't even offer to help her up."

I laughed. "We were all yelling and jumping around when Bobby made that fantastic catch with time running out. He's the one who really won the game for us."

She smiled coyly. "I heard about Linda and Allen. So have you found yourself another steady girl yet?"

"I'm … reviewing my options …"

"All us girls are wondering what we've gotta do to get your attention."

My smile froze as warning bells jangled. *First off, you've got to be street-legal.* I flashed my best flirtatious leer. "You're what, about sixteen? As pretty as you are, I'd be tempted to wait around for you, but I'm sure you've got dozens of guys standing in line."

"I just broke up with my boyfriend. All he ever wanted us to do was get in the backseat of his mother's car."

"You can get in trouble back there if you're not careful."

"I know all about the birds and bees, and besides, I'm on the pill. So how about that ride?"

"I don't think your parents would approve."

"What they don't know won't hurt them."

"I think we'd better wait a few more birthdays."

"That's like, forever."

"I'll try to make it worth the wait. In the meantime, I'll have—"

"A cheeseburger and strawberry malt, right? Tonia told me that was your favorite. All the way, right?" She batted her lashes. "I heard you was an *all the way* kind of guy."

My ego loved this even if she was a teenybopper. "You keep that in mind, Gail, and we'll see about that ride someday soon."

She smiled brazenly. "I know you're just kidding around with me, Paul Henry, but you don't have much of a backseat in this thing to crawl into anyway."

She sashayed off as I stared after her in amusement, finding it stimulating to be the most eligible bachelor around with the coolest car in town. The younger girls had definitely grown bolder while I was away. I'd heard about the sexual revolution sweeping the country. When I left, good girls generally *didn't*, but apparently the pill had set them free. Now it seemed that most girls *did*. It was somewhat intimidating up close. The passenger door opened as I sat admiring Gail's wiggle thinking unpure thoughts and Barbara slid onto the seat with her lips pooched out.

"I waited all day for you, Paul!"

My stomach sank. "Sorry, I got sidetracked."

"You can make it up to me tonight." She slid over and laid a lip-lock on me, thrusting her tongue halfway down my throat.

I pried her off. "Uh, I've already got another engagement tonight. I promised one of my old buddies we'd have a beer together."

"I like beer, too."

"It's kind of a guy thing, you know, to catch up on old times?"

Her eyes narrowed. "Are you putting me off? Stand him up like you did me. I can make things a lot more interesting for you than he can."

"Maybe we can get together tomorrow."

"*Maybe?*"

"I haven't talked to my mother since this morning. I promised her I'd take her to visit my father's grave. She hasn't been there in years." *Damn, I was smooth!*

She scowled. "Liar!"

"Now, why would I lie about visiting my father's grave, for Pete's sake? I'll try to call you tomorrow, okay?"

She snuggled in close to me. "We could go somewhere real quick like before you meet your friend. My panties have been in a wad all day from squirming around thinking about you."

Nymphomaniac flashed through my brain, which I admit aroused me on a basic level, but frankly, I didn't know if I had it in me with my mind still preoccupied with Elaine and those long, tanned legs. "I thought you weren't going to wear any panties."

"I didn't!" She grabbed my hand and thrust it up under her skirt. "See?"

I had it in me. "Okay, but afterward I've got to meet my friend …"

She slid across the console into my arms.

* * *

"*Paul!*" The knock on my door was insistent. "Paul! Are you in there?"

I pulled the pillow over my head. "Momma, I'm trying to sleep! I don't want any breakfast!"

"You've got a phone call. It's the third one this morning. A girl named Elaine. I think it's that Duckworth girl."

"Tell her I'll call her back later."

"You also got a call from a girl named Gail, and another from someone named Tonia. What's going on, Paul?"

Darned if I knew. "Never mind, I'm getting up." I pulled on my pants and hurried out to the hall to pick up the receiver lying on the table. "Hello?"

"*Good morning, Paul. I had a good time yesterday. Have you got any plans for today?*"

My immediate plan was that I damn sure wasn't giving any lessons in the art of Chinese lovemaking today: I hadn't gotten away from Barbara and her "quickie" until sometime after three this morning. "Uh, well, I …"

"Paul, where did you get those scratches on your back?" my mother gasped from behind me. "My goodness! I'll get some disinfectant!"

"*Paul?*" Elaine inquired as my mother rushed off down the hall. "*What scratches on your back?*"

21

"Uh, Elaine, I promised my mother I'd take her to visit my father's grave today. She hasn't been there in years and ..."

"Paul, I never asked you to do any such thing!" my mother intoned sharply as she slipped back up behind me.

I whirled around and raised my finger to my lips to shush her.

Her eyes widened as she saw the purple mass of crinkled skin on my upper torso. "Oh, my gracious!"

"*Paul?*" Elaine demanded. "*What's going on?*"

"Can I get back to you, Elaine?"

"Oh, my poor baby," my mother wailed as she hugged me. "When they said you were wounded ... I never imagined ..."

"It looks worse than it was, Momma. Here, don't cry now."

"*Paul? What's wrong with your mother?*"

"Elaine, I can't talk right now. Momma is upset. She just saw my scars for the first time."

"*Poor thing. I'll come right over!*"

"No!" The receiver went dead. "Elaine?"

I hung up and tried to peel my mother off. "*Shish*, Momma, *shish*, quit crying now. Look, they're all healed. See—I'm as good as new." I slapped my chest as the phone rang behind me and turned to snatch up the receiver.

"Hello?"

"*Hi, Paul, this is Gail. Your mother sounded real surprised this morning when I told her you were going to make me her daughter-in-law someday.*"

"What?"

"*I'm just kidding.*"

"Uh, Gail, you've caught me at a bad time. *Ouch*! Damn!"

"Be still, Paul!" my mother fussed as she scrubbed at the nail marks on my back with the alcohol-saturated cloth, spreading liquid fire as I squirmed and sucked in my breath. "And don't use coarse language."

"*I've got the three-to-nine shift today, Paul. Will you stop by to see me?*"

"Uh, sure thing. Catch you later, okay?"

"*Promise? Promise? Promise?*"

"*Ouch*! Easy, Momma, you're killing me! Yes, Elaine, I promise."

"*I'm not Elaine. I'm Gail.*"

"Oh, uh, I mean, Gail. Sorry. *Ouch*!"

"You triple-promised, so you better come by or I'll tell all your secrets."

"All my secrets?"

"My uncle told my Daddy last night that you spent all day at Rocky Fjord with Elaine while Barbara was going around town looking for you and telling everybody you're her guy now. I bet she'd be real mad if she knew you were two-timing her. You said you was gonna wait for me, remember?"

"Hey now, I never …"

"Bye, Paul, darling! See you later." The receiver went dead.

I replaced the phone in the cradle and stiffened as my mother applied iodine to the alcohol-cleansed scratches. The phone rang again and I snatched it up.

"Hello?"

"Hi, Paul, this is Tonia. Did you really tell Gail you would wait for her forever?"

"What?"

"You told me to call you on my birthday, remember? Why should I call you then when you promised Gail you would wait for her forever?"

"Tonia, I didn't … uh, look, I was just kidding around with her."

"Were you just kidding around with me too?"

"Look, Tonia, all I promised was to give you a ride when you turned sixteen, right?"

"Paul!" my mother exclaimed. "Is that a child you're talking to?"

"Look, Tonia, you've caught me at a bad time. I'll stop by later, okay?"

"Triple-damn-promise?"

"Uh, sure …"

"Say it then."

"I triple-damn-promise."

"Paul!" my mother chastised. "Don't use crude language around a child!"

"I gotta go now, Tonia." I hung up the phone. When it rang again almost immediately, I snatched it back up. "Tonia, I told you it's a bad time right now."

"Who's Tonia?" Barbara asked.

"Oh, hi, Barbara, Tonia's my aunt."

"You don't have an aunt named Tonia!" my mother scolded.

"Can I call you back, Barbara? You've caught me at a bad time."

"Is that the McDougal girl again?" my mother demanded.

"Come get me, lover! Let's spend the whole day naked in each other's arms!"

"No! I mean, I can't! I've got to carry Momma … somewhere."

"Well, it's time I met her anyway. I'll go with you. What time are you going to pick me up, lover boy?"

"I'll try to call you later! I've got to go now." I slammed the receiver down.

"Paul, what's going on with all these girls calling? You're not getting involved with *young girls*, are you? Or that *McDougal* girl either, I hope? Now Elaine Duckworth is from a good family and—"

"Momma, I've got to get out of town for a few days."

"Get out of town?"

"Where is my father buried?"

"In the Clayhill Cemetery. Why?"

"Let's take a small vacation and go visit his grave."

"Why do you want to visit his grave? Why do you need to get out of town? Why are all of these girls calling?"

"We'll talk on the way, Momma. Hurry now, Elaine's on her way over here."

"Why is she coming over here?"

I tugged at her arm. "I'll explain later. Let's go!"

She pulled back. "Paul, I can't just pick up and leave, and … and I'm not going to your father's grave!"

"Why not?"

"Because I … just can't …"

"Okay, I'll go alone then."

"Paul, please …"

I headed for my room. "If the phone rings again, tell whoever's calling I've left town and you don't know when I'll be back!"

* * *

I packed my few civilian clothes, tossed the suitcase in the trunk, waved at my troubled mother standing in the doorway with a bewildered look, and lurched out of the driveway. When I hit the North Highway and cleared the city traffic, I opened the Cobra up, which responded like a colt let out to pasture by leaping forward with a throaty roar. At 115 miles per hour and still climbing, I eased off the throttle and drifted back down to a serene 70 as Jasper vanished in the distance in my rearview mirror. I was cruising along enjoying the feel of freedom and open spaces until I blew by a police car sitting just inside the city limits sign of Pineland, which boasted a population of 940. I groaned when it roared out behind me with lights flashing and found a place to pull over to wait for the cruiser to coast in behind me. The cop got out with a clipboard in his hand, loosened the pistol in his holster, and eased up to the driver side of my Cobra.

"Hi, Officer," I greeted the short, stocky man in his mid-fifties wearing a cowboy hat, western boots, khaki pants, blue western shirt studded with white pearl buttons, and a shiny badge in the form of a star pinned to his chest just below a plastic name tag reading Deputy C. A. Johnston.

He surveyed my Cobra. "You in a hurry, boy?"

"No, Sir, Officer Johnston. I was daydreaming and didn't see the city limits sign until it was too late. I don't suppose you could see fit to just give me a warning, could you?"

"You was doing 65 in a 30. You don't have much respect for us, now do you, boy? Where you from?"

"Jasper. I'm just passing through on my way to Clayhill. I didn't mean any disrespect."

"Is this one of those fancy cars built to outrun us *po-lice*, boy?"

"I didn't buy it to outrun anybody."

"Since you're a city boy, you probably think we're just a bunch of hicks, don't you?"

I put on my best shit-eating grin. "I love Pineland, Sir. My grandmother lived here for almost twenty years before she died."

The officer tipped his hat back with his thumb. "Yeah? What was her name?"

"Me-maw Taylor. She lived just outside—"

"I know where she lived, boy. Do you think I'm stupid? I know everybody in this town. Been here my whole life."

"I didn't mean to imply ..."

"So you're kin to Mrs. Taylor?"

"She was my grandmother."

"Mighty fine woman. She'd be disappointed to know you don't respect the law."

"I *do* respect the law. I just wasn't paying attention and—"

"You gonna have to post bond or go to jail."

I swallowed. "Jail?"

"That's what I said, didn't I?"

"Is that really necessary, Officer?"

"I'm getting damned tired of having to repeat myself, boy. Are you angling to get yourself a resisting-arrest charge as well? Keep mouthing off and I'll add that to the list."

"The list? All I was doing was speeding. What other charges are there?"

"Reckless driving."

"I wasn't driving reckless!"

"I had to chase after you almost a mile and you ain't done nothing but back-talk me since I ran you down."

"Ran me down? I—"

"Shut up, boy. I done heard about all the mouth out of you I'm gonna listen to."

"Look, Officer Johnston, I admit I didn't see your speed sign, but I pulled over at the first spot I could find when I saw your lights flashing."

"You're being charged with speeding, reckless driving, and resisting arrest. How do you intend to plead to these charges?"

"I was speeding, but I wasn't driving reckless and I'm not resisting arrest."

"You are hereby fined ten dollars for the speeding charge. You'll need to post a ten-dollar bond for the reckless-driving charge and a fifteen-dollar bond for the resisting-arrest charge. If you fail to appear at your hearing, you'll be judged guilty and forfeit the posted bond. Do you understand me, boy?"

I almost swooned in relief. The bond money was as good as gone. There was no way I was coming back to this hick town to stand trial.

"I understand."

"Good. Are you prepared to post the bond now, or do you need to make arrangements? You're allowed one phone call."

"I'm prepared to post the bond now." I counted out thirty-five dollars from my wallet.

He wrote me a receipt. "You'll get a court appearance date in the mail. You're free to go now. Have a nice day."

I bit my tongue. "Much obliged."

I headed east toward Clayhill, paying close attention to my speed as Officer Johnston warily watched me depart before doing a U-turn and sprinting back to his speed trap. When I passed the city limits sign on the outskirts of town, I hit the throttle, playing with the curves on the old farm-to-market road enjoying the Cobra clinging to the asphalt as I swung into the turns at twice the posted speed limit anxious to get away from the little burg. Twenty minutes later a sign welcomed me to the city limits of Clayhill, and I eased off the throttle to drift into the tiny town claiming a population of 813 at a sedate 30 miles an hour.

I judged the municipality to be well on its way to extinction as I circled the central block square, which held a gray two-story courthouse with a smaller gray brick city jail perched on the corner. Dilapidated storefronts, most hosting sale or rental signs in their dirt-streaked empty display windows attesting to the sluggish economy of the area, surrounded this in an outer square. A cluster of battered old cars and beat-up pickup trucks were parked nose-in to the curb near the only visible people, a half-dozen elderly men playing dominoes on a cement table under a shade tree beside the old courthouse, whose every head lifted to stare at me as I drove by.

I turned onto the road leading to the Clayhill Cemetery and within two miles came to the graveyard. I parked in front of a small office just to the right of the entrance with the United States and Texas flags flying side by side. A plump, middle-aged woman with blue hair sitting behind a desk looked up as I entered.

"Good afternoon, Sir. May I assist you?"

"I hope so, Ma'am. Could you help me locate my father's grave?"

"I'll certainly try, Sir." She reached for a large, leather-bound registry book. "What is your father's name?"

"John Allison Henry. He died in November, 1947."

Her smile faded. "I see ..." She set the registry aside without consulting it. "John Allison Henry would be interred in the older family plot containing the founding members of the family located in the northeast corner."

I frowned. "There are two family plots? Where is the newer one located?"

"In the southwest corner." She pressed her lips together and fidgeted with her hair.

I turned to the door. "Thank you, Ma'am."

I drove to the back of the cemetery and parked next to a small, well-manicured area bordered by a black iron gated fence holding a collection of tombstones with fresh flowers placed at the base of each. I walked down the rows checking the names. At the end of the line, I found a small flat stone almost flush with the newly cut grass reading *John Allison Henry, 12 January 1922–14 November 1947*. I stared at the marble block wondering why my father hadn't been given a raised stone like all the others. Were they ashamed of him for committing suicide? I stood over the grave and waited for a reaction, an emotion of some sort, but only curiosity prevailed. Who was this man who ended his life on the day mine began? I walked back to the larger stones, closely inspecting the names and dates: *Robert Allison Henry, 10 July 1898–27 August 1946*, most likely my grandfather, and *James Allison Henry, 14 April 1875–29 May 1945*, probably my great-grandfather from the dates indicated. I thought it odd that all three had died within a year of each other, first my great-grandfather, then my grandfather, and then my father. Both elaborate white markers befitted influential members of the Henry family, which only heightened the mystery of why a flat stone marker adorned my father's grave. I walked around the other markers trying to match the names and dates to family members, picking out what I thought to be my great-grandmother and grandmother, but a child's grave baffled me.

I drove to the opposite end of the cemetery to a smaller, weed-infested parcel surrounded by a rusty iron fence decorated with iron baby angels and containing a single headstone. Knee-high grass grew wild in the plot, and stale artificial flowers adorned the small marble headstone with the inscription *Cathie Olivia Henry, 8 March 1917–16 June 1950, Loving wife of J. R. Henry.* So this was the wife of the man my father had gotten thrown into jail over before he committed suicide. But why was she buried way over here all by herself?

A gray Cadillac pulled up and a tall, distinguished gentleman with gray hair dressed in a dark suit got out and paused at the iron fence. "May I be of assistance to you, Sir?"

"Do you work here?"

"I'm Grady Farr, the owner and caretaker."

"I'm Paul Henry. I came to visit my father's grave."

"I believe your father would be located in the *other* family plot."

"Yes, I found his grave there. Why doesn't he have a headstone like the others?"

Mr. Farr pulled a handkerchief from his pocket and mopped at his forehead. "Sir, no one ever ordered a headstone for his grave."

I turned to stare at the weed-infested grave in the new Henry plot. "Why is this area so run-down and the other one so well maintained?"

Mr. Farr mopped at his brow again. "The two family plots are maintained privately, Sir."

"Why are there two Henry family plots on opposite ends of the cemetery? There seems to be plenty of space left in the old one."

"That is for the family to say, sir. Perhaps I could escort you back to your side?"

"*My* side? Isn't this woman my kin as much as the others?"

"Sir … it is rumored that the family is … estranged."

I walked through the sagging gate. "What are we *estranged* about?"

"That would not be appropriate for me to comment on, Sir."

"What does a marble headstone cost?"

Mr. Farr brightened. "We have several different prices, depending on size and inscription. If you would accompany me to my office, I would be glad to show you our catalog."

Mr. Farr seated me at a conference table while his blue-haired assistant, Matilda, produced a catalog. After some deliberation, I selected a moderate white marble headstone somewhat smaller than the large ones over my great-grandfather's and grandfather's graves in the old Henry plot. After hesitant analysis, I ordered the dedication to read *John Allison Henry, 12 January 1922–14 November 1947, Father of a son unknown to him.* The cost was just short of four hundred dollars. Mr. Farr assured me he could have it inscribed and installed within two days.

I started for the door and paused. "How much would it cost to get the new Henry plot spruced up? You know, grass cut, perhaps the fence straightened and painted as well?"

Mr. Farr and Matilda exchanged stunned glances. "Sir, it would run around twenty dollars. It's been neglected for some years now and ..."

I reached for my wallet. "Please see to that as well, Mr. Farr. Have it coincide with the placing of my father's headstone, if you will."

"I'll ... see to it, Mr. Henry. Thank you, Sir. It's ... been a pleasure."

I walked out somewhat perturbed by the neglect of the new family plot and the seeming unease of Mr. Farr and Matilda with my having it cleaned up.

THREE

I drove back to Clayhill and circled the courthouse square where the old men were still playing dominoes at the bench under the shade tree. They paused to watch as I nosed the Cobra against the curb half a block from the police station and sauntered into the drugstore to grab a bite of lunch, somewhat amused at being the sole attraction in this one-horse town.

I ambled along to an antiquated soda counter and short-order grill situated on the left side of the prescription department, which was located on the right side separated by rows of medical staples. A striking young lady behind the counter watched me expectantly as I slid onto one of the old-fashioned swivel stools brazenly appraising her startling green eyes, short, bob-style silky black hair, athletically slim figure with moderate breasts, and proud, erect stance.

"Hi, Gorgeous. Do you serve burgers here?"

Her faint, alluring scent teased my senses in a giddy surge as she stepped forward cautiously. "That's a beautiful car. What kind is it?"

I attempted to ignore the charge of whimsical enchantment her sensuous voice sent rippling through me in a heady wave. "It's not nearly as beautiful as you are. It's a Shelby Cobra, Limited Edition."

Her lips twitched in wary amusement. "I've never seen anything like it before. It sure turns people's heads."

"And you sure turn mine." I found her frank, censorious appraisal of me cheeky but appealing, as I focused on her lips, gauging the taste of their rich ripeness before shifting back to her remarkable eyes, more than willing to liven up the day with a little innocent flirtation. "How big is your boyfriend?"

"My boyfriend?"

"I'm gauging the risk of offering you a spin in it."

"Are you coming on to me?"

"Definitely." I held out my hand. "I'm Paul Henry."

A swift chill pass through her as she jerked her hand back just short of taking mine. "What can I get you, Sir?"

"*Ouch!*" I shook my hand as if burned. "Have they posted my picture in the post office or something?"

"I haven't seen you around here before."

"I didn't catch your name …"

"Eva … Eva Marie Sherrill."

"Well, Eva-Eva Marie Sherrill, that could be because I've never been here before."

"Are you kin to the Henrys that live here?"

"Apparently so, but I've never met any of them. I came here to visit my father's grave."

Her features softened. "Oh, you're one of the *other* Henrys."

That sounded like a slight plus for whatever reason. "My mother was originally from here as well, but her parents, the Taylors, moved to Pineland shortly before I was born, and she and I moved to Jasper."

"I don't know the Taylors, but you'd probably do well to go on back to Jasper now that you've visited your father's grave."

I arched my eyebrows. "And why is that?"

"It's probably just best, is all."

I smiled, bemused. "Could I at least get a strawberry malt and a burger before you run me out of town, Eva-Eva Marie?"

Her eyes darkened. "Yes, if you'll stop making fun of my name."

As she turned to the grill to prepare the burger, a man in his early forties entered wearing brown cowboy boots, dark brown pants, a holstered revolver, a tan shirt with a sheriff's badge on the left breast pocket, and a brown cowboy hat.

He sat down on a stool a couple of spaces away. "Coffee, Eva Marie, when you get a minute." He swiveled to face me. "I understand you're Paul Henry and that you drive that car outside."

I turned to him. This was indeed a small town considering that outside of Eva Marie, I had introduced myself only to Mr. Farr and

Matilda at the graveyard. "I didn't catch your name, Sheriff, but I'm guilty on both counts. Is either one of them a crime here in Clayhill?"

"Pardon me; I'm Sheriff Tate." He waited for Eva Marie to set a cup before him and pour his coffee. "How long are you planning to visit with us, Mr. Henry?"

I swiveled back to the front. "That all depends on this pretty little lady behind the counter here, Sheriff. Is there a problem?"

Sheriff Tate studied me, his face impassive. "There might be. The old Henrys have pretty much left these parts. That's probably for the best, the way things are around here now."

I locked eyes with him in the mirror behind the counter. "I could care less about what's for the best or the way things are around here now, Sheriff."

"I don't cotton to trouble, Mr. Henry. If and when it comes, I tend to hold those behind it personally accountable. Do you get my drift?"

Anger swelled within me. "*If* and *when* trouble comes, Sheriff, please feel free to hold *those behind it* personally accountable. Do you get *my* drift?"

"Enjoy your stay, Mr. Henry." He placed fifteen cents on the counter beside his untouched coffee. "I recommend your visit with us be a short one. Good day."

I swiveled to his back as he walked away. "I'd like to visit your jail before I leave, Sheriff. Do you find that to be a problem for you as well?"

He turned to me. "For what purpose, Mr. Henry?"

"It's a personal matter."

"Drop by on your way out of town." He tipped the brim of his hat to Eva Marie and walked out.

Eva Marie placed my burger and malt on the counter.

"What was that all about?" I asked as I salted and peppered the burger.

She met my eyes. "Sheriff Tate is a good man, Mr. Henry. He meant you no disrespect, which is more consideration than you gave him."

"Call me Paul, Eva; *Mr. Henry* sounds funny. Sorry if I came across as a smart aleck; I've just had my fill of back-county sheriffs today. So ... how about that ride in my Cobra?"

"There could be trouble if you stay around these parts. You'd probably do best to go on back to Jasper."

I took a bite of my burger. *What was with the people in this place?* "Mmm, this is good. You and your sheriff are pretty free with your advice. Why could there be trouble?" This whole weird scene was becoming tedious, but she *was* one damn fine-looking girl.

She bit her lower lip indecisively. "You're from the wrong branch of the Henrys. Like Sheriff Tate said, your side has pretty much left these parts now."

"Why did they leave these parts?"

She lowered her eyes. "Some folks claim the new Henrys ran them off."

I stifled the growing tide of irritation as I wiped my lips with a napkin. "Well, for the record, I don't plan on *anybody* running *me* anywhere." I dug some change out of my pocket and placed the coins on the counter. "So what time do you get off work?"

She looked out at the Cobra reflectively. "We close at six."

* * *

I near waltzed to the corner with a jaunty step, my thoughts on the green-eyed beauty back in the drugstore, and crossed over to the jail. A sign above the door announced *Clayhill Police Department*. A brass plaque beside the door read *Bricks donated by James Allison Henry to the town of Clayhill circa 1905*. Interesting: my great-grandfather built this jail and my father hung himself in it. I entered to find Sheriff Tate sitting at a battered desk across the room reading a newspaper with his boots propped up on the corner facing a small window air conditioner rattling away on high speed.

He dropped his boots to the floor, swiveled around to face me, and laid his newspaper aside. "Mr. Henry?"

"Call me Paul, Sheriff. I'm too damned young to be a mister."

"How can I help you?"

"Twenty-something years ago my father killed himself in your jail here. I'd like to see where it happened."

He frowned. "Why?"

"I'm curious."

He came around the desk and opened the door on the right side of the room. I followed him inside to a large space divided by three ten-foot by ten-foot empty square cells with steel bars running floor to ceiling. A narrow passageway led to the left, fronting the cells.

"Your father was in cell number three, the last one on the end there."

I walked down the narrow passageway, my footsteps echoing hollowly on the cement floor, and entered cell three through the open door. The left and rear walls were brick. The right and front walls consisted of iron bars. A single dirty window covered with wire grating, located high up on the rear brick wall, offered a modicum of weak outside light. A lightbulb covered with steel grating hung high overhead. There were no visible signs of heat or air conditioning, though the air was damp and cool. Two battered metal bunk beds stood one above the other against the rear wall holding thin cotton mattresses without sheets, pillows, or blankets. A stainless steel commode without a lid and a stainless steel sink stood beside the bunk beds. The place reeked of sweat and urine.

I stood in the center of the cell and turned in a circle as goose bumps fleshed out on my arms and my pulse increased tempo. "Were you the sheriff back then?"

Sheriff Tate leaned against the steel bars outside the cell. "I was a deputy. I'd been on the force about three months."

"How did he do it?"

He looked up to the corner formed by the brick wall and the steel bars. "He tore strips from the mattress and tied them next to the ceiling on that crossbar."

I stared up at the spot and tried to imagine my father hanging there. "Why did he do it, Sheriff?"

He shrugged. "Beats me. He got into a scuffle with one of his kinfolks over at the grain store. Sheriff Allston got there soon enough to head off anything serious and arrested him for disturbing the peace. At most he would have paid a small fine and been released. I've got a fresh pot of coffee back in the office."

I followed him back to his office and sat in a wooden chair in front of the desk. "Who found him?"

Sheriff Tate drew two cups of coffee from the pot and set one cup in front of me as he sank down in his chair behind the desk. "Sheriff Allston found him. I was out on patrol at the time. Helped cut him down afterwards. It never made sense to me."

"Did you know my father well?"

"I knew him well enough."

"What can you tell me about him?"

"We were about the same age, but the Henrys were too affluent for my poor upbringing, so we weren't pals or anything. I liked John. He always seemed to be a decent sort. He came home a war hero and something of a hellion, but I guess we all were back then since we'd just kicked Hitler's ass and the Japs too and were so full of ourselves. I knew your mother too. Every eligible male in the county was sweet on her before your father came back and swept her off her feet. How is Susan these days?"

"Mom's fine. What was the argument with my father and his kinfolk about?"

Sheriff Tate pursed his lips. "Well, it appears it didn't sit well when your grandfather died under peculiar circumstances while John was off to war and the family fortune, which consisted of just about everything in Clayhill, passed to J. R. shortly afterward."

"What was peculiar about my grandfather's death?"

Sheriff Tate shifted. "Shot in the chest in his home with a 10-gauge shotgun by an unknown assailant. That was before my time as a lawman."

"My grandfather was murdered?"

"I was in the Navy when it happened, so I don't know much about it, other than they never discovered who did it."

"So how did J. R. end up with the Henry fortune?"

"Your grandfather married Cathie Fields, who was much younger than him, a few years after your grandmother died. Shortly after his death, Cathie remarried J. R., who was about the same age as her. J. R. gained control of the estate through their marriage."

"So the disheveled grave in the new Henry plot belongs to my stepgrandmother, who remarried J. R. Interesting. How did she die?"

"The coroner's report said she died of a cerebral brain hemorrhage possibly as a result of her falling and hitting her head."

"So my grandfather remarried a younger woman and then was murdered by an unknown assailant. My stepgrandmother remarried J. R., one of my grandfather's distant cousins from Arkansas. My father returned from the war and found he no longer had an inheritance and committed suicide."

Sheriff Tate watched me with narrowed eyes. "That's the gist of it. Why are you so interested after twenty years?"

"I'm just curious about my father."

"Will you be leaving town now?"

"They said the tombstone for my father's grave would be ready in a couple of days. I guess I'll hang around until then. Have you got a good motel around here somewhere?"

"North side of town: the Pine View Inn. It's not much, but it's all we've got. Clean enough, I guess. I'll see what I can do to help get the headstone put in for you tomorrow."

"You folks sure have a way of making me feel welcome around here. Where's a good place to take a gorgeous girl out to dinner?"

His eyebrows arched. "Eva Marie?"

"She likes fancy cars."

Sheriff Tate frowned. "The only place open in the evening is Pearle's Grill. Eva Marie will know where it is. This is a small town, Paul. Proceed with caution so you don't stir up any unnecessary aggravation."

I stood. "I'll try real hard not to cause anyone any unnecessary aggravation, Sheriff."

"You do that," he replied to my back as I left.

* * *

I drove to the Pine View Inn, my thoughts on my father as I tried to visualize him hanging in the cell from the crossbar. I could not bring the image into focus. I went into the office and checked in. My unit, one of eight stand-alone structures, consisted of one small room with a blackand-white TV and a tiny bathroom with a shower. Linoleum covered the floors with throw rugs scattered about. A sickly window air conditioner supplied a semblance of cool air to the interior. I showered, changed clothes, and drove around for a half hour until it was time to meet Eva Marie, parked in front of the drug store, and leaned across to open the door for her when she came out.

"I understand there's a restaurant around here somewhere called Pearle's? Hungry?"

She half smiled. "Are you asking me out to dinner?"

I grinned. "Yep, I checked out all of the other women around here and you're the prettiest by far, so you win a free meal with the best-looking guy in town."

"Lucky me. Aren't you concerned about my big boyfriend?"

"If it comes to it, I figure we can outrun him in this thing. Hop in."

"I'd like to freshen up first. You can talk to my mother while I change. I'll see what you're made of if you survive that."

"Mothers are a piece of cake. I can charm the best of them."

Eva Marie laughed. "You're so full of yourself. You can follow me home. I live on a farm just outside of town."

"I like farm girls. Do you have any haystacks we can romp around in?"

"No, but my father does have the proverbial shotgun."

"*Oops*! Do I have to charm your daddy too?"

"Yes, but he's the easy one. Mother will decide if you're to be shot or not."

"That's reassuring. Does she often elect to have your beaus shot?"

"Only on rare occasions to serve as a warning to those who come sniffing around with less than honorable intentions."

"Geez, sounds like you might be the only virgin over eighteen still left in Clayhill."

"I can't imagine you ever having the opportunity to find out," she tossed back impishly as she climbed into an older-model Plymouth parked beside my Cobra.

I followed her to her farm and parked in front of a modest white clapboard house with a large pond in front. Her parents looked startled when she introduced me. Mrs. Sherrill ushered me to a seat in the cozy living room and hurried into the bedroom with Eva Marie as her father settled into an easy chair across from me. I looked around at photographs depicting Eva Marie at various ages littering the tables and walls as Mr. Sherrill, a short, balding, agreeable-appearing man, studied me.

"So, Mr. Henry, you've finally made your way back to Clayhill. I understand you have ordered a headstone for your father. That was very decent of you."

This was a *very* small town. At least he hadn't inferred that my mother and I had been run out of Clayhill—or that I should leave town immediately. "Please, call me Paul, Sir."

"How is Susan? I haven't heard from her since she moved away."

"Mom's fine. She lives in Jasper now."

"I went to school with your parents." Mr. Sherrill lowered his voice. "Your mother was a real beauty."

I'd never thought of my mother in that manner, but in retrospect, I supposed men would find her attractive. Somehow, that didn't sit well with me.

Mrs. Sherrill, a striking brunette with a shade lighter green eyes than Eva Marie's and still holding her trim figure, swept into the room with a tray. "Coffee, Mr. Henry?"

"Yes, Ma'am, thank you, and please call me Paul."

She placed a cup before me and offered cream and sugar, which I declined. She served Mr. Sherrill and seated herself across from me. "You're the spitting image of your father. Seeing you come courting our daughter was unsettling."

Time to turn on the charm—my forte. "When I met her at the drugstore today, Ma'am, I sensed she was a remarkable girl. Having met you now, I understand why." *Smooooothhh!*

She watched me skeptically over the rim of her cup. "Tell us about yourself."

"There's not a lot to tell. I got drafted into the army right out of high school and was medically discharged a week ago."

"You served in Vietnam?" Mr. Sherrill asked.

"Yes, Sir, I spent twelve months there."

"I'm a veteran," Mr. Sherrill offered proudly. "Is it as bad as they say it is over there?"

I shrugged. "No worse than what you faced, I guess. They say there's no war that's a good war."

Mrs. Sherrill placed her cup on the saucer in front of her. "That's an unusual car you drive. What kind is it?"

"It's a Shelby Cobra, Ma'am. It's very unique."

"But not very practical, it would seem."

Shades of Eva Marie, for heaven's sake! I rationalized dolefully.

"Now, Mother," Mr. Sherrill cautioned hastily. "To each his own; judge not lest you seek judgment thyself."

"I knew your father well, Paul. John was a fine man. Such a shame." She shook her head. "The Arkansas Henrys aren't fooling anybody but themselves. The *Texas* Henrys didn't put on such airs."

"Mother!" Mr. Sherrill protested.

"It's a shame he was killed at such a young age."

I stared at her, stunned. "I ... was led to believe he took his own life ..."

She hesitated. "Yes, of course, that's what they say. But he was the most practical man I ever knew. I went to school with him my whole life. He was a hero in the war and married to a decent girl who was expecting you any day. He had his whole life ahead of him. Why would he kill himself in such a cowardly manner?"

"Mother! That's enough!" Mr. Sherrill urged.

Mrs. Sherrill fixed me with a hard look. "If you were one of the Arkansas Henrys, I'd have done set the dogs on you. But I had the greatest respect for your family, the *real* Henrys. What are your plans with Eva Marie tonight?"

The sudden change of direction disoriented me. "Uh, we're going to dinner, Ma'am. At a place called Pearle's, I believe."

She grimaced. "If Eva Marie had given me some notice, I could have fixed you a fine supper right here. All you'll get at Pearle's is indigestion."

"Mother! What must he think of us?" Mr. Sherrill protested.

Eva Marie swept into the room wearing an alluring light green dress, matching shoes, and a ribbon around her throat suspending a green pendant. "Do you need rescuing yet?"

Her cheeks darkened under my appreciative gawk as I stood. "Uh, no ... I just about had your mother charmed into inviting me to dinner. You look ... dazzling ..." *And mouth-wateringly edible ...*

"Don't wait up for us, Mother." Eva Marie bent down to kiss her father's cheek and then hugged her mother. "Paul is going to poison me at Pearle's and then we're going to drive up to the lake for a while."

"I'll leave the porch light on. Don't be out late now," her mother cautioned.

My senses were vapor-locked by the enchanting fragrance she wore as she guided me to Pearle's, which was more of a small-town café than a restaurant. We seated ourselves at a table with wooden chairs and a Formica top. The handwritten menu offered one of three meats and a choice of three of five vegetables. I ordered the chicken fried steak with cream gravy and fries. Eva Marie selected the chef's salad.

I stared at her in open admiration. "You're way too stunning to waste on a mundane place like this."

She grimaced. "I hate this place."

"Pearle's?"

"Clayhill."

I smiled into her green cat-eyes. "What do you do for entertainment around here?"

"Go to the lake and watch the moon. That's about as exciting as it gets."

"Sounds romantic."

She laughed. "Not when everyone in Clayhill is parked within twenty feet of you. Half of them will be sitting on their hoods drinking bootleg beer, and the other half will be in the backseats of their cars making out."

I slumped in mock disappointment. "Darn! We don't have any beer!"

She giggled, her eyes glinting. "And your backseat isn't big enough to make out in. What*ever* will we do?"

I snapped my fingers in sudden inspiration. "I'll trade for a Cadillac on the way!"

"How long will you be in Clayhill?"

"A couple of days, I guess, until they place my father's headstone."

"Where are you staying?"

"The Pine View Inn."

"Is your room comfortable?"

"No. Want to see it later on?"

Her eyes danced. "Is that a proposition?"

"Of course—and I've got a black-and-white TV that gets two snow-filled channels for additional entertainment at intermission."

"I think we'd better stick to the lake tonight."

"Do you want to pick up some beer on the way?"

"I don't drink beer."

I was getting my signals crossed with her. From the mischievous gleam in her eye, I suspected that was exactly what she intended.

"From all of the pictures, I assume you're an only child?" I suggested as the waitress served our food.

She rolled her eyes. "Heavens, yes. And you?"

"Smothered to death all of my life by an adoring mother," I affirmed.

As we ate, we exchanged humorous stories of growing up as an only child of doting parents. I paid the tab, left a generous tip, and escorted her to the car.

"Which way to the lake?"

"I hope you're not disappointed."

I lifted my eyebrows. "With a quixotic lake bathed in romantic moonlight and the prettiest girl in Clayhill? Gee, I'll try to manage."

Her laughter was warm and comfortable. I decided I could really get to like this gypsy-looking girl as caution blinked in the recesses of my mind.

FOUR

I followed Eva Marie's directions to the lake and parked near a large log cabin containing bathrooms and a snack bar with a porch running along the front facing the dark water, where a long pier jutted out. A variety of cars and pickups clustered at the rear with groups of girls and boys gathered around them. Everyone paused to stare at the Cobra as I opened Eva Marie's door.

"We seem to have everyone's attention," I observed. "What should we do for an encore?"

She took my arm. "Let's walk down to the pier. It's cooler near the water. I hope this wasn't a bad idea."

I inhaled her faint perfume as she glided along beside me, the warmth of her arm hooked through mine sending tingles through me. "Are you concerned about being vulnerable to my irascible charms?"

"That and the fact there are more people here than usual."

"Want me to ask them to scram?"

"It's too late now. The word will get out that you're here."

"Why would anybody care where I'm at?"

She guided me out onto the pier and sat on a wooden bench near the end. I settled in beside her. The three-quarter moon cast a silver path across the water. A couple near us kissed in rapture with their arms wrapped around each other. Water lapped against the pilings as the feathery reflection from the lake sent shadowy images dancing around us.

"This is nice, Eva. So, tell me about yourself," I encouraged.

A gentle breeze ruffled her short hair. "I graduated from high school in May. I've dated a couple of the boys around here, but nothing serious.

43

I'm desperate to get out of this place. That about sums it up for me; tell me more about yourself."

"I'm trying to decide what to do with the rest of my life now that I have my service obligation behind me."

"Is your side of the family wealthy like the Henrys here in Clayhill?"

"Actually, my mother is a schoolteacher and owns a small house in Jasper."

"How can you afford such a unique car?"

"I saved most of my money in the Army, and I was good at poker. Are you disappointed that I'm not one of the rich Henrys?"

"I'm crushed. What did you do in Vietnam?"

"I was in the Infantry."

"Maybe I'm not supposed to ask, but is that where the scar on your cheek came from?"

"Yes, along with a couple of others that aren't as visible."

"It looks kind of sexy."

"That's some consolation, I suppose."

"What was it like over there?"

I hesitated, searching for an answer. What *was* it like over there? My mind raced back through the experience like a movie reel, images flashing across my mind's eye in rapid sequence. Bleakly, I realized there were no words to describe the experience adequately, especially to a civilian.

"I ... don't want to rush back anytime soon," I replied weakly.

"I assume it was a bad experience you don't like to talk about. I'm sorry, I shouldn't have asked."

"No, it's not that ...it's ... it's just hard to explain ... especially to someone who hasn't been there. There were some really good times ... and there were some very bad ones. Mostly I remember the guys I served with. It's a brotherhood like no other experience in the world. And sometimes I think of the ones who didn't come back ... and it almost kills me inside ..."

"Because you feel guilty about coming back when they didn't?"

"Possibly ... I guess ... look, I really don't want to overanalyze this, okay?"

"Okay. So do you agree with why we're there?"

"To stop the communist expansion? I agree with the theory of why we're there, but I don't agree with how we're conducting the war."

"What do you disagree with?"

"We don't have any clear military objectives. We go out on patrol, shoot up the world, and then go back to our base camp. The next day we go out and do the same thing in the same place. We don't seem to be getting anywhere. Hey, no offense, but talking about Vietnam bores the hell out of me."

"Okay, we'll change the subject. So why are you so confused about what you want to do with your life now?"

"We're still talking about Vietnam," I said, laughing. "Seriously, I don't know if I can answer that. I feel out of sorts since I've been back. Combat has a way of instilling such intensity into your every thought and action that being back in a safe environment again tends to make the mundane things seem unimportant. It's hard to explain, but when your every movement could be your last, I mean, when you spend every day trying not to get killed, it's hard to care about anything that isn't of an immediate, life-threatening challenge to you."

"I can only imagine how happy you are to be back home now."

"That's just it ... I'm not sure I am back home yet. Or if I am, I don't recognize it anymore."

"That's so sad. Is that why you decided to visit your father's grave after all this time? To search for your roots?"

"Part of it, I guess. Mostly I'm just curious. I've never known anything of my family on the Henry side because my mother refuses to talk about them."

She slipped her arm through mine and rested her head on my shoulder. "I'm a sucker for lost little boys."

"Hey, whatever works! You know, it's really interesting to see how people react around here when you say you're a Henry."

"You'd have to be from here to understand it."

We sat in thoughtful silence mesmerized by the stars reflecting off the lake in a million points of light. *Screw it. I'm going to kiss her and to hell with the consequences.* I tilted her chin up with my fingertips and lowered my lips to hers. When she responded, I pulled her into a full embrace, her soft, warm lips inviting swirls of delight. I was almost panicked when we parted, wanting on the one hand to run for my life, and on the other to dive back into that bottomless pit of ecstasy and stay in her arms forever.

She shifted away from me. "You're pretty bold, aren't you?"

"Are you angry?" I asked, breathless.

"No. I liked it," she replied softly. "So keep your distance."

"Okay," I agreed, shaken, as the couple near us departed, leaving us alone on the pier.

We sat for a time discussing nothing of consequence, comfortable in the near darkness gazing at the white moonlight rippling across the lake, each careful to avoid touching the other. I was near the point of throwing caution to the wind and taking her in my arms again when she stiffened and looked beyond me toward the lodge.

"We need to go now!"

"Why?"

"Bruce is here. I should have known better than to bring you out here."

"Is Bruce your big boyfriend?"

"He's one of your kinfolks."

"Oh. So does he have a claim on you?"

"No, of course not, but there's sure to be trouble if we don't leave."

"You're kidding. Why?"

"Please, could we just go now?"

She took my hand and led me back to the lodge, the touch of her palm and the interlocking of her fingers leaving me wanting more. A group of people clustered around the front porch quieted as we approached, and the hairs on the back of my neck rose, a sure sign of danger.

"That your blue fag-car parked out back there?" a voice chided as Eva Marie squeezed my hand and hastened her pace.

"Hey, I'm talking to you," the voice taunted. "Are you deaf?"

"Would that jackass I hear braying be Bruce?" I asked Eva Marie.

"Please, Paul, let's just leave, okay?" she pleaded.

"*Please, Paul, let's just leave, okay?*" the voice mocked as the group chortled. "Is that what it takes to get in those pants of yours, Eva Marie, a fancy fag-car?"

I released Eva Marie's hand and turned back to the group.

She clutched at my arm. "Paul, please!"

"*Paul, please!*" Bruce, a few inches taller than me, slim and wiry, with shoulder-length dark hair, a scraggly goatee, and a baseball cap turned backward on his head, echoed as he stepped forward, smirking over his shoulder at those behind him.

As I closed the gap, I knew two things conclusively: Bruce had too large an audience to back down, which meant we would fight, and due to my long recovery in the hospital, I was still too weak to go toe to toe with him in a physical contest. That meant a quick, decisive victory was paramount. He was still smirking at the group behind him when I kicked him in the crotch.

He doubled over with a strangled gasp, clasped his groin, and collapsed onto his knees, his eyes gaping in shock.

I slapped his hat off, grabbed a handful of his hair, and jerked his head up. "Nice to finally meet one of my relatives, Bruce. I believe you owe an apology to this lady."

White foam covered his lips. "*Screw … you!*"

"I expected you to show better manners, since we're kinfolks and all." I released his hair, stepped back, and kicked him in the face.

His hands flew to his mouth as he flopped over onto his back and rolled onto his side. I stepped forward and kicked him in the stomach.

"I suggest you work on your etiquette a bit, Bruce," I advised as he curled into a fetal position, gasping. "You're proving to be an embarrassment to the family." I took Eva Marie's arm and steered her to the car as the group rushed forward to hover over him.

Eva Marie slumped against her door with her arms crossed, her eyes straight ahead as I pulled away.

"Are you upset?" I asked in the strained silence.

"Was that really necessary? You may have seriously injured him."

"Is there someplace we can get a cup of coffee?"

"I'd prefer to go home now."

"Let's don't let him spoil our evening, Eva."

"I really don't feel well. Please take me home."

When I parked in front of her house, she opened her door. "Good night, Paul. I can see myself to the door."

I drove back to the Pine View Inn certain Bruce Henry wasn't worth the emotional turmoil I was suffering. It had been a pleasurable evening with Eva Marie until that loud-mouthed lout came along. What was with the Arkansas Henrys anyway? Were they crazy as hell? I didn't give a damn about their feud, but they were beginning to piss me off. I hadn't wanted any trouble. But a man couldn't walk away from it either. Trouble always followed if you ran from it. You had to stand and face it when it came. Sometimes violence was a necessary, if unwelcome, evil. Eva Marie needed to understand that so she wouldn't be so upset with me … so she could glide back into my arms and lift her lips to mine …

What the hell? I needed to get a grip before this thing with her got out of hand.

* * *

When I pulled into the Pine View Inn, a police cruiser slid in behind me. I got out of the Cobra as a huge, heavyset deputy emerged from the driver's side of the cruiser and leveled a pistol over the frame of the door.

"Paul Henry?"

I raised my hands, palms out, as my heart hammered. "Could you point that thing someplace else?"

The pistol didn't waver. "Turn around and place your hands on top of your car and spread your legs."

I leaned into the car and spread my feet obediently. "What is this all about?"

The deputy, a young mammoth of a man well over six feet tall shaped like an egg, hooked one of his boots around my ankle as he frisked me. "Place your right hand behind your back." He snapped the handcuff around my wrist, pulled my left hand behind my back, and cuffed that wrist also before turning me around to face him. "Paul Henry, you are under arrest for assault and battery. Anything you say or do can be held against you in a court of law. You have the right to remain silent …" he continued through the whole Miranda warning as he steered me to the patrol car and guided me into the backseat.

At the police station he removed my handcuffs, fingerprinted me, and took my mug shot with a Polaroid as I stood beside a height scale painted on the wall. He then inventoried the contents of my pockets, and I signed a form confirming the personal items. After I surrendered my belt, he escorted me to the first cell inside the holding area.

I stopped. "Could you put me in the cell on the end?"

He hesitated. "Why?"

I smirked. "It's an old family tradition."

He shrugged, turned me to the last cell on the end, and locked the door.

I grasped the bars. "Where is Sheriff Tate?"

"He'll be in before you go to the magistrate at ten thirty." He waddled out and closed the door behind him.

I looked around in dismay, absorbing the putrid odors of the cellblock. A drunk sprawled on the bunk in the center cell next to mine, exhaling the aroma of sour whisky in harsh, rattling snorts. The smell mingled with that of a rancid pool of vomit on the floor beside his bunk. I sat down on the soiled, thin mattress of the bottom bunk and stared up at the corner where my father had hung himself almost twenty-one years ago and then averted my eyes, still unable to visualize the scene as I reflected back on what Mrs. Sherrill had implied about his death being something more than a suicide.

Sometime later the outer door opened and a tanned, medium-sized man in his early sixties with slicked-back gray hair and a well-groomed mustache, dressed in a black suit and expensive shoes, entered. The big deputy hovered behind him in a subservient manner as the man paused outside my cell.

I sat up and met his impassive brown eyes staring at me through the bars. "Who the hell are you?"

His lips lifted in a tight, satisfied smile before he turned on his heel and departed. The deputy followed him out and closed the door behind them. I flopped back on my cot and tried to breathe through my mouth to ward off the stench waftling around me. Eventually I slipped into a restless, dreamless slumber, and awakened to a red dawn filtering through the dirty windows. The drunk sat on his bunk with his elbows propped on his knees and his hands clasped on each side of his head. I swung my legs over the bunk and sat up, itching all over.

The drunk, in his mid-twenties, six feet or better in height, thin and wiry, dressed in soiled jeans, scuffed cowboy boots, and a torn, threadbare western shirt, lifted his red-rimmed, bleary eyes.

"'Lo," he mumbled.

I nodded curtly. "Hello."

He raked his hands through his unruly black hair. "Ain't seen you around here before, Sport, what'd you do to get thrown in the tank?"

"I kicked a wise guy's ass, *Sport*, but it wasn't worth smelling your puke all night."

"Whose ass did you kick?"

"Bruce Henry's; not that it's of any concern to you."

"Could've told you not to do that. That bunch owns this town. What'd he do to piss you off?"

"Are you writing a book or something?"

"Just curious."

"He insulted the girl I was with."

"Thirty days. Sorry about that."

My pulse quickened. "Thirty days? What the hell do you mean by that?"

"Old Judge Handley's gonna nail you for thirty days in the slammer. He'll probably fine you a hundred, too. Your goose is cooked for sure."

"How do you know that?"

"J. R. owns him. Thirty days is the max he can give you."

"Are you a lawyer?"

"No. I beat up Bruce's younger brother Jimmy once. J. R. don't like his boys getting their asses kicked. Who was the girl?"

"Eva Marie Sherrill."

The drunk whistled. "How'd you get up with her? She don't take to guys around here much. Hey … you're that Henry that drives that strangelooking race car—the blue something or other?" He walked over to the bars. "You don't look like a Henry, Sport."

"What is a Henry supposed to look like?"

"You're too light and skinny. The blond hair and blue eyes don't fit either."

"Sorry to disappoint you, pal, but I'm definitely a Henry."

"Your bunch got run off years ago. Why did you come back?"

I glowered. "No one in this hick town has ever run *me* off from anywhere, *Sport*, and it ain't *likely* to happen anytime soon either!"

The drunk laughed. "You're a Henry, alright; arrogant as hell." He shoved his hand through the bars. "I'm Hal Sutton. I was hoping to meet up with you. Where'd you get that scar on your face? Knife fight?"

I ignored his hand. "I'm Paul. Why were you hoping to meet up with me?"

He withdrew his hand. "If you've come back to claim your kingdom, I can be of help to you."

"What damned kingdom? You don't make sense."

"Sorry about the puke you had to smell all night."

"It's to be expected from the town drunk, I suppose."

Hal flinched. "I just got hold of some green whisky, is all."

"You're confusing me with somebody who gives a damn."

The fat deputy entered carrying a bucket of water and a mop, opened the door to Hal's cell, and set them on the floor. "Clean up your mess, Hal. It's got the whole jail stinking. Sheriff Tate will raise hell if he comes in and finds the place smelling like this."

Hal grabbed the mop and dipped it into the water. "Much obliged, Joe. I was just apologizing to Paul here about that. I got a jug of bad whisky last night." He smeared the mop around in the puddle beside his bunk, which only served to heighten the noxious fumes.

"Don't call me *Joe*, call me Deputy Miller, like you're supposed to. I done told you that about a hundred times now."

"Now don't go putting on airs with me, Joe," Hal chided as he swabbed the floor. "I've known you since the first grade when I used to beat you up and take your milk money."

"We were kids then. We're adults now, and you need to start acting like one."

I walked to the front of the cell. "Who was that man who came in here last night, Deputy?"

He shuffled around to face me, his bulk filling the narrow corridor between the bars and the brick wall. "That was Mr. J. R. Henry, the father of the man you assaulted."

"Shouldn't you be using the phrase 'allegedly assaulted' until it's proven otherwise?" I demanded.

His double chins quivered. "Proving it'll take about five minutes after you get to court this morning. Bruce is still in the hospital with a busted jaw and a bruised spleen."

I met his eyes. "He was looking for trouble. He kept letting his mouth overload his ass. Your investigation should show that."

He shrugged. "Yeah? Well, he's got about ten witnesses that say you attacked him first. They claim he never laid a hand on you." He turned and waddled out of the cell block, breathing hard from the exertion.

"Lard-ass!" I chided as the door closed behind him.

Hal placed the mop in the bucket and leaned the handle against the bars. "He's okay, Paul, just dumb as a rock. You got any money to get yourself a lawyer? You don't mess with the Henrys in this town."

"*I'm* a Henry, remember?"

He grinned. "But you ain't one of *The* Henrys. Get a lawyer."

"I don't know any damn lawyers!"

"I recommend Jason Jackson. He's the only one that will stand up to the Henrys."

The thought of thirty days in this foul-smelling place was unsettling. "*Hey, Deputy!*" I yelled. After a moment the door opened and the deputy looked in with arched eyebrows above his pudgy jowls. "I'm entitled to a phone call. I want to talk to a lawyer named Jason Jackson."

The deputy's eyes narrowed. "Hal, you'd do best to keep out of this."

"Do I get my phone call or not?" I demanded.

The deputy looked at me with some trepidation. "I'll place a call to Mr. Jackson and inform him that you want to talk to him." He closed the door.

I washed my face in the small stainless steel sink and paced around the cell irritably to air dry since there were no towels. The door opened, and the deputy reappeared to thrust a small brown paper sack through the bars at Hal.

"Enjoy," he called as he departed.

Hal dug into the sack and handed me a cup of black coffee and a fried egg sandwich. He then extracted a piece of paper, read it, and poked it through the bars.

"I believe this is for you, Sport."

I took the scrap of paper and read:

"*Paul,*

Maybe under different circumstances we could have been friends. Please go back to Jasper and leave these troubles behind you.

Eva Marie"

"They get our breakfast from the drugstore," Hal offered as he munched on his fried egg sandwich. "Looks like you just got dumped, Sport. It's probably for the best."

I crumpled the note and tossed it aside. "What's for the best?"

"That she discarded you. By the time you get out of this septic tank she'll have forgotten you anyway and I'll probably have done married her myself."

I scowled. "I barely know her, so have at it, *Sport!*" *Damn, I needed to get out of this burg*!

"Since I'm gonna be working for you, I'll need an eleven-dollar advance, if you don't mind."

I turned to him, incredulous. The man was a nut case. "How do you figure you're going to be working for me?"

"You need me to cover your back and advise you in your feud with the Henrys. I know everybody in this town. Even if the folks around here would talk to you, you wouldn't understand what they're saying. See, it takes a bit of interpreting because they more or less talk *around* things, not *about* them."

"I don't have a feud with the Henrys, and I don't need anybody to cover my back, thank you very much. Nor do I need an interpreter, especially one I can't understand myself. As soon as they lay my father's headstone, I'm outta this hick town, and good riddance."

"So you're gonna cut and run, huh?"

I clenched the bars between us. "*I'm* not cutting and running anywhere, *pal!*"

"Sounds like it to me, Sport. I was hoping you'd have a little more staying power."

"Staying power for what?"

"The Henrys. I was hoping you'd stand up to them. I'm disappointed."

"Do you always talk in riddles?"

"You said you were leaving."

"Well, I'm *staying* until I'm *ready* to go!"

"You'll need my services then, but I can't afford to work for nothing, you understand, even if we are friends."

"Friends? How do you figure that? Quit talking in circles."

"I need ten dollars to pay my fine so I don't have to spend the next five days in here with you. They only give credit at two dollars a day for time served, and frankly, I find your crabby disposition somewhat lacking, I'm sorry to say."

"You said you wanted eleven dollars."

"I need some operating capital if I'm going to be of any use to you. The extra dollar is for my lunch and a pack of smokes."

"I hate to dash your employment plans, but I'm not in a feud with the Henrys and I don't plan to be. I just had a problem with one little wiseass."

"Wrong, Sport. If you've got a problem with one of them, you've got a problem with all of them. You're gonna have to either fight or break and run."

I sat down on the bunk in disgust. "Are you crazy in addition to being the town drunk, by chance? I don't need your help, and I'm real choosy about who my friends are."

"Why are you Henrys so cantankerous? Is it a family trait or something? Hey, if you'll give me the keys to that fancy car of yours, Eva Marie and I'll drive it around and keep the battery charged up for you at no extra charge."

"I think that bad whisky has addled your brain!"

The door opened and Sheriff Tate walked down to my cell. "Good morning, Mr. Henry. I see your pledge to cause no trouble was meaningless."

"I wasn't given much choice in the matter," I retorted.

"I understand you've retained Mr. Jackson to represent you. He'll meet you in court."

"I would have preferred to meet him *before* court."

"They're laying your father's headstone this morning. If Mr. Jackson is successful in getting you out on bail, I suggest you go on back to Jasper after visiting the site. I recommend you forfeit the bail and never come back to Clayhill. It would be in your best interest."

"I'm getting damned tired of everyone around here telling me what's in my best interest, Sheriff."

He turned to Hal. "Welcome back, Mr. Sutton. I understand you broke up Maybell's place again last night."

Hal grinned. "I don't recall, Sheriff, to be honest with you. She was selling green whisky again. You know how that stuff makes me crazy. You need to get us a new bootlegger for this county. She's gonna poison somebody one of these days."

"Do you have the money for the fine, or are you going to need accommodations in my hotel for a few days?"

Hal glanced at me. "Paul and I just cut a deal. I'm working for him now."

Sheriff Tate turned to me, perturbed. "I see. That doesn't sound like you'll be leaving Clayhill anytime soon, Mr. Henry. That's disappointing." He walked out of the cell block.

"Why did you tell him that bullshit?" I demanded.

"It's easier on the both of us if you advance me the money. That way I don't have to fret about chiseling you out of it, and it allows us to focus on the more important matters at hand."

"Such as?"

"Such as the Henrys. If you hang around here, you're gonna need me. Otherwise, you'll be back here in that cell in no time on another trumped-up charge. You could even end up hanging from that crossbeam up there like your Daddy did."

I spun to face him. *"My father is none of your damned business!"*

He grinned. "You've got a lot to learn about this place, Sport, but first let's focus on getting you out of here."

FIVE

In due course the deputy returned to escort Hal and me to face the magistrate. He handcuffed me for the short walk from the jail to the courthouse after explaining that it was regulation for anyone charged with assault. He seated us on a bench off to the side of the courtroom and removed the handcuffs. We waited half an hour before a tall, thin, white-haired gentleman in his mid-seventies dressed in a worn three-piece gray suit came in. He glanced in my direction, nodded curtly, placed his battered briefcase on the floor beside the table, and settled down in the chair.

Hal nudged my arm. "That's your lawyer, the honorable Jason Jackson."

A short, pudgy man in his mid-forties wearing a blue suit came in, shook hands with Mr. Jackson, and settled in at the table on the right.

"That's the prosecutor, Mr. Hard-ass Jordan," Hal mouthed as the man ignored us.

The main door to the courtroom opened. J. R. Henry, looking serene in his tailored dark suit and coiffed hair, entered with two younger men in tow. One of the men was of medium height, slim of build with dark features, and roughly my age. The other was a year or two older, blond headed, powerfully built, wore jeans and a sweat shirt, and scowled intently as he locked eyes with me. They seated themselves near the front on the right side behind the prosecutor.

Hal leaned toward me. "The dapper gent is J. R. Henry himself, who I believe you met last night. The younger one with the slim build is Jimmy, his son. The other one with the attitude is a local tough named Garland Sanders. He works for J. R."

"All rise!" the bailiff intoned.

We rose as an elderly fat man in his mid-sixties dressed in a black robe with white curly hair covering the sides of his bald head framing his bibulous facial features entered through a door behind the elevated judge's platform.

"The Honorable Judge Steward Handley, presiding," the bailiff droned through his nose.

We waited patiently for the judge to settle into his chair and study the room with glassy, unfocused eyes. "Be seated," he finally directed in a thin, nasal voice.

The prosecutor stood. "If Your Honor pleases, the first case before you this morning is a drunk and disorderly charge filed by Deputy Joseph Miller against Mr. Howell Tater Sutton."

I glanced at Hal. "*Tater?*"

Hal grimaced. "My Daddy had a warped sense of humor."

"Mr. Sutton, please stand before the bench," the fat judge ordered. Hal walked to the center of the court and faced him. "As to the charge of drunk and disorderly, how do you plead?"

"Innocent by reason of temporary insanity, Judge," Hal offered without pause.

The judge frowned. "That is not an acceptable plea, Mr. Sutton."

"It's the truth, though, Judge. If I wasn't temporarily insane, I wouldn't have busted up Maybell's. For the record and as a second line of defense, she was serving green whisky again. Somebody ought to reprimand her for that. It makes me nutty as a loon, and she knows it. How can I be held accountable when everybody knows green whisky makes me crazy? I recommend the court order the sheriff to allow another bootlegger into the county. If Maybell had a little competition she wouldn't be so willing to serve a man bad whisky."

"Is that your defense, Mr. Sutton?" the judge demanded.

"That about sums it up, Judge."

The judge pounded his gravel. "Ten dollars or five days! Next case."

The prosecutor stood. "The next case, Your Honor, is a charge of aggravated assault and battery levied against Mr. Paul Henry involving a vicious physical attack without justifiable provocation upon Mr. Bruce Henry."

"Paul Henry, stand before the bench," the judge ordered. I walked to the center of the room as Hal was led out by the deputy.

Jason Jackson stood also. "If it so pleases the court, Your Honor, I am the attorney of record for Paul Henry."

The judge nodded. "So noted; how does your client plead to the specified charge?"

"My client pleads not guilty to the charge and specification. We request a jury trial and further request that Mr. Henry be released on his own recognizance until such trial is convened."

The prosecutor rose to his feet. "I object, Your Honor. The defendant is not from this county. As such, that is an open invitation for him to flee the justice of this court in this matter. I move that the defendant be remanded to the custody of the sheriff until a trial is conducted."

Mr. Jackson rose. "That is absurd, Your Honor. Mr. Jordan knows perfectly well that it will take two months for a trial by jury due to the schedule of the circuit court judge. Even if my client were convicted, he would face a maximum sentence of thirty days in jail and a $150 fine. Remanding him to the custody of the sheriff would require him to be held beyond the maximum sentencing guidelines for the crime for which he is charged. I further submit to the court that my client is more than eager to face the justice of this court because he is innocent and more than willing to answer to the bogus charge. Therefore, he has no motivation to flee and should be released on his own recognizance."

The judge consulted a calendar on the desk in front of him. "Trial by jury will tentatively be set nine weeks from today, pending confirmation by Judge Ferguson. Bail is set at $250. Court is dismissed."

"All rise!" the bailiff ordered as the judge departed.

Mr. Jackson moved next to me. "Do you have the funds to post your bond?"

"Yes, back in my billfold at the jail."

"Post your bond with the clerk of court, get cleaned up, and meet me in my office at two this afternoon. I'm across the street on the second floor above the hardware store." He walked out of the courtroom as Sheriff Tate moved up to me with his handcuffs.

"Do you think I'm going to try to escape before I post bail, Sheriff?"

"It's procedure, Mr. Henry. Turn around please." Sheriff Tate locked the cuffs around my wrists and led me out the side door as J. R., Jimmy, and Garland Sanders sat impassively.

Back at the jail Sheriff Tate pulled the manila envelope containing my personal items from the safe, jointly inventoried it with me, had me sign a receipt, and then escorted me back to the courthouse to post bail with the clerk of court. While there, I impulsively paid Hal's ten-dollar fine as well. I walked out a semi-free man and stood in front of the courthouse in the heat getting my bearings. My Cobra was still back at the Pine View Inn a mile away. With misgivings, I walked across the street to the drugstore. An old codger in his eighties sat at the counter drinking coffee from a spoon, which he dipped into the cup, blew on several times, and then sipped with a rasping, sucking sound.

Eva Marie watched with a bland expression as I seated myself. "May I help you, Sir?"

Butterflies swarmed in my stomach as I locked eyes with her. "*Sir?* Eva, I've been 'Mister-ed' and 'Sir-ed' to death since I got to this damned town. Do you have a taxi service here? I need a ride to my motel. I'm nasty and covered with jail lice. I need a shower and a change of clothes."

She turned to the telephone beside the cash register. "I'll call one for you." After she hung up, she turned back to me. "It'll be here in about ten minutes."

"Thanks. Could I get some coffee while I'm waiting?"

The old man nodded at me as she placed a cup before me and poured, keeping her eyes averted from mine. She refilled the old gentleman's cup, returned the container to the burner, and drifted to the end of the counter to adjust a display as he heaped sugar and cream into his coffee.

I sipped my coffee as I watched her pretend to be busy. "Eva, why are you being so formal and ignoring me?"

She glanced in my direction. "What should I be with you? I barely know you."

"You know me well enough to call me by my name. Are you still angry about last night?"

"I don't like violence and dissension, especially where the Henrys are concerned. This is my home, Paul. We're a small community. I have to continue to live here after you're gone."

"I wasn't looking for trouble and you know it. Bruce was determined to provoke me. Can I take you to dinner tonight to make it up to you?"

"Go back to Jasper where you belong. Only bad things will happen if you stay here."

I sat back, exasperated. "Why is everyone so intent on me leaving? This is the craziest damned town I've ever seen. I'm a Henry, but not really. There's a family feud that's been raging for twenty years, but I don't know what it's about, even though I seem to be caught up in it now. I've got kinfolks I've never met who insult the woman I'm with in order to pick a fight with me, then they put me in jail for standing up for her honor, and now she won't even talk to me. Even the damned cemetery here has got the Henrys split into two groups."

She looked out to the street. "I believe your taxi is here."

"Can I see you tonight?"

"Your taxi is waiting, Mr. Henry."

I tossed a quarter on the counter. "You have a nice day, *Miss Sherrill*."

* * *

At the motel I took a long, hot shower, soaping down and scrubbing twice before I felt clean again. As I dressed, a hearty knock beat at the door. I opened it to find Hal grinning at me.

"You forgot my extra dollar advance for lunch and smokes, Sport."

I grabbed my wallet and handed him a dollar. "Consider this a loan." I closed the door in his face. When I finished dressing, I walked out to find him leaning against the front fender of my Cobra smoking a cigarette.

"You're slower than an old woman. Give me a ride to my place so I can get myself presentable before we go to the cemetery."

"What makes you think I'm going to the cemetery?"

"They put a marker on your daddy's grave this morning. Half the town has already been out there to check it out." He pushed off the fender and walked around to the passenger door.

I shook my head in disbelief. "Does everybody mind everybody else's business in this damned flea-bitten town?"

"Yep," he replied as I slid in behind the wheel. "When are you gonna let me drive this little beauty?"

"Never. Where the hell do you live, anyway?"

"Head north and I'll give you directions. Hope I've got a clean shirt around somewhere. Did you go by the drugstore to check on Eva Marie?"

"It was like walking into a deep freeze," I allowed as I drove out of town.

"What did you expect? You gave her to me, remember? She's not the two-timing type."

"Give it a rest, Hal; I'm not in the mood."

"Pull into the dirt road there on the right. My place is just a piece further along."

I navigated the washed-out dirt road, which soon turned into a rutted lane, and arrived at an unpainted, rusty-tin-roofed affair with a sagging front porch that leaned to the left as if ready to fall over at any moment. Half a dozen hound dogs loitered around barking as we pulled up in front of the weather-beaten structure. I surveyed the piles of scrap metal, used tires, mounds of rotting rubbish littering the knee-high weeds in the front yard, and the several rusted old cars and pickup trucks perched about on rickety blocks with their tires removed as a flock of chickens scratched at the matted vegetation pecking at whatever chickens peck at in the dirt.

"Watch out for Old Billy," Hal advised as he stepped out. "He don't take to strangers much."

I looked across the top of the car at him as I got out. "Who the hell is Old Billy?"

"Oh shit! *Run!*" he shouted as he took off for the porch.

Hoofs pounded behind me. I leapt after him in panic, afraid to look over my shoulder to see what was chasing us as I darted for the raised porch a half-step ahead of the snorting at my heels and jumped up next to Hal. Gasping for breath, I turned to see a scraggly goat, his head lowered, snorting and stamping his hoof in the dirt.

"That old coot is getting too damned territorial for his own good," Hal observed. "I'm gonna have to do something about him one of these days."

"Now's as good a time as any," I panted. "Go get your gun!"

"Aw hell, I ain't got no bullets for it."

I followed him into the living room of his shack and paused just inside the door to assess the rough-cut wood flooring strewn with old clothes, heaps of magazines, newspapers, and other assorted paraphernalia of questionable origin. A ragged sofa and easy chair stood in the debris with two mismatched end tables holding dirty plates and opened cans of stale, green-fuzzed food.

"Besides, Old Billy eats all the bad snakes around here," Hal continued.

"*Bad* snakes?" I looked at the rubble at my feet trying to envision what a *good* snake might be.

"Oh, don't worry about the ones in here; they're friendly little rat snakes for the most part," Hal reassured me. "It's the ones out in the yard you gotta watch out for. Old Billy keeps them pretty much et up."

"The *goat* eats the *bad snakes*?" I asked, my head swiveling about in alarm. "The *good snakes* eat the *rats*?"

Hal studied me. "You ain't no country boy, are you?"

"Why don't I just wait in the car?"

"Okay, I won't be but a minute. Watch for Old Billy on your way out, though."

I turned to Old Billy standing in the middle of the yard glaring back at me. "Uh, never mind, I'll stay in here."

"Suit yourself. Throw some of that junk on the floor and have a seat."

I eyed the threadbare sofa covered with trash, which provided numerous potential hiding places for the rats and their nemeses, the rat-eating good snakes. "I'll just stand, thank you. Do you actually *live* here?"

"Yep, home, sweet home. My Maw left it to me. I had forty acres at one time, but I lost most of it to J. R. when he sued me. I wasn't much of a farmer anyway. I only got three acres and this house left. Be right back; make yourself comfortable."

I hovered near the screen door keeping my eyes on the rubbish on the floor looking for anything suspicious and mentally weighing the odds of making it safely past Old Billy to the car should a varmint suddenly materialize out of the refuse. Mercifully, a short time later Hal emerged from the shambles of his bedroom wearing a clean set of worn Levi's and holding a cowboy shirt in each hand. He sniffed at each before choosing the cleanest dirty one and slipped it on before he sat down on the sofa to pull on a pair of western boots.

"Ready if you are," he advised as he buttoned the snaps on his shirt and reached for a gray Stetson hanging on a peg by the door.

I looked over my shoulder at the goat, whose disposition hadn't changed in any significant manner. "So what's the plan?"

"The plan?"

I nodded at the goat. "How are we gonna get by him?"

He looked at Old Billy, his expression thoughtful. "Umm, I usually just make a run for it; most of the time it takes him a minute or two to get cranked up—unless he's feeling especially frisky. He's about half blind."

"What if he *is* feeling especially frisky?"

"Oh hell, Sport, he can't run that fast anymore, he's too old. I think he's got the rheumatism or something. We should be able to outrun him."

"I've got a better plan. *You* go outrun him down the road a piece. When it's safe, *I'll* get the car and meet up with you after you've worn him out."

"That's not much of a plan, Sport."

"It's *your* billy-goat, *Tater* ..."

He grimaced. "I thought we were friends."

"*I* thought you were my *employee*."

"I envisioned us working as a team."

"This *is* teamwork, where my life and your old goat are concerned."

He sighed. "Oh, all right. When I get his attention, you make a run for it." He opened the screen door and edged out onto the porch as Old Billy braced him.

"*Yee-haw!*" Hal yelled as he jumped off the porch and rambled down the rutted lane at a mad gallop. Old Billy fell in behind him in a determined trot, head lowered and nostrils flaring. The hound dogs chased after the both of them yelping in excitement. I opened the door, jumped off the porch, and dashed for the car. Old Billy whirled around and came charging back at me as I yanked the door to the Cobra open, slid in, and slammed it in his face. The old goat pawed the ground and snorted at me in disgust. I waved at him as I fired up the Cobra. Hal and his pack of dogs were waiting for me at the end of the lane.

He slid in smiling smugly as the dogs milled about. "See, I told you Old Billy couldn't run very fast. I probably need to get the vet to check him out."

"Why? So he can run fast enough to catch you? You're seriously Looney Tunes, do you know that?"

"He might be in some pain or something."

"I'll advance you the money to buy a bullet so you can put him out of his misery."

"Aw, I couldn't do that. Old Billy's been around as long as I can remember. He's like family."

"Yeah, like my own crazy damned family in these parts. What is it with this place? Have you people ever had your water checked?"

"Checked for what?"

I sighed. "You mentioned that J. R. sued you and took your land?"

"Yeah, he got everything I owned except the old homestead."

"What were you and Jimmy fighting about?"

"A girl."

"Was she worth it?"

"I guess not; she married him."

"Were you drunk at the time?"

"No, I didn't drink back then."

"How long ago was that?"

"About five years back."

"What did he sue you for?"

"Malicious personal injury—they said I stomped him when I got him down."

"She must have been some girl."

"I thought so at the time. It was a bogus lawsuit. Jimmy and I fought for her fair and square. He busted a couple of my ribs and fractured my skull."

I snickered. "I guess that explains it."

"Explains what?"

"Uh, that love sucks."

"It does at that. I hope you stay long enough to set things right around here. The Henrys have screwed over a lot of people in these parts. You'd do a lot of good by bringing them down."

"I'm a Henry too, remember. Why would I want to bring my own kin down?"

"Because you're one of the *good* Henrys. Folks haven't forgotten that. Your clan was proud and honorable people. They took care of the little people. You've got more friends around here than you know about, but most folks will sit by the wayside and wait to see what you're gonna do at first. They wanna make sure you're gonna stay and fight."

"That's bullshit, Hal. Fight who about what? You're talking crazy again."

"Why, fight the Henrys for what's rightfully yours. To restore the balance of power around here, to cast off the heavy cloak of the evil Henry clan, to bring righteous truth and justice back to the land."

"You *are* crazy! One minute you talk like a country hick, the next you sound like a damned scholar or something. Which is the real you, anyway?"

"I'm a little of both, I guess. I'm a sophisticated country hick, thanks to my Maw."

"Well, you need to pick one or the other so I can keep up with you. And I've told you, I have no quarrel with the Henrys."

"Folks are counting on you, Paul. You're like royalty to them. They've been waiting for you to get grown and come back for years. They expect you to right all the Henry wrongs."

"Do I look like Robin Hood or something?"

"It's not a taking from the rich and giving to the poor kind of thing. It's more like not letting the Henrys take advantage of them. See, in the old days if you got down, the old Henrys took care of you until you got back on your feet. Nowadays if you get down, the new Henrys take advantage of you. In some cases they actually create bogus problems so they *can* take advantage of you, like in my case."

"That's none of my business, Hal. I don't intend to get involved."

"You don't have a choice, Sport, unless you cut and run. Like I said, you're royalty. You're like a baron or something."

"A *baron*? Bullshit!"

"I mean it. These folks are depending on you."

"I say again, bullshit! It's not my problem."

"But it *is* your problem, don't you see, Paul? You've got to fight for what's yours. You're the only one that can change things. If you beat them, we all win."

"*Them* and *we* who? You and this whole damned hick town are nuts."

I pulled into the cemetery parking lot. Hal followed me inside, where Matilda beamed at us as Mr. Farr rushed to greet me.

"Mr. Henry, so good to see you again. Your father's headstone was set first thing this morning. We worked all night on the engraving. I think you'll be pleased."

"Thank you, Mr. Farr. How about getting the other plot spruced up?"

Mr. Farr's smile thinned. "I've got a couple of men coming in this afternoon to take care of it, Mr. Henry. It took some doing to find someone willing. The others are up there now taking care of your family plot."

"What others?"

"They wanted everything to look nice when your father's tombstone was set."

"They who?"

"Well, Sir, I guess you'd call them volunteers. They've taken care of the old Henry plot all of their lives, as regular as clockwork."

I stared at him blankly. "Why would they volunteer to do that? Who are these people?"

"They're old friends of your family, Mr. Henry. They're quite excited about you being back."

"Is this some sort of a joke? What are they excited about?"

"Oh, it's no joke, Sir, I assure you. They always expected you would return one day."

Hal took my arm. "I told you, you have a lot to learn, Sport. Come along now; let's go meet some of your loyal subjects."

"Would you quit talking crazy, Hal?" I jerked my elbow from his grasp. "You ain't made a lick of sense since the day I met you."

He grinned. "That was just this morning, My Lord. Give it time."

"I think I wasted ten dollars. I should have left you rotting back there in that jail cell."

"Eleven," he reminded me as he pushed me toward the door. "Now quit being so contrary. I've been trying to tell you how things are ever since I met you. You are one stubborn hombre! I sure hope you turn out to be worth all the trouble you're puttin' me through."

* * *

We drove to the back of the cemetery, where we found two beat-up pickup trucks parked next to the old Henry plot and a dozen black people scattered about working. I got out cautiously surveying the iron fence shining with a fresh coat of paint, the newly mowed grass dotted with flowers adorning each gravesite, and the bright marble tombstone standing on the end above my father's grave. An old, weathered man removed his sweat-streaked, ragged straw hat and shuffled over as the others paused to stare at us.

"Mr. Henry, Suh, it be a pleasure to serve you and your family again. Indeed it do."

I extended my hand. "My name is Paul. And you are …?"

The man wiped his sweaty palms on his pants before taking my hand. "I be Rufus Washington, Suh." He turned to the others. "This be my wife, Agnes, who was the midwife to your mother, Mrs. Susan, when you was born. She be the one who bring you into this world." He went on to introduce three of his grandchildren, Mr. and Mrs. Jacobs, their son and grandson, the Jefferson family, and one of their granddaughters.

I shook hands with each as they stepped forward to be introduced. "Mr. Washington, Mr. Farr said you volunteer to maintain the family plot. Why?"

Mr. Washington bowed his head. "Our families go all the way back to when your great-granddaddy first come to Texas, Suh. We worked in the Henry brickyard before the troubles came. We still live on Henry land 'cause your granddaddy provided for us in our lifetime, bless his soul. We sure be glad you come back home, Suh. Aunt Elsie said you come back someday. Said you be riding a powerful serpent. Said you bring truth and justice when you come. Said things gonna change around here when you come. We be mighty grateful to you for that, Suh."

I looked at Hal in bewilderment, who stood off to the side with a huge grin plastered on his mug, and turned back to Rufus Washington. "Uh, you and the others have done a superb job on the family plot. I thank you for that and insist on paying you for your labors."

Rufus shook his head. "It be our pleasure to serve the family, Suh. We don't want no money for such. We grateful you done come home. We thanks you for that. We surely do."

"Can I at least pay you for the flowers? They provide a nice touch."

"Thank you kindly, Suh, but the flowers come from our yards. They our way of saying welcome home to you. Things gonna change around here now. Old Aunt Elsie said so. She got the magic eye."

Hal winked at me as I stared at him, perplexed. "I feel awkward in the face of your generosity, Mr. Washington. I'm ashamed to admit that I know very little about my family."

Rufus took my arm and led me to the line of headstones. "Come on, Suh. I be happy to introduce you to your ancestors." He stopped before the first tombstone, which was also the largest. "This here be Master James Allison Henry, your great-granddaddy."

I stared at the monument with the dates *14 April 1875–29 May 1945*.

"He moved here to Clayhill from Little Rock, Arkansas, in 1895, when he was twenty years old. He be the one that hired my daddy to work for him in the brickyard he built."

Hal stepped forward. "They say he was a right feisty old gentleman in his time, and there are some colorful stories told about him. It's said he could be a hard man, but there's also a lot he did for the local community, such as building the jail in Clayhill and a school for the black folks, among other things."

Rufus moved to the next gravesite. "That be right, Mr. Henry. He be a hard but fair man. He married your great-grandmomma, Mrs. Rosemary here, in 1896, the same year he started the Henry brickyard. She be a fine lady in her time, with a kind, generous heart."

Hal nodded. "The Higgins family owned thousands of acres of land in these parts. Rosemary was their only child. Most of the early Henry wealth came from her."

I looked at the dates on her tombstone, which read *4 December 1867–20 March 1900*, and compared them to James Allison's dates. "It appears my great-grandmother was older than my great-grandfather."

Hal nodded. "Folklore says she waited a long time to marry. She was a beauty, or so they say. She was very wealthy and could have had the pick of any man in the county. Old James Allison didn't have a dime in his pocket when he got here, it's been said. He must have been a real charmer to win her hand."

Rufus moved to the next grave, which had a small tombstone on it reading *Rose Marie Henry, 20 March 1900–3 April 1900*. "Mrs. Rosemary passed on giving birth to little Rose Marie here, Suh. It was a breech birth and hard on both of them. My Momma do the best she could for them, but it not enough, I sorry to say."

Rufus paused at the next gravesite beyond the baby Rose Marie. The tombstone read *Robert Allison Henry, 10 July 1898–27 August 1946*. "This be your granddaddy, Suh."

Hal chuckled. "If the gossip is right, your great-grandfather was right colorful, but your grandfather was a pure rascal. He was a bootlegger during the thirties and forties. Rumors still abound about all his money being buried somewhere around the old Henry homestead."

"Why did he bury it?" I asked.

Hal shrugged. "Like most folks, he didn't trust banks due to the recession of the thirties. The revenuers were keepin' a close eye on him as well, so he couldn't put the money in the bank even if he had trusted them. No one knows what happened to his stash of cash when he was killed. Some folks claim he was murdered over it. If you visit the old homestead, you'll see holes in the ground everywhere. The new Henrys and just about everybody else in the county have dug the place up looking for it over the years. Hell, I admit I dug a few of those holes myself as a kid. But nobody ever found any of his buried money. Or if they did, they damned sure didn't tell anybody." He grinned. "But come to think of it, I wouldn't have told anybody if I'd of found it either. Most likely whoever killed him took it."

Rufus stepped to the next grave, which read *Olivia Jane Henry, 12 August 1899–9 February 1943.* "This be your grandmomma; Mrs. Jane, she be called. She be a kind and God-fearing woman. She have two daughters as well as your daddy. They be Miss Alice Jane and Miss Rose Olivia."

Hal shrugged. "I don't know much about her. She was a Simms before she married Robert Allison. The Simms were hardworking but relatively poor people. They've all died out or moved on now."

"Where are the two daughters?"

Hal shoved his hands in his pockets and hunched his shoulders. "Nobody knows for sure. I heard a rumor that one of them was married and living in Tyler, but I don't know that for a fact, or what her married name might be now if she is living there. The other one supposedly moved to California. No one has ever heard any more from her. I do know that your grandfather remarried after your grandmother died. Your stepgrandmother, Cathie Fields, came from poor white trash and was considerably younger than your grandfather. They had one son named Jerry Calvin Henry, who was born after your grandfather died. She remarried J. R. Henry just before Jerry was born and later bore Bruce and Jimmy by J. R. before she died. She's buried over in the new Henry plot that you're having fixed up, though nobody can figure out why you're doing it."

"She's family. Why wouldn't I do it?"

"She was your stepgrandmother, Paul. She lost the whole family fortune to J. R. and his clan. She's not well thought of around here, if the truth be known."

Rufus stopped before my father's new headstone. "Your daddy be a young man when he died. He be a fine man with high spirits."

Hal snorted. "That's putting it kindly. They say he was a pure hell raiser. He hated J. R. and your stepgrandmother. He was suing them when he died."

"On what grounds?" I asked.

Hal shook his head. "Mr. Jackson can tell you all the legal crap. He's been the Henry family lawyer all his life."

"You didn't bother to tell me he was my family's lawyer when I was going to court," I retorted. I looked at my watch. "Speaking of which, I guess we better get going. I'm supposed to meet him in half an hour." I turned to Rufus as the others gathered close behind him. "I've enjoyed meeting you and appreciate all you've done for my family over the years."

Rufus shook my hand. "It good to have you home, Mr. Henry. We be waitin' a long time for this day. Things gonna change around here now, old Aunt Elsie say."

"Good day to all of you. Again, I appreciate all you've done for the family plot."

Hal followed me back to the car, and the group stood watching as we drove off.

"*Weird*!" I groaned when I turned out of the cemetery back onto the road to Clayhill. "What the hell do you make of that? Who the hell is this Aunt Elsie with the magic eye? What kind of witchcraft is she spouting about me coming back riding on a serpent spewing out truth and justice? What bullshit!"

Hal arched his eyebrows. "She's considered to be a great fortune-teller around these parts, Sport. Lots of folks seek her out. My own mother went to her more than once and swore by her."

"Don't tell me you believe in that crap! Even *you* aren't that dumb."

"Stop the car, Paul," he commanded.

"Do what?"

"Pull over, damn it!" He walked around to the front of the car. "Come here, Paul." When I got out and went around to the front of the car, he pointed at the hood. "What do you see there?"

I looked at the car. "A car, Hal, what the hell am I supposed to see?"

He tapped the emblem with his finger. "What is *that*, dumb ass?"

I stared, stunned. "A ... cobra ..."

"Would you call that a *serpent*?"

Chills chased down my spine as I stood staring at the snake emblem. Hal got back into the passenger seat. I silently followed and drove us back to Clayhill.

Hal turned to me as I parked in front of the hardware store. "Freaky, ain't it?"

I shrugged. "Coincidence; you have to admit it's a rather broad interpretation of this Aunt Elsie's vision or whatever."

He sighed. "You Henrys are stubborn cusses. Let's go see our lawyer."

"*Our* lawyer?"

SIX

Hal led me past the entrance to the hardware store into a steep stairwell leading up to the second floor. A narrow hallway guided us to a door framed in frosted glass with *Jason Jackson, Attorney at Law* printed across it in gold lettering. The door opened into a small reception area where a trim, older woman sat at a desk typing on a manual typewriter.

She turned to us. "Good afternoon to you, Mr. Sutton. How are you, child?"

Hal grinned. "I'm just fine, Miss Gladys, and how are you?"

"Thank you for asking, Mr. Sutton. I'm getting the rheumatism in my fingers. I keep telling Mr. Jason to hire a younger girl to do his office work, but he won't hear of it. You would think that after forty-two years he'd allow me to retire."

"Gladys? Is that Mr. Henry?" Jason Jackson called from the adjoining office.

"I don't know, Mr. Jason. You haven't given me time to get through the pleasantries yet," she called back. "He's always so impatient. Mr. Henry, I presume?"

"I'm Paul Henry, Ma'am. Glad to meet you."

She smiled. "My, my, but you're such a handsome young man. You look just like your daddy. Now he was a real lady-killer. Why, he had every girl in the county chasing after him."

"Gladys?" Jason Jackson called.

"I'm still doing the pleasantries, Mr. Jason. How is your mother, Mr. Henry? Now she was a woman who could hold a man's eye."

I laughed. "She's just fine. I'll tell her you inquired about her."

"Please do. She's such a fine woman."

"*Gladys!*" Jason Jackson called.

Miss Gladys punched a button on an old intercom box on her desk. "Mr. Jason, you have two gentlemen, a Mr. Sutton and a Mr. Henry, to see you," she yelled into the box.

"For goodness sakes, Gladys, I can hear you without that contraption—my door is open!" Jason Jackson bellowed. "Send them in before you talk them to death."

Miss Gladys smiled up at us. "You may go right in now, Mr. Jason is expecting you."

"Thank you, Ma'am," I replied, stifling a grin as Hal led me into the office.

Jason Jackson sat at a large dark oak desk in his white shirt and gray vest surrounded by memorabilia cluttering the end tables and lining the built-in bookcase behind him, with framed diplomas and pictures of him as a younger man posing with other people littering the walls. A deep, musky texture of old-world tang permeated the room as he stood and extended his hand.

"Mr. Henry, I trust your visit to the cemetery was agreeable?"

I shook hands as Hal settled into a worn leather chair beside me. "They placed the tombstone this morning. A strange thing occurred there. There was a group of black people cleaning up the plot. They wouldn't allow me to pay them for their services. They said they once worked for my great-grandfather and my grandfather in some brickyard."

Mr. Jackson indicated for me to be seated and sank into his own high-backed leather chair behind his desk. "That would be the Washingtons, Jeffersons, and Jacobses."

I nodded. "Yes, along with some of their children and grandchildren."

He clasped his hands on his desk and chuckled. "Your grandfather gave them a lifetime estate in their sharecropper shacks, along with three acres of good farm land, on the old Henry estate. It drives J. R. crazy because he can't get control of those patches of land until they die or choose of their own accord to move on. What are your plans now, Mr. Henry?"

I shrugged. "I came here to visit my father's grave. I hung around to see his gravestone placed. I have nothing to keep me here now other than the charges filed against me."

Jason Jackson leaned back in his chair. "You've posted bail. The worst that could happen is that you would be convicted if you failed to show for trial, at which time you would forfeit the bond. That's what everyone expects you to do. Standing trial serves no purpose. Staying here any longer could only invite additional problems for you."

"Are you advising me to leave town as well, Mr. Jackson? Everyone else seems to want me out of here."

"Not at all, Mr. Henry, I was simply advising you of the legal ramifications concerning the charges brought against you by your, uh, *family*."

I scowled. "Friendly bunch, aren't they? What do I owe you for your services, Mr. Jackson?"

"Fifteen dollars will cover my court appearance on your behalf, Mr. Henry. I've done nothing else up to this point to prepare for trial. However," he continued, fixing me with a benign stare as I reached for my wallet. "There are several pending legal issues concerning the Henry estate that I feel compelled to seek your guidance on."

I counted out fifteen dollars and placed the money on the desk. "What legal issues concerning the estate? J. R. owns everything now, doesn't he?"

Mr. Jackson wrote out a receipt and handed it to me. "He does and he doesn't, Mr. Henry. Your grandfather's will specifically bequeathed the bulk of the estate to your father. Cathie, perceptibly under J. R.'s tutelage, moved to have the will invalidated because it was written prior to your grandfather's marriage to her."

I stared at him. "Which means?"

Mr. Jackson arched his eyebrows. "In *theory*, J. R. became the owner of the Henry estate by virtue of his marriage to, and the subsequent death of, your stepgrandmother, Cathie. But the estate never went through probate, as is the custom."

"So?"

"When your father returned from the war and discovered he was virtually penniless, there was naturally bad blood between J. R., Cathie, and your father. Your father filed suit against the estate claiming the will was in fact valid and should therefore be probated as written. That would have made your father the heir to the Henry fortune."

"What happened to his suit?"

"Your father died before it came to probate and the proper legal rights of the estate were established. At the time, only your mother could continue the legal action he started. Susan refused to do so, therefore it has been held in abeyance for over twenty years now waiting for you to come of age."

"What does that mean?"

"It means the issue before the court is still open. Your father's rights, if any, are extended to you if you should wish to continue the suit he started."

"Are you saying I have a legitimate claim to the Henry estate?"

Mr. Jackson paused. "That is partly correct. There is one other potential heir that I know of. Jerry Henry is Robert Henry's legitimate son and your father's half brother, though he was unborn when your grandfather died and Cathie remarried J. R. He would have rights as well."

"Even though my grandfather had not married Cathie at the time he wrote the will?"

"That is correct."

"This is giving me a headache. Why didn't Jerry pursue his rights?"

"He probably isn't even aware of his potential rights because he has never had reason to question his stepfather's ownership of the estate. I only make you aware of this because if you do pursue your legal rights and are successful, he in turn could have rights as well. I inform you of these facts now out of simple courtesy to you."

"Hal said you were once my side of the family's lawyer."

"My father served as the Henry legal counsel for some thirty-odd years until he retired and turned the practice over to me shortly after I graduated from law school. Subsequent to your father's untimely death, my services to the family were discontinued. I await your instructions, Mr. Henry."

I shifted, bewildered. "I don't know what to say. I need some time to think about this."

Hal sat forward in his chair. "What the hell is there to think about, Sport? You own the estate by right. J. R. stole it from your daddy. Why do you think J. R. and his brood are so upset about you coming back here?"

I hesitated, my mind swirling with the confusing information. "Why didn't my mother pursue the issue? She must have had a reason. What is the estate worth, Mr. Jackson?"

Mr. Jackson shrugged. "It's hard to say in today's dollars. At the time of your grandfather's death, the Henry estate consisted of over two thousand acres of prime timber and farmland, as well as the brickyard. The brickyard has been sold by J. R. and closed down, but you would still have a claim for the moneys he received for it. I'm told it was over a half a million dollars."

"Why is it closed now?"

Mr. Jackson shrugged. "A rival company bought it. Closing it down gave them a monopoly in this area. In any case, if you should prevail in court, you would not be bound by the terms of the contract of sale if you chose to return the money. In essence, you could have the ownership reversed and reopen the business. It was quite prosperous in its time."

"Then why didn't J. R. run it? Why sell it, even for half a million dollars?"

Mr. Jackson paused. "I ... assume J. R. had no real desire to run it himself. I suspect it held bad memories for him. In any case, it's doubtful he had the required skills to continue the operations of the facility since he'd had no training in the administration of the business."

I sank back in exasperation. "What kind of bad memories, Mr. Jackson?"

Jason Jackson leaned back in his chair and chose his words carefully. "Apparently, the Arkansas side of the Henry family is very poor, though I know little of them. When your great-grandfather drifted to Clayhill from Little Rock in the late 1800s seeking his fortune, he met and married your great-grandmother, who came from a wealthy family. Over the years he founded the brickyard and vastly expanded the original landholdings of his wife's estate. When J. R. appeared in Clayhill in 1942, your great-grandfather, for whatever his personal reasons, was not particularly enamored with him. As such, he reluctantly put him to work in the brickyard as a lowly common laborer. J. R. worked there virtually ignored by the rest of the family until both your great-grandfather and your grandfather died and he married Cathie. Overnight he became the boss, going from rags to riches, as the saying goes, but in any case, it appears he did not enjoy the respect of the other workers."

Hal turned to me. "So what're you going to do about all this, Sport?"

I stared from one of them to the other. "I'm going back to Jasper to talk to my mother. I need to understand why she didn't pursue the issue herself."

Mr. Jackson nodded. "As I stated, Mr. Henry, I await your instructions."

* * *

When we reached the street, Hal sauntered past the Cobra toward the drugstore. "I assume we've got time for you to spring for a cheeseburger before we set out for Jasper, Sport?"

I drew up short. "Before *we* set out for Jasper?"

"I figure I'd better go with you so you don't forget your way back," he answered over his shoulder.

I followed him in with misgivings as Eva Marie watched us approach with troubled eyes.

"Hey, beautiful!" Hal greeted as he leaned across the counter to embrace her. "I hear Paul's been trying to get you to two-time me!"

Her eyes danced. "You haven't been by in ages! I thought you'd given up on me."

"Never happen. You'll always be my favorite girl!"

She darted a quick glance in my direction as her smile faded. "Mr. Henry."

"Miss Sherrill," I replied.

Hal looked from one of us to the other, bemused. "Honey-child, I want the biggest cheeseburger you've got, with all the trimmings, and a chocolate malt to go with it."

"Cheeseburger and strawberry malt," I added.

"So why haven't you been by to see me, Hal?" Eva Marie teased as she turned to the grill.

"I've been busy, darlin', but that don't mean you're not still the one and only for me."

I sat down at the counter as they bantered, circumspectly watching Jimmy Henry, dressed in slacks and a sports shirt, and Garland Sanders, in jeans and a jersey with the sleeves cut off, in the mirror behind the fountain as they strolled past and selected a booth next to the counter.

Garland's eyes locked with mine in the mirror in a telepathic, scornful taunt. "Hey! Can we get some damn service around here?"

I swiveled on the stool to face him. "Can't you see the lady's busy?"

Garland's face turned an angry red. "You talking to me?"

"You're the only one making a racket. Be patient, Fat Boy, she'll get to you when she's finished with us."

Garland lunged up from the booth coiled in rage. "Who the hell you calling 'Fat Boy'?"

I stood. "You don't have to make a total ass of yourself—if you're looking to start some shit with me, I'm more than willing to oblige you!"

Garland blinked and looked beyond me as the door opened. I glanced over my shoulder to see Sheriff Tate ambling toward us and eased back down onto my stool as Garland slunk back into his booth.

The sheriff sat on a stool beside Hal and tipped his hat back. "Good afternoon, Eva Marie, a cup of coffee when you get the chance, please." He turned to Hal and me. "Howdy, boys; sure is a hot one today, ain't it?" He looked beyond us to Jimmy and Garland in their booth. "Jimmy, Garland, you boys must have knocked off work early today."

Hal looked at the sheriff in the mirror. "It is hot at that, Sheriff. Hot enough to fry an egg on the sidewalk. This kind of heat makes tempers flare up."

Sheriff Tate's calculating eyes met mine in the mirror. "It does at that. Makes people all mean and nasty when it gets this humid. How was your daddy's headstone, Mr. Henry? Meet with your satisfaction, I trust?"

I held his gaze in the mirror. "The work was suitable, Sheriff."

He smiled without humor. "Glad to hear that, Mr. Henry."

Eva Marie set a cup before him, poured his coffee, replaced the pot on the burner, and hurried to Jimmy and Garland with her order pad in hand. She rushed back, drew two fountain sodas, turned to the grill, flipped the burgers, placed a slice of cheese on each, and then hurried back to Garland and Jimmy with their drinks. She hastened back to the grill to spread mayonnaise on the buns in the profound hush.

Hal cleared his throat. "A man ought to be fishing on a day like this, as hot as it is."

The silence grew deeper as Eva Marie slid the burgers and malts before Hal and me. "Do you need ketchup?"

Hal bit into his burger. "Umm, you're gonna make me a wonderful wife someday."

She half smiled. "You should be so lucky."

The sheriff dropped his hat onto the stool beside him. "Eva Marie, darling, I'll take a refill, if it's not too much trouble. It's so cool in here, I might stay awhile."

Jimmy placed two quarters on the table. "Come on, Garland."

Garland drew on his straw. "But I ain't finished my Coke yet!"

Jimmy nodded as he passed. "Sheriff."

The sheriff nodded back. "Jimmy."

Garland sucked air through his straw from the bottom of the glass, slammed it down on the table, and rushed out after Jimmy.

The sheriff smiled in the mirror. "Do I detect a level of tension in the air?"

Hal grinned, his mouth full. "I admit it's one of the rare occasions in my life when I'm delighted to see 'Johnnie Law' happening along."

Sheriff Tate studied me in the mirror. "Do you plan to stay in Clayhill longer, Mr. Henry?"

"You know, Sheriff, it's annoying as hell to have to keep answering that question, but in fact, I am going back to Jasper today." I imagined the faintest hint of disappointment cross Eva Marie's face. "But I intend to return. This is such a friendly little town it plumb makes me feel right at home." I pushed my untouched burger away and tossed two dollars beside the plate. "I'm outta here, Hal. If you're coming, get a move on."

Hal grabbed both cheeseburgers before hurrying after me. "You sure got a short fuse, Sport," he complained as I backed out. "Do you want this?" He held my cheeseburger out to me.

"I've lost my appetite. You damned people around here are getting on my nerves. I'm tired of everyone wanting to know my business."

"Don't take things so personal. Hell, anything that happens around here out of the ordinary is cause for speculation. You see those old men over there playing dominoes under the shade tree? They'll start a conversation today about the weather and finish it tomorrow. You're the only real entertainment we've had around here in ages."

"The only reason Jimmy and Garland came into the drugstore was to start some shit. If they want a piece of me, I'm ready to get it on."

Hal swallowed the last of his burger and bit into mine. "You made that perfectly clear to them, Sport. Poor old Garland didn't know what to make of it. He's a little dense. But don't go underestimating him. If he gets his hands on you he's capable of doing some serious damage."

"That fat piece of shit?" I scoffed. "He's a tub of lard that lives on intimidation. I'd love to bust that jerk-off's ass!"

Hal cut his eyes at me slyly. "This couldn't be about little Eva Marie, now could it?"

"What the hell do you mean by that? She's just another Clayhill fruitcake, as far as I'm concerned."

He chuckled. "Yep, it's got a little something to do with Eva Marie, for a fact."

I stomped the throttle, and the Cobra jumped forward. "What's her damned problem anyway?"

"She's a princess, Sport. She's royalty too, the same as you. She doesn't have to stoop and bow to you like the rest of us do. You're going to have to win her over through merit, and work hard at it at that, to prove yourself worthy of her fair hand."

"Give me a break!" I grated.

Hal pointed. "Turn left here. I want you to take a little detour for me."

"A detour to where?"

"To better understand your roots."

"Do you always talk in riddles?"

"You'll understand when we get there. Sometimes you have to know where you came from to know where you're going."

"Would you mind translating that into comprehensible English?"

"I'm going to show you the old Henry mansion, your ancestral home. It's about a mile on the outskirts of town."

"Won't J. R. object to us traipsing through his living room?"

"J. R. doesn't live there. He never has. It's been vacant for over twenty years now."

"Why doesn't J. R. live there?"

"They say it's haunted by your grandfather."

I rolled my eyes. "Bullshit!"

At Hal's direction, I slowed and turned onto a gravel lane with two large *No Trespassing* signs posted on each side. A massive, three-story white brick house with a sweeping wraparound cement porch on the lower level and big columned balconies on the two upper levels loomed before us. I eased up the lane through the once- magnificent grounds now in disrepair with raised flower gardens choked by weeds and vines beyond the shaggy, unshorn hedges. Three white fountains, discolored and silent, forlornly lined the center of the once-lush front lawn.

I got out and stared up at the huge dwelling in wonder, for the first time appreciating the wealth and power of the once-mighty Henry clan. "How many rooms do you think this place has?"

Hal led me around the structure. "I'm not sure, I've never been inside. In back's a bathhouse and swimming pool with a double tennis court. Beyond is a ten-horse stable with an attached barn and harness room."

The years had left the stable, barn, and bathhouse with their red cobbled roofs and white brick walls matching the main house in considerable disorder, as well as the pool, which featured diving boards on each end of its waterless, leaf-clogged bottom.

"I've snooped around the grounds here lots of times," Hal continued mystically. "The Henrys used to throw a summer bash on the 4th of July and invite everyone in Clayhill, rich, poor, or in-between, black and white. No one was excluded. It was the social event of the year. The rich would dress up in their tails and gowns to waltz around the ballroom and eat in elegance in the main dining room. The peasants huddled around outside here amongst tubs of baked beans, hundreds of desserts, huge pits of smoldering barbeque, and several bands playing above wooden platforms for dancing. Of course, J. R. stopped all that. Impressive, ain't it?"

I shrugged. "Personally, I think this place is too damned big and impractical for anyone to live in." As we stood staring up at the back of the main house, my attention was drawn to one window in particular. "Hey, somebody's watching us."

Hal followed my focus. "Where?"

"Second story window on the corner—I can't make it out, but something moved."

"It could be your grandfather's ghost. Some say that's why J. R. and his clan chose to build a new home down the road a piece."

"Or it could have been a shadow or a reflection," I scoffed.

Hal shrugged. "You're the one who saw it, Sport."

I studied the window. "Or it could be a vagrant. With this place standing empty for so long, anyone could have moved in."

"Could have, but I don't want to go in and check it out."

I chuckled. "You don't really believe in ghosts, now do you, Tater?"

"Don't call me *Tater*, damn it. Let's get on down the road to Jasper. I just wanted to show you the old place so you could get a feel for where you came from."

"Sorry to disappoint you, pal, but it still doesn't give me a road map to where I want to go."

Hal turned back to the Cobra. "Give it time, Sport."

* * *

I slowed to the posted speed limit through Pineland and waved at Sheriff Johnston sitting in his speed trap as we drove by. On the open highway again, I let the Cobra have its lead, blowing by the light traffic in a howling blur as Hal sat with his feet braced against the floorboard. Twenty minutes later I eased off the throttle and coasted into Jasper, my hostility fading.

"Do you know any women around here we can hook up with?" Hal asked.

"Do you know any Chinese love-making techniques?" I countered.

"Chinese what?"

"Never mind. I know a couple of girls that might be available for the evening."

He rubbed his hands together. "Now you're talkin'! The pickings are mighty slim around Clayhill. I've always wanted to see what city girls are like."

"They're like girls everywhere—their sole objective in life is to make you miserable."

Hal's eyes twinkled. "Still smarting over little Princess Eva Marie blowing you off, Sport?"

I glanced at him as I pulled into my mother's driveway. "You're working your way right up to the top of my shit list, pal."

My mother rushed to hug me when we walked in. "Paul! I was so worried about you."

"Momma, this is Hal Sutton, a friend of mine from Clayhill."

She turned to him. "Mr. Sutton, I'm glad to meet you."

Hal swept his cowboy hat off his head. "I'm delighted to meet you, Mrs. Henry."

"I'll call your Aunt Kathy and cancel bingo for tonight. I know you boys are hungry. We'll fix you a big supper of fried chicken and mashed potatoes with corn and black-eyed peas."

"Don't bother, Momma, Hal and I've got other plans. We'll grab something at the Dairy Queen."

"You probably haven't eaten a decent meal since you left!" she protested.

"Go to bingo, Momma! We'll be fine. There's a lot we need to talk about concerning the Henrys and Clayhill, but it can wait until tomorrow."

Worry lines creased her forehead. "What things, Paul?"

"We'll talk later, Momma. Do I have a clean shirt?"

"The one you left is hanging in your closet. Give me your dirty laundry and I'll get started on it before I meet Kathy. I can make your friend a bed on the couch for tonight."

"I don't want to be any bother to you, Ma'am," Hal insisted.

"It's no trouble at all, Mr. Sutton. I'm just embarrassed that I won't be fixing supper for you. Paul is so hard to predict. He never gives me any warning about these things."

"Don't you fret about that, Ma'am; we'll be just fine. You go on and enjoy your bingo."

Hal followed me into the bedroom as I headed for the shower. When I came out, he was studying the pictures and newspaper clippings on the wall with the frame containing my medals from Vietnam in his hands.

"Where the hell did you get that?" I demanded.

He stared at the scars on my bare upper torso. "From your mother; you didn't tell me you were an All-Star quarterback and a bona fide war hero."

I rummaged through my closet for my shirt. "That's probably because it's none of your damned business."

"Oh my, and he's modest, too," he chided.

"Are you going to shower? You can borrow one of my old jerseys from high school."

"But his personality still sucks ..." he added on his way to the bathroom.

I searched through a drawer, found one of my old football jerseys, which was the best fit I could come up with for Hal's larger physique, tossed it on the bed, and went back into the living room, where my mother confronted me.

"Elaine Duckworth called, and that *McDougal girl* has been calling three times a day every day ..."

"No problem." I turned to the hall phone and dialed. "Hi, Elaine."

"Paul! Where have you been?"

"What are you doing tonight?"

"Why are you asking?"

"I've got a friend with me. We thought we'd meet up with you at the Dairy Queen, if you don't already have other plans."

"Paul ... Barbara heard something about us being together ..."

"Don't worry about it. We'll see you at the Dairy Queen in half an hour. Maybe we can discuss that Chinese thing some more. Bye now." I smirked as I dialed Barbara's number.

"*Paul? Where have you been?*"

"I had some business to attend to. Look, I brought a friend back with me. Do you want to meet up with us and Elaine in half an hour at the Dairy Queen?"

"*I know all about you and Elaine, you asshole!*"

"What's that supposed to mean?"

"*I thought I was your girl.*"

"Why?"

"*Well … because … you know … we … you know …*"

"I don't remember any lifelong commitments being made."

"*Who are you going to be with tonight, me or Elaine?*"

"We'll work that out when we get there."

"*You want things all your own way, don't you, Paul Henry?*"

"I'm just out for a good time."

"*I'd like to think I'm more than just a good time.*"

"Look, if you have other plans …"

"*I'll be there in half an hour!*"

"See you there."

"*I've missed you, Paul. When I see you I'm gonna –*"

"Uh, Barbara, hurry now, okay?"

"*I ain't wearing any panties. You just keep that in mind when you're trying to decide on me or Elaine …*"

"Bye, Barbara." I hung up the phone.

My mother wrung her hands. "I hope you meet a *decent* girl soon …"

"Why, Momma, decent girls aren't half the fun!"

"*Paul Allison Henry*! I raised you better. You better start acting like it too, young man!"

I kissed her forehead as Hal stepped out of my bedroom. "See you later. Hal's anxious to get at our city girls."

"I declare, I worry myself to death over you," she fussed.

I turned to the door. "Don't be waiting up for me, Momma!"

"So did you get us a date?" Hal asked as we climbed into the Cobra.

"Well, actually, I got *me* two dates. I'll do my best to pass one off to you, but no promises: they're both pretty smitten with me."

"Hell, I'm not picky. I'll take either one."

"Good. I want Elaine. You can have Barbara."

"Why do you want Elaine?"

"She's better looking and she's got class. Barbara is more your type."

"What's my type?"

"You know, raw and ready. Me, I like the subtle type, the ones that can carry on a conversation. You'd be lost with Elaine. Barbara is an alley cat better suited to your style."

Hal preened. "Let's roll!"

We pulled into the Dairy Queen, where Elaine waited in her old brown Pontiac. Her eyes lit up as she took in Hal's tall frame, broad shoulders, and narrow hips as he in turn sized up her slim figure, liquid brown eyes, and dark curls with a broad grin of appreciation. By the time Barbara arrived, Elaine was so thoroughly enamored by Hal's corny jokes and hillbilly humor she didn't even seem to notice Barbara rush into my arms to stake her claim for the night.

I was left to wonder about fickle women: less than an hour earlier I had all but promised Elaine an education in the ancient art of Chinese lovemaking, and now she was making goo-goo eyes at a bummed out, half-assed cowboy who didn't have two nickels to rub together or a clean shirt to his name.

After burgers and fries, we departed in Elaine's Pontiac to the local bootlegger. We then drove to Rocky Fjord, where I sat on the far side of the pool with Barbara draped all over me in an eager tangle and drank more than my share of the whisky as Hal and Elaine frolicked in their underwear in the moonlit water, my thoughts drifting dully to Eva Marie.

SEVEN

I lay tangled in the sheets with harsh sunlight streaming through the curtains staring at the clock on the nightstand, which indicated it was well past noon, my head exploding and my mouth covered with a thick layer of algae. I stumbled up on quaking legs, dressed, and made my way to the living room, where I found Hal snoring peacefully on the sofa, his freshly laundered jeans and shirt folded on the coffee table beside him.

My distraught mother sat at the kitchen table. "You got in late last night."

I poured a cup of coffee with trembling hands and sat down across from her. "Actually, I got in early this morning."

She shifted her eyes downward. "I worry so much about you."

"Are we going to go through this again, Momma?"

"I could smell liquor. That's against the law, Paul."

"Drinking is not against the law. Selling liquor is against the law— that's why bootleggers have to bribe the law to sell it."

"You've got your whole life before you. Drinking and staying out until all hours of the night with women of questionable repute—"

"Drop it, Momma! I mean it. I want to talk about my father. I know it's painful for you, but the time has come. You need to tell me everything."

She hesitated as Hal got up from the sofa and made his way to the bathroom. "There are things in the past I don't understand, Paul. Your father was not one to share his troubles for fear of worrying me."

"Why didn't you continue the lawsuit against J. R. and my stepgrandmother?"

"You've been talking to Jason Jackson."

"Miss Gladys sends her regards."

She brightened. "She's such a dear lady."

"She wants to retire now, but he won't let her."

She laughed. "He couldn't practice law without her. She wouldn't leave him anyway."

"Why did you refuse to pursue the suit against the Henry estate?"

She grew somber. "Things were very confusing at the time. When I visited your father in jail, he was extremely angry. He gave me instructions to get him out on bail. And then he was gone. It was so quick. I couldn't believe it. I couldn't understand how … he could do that to himself … to me … to you. When I went to the mortuary to … identify him … I collapsed. I almost lost you too. You were born premature. You were weak and wouldn't take my milk. I was terrified. You were all I had left. I had to pull myself together to protect you. I had to get us out of Clayhill."

"Why did you feel Clayhill was a danger to us?"

She wiped at her tears. "After you were born, J. R. and the sheriff came to visit me. J. R. insisted that your father had no legal claim to the estate. He offered me twenty-five thousand dollars to start a new life if I would sign a paper dropping my claim to the estate and move away from Clayhill. I was frightened. I had no money and nowhere to go, except back home to my parents. Twenty-five thousand dollars was a lot of money. I used half of it to buy this house so you would have a decent home. You were all I cared about."

I leaned forward. "Did J. R. and Sheriff Allston threaten you?"

"Not … directly … but I felt something bad might happen if we stayed in Clayhill. It's difficult to explain."

I took her hand. "I understand how hard this is for you, but I need to know everything."

She lifted misery-filled eyes to me. "Why is this so important to you, Paul?"

"If we have a legitimate claim to the estate, then we should pursue it. Do you know what the estate was worth at the time?"

"There was land involved, and the brickyard of course, but I knew little else."

"The estate was worth in the neighborhood of a million dollars. That was twenty years ago. It's probably worth three times that now."

"I had no idea ..."

"J. R. gave you a paltry twenty-five thousand dollars to drop your claim, and then he intimidated you into leaving Clayhill."

"Is the money that important to you, Paul?"

I sat back in my chair. "It's more personal than money."

"Personal in what way?"

"My father seemed to think J. R. cheated him out of what was rightfully his. There are even some in Clayhill who don't believe my father committed suicide."

"Are you saying they think J. R. had something to do with his death?"

I shrugged. "You admit you left Clayhill because you were concerned J. R. might harm us in some way, right? And you're concerned even now that if I pursue this lawsuit with J. R., he may still try to harm me, aren't you? If my father didn't hang himself in that cell, I want to try and prove it."

Her eyes filled with pain. "Oh, Paul, please don't be foolish about this."

"What was my father's relationship with Sheriff Allston?"

She collected herself. "Your father didn't trust him. He thought J. R. had some kind of hold over him."

"He told you that?"

"He accused Sheriff Allston of being J. R.'s puppet when I was at the jail. Sheriff Allston got very angry. They shouted at each other. Your father was very direct about things." She reached across the table and clasped my hand. "The Henry estate is not worth the risk, Paul. We've managed to make a new life for ourselves without their money. I beg you to leave things as they are. Please don't get caught up in this. If Sheriff Allston really is on J. R.'s side—"

"Sheriff Allston is retired now. Sheriff Tate is in office. He inquired about you as well."

Her eyes softened. "Nelson Tate? He was only a deputy when ..."

"His main focus now seems to be that I'll cause trouble for the Henrys."

"I ... always knew him to be a good, honest man ..."

"People can change. I met Bruce, and I saw J. R. and Jimmy." Fighting Bruce, spending the night in Sheriff Tate's jail, and the assault-and-battery charges pending against me were better left untold.

She squeezed my hand. "Stay away from there, Paul. That place will only bring you trouble."

"I've never been one to run from trouble, Momma. You know that. Is there anything else you can tell me that might help?"

She bit her lip. "Your father always felt that J. R. ... was somehow involved in the murder of his own father, Robert."

I sat back in my chair. "Did he have any proof?"

She shook her head. "Not that I know of; as I said, your father didn't discuss those things with me. I overheard him talking to someone else. But if J. R. was involved in the death of your father as well, then you can understand why I don't want you to become mixed up in this estate thing. It's not worth your life."

Hal emerged from the bathroom with his hair slicked back from his shower and entered the kitchen buttoning his shirt and looking radiant after his night with Elaine, which only served to aggravate me further as I recalled my sticky, groping time with Barbara.

"Am I interrupting anything?" he asked in the silence.

I scowled. "No. Sleep well?"

"Like a baby. I sure appreciate you laundering my things, Mrs. Henry. I hope it wasn't too much of a bother for you."

"No problem at all, Mr. Sutton. Are you hungry?" She poured him a cup of coffee and placed it before him as he seated himself at the table.

"Yes, Ma'am, I'm starved. Can I help you with anything?"

"No thank you, Mr. Sutton, I've got everything under control." She turned to the counter to prepare soup and sandwiches for us.

"Could we please dispense with all the 'Mister' crap, Momma? Call him Hal. I've heard all the 'Misters' I want to hear for a while."

"Proper manners are the mark of a man," she chastised as she worked. "You'd do well to practice what you've been taught." She smiled sweetly at Hal. "Are you Doris and Wilbur's son, by any chance?"

"Yes, Ma'am. Dad died in a logging accident about ten years ago. My mom passed on six years later from the fever."

She turned to him. "I'm sorry to hear that. They were both fine people. You were just a baby when I left, but your mother was so proud of you and showed you off every chance she got."

Hal laughed. "She did that 'til the day she died. It was hard to live up to her expectations. I hope I didn't disappoint her too much along the way."

She slid our sandwiches before us and turned to ladle up bowls of soup. "You seem to have turned out to be a fine young man."

I rolled my eyes. "He's just good at fooling people when he's putting on the dog, Momma. I'm surprised you can't see what an outlaw he is. You should know he's a bad influence on me and always trying to lead me down the path of sin and self-destruction."

She laughed. "Oh, Paul, I imagine if there's any leading going on, you're in the forefront."

I scowled at Hal. "Now you've turned my own mother against me!"

Hal grinned as he bit into his sandwich. "Sounds like she's got your number, Sport. So, what are our plans for today?"

"Why? Have you got something *personal* in mind?"

He twitched in a noncommittal shrug. "Elaine said she might call this morning."

"It sure didn't take you long to whisk her off her feet. What is it with you and women? Can't they see through all that phony charm to the snake underneath? By the way, you were supposed to take Barbara."

"I don't remember agreeing to that. Besides, Barbara appears to be a little raw for a man of my genteel persuasion."

My mother lifted her eyebrows triumphantly. "You see, Paul, even a stranger can spot the flaws in someone like that McDougal girl. I don't know why you can't see that for yourself."

I glared at Hal's smug expression. "Well, *Sport*, do you want to hang around here and keep scoring points with my mother all day, or are you ready to roll?"

He scooped up the last of his soup. "Where are we off to?"

"Clayhill."

My mother's lips thinned. "Paul, I wish you'd give this more thought."

"What's the hurry?" Hal urged. "If your mother feels you need more time to think this thing through …"

"Thinking things through doesn't have anything to do with it, *Sport*. You're trying to stall, hoping Elaine will call."

"Well, I *would* like to tell her goodbye proper like, if you don't mind. There's no need to rush on back to Clayhill since nothing is going to change in a day or two that hasn't changed in the last twenty years."

My mother turned from the counter. "He's right, Paul. We need to talk further about this before you do something rash."

The phone rang and she hurried out to answer it. "Paul?"

I went out to the hall and took the phone. "Hello?"

"Paul, this is Elaine, but call me Sheila, okay?"

"Sheila?"

"Is Hal where he can hear?"

I looked over my shoulder to him seated at the table. "Uh, sort of. Why?"

"I really like him a lot. Have you told him about us?"

"Us?"

"I wouldn't want him to get the wrong idea. Do you know what I mean?"

"Uh, no …"

"Please don't ever tell him about us. Okay? Promise?"

I grinned. "Ever? That's a long time, Sheila. I might need some sort of inducement to keep a secret that long."

"Inducement?"

"Yeah, like, what's in it for me if I do this favor for you?"

"Oh, well … I'll keep one of your secrets for you in return."

"I don't have any secrets."

"Sure you do," she insisted.

"Such as?"

"Getting into a fight with your cousin and spending the night in the Clayhill jail."

"What!" I turned to glare at Hal, who was busy charming my mother with some outlandish tale, his arms spread wide for emphasis.

"Is that inducement enough?" she purred. *"I don't tell your mother your secrets and you don't tell Hal mine. Deal?"*

"Deal," I growled.

"Good. I'm going to hang up now and call him back in a few minutes. Thanks, Paul. Now say 'goodbye, Sheila.'"

"Goodbye, Sheila!" The receiver went dead. I hung up and turned back to the kitchen.

"Who was that, dear?" my mother asked.

"Sheila," I mumbled.

"Sheila Grooms? Isn't she married to Tom—"

"Not *that* Sheila."

"I don't know any other Sheila in Jasper ... unless she's another one of those young—"

"*Momma*, can we just *drop* it?"

"But, Paul ..."

"I'm going to take a shower." I hurried out of the kitchen as the phone rang again.

She answered it and called Hal to the phone as I closed my bedroom door.

* * *

I stopped by the bank to replenish my cash supply from my meager savings, which were running seriously low now due to all the unplanned expenditures. Afterward I drove toward Pineland at a sedate pace as Hal leaned against the passenger door humming happily, lost in his own world.

"You're sure in a mellow mood," I grumped.

He flashed me a goofy grin. "I sure like city girls."

"You've only met *one*, for Christ's sake."

"I think I'm in love—*good grief*!" He grabbed for the dash as I gaped at him in astonishment and swerved off the road. "I've decided to give Eva Marie back to you since I stole Elaine," he mused after I stabilized the Cobra and regained the asphalt.

"What a pal!" I choked.

"Obviously it's the right thing to do under the circumstances."

"Obviously," I sneered.

"You sound pissed. You shouldn't be. You've still got Barbara on the side, too."

"Oh, clearly I'm pissed—I can't stand Barbara, and Eva Marie can't stand me. What a deal!"

"When I first saw Elaine, I knew she was special. I knew then why you were trying to pawn Barbara off on me. The minute I looked into her eyes, I was a lost man. I think it all turned out for the best."

"I'm sure it did."

"Elaine's clearly a woman who values high principles in a man. You would never appreciate her like I do. I mean, you're an okay guy in some ways, but the fact is, when it comes to women, you're pretty shallow. Know what I mean?"

"Oh, sure; I know exactly what you mean. By the way, the next time I find your drunk ass rotting away in a jail cell, I'm going to leave you there. *Know what I mean?*"

"You're a poor loser, Paul."

I slowed as we approached the city limits of Pineland. "Wave at Sheriff Johnston as we go by; he and I are *real pals* too."

"You're being cynical," he accused.

I waved at Sheriff Johnston, who glared at me. "Who, me? Why would you think such a thought?" When we cleared Pineland, I let the Cobra sail toward Clayhill as Hal swayed through the turns clutching at the dash.

"I assume you've reached a decision on the Henry thing for us to be rushing back so soon?"

"I'm still thinking about it," I snapped. "Mostly I just wanted to get you away from my mother before she disowns me."

"I know you've got the backbone to stand up to them, so what's your real reluctance?"

"For starters, in case you didn't notice, my mother's dead set against it."

"It appears to me you've never given your poor old momma's wishes much consideration in anything you've ever done before."

"*Stuff* it, *Tater!*"

* * *

I eased into Clayhill and made the obligatory circle around the courthouse square so everyone could stop and gawk at us. Sheriff Tate stepped out of his office and motioned to me. I parked in front of the hardware store, and he ambled over.

"Mr. Henry? I'd like you to ride out to the cemetery with me, if you have the time."

"Why?"

"I'm afraid we've experienced a little vandalism here in Clayhill. Your father's grave was desecrated by vandals last night. I'll need you to file an official complaint to go with my report."

Hal whistled as we followed Sheriff Tate across the street to his patrol car. "I have a feeling things are gonna get downright interesting around here now, *for sure!*"

Mr. Farr hurried out of the office and climbed into the back with Hal when we pulled into the cemetery.

"I'm so sorry about this, Mr. Henry. I've never had such a thing happen before."

When we pulled up to the family plot I saw rutted tire tracks in the grass indicating someone had used their bumper to push the fence over on one side, leaving the other sides sagging. I walked down the row of graves to my father's marble headstone, which lay smashed in several pieces. A mass of raw human feces spotted with flies festered in the center of the burial mound.

I turned back to the car in a burning rage. "Only a sick, deranged mind would do something like this to strike at me," I gritted as the others climbed into the car.

Mr. Farr cleared his throat. "I'm deeply embarrassed by this terrible deed, Mr. Henry."

"I can guess who's behind this," I spat back.

"Don't go jumping to conclusions, Mr. Henry," Sheriff Tate warned as we pulled away. "It'll serve no useful purpose for you to go off half-cocked on this before I've completed my investigation."

"I'll have the mess cleaned up immediately," Mr. Farr assured me from the backseat. "Do you want to order a new headstone?"

"Leave things as they are for now!" I muttered. "I want the people around here to know that a perverted psycho lives in their midst."

"As you wish, Sir."

The sheriff dropped Mr. Farr off at the office and then drove us back to Clayhill. "I'll need you to come in and sign a complaint," he advised as he parked in front of the jail.

I turned to Hal. "Why don't you grab a burger?" I took out my wallet and handed him ten dollars. "Be ready to roll in half an hour."

"Do you want me to say anything to Eva Marie?"

"I'm sure she already knows. There aren't any secrets in this damned town unless you're an outsider, and then nobody is willing to tell you anything."

He hesitated. "What I meant was … do you want me to tell her anything *personal*?"

I turned to the jail. "Tell her you traded her back to me for Elaine— that ought to curl her toes!"

Sheriff Tate seated himself and pushed a typewritten form across to me. "It's pretty self-explanatory. You're filing a complaint with the county for an act of vandalism on personal property. I have another complaint signed by Mr. Farr on the cemetery's behalf."

I signed the complaint. "Anything else?"

He cleared his throat. "How is Susan?"

"She's beside herself because I came back to Clayhill. I've decided to fight J. R. I'm informing you of this so you don't have to keep asking when I'm leaving."

His expression shifted to neutral. "I hope you know what you're letting yourself in for."

"I'll play by the rules as long as he does. But if he crosses the line, I'll do the same. I'll fight him on his ground using his rules if necessary. I want you to know that up front."

His eyes narrowed. "I don't like the inference in that, Mr. Henry."

"If trouble comes my way, you just call it as it stands, Sheriff, without bias."

His jaw clenched. "You don't beat around the bush, so allow me the same latitude. I tend to take it personal when it's implied I would use my badge in anything but a neutral fashion to uphold the law."

"I simply want to ensure we have an understanding, Sheriff."

His face darkened. "Before I completely lose my cool, would you give me the courtesy of explaining why you have doubts about my personal integrity to begin with?"

"My father accused Sheriff Allston of being J. R.'s puppet. J. R. more or less threatened my mother in his presence if she didn't leave Clayhill. Where were *you* when that went down?"

He stood abruptly. "I think it best if you leave now, Mr. Henry."

I stood. "For the record, I don't think my father committed suicide in that cell. I think he was murdered. You were part of the police force back then—what do *you* think happened?"

He walked around the desk. "Take your insinuations and get out of my office before I forget that I admire and respect your mother. This one is on the house, but if you ever insult me to my face again, I'll take this badge off for a few minutes. That's not a threat; it's a guarantee."

I held his stare. "And *I'll* guarantee *you* that I won't spend another night in your stinking jail on some trumped-up charge, Sheriff, nor do I plan to find myself hanging from one of the crossbeams in there like my father did!"

"Get out, Mr. Henry, before I throw you out."

I turned to the door. "I'll be seeing you, Sheriff."

"You can count on it," he replied as I closed the door behind me.

* * *

I walked across the street to the drugstore, where Hal sat at the counter munching on a burger and talking to Eva Marie. When her stunning green eyes lifted to mine, I experienced an involuntary flutter in my stomach in spite of the annoying sympathy I saw reflected there.

"Good afternoon, Mr. Henry. I'm sorry to hear about your father's grave."

"Good afternoon, Miss Sherrill. Thank you for your concern. Hal, wrap that thing in a napkin and let's get going."

Hal scowled. "I'd sure appreciate it if you two would sort things out so I could finish a meal sitting down. What's the hurry, anyway? You said half an hour."

I turned to the door. "The sheriff wasn't in a sociable mood."

He hurried after me. "Now, why do I feel like you went and insulted him in some way?"

"We just needed to clear the air on a few things." I turned to Jason Jackson's office. "I've decided to file claim to the Henry estate."

Hal followed me up the steps to Jason Jackson's office, where we exchanged the necessary pleasantries with Miss Gladys before she ushered us in.

Mr. Jackson stood and offered his hand. "Mr. Henry, please accept my sympathy for the despicable act at the cemetery. It reflects badly on all of the good citizens of Clayhill. Does the sheriff have any suspects yet?"

"He says he's investigating."

"He's a very capable law officer. I'm sure he'll get to the bottom of things. How was your trip to Jasper?"

"My mother sends her regards."

He smiled. "I'm sure Susan wasn't pleased with my discussing the estate with you."

"She's concerned that I might get in over my head."

He nodded thoughtfully. "Have you made a decision then?"

I shifted in my chair. "J. R. paid my mother twenty-five thousand dollars to sign a piece of paper dropping her claim to the Henry estate and to leave town."

He nodded. "I suspected there was something like that behind her reluctance to continue the suit action."

"In view of that, what do you think the odds are of me winning?"

"She could only sign away her rights by way of a quitclaim deed. As such, it would not affect your rights in a probate proceeding because a parent cannot sign away the rights of a minor child. As for winning the suit, in the legal world there are no certainties, as such, but in my opinion, you have a strong argument. I've studied the case law involved, and it's as solid as any position I've seen."

I locked eyes with him. "My mother thinks I might be in some sort of danger if I pursue this. What is your opinion?"

He leaned back in his leather chair, propped his elbows on the padded armrests, and formed a pyramid just below his chin with his fingertips. "That is an issue you will have to evaluate for yourself, Mr. Henry. There is certainly a lot of land and money at stake. I'm sure the emotions will run high as the case progresses."

"Do you have any reason to believe my father did not commit suicide?"

He fixed his gaze on the dirty window. "I don't have a legal opinion on that, Mr. Henry."

"Give me your personal opinion then."

"I don't offer my personal opinion to clients in such matters."

I sighed. "Mr. Jackson, everyone around here seems to think they know something, but no one is willing to say what they think they know. Why is that?"

He turned back to me. "This is a small town, Mr. Henry. People have long memories and harbor ill feelings for extensive periods of time. In most cases, the feuds of the fathers are handed down to their children, who weren't even born when the original dispute occurred. In such an environment, it is wise for one to move carefully and choose his stances solidly since it will likely be with him for years to come after the fact."

I turned to Hal. "Okay, you said you could interpret what was being said, so interpret."

Hal shrugged. "You can't expect to pick a fight and ask people to stand with you unless they believe you're willing to finish the fight."

I turned back to Jason Jackson. "What would be the legal costs of pursuing this action?"

He pulled out a ledger. "Your father paid most of the filing fees up front, as well as a most generous retainer for my services. At worst, any additional costs should not exceed five hundred dollars, if that much."

I opened my wallet, counted out five one hundred dollar bills, and laid them on the desk. "Please proceed with the legal claim on the Henry estate, Mr. Jackson."

He nodded. "As you wish, Mr. Henry."

EIGHT

I clomped down the stairs from Mr. Jackson's office with Hal trailing after me.

"So now that you've decided to stand and fight, what's next, Sport?' he asked.

"Find a place to live," I replied over my shoulder. "It's too much of a hassle to commute between here and Jasper, and I've had about all of the Pine View Inn I can stand."

"Why don't you move into my place?"

"You're kidding, right?"

"Outside of the Pine View Inn, we don't have much else to offer around here."

"I'm sure Old Billy would just love that."

"Aw, he'll get used to you eventually."

"Actually, he's the least of my qualms. Your pet rats and snakes scare me even more."

"They're harmless enough. Besides, it'll be easier for me to keep an eye on you if we're under the same roof."

I turned to him when we reached the street. "I'll consider it if you'll allow me to hire a maid to clean the place up and a carpenter to do a few repairs first."

"That's not necessary."

"It is if I'm going to stay there. You can deduct it from my rent."

"I don't expect you to pay rent, Paul."

"Consider it an insurance premium then."

"Insurance for what?"

"Insurance on me not getting bit by some damned varmint lurking around inside or the damned place falling down on my head while I'm asleep."

He winced. "You sure make it hard on a man to be a friend. What happened between you and the sheriff that's got you so pissed?"

I yanked open the door to the Cobra as he hustled around to the passenger side and slid in. "We reached an understanding. It's nothing to worry about. Where do the Washingtons live?"

"Out near my place. Sheriff Tate's a good man, Paul. Don't alienate him; you're going to have more than enough trouble with the Henrys as it is."

"You're just chock-full of advice, aren't you?"

"That's why I'm here, ain't it?"

We drove in silence until he indicated a gravel road intersecting the pavement. "Turn here, the Washingtons live about a mile out."

I pulled up in front of a weathered, well-kept house with a tin roof, where a pack of hounds greeted us in a howling clamor.

Rufus Washington stepped out onto the porch. "*Get on back there, Rosie! You too there, Red! Get on back now!* Mr. Henry, Suh! What bring you all the way out here?"

I eyed the hounds warily as I eased out of the Cobra. "How are you, Mr. Washington? I was hoping you could help me find some labor. I'm willing to pay top wages."

"What you need doin', Suh?"

"I need a dump of a house cleaned, a few carpenters to fix the place up, some weeds cut, a ton of trash disposed of, and some junk cars hauled off to the scrap yard."

Mr. Washington cut his eyes at Hal. "You talkin' about the old Sutton place, Suh?"

"It's in pretty bad shape, inside and out."

"Yes, Suh, I be by there just a while back to mate one of my coon dogs up with one of Mr. Sutton's there. Place sure do need some work. When you want us to start?"

"The sooner the better."

"I be by there first thing in the morning with a good crew. We get that old place fixed up in no time. Thank you for the work, Suh. Things be slow around here these days."

"Thank you, Mr. Washington. I appreciate your assistance." I turned back to the car and drove off. "We'll stay in the Pine View Inn tonight."

Hal frowned. "Why do we need to stay there?"

"I don't think my vaccinations are up to date. Where's Maybell's? I need a drink."

Hal pointed. "Turn here. She charges a dollar a pint for her homemade brew, but her stuff will make you go blind. I recommend the two-dollar distilled booze she ferries in from Louisiana."

He directed me to a weathered shack set back in the woods at the end of a well-traveled dirt road, where we entered a room masquerading as a lounge with a rough-cut wooden bar, from behind which a large, busty woman fixed a mean set of eyes on Hal.

"What the hell you doin' back here? And who the hell you got there with you?"

Hal edged behind me. "Now Maybell, we ain't staying or anything. We just want a couple of pints of your imported finest."

Maybell's steely eyes shifted to me. "And how the hell do I know this son of a bitch ain't no revenuer you're siccin' on me?"

Hal looked pained. "Now, Maybell, you know me better than that! We go way back."

"Yeah, all the way back to you tearing up my whole joint the other night!"

"Now, Maybell, you know that stuff you brew makes me plum crazy! I'd never do anything like that if my wits weren't scrambled! Why, I've always adored you, and you know that for a fact. If you weren't already married, I'd be chasing after you night and day."

Maybell's disposition softened somewhat. "Hal Sutton, you're as full of shit as a Christmas turkey, but you *are* a charmer. I'll get you a couple of pints of Old Crow, but you better not break the cap on them till you hit the highway. You understand me?"

Hal hurried around me to hug her large body to his chest. "You're my favorite gal, Maybell! I'm sure sorry about the other night!"

I bought two pints of the good stuff, put one of them in the glove compartment, and drove to the Pine View Inn, where I checked us into a double room after dispatching Hal to a corner store to purchase a six-pack of Coke and a small bag of ice. When he returned, we settled in to watch a rerun of *I Love Lucy* on the snowy, static-filled black-and-white TV while we drank the whisky.

I lay in a half daze, my thoughts wandering. Had I lost my mind? What was I trying to prove by staying in Clayhill and stirring up a family feud that had been brewing for twenty years? It was for justice, I decided grimly. J. R. needed to be brought down for cheating me out of ever knowing my father. And they had no right to desecrate my father's grave. I sipped at the distilled poison, growing eager for the confrontation to come.

* * *

I drove us to Pearle's for breakfast to settle our nauseous, whisky-soured stomachs. When I turned into Hal's lane afterward, we found several trucks parked about with men hustling around busily. Old Billy, tied to a tree with a rope, looked none too happy about the activity swirling around his domain as we climbed out of the Cobra appraising the men cutting weeds and dragging mounds of rubbish to a fire built off to the side. Others piled scrap iron into the back of two pickup trucks as several more busied themselves winching the junk cars up onto a flatbed truck. Half a dozen men labored on the frame of the house, straightening it with jacks and rebasing the studs. Others ripped off rotten boards from the porch and sides of the house while still others pounded on the old tin roof. Several women hauled trash from the house to the fire outside while others scrubbed the floors and windows inside.

Rufus Washington hurried to greet us. "Mornin', Mr. Henry, Mr. Sutton. The women be needing you in thu house to tell 'em what need to be thrown out and what need to be kept. We gettin' the foundation straight and the roof patched. I got lumber comin' to patch the rotten wood and such. Had to tie your goat up. Hope you don't mind. He be mighty particular about folks being in his yard."

I grinned. "He's a rascal, alright. I'd like to rent one of your pickups and a driver to pick up some things from town."

"Yes, Suh. I send Thomas over there with you."

"Thank you, Mr. Washington." I walked into the house. "Good morning, Ma'am," I greeted Mrs. Washington. "Throw away anything that can't be used, to include the sofa there and the mattresses on that bed in the spare bedroom. Burn all the trash lying on the floor."

"Yes sir, Mr. Henry. Jake got the old washing machine working. It just slipped a belt, is all. Mildred be doing the washing now. She be ironing the curtains and the sheets and such when we get them cleaned. We have the place spick-and-span before we done, don't you worry none."

"I'm grateful to you, Ma'am."

Hal shook his head. "This place ain't never seen the likes."

I turned to the door. "Let's go do some shopping to put the finishing touch on things."

* * *

When we returned, the place had taken on a remarkable appearance. The trash had vanished from the front yard, the weeds were cut, and the old cars hauled off. The house no longer leaned to the left. The rotten boards had been replaced. The roof held new tin in places and patches of hot tar drying in others. New screens covered the doors and windows. The old tires and rubbish burned off to the side. Clean linen flapped in the breeze on the clothesline out back. Several of the men hurried to unload the new mattress, sofa, easy chair, color TV, and two new throw rugs for the living room and my bedroom. The rooms were spotless inside, with the bathroom sparkling clean and the kitchen scrubbed to a shine. A woman stood at an ironing board pressing the curtains as another strung them over the windows. Hal's washed and pressed clothes hung in the closet of his bedroom, which was organized to perfection. As a couple of men set my new bed up in the tidy, spare bedroom, I found Rufus Washington supervising some men in the backyard hauling the last of debris to the fire and finishing the screening of the back porch.

"Mr. Washington, you and your crew have done a magnificent job. If you'll figure out what I owe you, we'll square up."

He removed his hat and wiped his forehead on his sleeve. "Yes, Suh, Mr. Henry. Labor for these folks here come to about $150, all total. I got the receipts for the lumber and other material right here. It come to about $212. We sold the old cars and scrap iron to the junkyard, so that fetch about $43. When that deducted, it run a total of about $319, all told."

I counted out $350. "Consider the extra as a bonus, Sir. It's been a pleasure doing business with you."

"It be our pleasure, Suh. If'n anything displease you, let me know and it be set right. We be grateful for the work."

Within the hour the workers loaded up and departed. Mr. Washington eased over, unhooked Old Billy from the tree, and made a dash for his pickup as the old goat snorted and trotted after him, his head lowered for combat.

Hal stood inside the living room as the color TV played in the background. "I wish Mom was here to see the old place. It's never looked this good since I lost her."

I surveyed the interior. "It cleaned up real good. Let's get some dinner at Pearle's. On the way back we'll stop off at the store for some groceries."

He held out his hand. "Thanks, Paul. I never expected all this."

I turned to the door. "Gee, Tater, you're embarrassing me."

"Asshole," he muttered as he followed me out, where Old Billy immediately braced us from the front yard pawing the ground and snorting, still greatly riled and ready to do battle for having been tied up all day.

I sighed. "This is ridiculous!"

"Oh, he don't mean no harm," Hal soothed. "I'll distract him while you dash for the car."

He took off down the road with Old Billy chasing after him in a stumbling gait while the hounds tumbled around the both of them in a howling pack. When I judged it safe, I ran for the car, thinking Clayhill was one damned peculiar place.

* * *

I awoke early the next morning to a hullabaloo of noise and lay for a moment in complete disorientation before realizing I was in the spare bedroom of Hal's shack lying in my new bed. The clamor came from the front yard, where the hounds were yowling over someone yelling in panic. I slipped on my pants and ran for the front door as Hal hurried out of his room across the living room.

We found a Clayhill police car parked in the front yard with Deputy Miller's massive frame sprawled on the hood with his feet kicking in the air as Old Billy pawed at the ground below him amid the pack of hounds running around them howling in excitement.

"What the hell, Joe?" Hal yelled at him.

"This damned animal just attacked me!" Deputy Miller yelped back. "He *attacked* me!"

"Take it easy now," Hal called. "He's harmless enough."

"Hal Sutton, you come do something with this beast or I'll be forced to shoot him!" Deputy Miller threatened.

"Don't do nothin' foolish now, Joe! *Here now, Billy! Come on away from that man*," Hal encouraged as Billy ignored him. "Try and make a run for it, Joe; he's too old to catch you!"

"Are you *crazy*? I ain't getting down off this car until you have that damned animal penned up or something," Deputy Miller howled. "I'll shoot him first! I mean it!"

"Now, you can't go shooting my animals, Joe; that's against the law!"

"*I'm* the law, Hal, and this crazy thing is *attacking* me." Deputy Miller quivered from his perch on top of the hood. "I'm allowed to defend myself in the line of duty, by God! Now, you come on out here and do something with him, or I'll do something myself!"

"Now you just hold on there, Joe!" Hal insisted.

I nudged Hal with my elbow and grinned. "I suggest you go distract Old Billy before things get out of hand."

"Why is it always *me* who has to distract him?"

"It's *your* goat."

"Are you going to do something or not?" Deputy Miller demanded.

Hal grimaced. "Damn. I guess I'd better lure him off down the lane a piece then before Joe goes and does something dumb."

I nodded. "Sounds like a plan to me."

Hal turned to the squirming deputy. "Joe! When I get him away from the car, you make a break for the porch. Okay?"

"Don't call me *Joe*! It ain't proper for you to call me by my first name since I'm an officer of the law now."

"*Yee-haw!*" Hal thundered as he leaped off the porch, his long legs churning. Old Billy got his bearings and charged off after him. Deputy Miller watched them until he gauged it was safe, slid off the hood, and waddled for the porch, gasping for breath. Hal circled around the car and ran back to the porch with Old Billy in hot pursuit, whereupon we hurried into the house and slammed the door behind us, leaving Old Billy snorting in the front yard.

"That thing ought to be shot!" Deputy Miller wheezed as he wiped his brow with a soiled handkerchief. "He's a menace to society!"

"Well, *society* can just stay the hell out of my front yard," Hal panted. "He's *my* goat, and this is *my* land, so *I'll* decide if he needs to be shot—which reminds me, why in tarnation are you out here this early in the morning anyway?"

"I'm out here because Sheriff Tate sent me out here because you're too damned cheap to install a telephone like regular folks. You don't think I'd come all the way out here for coffee, do you? By the way, do you have any made?"

"No, I don't have any made, Joe, but even if I go and make some, I ain't gonna give you any until you apologize for threatening to shoot Old Billy."

"Well, you're sure in a sour mood. You need to go on back to bed and get up on the other side. Besides, shooting that old goat would be doing you a public service, if you ask me."

"I'll make the coffee," I offered and turned to the kitchen. "Why did Sheriff Tate send you out here?"

Deputy Miller lumbered into the kitchen behind me. "Sheriff Tate would like to see you at your earliest convenience, Mr. Henry."

"Paul ain't done nothin' wrong for the sheriff to go sending for him," Hal insisted as he followed us into the kitchen.

Deputy Miller grimaced in exasperation. "Now, ain't nobody said he *did*, Hal!"

"Well, what's the sheriff want to see him for then?"

"The sheriff don't always tell me his business, thank you, and even if he did, I wouldn't be obliged to discuss it with you. I guess it really ain't none of our business, if you want to get right down to it."

"Well, you don't have to be so hoity-toity about it, Joe!" Hal bristled as I filled the pot with water.

I turned the flame down under the coffee pot so it wouldn't scorch. "I'm going to get dressed. Help yourself when the coffee's finished perking. Cups are in the cabinet over there."

When I came out later, the deputy sat at the table. "You make good coffee, Mr. Henry."

I poured myself a cup. "Call me Paul. How long have you been on the police force?"

"About two years now. I'm the only full-time deputy they got. We got a part-time deputy that works when one of us is sick or needs a vacation, though."

"What do you think of Sheriff Tate?"

His eyes narrowed. "He's about the finest lawman I've ever known. He's honest and he's fair. Most of all, he's smart. Why you asking?"

"Just wondering. Did you know Sheriff Allston?"

"I was a part-time deputy under him just before he retired."

"What did you think of him?"

"He was okay, I guess. Why you wanting to know about him?"

"Was *he* honest and fair?"

"I've never known anything dishonest or unfair he ever did, no matter what some may say about him behind his back. It don't matter no more anyhow, 'cause he's done retired now." He lifted his ponderous frame as Hal rejoined us in the kitchen. "I better get on back. Hal, you need to come do something with that old goat so I can get back to my car."

Hal set his cup on the table. "I'll draw him around to the back of the house. You make a run for it as soon as he turns the corner."

I poured myself a second cup of coffee as they headed for the front door together. A moment later I heard a yell, and soon afterward Hal rushed in through the back door as Deputy Miller lumbered out the front door for his car. When the vehicle was out of sight, the yammering hounds settled down, restoring a measure of tranquility to the morning.

* * *

I nosed the Cobra into the visitor's parking space in front of the jail.

Hal met me on the sidewalk tucking in his shirttail. "Do you want me to come in with you?"

"It might not be a bad idea since the last time the sheriff and I met, it was on something less than amicable terms."

"You *do* have a way of pissing folks off, Sport, I'll give you that."

Sheriff Tate sat at his desk reading the paper. "Thank you for stopping by, Mr. Henry. I hope I haven't inconvenienced you?"

"The only inconvenience is that I have to keep reminding you to call me *Paul*."

He folded his paper and set it aside. "I took the initiative to call Susan last night. She's concerned about your decision to challenge the will in probate."

"I'd appreciate it if you'd leave my mother out of things."

He pulled a faded, battered file from a drawer. "We talked at length about her decision to leave Clayhill. This is the official investigation of your father's death. I don't have the authority to allow you to read it, of course." He stood. "I think I'll just mosey on over to the drugstore and buy Hal here a cup of coffee." He started for the door.

"Why are you doing this?"

He hesitated. "We seem to have gotten off on the wrong foot. I'd like to rectify that."

"Is that the only reason?"

He pondered the question a moment as he scuffed at the floor with his boot. "I've never felt at ease about your father's death. Maybe I should have questioned it deeper at the time. I was a young, dumb deputy back then." He ushered Hal out and closed the door behind them.

I sat down in the chair in front of the desk and pulled the thin file to me. Surely my father's death warranted more than this? I picked up the first page, an arrest report filed by Sheriff Allston, the sheet aged and written in fading blue ink, making the scrawling script almost indistinguishable, dated November 14, 1947:

Received complaint by telephone at 9:30 A.M. from George Hiller, owner of Clayhill Feed and Seed, about disturbance on premises. Proceeded immediately by squad car to location. Found John Allison Henry engaged in verbal confrontation with J. R. Henry, each known to be relatives on bad terms. During this officer's attempt to intercede in confrontation, John Henry physically attacked J. R. Henry, striking several blows to and about the head and face of J. R. Henry. In the ensuing confrontation this officer was jostled and shoved to the ground. Other witnesses, one Jarvis Holderman and one Malcolm Grant, subdued John Henry until this officer could place handcuffs on individual. Victim J. R. Henry was transported to the Clayhill Clinic for treatment of injuries received. John Henry was transported to the Clayhill City Jail and incarcerated on initial charges of disturbing the peace. It is anticipated that victim J. R. Henry will file additional charges.

Samuel Allston
Sheriff, Clayhill

I turned the page. The second sheet contained an inventory of personal property for detainee John Allison Henry and read:

One brown leather billfold containing driver's license issued to detainee, one hundred and fifty three dollars in denominations as follows: five twenty dollar bills, four ten dollar bills, two five dollar bills, three one dollar bills, and various photographs.

One brown leather belt with silver buckle.

One wristwatch with leather band.

Contents of detainee's pockets as follows: one silver dollar, two quarters, one dime, three nickels, one three-blade K-bar pocket knife with yellow bone case, one key ring with three keys, one Zippo lighter, one open pack of Camels containing five cigarettes.

Articles confirmed by
John Allison Henry

I experienced a jolt as I studied the smooth, deliberate signature. It was the last time my father had put pen to paper. It was a bold, swooping autograph, much as I was beginning to envision my father to have been. I turned the page. The next sheet was an incident report:

Initial Incident Report filed by Sheriff Allston
November 14, 1947, 5:30 P.M.

This officer entered the Clayhill Police Department holding area on a routine inspection at approximately 3:30 P.M. and found detainee John Allison Henry hanging by the neck from a makeshift cloth cord suspended from the top crossbar of cell number three where detainee was incarcerated earlier this A.M. Upon examination by this officer the detainee showed no detectable signs of life. This officer elected to leave detainee's body in present location to facilitate further investigation into the cause of death. This officer then contacted the County Coroner to verify death.

The report was not signed. The next sheet contained a coroner's certificate verifying the death of John Allison Henry of probable self-induced strangulation in the Clayhill City Jail dated at 4:12 P.M., on November 14, 1947. The certificate authorized the body to be removed to the county morgue and was signed by David Greene, County Coroner.

A two-page autopsy report came next, filled with medical jargon, indicating that John Allison Henry had died from strangulation induced by a cord around the neck. It contained references to trauma on the body inflicted by unknown blunt objects to the head, shoulders, and back, as well as severe bruising of the wrists and heels.

A final three-page report from Coroner David Greene following a formal coroner's inquest into the death of John Allison Henry was next. Sheriff Allston's testimony and his reports were summarized, along with the autopsy. The coroner concluded that John Allison Henry had committed suicide by hanging himself in his cell at approximately 3 P.M. on the afternoon of November 14, 1947. It noted that strips of cloth had been torn from the mattress in the cell and tied together to form the noose. The trauma to the wrists was attributed to the handcuffs used to restrain him upon his arrest by Sheriff Allston. The trauma to his head, shoulders, and back was acknowledged as coming from his scuffle with J. R. Henry and the two witnesses who helped subdue him. The trauma to his heels was accredited to his death throes as his feet kicked against the iron bars after he hung himself.

When I turned the last page of the coroner's report, I found a series of eight-by-ten glossy black-and-white photographs, each somewhat grainy and faded by age. The first photo showed a man hanging with his back to the iron bars in cell number three, his face contorted in a death grimace. His tongue hung partly out of his half-open lips. His lifeless eyes stared from their bulging sockets. His arms dangled limply by his sides. He was shoeless, clad in a rumpled plaid shirt and a pair of dark pants. I shivered. This was the first picture I had ever seen of my father. It was an image I had never visualized. It was an image I would never forget. I turned it over.

The second photo showed a mattress on a bed with a large section of the fabric missing. The third photo depicted the interior of the cell, little changed from when I had been incarcerated there, the only discernible difference being the commode and wash basin, which were of white ceramic instead of today's stainless steel. The cell looked even dingier in the black-and-white picture. The last photo framed a thinner, younger Nelson Tate with his arms wrapped around my father's legs to support his body as Sheriff Allston stood on a chair outside the cell and worked to untie the knot from the noose suspending the body. A younger J. R. Henry stood to the right of Sheriff Allston looking up as the sheriff worked.

I turned back to the first photo of my father. I could tell little of his facial features because of the distortion. He appeared to be of medium height and slim of build, not unlike myself. I had an overwhelming desire to know what he had looked like in life. Both Miss Gladys and Mrs. Sherrill had alluded to the fact that he had been handsome. There was nothing endearing about my father's face in the grotesque picture I held. I skipped through the pictures again and picked up the last sheet in the file, a simple statement filed by Sheriff Allston supporting the coroner's report of suicide and closing the case. I pushed the file aside and sat back in my chair, heavy with sorrow.

Who was this man who gave me life? Why would he have taken his own life in such a fashion? What would my own life have been like if he had been there to guide and teach me? What different paths would I have chosen to walk with the benefit of his knowledge and wisdom? A deep ache grew inside me as I suddenly realized I had always wanted to be like the other boys who'd had their fathers to hunt and fish with, to come to their games and cheer for them, to practice with them at home to perfect their sporting skills. I wiped at the tears sliding down my cheeks, embarrassed because they were born of self-pity. I'd never known this man they called my father, yet I had always longed to do so. A cold anger grew. Had he really killed himself, or had others only portrayed it as such? I wanted to know the truth of what had happened on that day twenty years ago—the day my father died and I was born.

I quickly swiped at my moist cheeks when the door opened and Sheriff Tate ambled in. He hung his hat on the rack and poured two cups of coffee, placing one before me before settling down in his chair behind the desk, averting his eyes to give me time to gather myself up.

"It's strong. I made it this morning," he said by way of apology as he sipped. "Is there anything more I can help you with, Paul?"

I swallowed the knot clogging my throat and drew a deep breath. "Tell me about that day, Sheriff. I'd appreciate anything you can remember about it."

"I don't reckon I'll ever forget that day. It's burned in my memory like a bad scar." He collected his thoughts, his eyes focused on the window beside him. "I was out at the Peters place. Somebody had shot one of his cows. I got a call on my radio to get back to the jail pronto. When I got here, I saw John hanging up there on the bars of his cell. I had talked to him less than an hour before, just after Susan came to visit him. I was shocked. He'd been mad as hell, ranting and raving about being locked up, but I sure didn't read him as suicidal."

"Did you see anything out of the ordinary when you got back here?"

He paused to reflect. "There wasn't anything *ordinary* about the scene as far as I was concerned. I'd never seen anything like it before. I was in shock."

"Who was here when you arrived?"

"Let's see, there was Sheriff Allston and the coroner, a photographer from the coroner's office, and J. R., as best I can recall."

"How were they acting?"

Sheriff Tate shrugged. "Sheriff Allston was agitated. He seemed out of sorts, almost panicky. The coroner and his assistant were all business. Seeing dead bodies was an everyday thing for them, I guess, but it was the first time I'd seen a dead man outside of a funeral home."

"How was J. R. acting?"

"J. R. was ... calm."

"Calm?"

Sheriff Tate frowned. "Yeah ... calm ... very much in control. He kept reassuring Sheriff Allston that everything would be okay. Strange, now that I think back on it."

"Why was J. R. there?"

Sheriff Tate's frown deepened. "Damned if I know. I was so shook up at the time I never even questioned it. I assume he was there to press charges against your father."

"My father accused Sheriff Allston of being J. R.'s puppet when my mother visited him. She said Sheriff Allston was very angry about it."

"Sheriff Allston and J. R. were friends, had been since J. R. came to town. They hunted and fished together. J. R. helped get Sheriff Allston elected a few months before. I don't know that he was J. R.'s puppet or anything, but they were close."

"How did J. R. help him get elected?"

"Money to campaign with, of course, but mostly with the Henry name. That went far around here back in those days. Sheriff Goodlow had been in office a number of years with Henry backing. After your grandfather died and J. R. came to power, so to speak, he shifted his support to Sheriff Allston. Allston was a shoo-in after that. Mostly, where the Henrys led the others followed."

I looked him in the eye. "So it seems, unfortunately."

His face darkened. "For the record, I got elected over Stan Guthrie, who was supported by J. R. when Sheriff Allston retired. *Fortunately*, I had enough support due to my own proven integrity over the years as a deputy to overcome the Henry onslaught and win this office by a grand total of *six* votes."

I broke eye contact. "I ... guess I was wrong to make inferences ..."

"That's about the weakest apology I've ever heard."

I shifted in the awkward silence. "It's obvious that J. R. had a motive to see my father dead because of the estate and the lawsuit. Can you think of any reason Sheriff Allston would want to see him dead?"

"Your father was well liked by most everyone around here. I never heard of any problem that existed between them."

"But you admit his suicide doesn't make sense, right?"

"Nothing about it made sense back then, and it still doesn't now."

"Unless you look at it as murder."

He sat back in his chair. "There's no evidence to support such."

"Why would a man with everything to live for kill himself? And if he didn't kill himself, who had the motive and the opportunity to make it look like suicide? J. R. had a motive in the Henry family estate. Sheriff

Allston had the opportunity because he controlled the jail. They were both here when you arrived. J. R. and Allston were good friends. Allston was sheriff because J. R. got him elected with his support. Just before my father died, he accused Sheriff Allston of being J. R.'s puppet. J. R. and Allston came to my mother after the fact to bribe and subtly threaten her into leaving town and dropping her claim to the estate."

Sheriff Tate frowned. "Even so, all that's not even in the realm of circumstantial evidence. I'd need a whole lot more to go on to reopen this case as a murder investigation versus a suicide after twenty years. Mere suspicion of foul play doesn't go far in a court of law."

"Then I'll get you something more concrete," I promised.

"Where would you even start?"

I stood. "I just did, by talking with you. I'd like to talk to the others who were involved. If I put enough pieces of the puzzle together, maybe it will lead to some hard evidence."

He stood also. "Go easy with your inquiries, Paul. J. R. won't like this. Do your best to steer clear of him and his brood."

"I'll do that, Sheriff."

NINE

I straddled the stool next to Hal in the drugstore as Eva Marie feigned indifference to my arrival.

Hal scraped at the last vestiges of liquid ice cream from the plastic boat that had contained a banana split and cut his eyes at me. "Hi, Sport. How'd it go?"

"Okay, I guess."

Eva Marie stepped forward tentatively, her green eyes sending a faint shiver through me before she cut them away. "Can I get you anything, Mr. Henry?"

I focused on her lips, recalling their texture against my own. "No thank you, Miss Sherrill. Let's go, Hal."

"What's the hurry?" He scooped up the last spoon of melted slush. "I wish you two would talk things out; this cat-and-dog act is getting tiresome."

"Paul ...?" Eva Marie called softly as I turned away.

I met her direct gaze, acutely conscious of the fact that no woman had ever affected me as this one did. Being near her made me feel like a schoolboy at recess trying to muster the courage to hand a girl a note that read *I like you, do you like me? Check yes or no below.*

Her cheeks flushed. "Hal is right ... we should ... try to be friends."

"I never understood why we stopped being friends," I challenged.

Hal sighed as we stood immobile, the air tense between us. "You two are hopeless. Let's grab some beer later and go to the lake for a swim. You can talk things out there."

Eva Marie studied me, her penetrating stare unnerving.

I shrugged. "Works for me."

She chewed her bottom lip for a long moment. "Pick me up at home around seven."

As I departed, her compelling emerald eyes mixed in with the darker image of my father's distorted, grainy features hanging by a cord in the Clayhill jail.

"I hate to be the one to break this to you, Sport," Hal groused as he slid into the passenger seat, "but when it comes to women, you're about as smooth as a porcupine."

"I don't think she and I are on the same wave length. She's as frigid as a block of ice when I'm around."

"You're wrong, Sport. She's attracted to you, and I know damn well you're attracted to her. You two are playing games with yourselves. It's sort of like a self-defense mechanism: you're both terrified of the other."

"And just when did you become such a philosopher?"

"Oh, it's wisdom born of pain, Sport, believe me. Over the years I've made about every mistake in the book when it comes to women, just like you're doing now. You're lucky you've got the benefit of my sage insight to save yourself the agony."

"Spare me!"

"I'm dead serious, Sport! She's hot for you, and that scares her because she's accustomed to guys chasing after her while she leads them on a merry chase. You're hot for her, and that scares the hell out of you because you're a lone wolf accustomed to plucking chicks out of the hen yard for snacks."

"Is there a point to all this?"

"She can't stand you ignoring her, and you can't stand her indifference to you."

"You're truly a flake, do you know that?"

He smirked. "You two have met your match in each other and don't have a clue how to proceed with the courtship. Neither of you is playing the game right."

"I don't like playing games, and I damn sure ain't chasing after her. Life is too short and there are far too many women in the world for such foolishness."

"You gotta admit she's one damn-fine-looking woman, though, Sport. She might be worth a little foolishness in the long run."

"I'm not into extended courtships. I like being a free bird and going where the wind blows me."

"You're making a mistake if you pass that little piece of heaven by."

"You're giving me a headache. Can we change the subject?"

"Tell me about the file the sheriff couldn't let you look at."

"I think my father was murdered in that jail. There was nothing in the file that supports that, but then I wouldn't expect there to be if Sheriff Allston was in cahoots with J. R."

"So what's the plan?"

"I've got a lead on some people who were involved in the events that day. I'd like to talk to them and get their version of the story. Can you help me find them?"

"That's the easy part, but you ought to consider buying some bullets for my guns. If you're right, things could get mighty interesting when J. R. hears about what's going down."

"Do you really think he's such a threat?"

"Damn almighty, Paul, you just *implied* you think he helped murder your daddy. There are a lot of people that won't say it, but they think he may have been involved with your granddaddy's murder too. If he's already killed two people to get the Henry estate, what would stop him from doing you in for trying to take it away from him?"

"What kind of guns do you have?"

"A Winchester rifle, a 12-gauge shotgun, and a .38 caliber pistol. Maybe you should give this Eva Marie thing a second look too, Sport, seeing as how you might not be around to enjoy such earthly pleasures much longer."

"Let's go get some ammo for your damn guns, Hal, and for the record, Eva Marie doesn't drink beer, I hate swimming, and I *damn well* plan on being around longer than J. R. Henry!"

Hal thrust his palms out and raised his head to the sky. "Lord, I'm *trying*, I *really* am!"

* * *

I pulled into the lake lodge parking lot as the red sphere of the sun eased into a magnificent orb in the far west. Eva Marie got out on the passenger side and pulled the seat forward to help Hal wrestle his tall frame out of the cramped backseat. Hal and I turned into the men's room to change into our bathing suits as Eva Marie slipped into the women's room. She rejoined us wearing a black bikini that left me spellbound as I stared at her smooth, well-toned body and long, striking legs, smooth midsection tanned an inviting golden hue, and perky breasts threatening to fall out of the skimpy cloth restraining them. Against her perfect beauty, I was acutely self-conscious when her eyes widened sympathetically as they swept my own disfigured torso.

Hal whistled under his breath. "You are one fine-looking woman, Eva Marie!"

She lowered her lashes. "Mother would die if she knew I even owned this thing." She wrapped a black silk top around her. "Let's go swimming."

She led the way out to the end of the dock, where she slipped the silk top off and dove in. Hal tossed his towel on the nearest bench and dove in after her. I jumped in feet first behind them. Eva Marie swam away from the dock in long, measured strokes toward a square wooden platform in the center of the lake. I splashed along after her in short, rapid thrusts, which passed for swimming but more closely resembled a panicked man drowning. She reached the raft and pulled herself up on top to sit with her feet in the water. I pulled myself up beside her in a grateful-to-be-alive heap of gasping flesh.

"You're a good swimmer," I sputtered.

"I thought for a minute there you weren't going to make it."

"That makes two of us." I nodded at Hal back on the dock. "He was smart enough not to even try."

She smoothed her wet hair with her hands as water trickled down her back. "He's actually a trained lifeguard."

"Hal? Really?"

"Years ago, when I was a little girl with braces and he was a teenager, he worked at the public pool in the park in the summers. He was so handsome I'd make a fool of myself trying to get his attention."

"You certainly don't have any problem getting his attention now," I quipped.

Back on the dock Hal reached into the cooler, extracted a beer, held it up to us in a salute, and took a long pull from the bottle.

"That explains it," I observed. "He didn't want to get too far from the cooler."

"He wanted to give us some time alone," Eva Marie corrected.

I met her eyes, trying not to get lost in them. "Do we need some time alone?"

She held my stare. "We need to understand each other ... to lay some ground rules."

"Ground rules for what?"

She sighed. "I'm not going to do this all by myself. It's difficult enough for me as it is."

I fought off my uneasiness, annoyed with the way she disarmed me so easily. "Fair enough. What are the rules?"

"I ... want us to be friends."

"Could have fooled me," I scoffed.

"Are you going to play the part of court jester or get serious?" she demanded.

"Sorry." I wanted to do anything but get serious, knowing I was vulnerable to my own jumbled emotions boiling just under the surface. "So what's the problem with us being friends?"

"You terrified me when you attacked Bruce. I abhor violence. And I was frightened when you confronted Jimmy and Garland in the drugstore. I don't understand that part of you."

"I've learned that violence is often a necessity of life, Eva. When faced with it, I react in a decisive fashion. But it's not something I go out of my way looking for, in spite of what you think about the situation with Jimmy and Garland. They came in looking for trouble. I was just willing to oblige them."

"I've lived a protected life, I guess. Maybe I'm wrong to judge you."

"Judgment should be tempered by circumstance."

"What do you mean?"

"I've seen and done things in my life I never imagined. Many of them I found appalling, both then and now, but under the circumstances at the time they were perfectly acceptable actions. I've even been praised and decorated for doing some of them. Just about anything is acceptable under the right circumstances, even brutal violence."

"But look at your scars, Paul. Don't you have regrets? Wouldn't you have preferred not to do those appalling things you did, and wouldn't you have preferred to avoid those bad things that were done to you, given what you know now?"

"My preferences were never a consideration. I did what I had to do under the circumstances. I would do the same thing again, even knowing what I know today. There's no good way to do a necessary bad thing. I don't feel good or bad about doing those things. What was done to me in return is the price I paid. But I admit that when I'm near someone as pure and innocent as you, I sometimes feel a little ashamed and unworthy."

"I'm not as pure and innocent as you may think, Paul, and I may even be naive in my views, but I do appreciate your honesty, even if I can't understand your reasoning. Please forgive my limitations."

"What are you looking for, Eva, where you and I are concerned?"

She lay back on the platform to stare up at the darkening sky, where the stars had not yet begun to appear in the purple murkiness as the last of the sun disappeared, leaving a red hue on the far horizon. "I'd like for us to be friends. I feel terrible about what they did to your father's grave. I'd like to help make that up to you."

I lay back beside her. "I don't need your pity. The world is a cruel place filled with a lot of nut cases. I can handle what it dishes out."

"Don't you want us to be friends?"

"Do you honestly want us to be *just friends,* Eva?"

She rolled onto her side to face me and propped her damp head in her palm. "You're brutally frank. That's refreshing in a way. The truth is … I'm attracted to you in spite of my dislike for your violent side."

I rolled on my side and propped my head in my palm. "Playing games frustrates me. I tend to throw everything up in the air and see where the pieces fall. The truth is, I'm attracted to you as well. But there are some things that concern me about you."

"Such as?"

"I plan to pursue the lawsuit my father started against J. R. over the Henry estate."

"How does that affect our relationship, Paul?"

"I could be putting myself in harm's way. I've been warned that it will lead to an adverse reaction from him. I'm not sure what that means, but you need to understand that violence is a real possibility in this issue, and that I will react violently if the situation calls for it."

"You're doing a good job of scaring me off. Is that what you want?"

"I just want you to understand the risk in us being … something more than friends."

"I'm tougher than you may think when the situation calls for it. What other concerns do you have about us being … something more than friends?"

"I'm also concerned about you running hot and cold every time something distasteful occurs. A relationship shouldn't be like a roller coaster fluctuating between the good times and the bad ones."

"That sounds fair enough. So where do we go from here?"

"I haven't a clue. Do you?"

She touched her lips to mine, softly searching, sending tingles through my body, and then pushed me back onto the platform as her lips devoured mine deeply and boldly before lifting to hover over me. "There's something else you need to know about me, Paul … I'm not the last eighteen-year-old virgin in Clayhill."

"You're not?" I gasped, trying to regain my equilibrium.

She laid her head on my chest. "Are you disappointed?"

"No," I replied, giddy from the taste of her and the heat emitting from her body.

"Should I tell you about it?"

"That's not necessary."

"There was a boy who came to work on our farm one summer two years ago. I was so in love with him. It was the most glorious summer of my life."

I stroked her back as she lay on my chest. "What happened to him?"

She tensed. "Near the end of the summer he went to another farm to help with their harvest. There was an accident. A tractor turned over on him. I was devastated. I've never told anyone about us."

"I'm honored. I'll treat the secret as a sacred trust. So what attracts you to me now?"

"I'm attracted to you because you don't put me up on some silly pedestal, or treat me as some sort of a saint. I'm also attracted to you because you've lived your life with few boundaries or regrets. Knowing that frightens me in a basic way ... but I also admit I ... find the fear somewhat stimulating."

"Now I understand why you're so baffling," I said, laughing. "You're all screwed up in the head. So where do we go from here?"

"What are the choices?"

"Distant friends or casual lovers would seem to be the only two choices. Anything in between would be extremely frustrating to me."

She lay very still. "I'm not a casual love kind of girl, Paul."

"And I'm not a committing kind of guy, Eva. Perhaps we should opt for distant friends?"

"I don't like that option either," she replied, lifting her head to kiss me before rolling over onto her back to stare up at the gathering stars beginning to fill the sky above us, a mere dark outline on the platform beside me. "So what are you thinking this very moment, Paul?" she whispered after a lengthy silence.

Devouring her with lusty gusto wouldn't bear the telling. "I'm thinking I'll probably drown trying to swim back to the dock. What are you thinking this very moment?"

"You're being evasive."

"Okay, this very moment I'm thinking I want to make love to you right here and now."

She tensed. "Wow. Maybe I should have let you remain evasive. Everybody in Clayhill will probably think we've ... been together ... anyway since we've been out here this long by ourselves."

"Do you want to head back now?"

"No."

I rolled over and kissed her. "Then if we've got to bear the gossip, shouldn't we sample the forbidden fruit?"

She giggled. "That's a corny come-on."

"Hey, I'm pulling out all stops here."

"Paul, would you play an imaginary game with me?"

I rolled onto my back and pulled her across my chest. "I'm not very good at games. I'm a poor loser and I tend to cheat."

"Imagine that we've just made love here on this raft," she whispered as she snuggled into me. "Now we're lying here entwined in each other's arms, sated and filled with wonder, just like in the romance books."

"I can get into this game," I replied. "But you've got too many clothes on to get my imagination really fired up." I tugged at the bow holding her bikini top together in back and the piece parted, spilling her breasts out across my chest. "That's better," I whispered as she caught her breath in surprise. "Okay, now I'm into the part. What's next?"

"We were supposed to be *imagining*!"

"I warned you I cheat."

She arched her shoulders as I kissed her breast. "*This is not how the game is played*!"

"Let's make up new rules then," I murmured as my lips found her other breast.

She shivered. "The *game*, Paul, is to decide how we would define our relationship *afterward*! I mean, if we make love, does it mean anything tomorrow?"

I kissed her neck as she trembled. "How would you want to define our relationship afterward, Eva?"

"I can't go around telling everyone we're *casual lovers*, as you define it," she moaned. "What would we say when someone asks?"

"What are the choices?" I devoured her lips in a bruising, swirling crush.

She rolled off me to regain her composure. "That's the whole problem I'm having here, Paul," she gasped. "I'm not trying to be pushy or anything; I'm trying to understand what it would mean after the fact."

I rolled over on top of her and kissed her. "Let's don't define it, Eva. Let's let things happen. We shouldn't put a tag on it. How we feel right now is all that matters."

"We can't let everyone go around guessing and gossiping about us."

"Sure we can—it'll be intriguing."

"Sure it will—right up to the point where my mother has my father shoot you."

I rolled over, my desire ebbing as I pictured her father with his shotgun. "Oh, yeah, there's always that." Things were getting too complicated; time to run. "But I'm not overly worried about it since there's a distinct possibility I'm going to drown trying to swim back to the dock tonight anyway. We should head back—Hal's probably drinking my share of the beer by now."

"A point well taken," she agreed coolly as she sat up and fastened her top back in place.

As we plunged into the dark, tepid water, I knew there had been some regrettable moments in my life, the kind of careless moments when I really hated myself afterwards, and that surely there would be more of those moments to come. But I was fairly certain that *this* moment would forever rank right up there at the very top of my *Most Regrettable Moments* chronicle.

I splashed emphatically along toward the distant, dim light at the end of the pier trying to ignore the alluring shimmer of Eva Marie's bronze skin as she stroked effortlessly at my side. She could be fatal to my free-spirited lifestyle if I wasn't careful. I had been wise to pull back from the brink of self-destruction back there on the raft when I discovered she was seeking something more than a casual fling. I had mercifully avoided the potential, lethal-to-my-independence, subtle entrapment of admitting that our lovemaking would have been anything more than light, recreational entertainment. It would take more than a pretty face and a gorgeous body to snare this wily old wolf, I congratulated myself smugly.

At the halfway point I was thrashing for all I was worth. My arms and legs felt like lead weights. I became genuinely concerned about making it to the wavering light on the end of the distant pier. The combination of my war wounds and the dreary months in the hospital in Japan had taken a heavy toll on my wrecked body, sapping it of strength and endurance. I sensed the Grim Reaper lurking near, waiting to snatch my exhausted carcass into the depths of the cold black void enveloping me. I purged my mind of the growing weariness in my limbs by recalling the taste of Eva Marie's lips, the texture and firmness of her taut breasts, the eager response of her body to my touch, bleakly realizing I should have given in to her meager request for assurance that our lovemaking would have meaning in the light of day. I should have reassured her softly, tenderly, ardently—and then taken her boldly, lustfully, and completely. I should have selfishly enjoyed the delights she had to offer then and there when I had the chance. If only I'd given her that one small assurance I would at least have that one last, enduring, sweet memory to cling to as I slipped to the murky bottom of this confounded damned lake. *Only to have that lost opportunity again*, I begged of fate as I clawed at the water in desperate, ineffectual thrusts.

"You're too stiff, Paul," Eva Marie coached from my side as she glided along like a sleek mermaid, making hardly a ripple in the dark water compared to my white-foamed, churning assault, oblivious to the demented, shameless thoughts of her I was using to pry back the jaws of death. "Relax, take long, slow strokes and kick your feet in rhythm to your arms. Let your body work in harmony instead of against itself."

"That's easy for you to say," I gasped. "You're not the one drowning here."

"I won't let you drown, I promise."

"Oh gee thanks; all I need is to have Hal see you hauling me back to the pier like a helpless baby."

"Would you rather drown?"

"*Yes*! Damn it, who keeps moving that damned light? It looks further away now than when we started."

"Save your breath, Paul. Don't try to talk. We're almost there. Just relax and take steady strokes. You're doing much better now."

Near the point of complete physical collapse, I chugged up to the end of the pier, where Hal sat with his feet dangling, beer in hand. Eva Marie slid up out of the water next to him as I clung to the wooden ladder attached to the end of the pier wheezing like a locomotive, too winded to raise my arms to pull myself up.

"He ain't much of a swimmer, is he?" Hal observed as he took a sip of his beer.

"I guess I should've asked him about that before I led him out that far," Eva Marie replied. "Have you got another one of those beers?"

"Sure do." Hal dug into the cooler. "Nice and cold too."

"*I … didn't … think … you … drank … beer!*" I gasped, trying to focus my bleary eyes on the two of them above me outlined by the dim light.

"I need something to calm my nerves," Eva Marie retorted.

"Was making up with him all that difficult?" Hal inquired as she tilted her head back and drank.

She wiped her lips with the back of her hand. "Things could have gone a lot smoother."

"But you two *are* friends again, right?" he inquired anxiously.

"Oh, we're a little further along than *friends*, I'd say," Eva Marie assured him and took another deep swallow of her beer.

"*Lovers?*" Hal asked, incredulous.

"Not quite," Eva Marie corrected. "He's terrified of commitment on any level."

"He's *such* a damned fool," Hal swore. "Maybe you should have let him drown."

"I considered it."

"I'd appreciate … one of them cold beers … if you don't mind," I gasped as I heaved myself up onto the end of the pier with the last of my waning strength. "And I'd also appreciate it … if you two wouldn't discuss … my character traits and love life … as if I wasn't here."

Hal handed me a beer. "Well, Sport, I hate to be the one to enlighten you, but your character traits make for a very brief discussion, and it sounds like your love life is an even shorter topic."

"Do you ever quit … running your mouth?" I gasped. I took a stiff slug of the beer, relishing the cool, biting liquid after my harrowing experience.

"That's the curse of being best friends with a philosopher. Endlessly expounding on the myths, mysteries, and shortcomings of life is our bane."

"*Endlessly expounding* is … certainly the right choice of words," I wheezed.

"Which carries us back to the subject at hand, Sport: if you and Eva Marie are something more than friends but something less than lovers, what do I tell people when they ask?"

"Tell them to mind their own damned business," I advised.

Hal turned to Eva Marie. "Then perhaps you can enlighten me, Fair Maiden. What would *you* have me tell the busy-bodies and tongue-waggers when they come prying?"

"Tell them we're …" She hesitated as she lifted her beer to her lips, frowning in concentration.

"For Christ's sake, if it's such a big deal around here, just tell them she's my damned girl now!" I growled. "Will that make everybody happy?" My stomach fluttered with the declaration. Was it abject fear of the pledge—or the electrifying thrill of future promise?

Eva Marie dribbled beer down her chin in a most unladylike fashion and fell into a fit of coughing.

Hal nodded, thoughtful. "Okay, that's a good starting point; Eva Marie is your damned girl now. Uh, for the sake of clarity, is that as in your *steady* damned girl? You know, like the *one* and *only* type of damned girl? Is it like as in being your *main squeeze* damned girl and all that other *committed* type stuff?"

"*Your ... damned ... girl ...*" Eva Marie repeated, rolling the words around, trying them out for substance and balance.

"Well, do you want to be my girl or not?" I demanded.

"Oh, he's *such* a pathetic romantic," Hal declared, rolling his eyes in exasperation.

"Why don't you mind your own damned business, Hal?" I demanded.

"Well ... I really don't know for sure, Paul," Eva Marie replied, cautious. "That was the whole point of our discussion out there in the middle of the lake, remember? Has there been any significant change in your mind-set from there to here?"

"I think it's called a near-death experience," Hal offered.

I shot Hal a go-to-hell look, recalling the snatches of heart-gripping terror I'd experienced in the murky water. "I've had time to ... put things in perspective, Eva. You're an intriguing woman. I mean, a guy could sure do a lot worse than you."

Hal grimaced. "How *heartfelt*! I'm sure Eva Marie is as deeply touched as I by the eloquence of your verbal presentation in asking for her secular companionship."

"*Huh?*" My dull mind tried to refocus. "Damn it, Hal, would you butt out of this! Eva, I guess I'm saying it all wrong, but what I mean is, I'd like for you to be my girl, damn it!"

"Ah, *finally*, and how *sweet*," Hal crooned. "That was much better, Sport; there may be hope for you yet."

"Damn it, Hal, stay the hell out of this!"

Eva Marie set her beer down, wrapped her arms around my neck, and kissed me in a slow, sensuous manner before pulling back to gaze into my eyes in the dim light. "Can I have some time to think about this, Paul? I'm old-fashioned and don't like to rush into things. Ask me again sometime real soon. Okay?"

"Sure," I groped, my emotions hanging out there somewhere between the soaring elation of escape and the bitter plunge of rejection. Damn, why did women always lure you right up to the threshold and then close the door in your face, leaving you feeling foolish?

"*Real* soon," she urged, her lips brushing against mine, teasing, seeking.

"Eva, will you be my girl?" I murmured, my eager lips against hers, tasting, searching.

"*Definitely,*" she moaned as her lips devoured mine.

"Hey, folks, am I *intruding* on anything here?" Hal demanded, feigning disdain.

"*YES!*" Eva Marie and I chorused together.

"Good!" he said, laughing as he opened new beers for everyone. "That's what chaperons are *supposed* to do!"

TEN

I languished between the sheets entertaining erotic fantasies of Eva Marie. It was a bad sign when a man went to bed with a woman on his mind and woke up with her still lingering there. I smelled coffee perking and bacon frying, pulled on my pants, and padded barefoot to the kitchen to find Hal scrambling eggs in a bowl by the sink.

"Good morning, Sport. Hungry?"

"Starved," I affirmed, yawning as I poured a cup of coffee.

He smirked. "Nothing like a new love to bring out the appetite in a man."

"Give it a rest, Hal," I threatened.

"What a grump." He forked the bacon out of the frying pan and drained off the grease into a mason jar. "What's the agenda for today?"

"I want to go to the Clayhill Feed and Seed to talk to George Hiller."

"What do you want to talk to him about?"

"He called Sheriff Allston the day my father got arrested. Do you know him?"

"I know him well. He's a good man. Honest as the day is long." He poured the beaten eggs into the skillet and lifted his head at the sound of tires crunching on gravel outside. "Now who the hell is that this early in the morning?"

I glanced at my wristwatch. "Early, hell, it's 10:30; we slept half the day away. I'd better go check it out before Old Billy scares them half to death."

I hurried to the front door and stood gawking as Elaine Duckworth got out of her old brown Pontiac and Barbara McDougal stepped out on the passenger side. Both smiled and waved.

"Hi, Paul!" Elaine called.

"Hi, sweetie!" Barbara trilled. "I bet you didn't expect to see us come driving up!"

Oh, shit! I was so shocked I forgot to warn them about Old Billy. I collected myself and shoved open the screen door as he lurched around the corner in a stiff-jointed gallop. "*No, Billy! Girls! Watch out! Run! There's …*"

"Oh, how cute! A little goat." Elaine knelt down to greet Old Billy as he lurched to a stop, confused. "Isn't he adorable, Barbara? Come on, boy, come on, I won't hurt you. Will you let me pet you? You're such a little cutie. Hal didn't tell me about you, little fellow."

I stood with my jaw unhinged as Elaine stretched out her hand and rubbed Old Billy's head. The old goat edged closer to her, bobbling his stubby horns and pushing against her hand, preening as she rubbed him.

Barbara hurried around to rake her fingers through the scraggly hair on his back. "Oh, he's such a little darling," she cooed as Old Billy arched his back for her fingers to comb through his shaggy old coat. "Do you like having your back scratched? Yes, you do, don't you, big boy?"

"Who is it, Paul?" Hal called from the kitchen.

"Come see this, Hal. You aren't gonna believe your eyes!" I called back.

Hal appeared beside me. "Well, my goodness! Elaine and Barbara! What a surprise!"

"I'm *talking* about your damned old crazy *goat*, Hal!"

"Aw, he *likes* Elaine," he swooned. "Look at him licking her hand. That says a lot for Old Billy to like her. Don't you think so, Paul?"

I sighed and turned back to the kitchen for my coffee. "I give up."

Hal stepped out onto the porch. "How'd you girls find us way out here?"

"A real nice girl at the drugstore gave us directions," Elaine explained.

Oh, shit! I did a U-turn in the middle of the living room and headed back to the door as Hal tossed me a baleful look.

Elaine and Barbara came up onto the porch with Old Billy following docilely after them. "She said she was friends with you guys," Elaine continued.

"What did you tell her?" I demanded as Hal and I exchanged alarmed glances.

Elaine stopped in puzzlement. "We told her Hal invited us up to visit. Since she knew you, we sat and talked for a few minutes. Why? Is there something wrong?"

I glared at Hal, who smiled meekly and cleared his throat. "Uh, Paul is, uh, well, uh ... he, uh, I'll let him explain it to you ..."

I stared at him in astonishment. "*You* explain it to them, Hal ... *you* invited them here!"

He swallowed. "Paul, uh, he, uh ..."

Elaine tilted her head. "Yes?"

He flushed. "The thing is, uh, Paul, uh, has to go somewhere ..."

Barbara stiffened. "Go somewhere?" Her face went through a contortion similar to her sucking on a lemon. "*We drove all this way to see you and you have to go somewhere?* When?"

I held my breath. "Uh, right away. I have to leave now. In fact, I'm running late ..."

"I just got here and you're running out on me?" Barbara wailed. "Where the hell are you going? I'll go with you."

"Well, uh, actually you can't ... uh, because I'm going ... uh, tell her, Hal."

"He's ... he's, uh, going far away, and he won't be back for some time, so you see, you can't go with him. Right, Paul?"

Barbara advanced on us. "That doesn't make sense! What are you two trying to hide?"

Hal backed up a step. "Hide? Us? Nothing! I swear. It's just that Paul's, uh, he uh, that girl and Paul, uh, you tell her, Paul ..."

She whirled on me. "Have you been two-timing me with that little green-eyed bitch at the drugstore, you sorry, low-life, egg-sucking dog?"

Egg-sucking dog? I hastened backward. "Well, uh, she and I ..."

"You bastard!" she shrieked, swinging at me in a flurry of clenched fists. "I'm supposed to be your steady girl!"

I held up my palms to ward off her blows. "Now damn it, Barbara, I've never implied any such thing and you know it!"

"Well, what the hell am I then?" she shrilled as she pummeled me. "Your *steady* little piece-of-ass-on-the-side when you're in the mood for it? I'll beat that little bitch's ass, by God!" She spun back to the car, panting. "Take me back to town, Elaine! How dare that jezebel go after my guy when my back's turned, that little two-bit tramp! I'll run that little whore's ass all the way out of this hick town, so help me God, I will!"

"*Girls, girls! Now hold on here a minute,*" Hal soothed. "Let's sort this thing out!"

Barbara collapsed onto a rickety chair on the porch wailing as Elaine hurried over to comfort her.

"You've got to be kidding me!" I groaned as Barbara squalled and called me names I didn't even know girls knew.

Elaine wrapped her arms around Barbara. Hal stood open-mouthed watching them. Old Billy trotted back around to the rear of the house where things were a little more peaceful. I fled into the bedroom to pull on my shirt and shoes. When I came back out onto the porch, Barbara was still sobbing, but thankfully all the screaming and cussing had subsided somewhat.

"Where are you going?" Hal demanded.

"To that faraway place," I called over my shoulder as I headed for the Cobra.

"What am I supposed to do?" he shouted after me.

"*You* figure it out!"

"Don't you need me to go with you?"

"*No!*" I slammed the door and fired up the Cobra with a throaty roar.

* * *

Eva Marie wore a pinched look about her lips visible all the way from the front door of the drugstore. I eased down to the counter like a cat in a dog kennel and slid onto a stool. She stood with her back against the half coolers lining the rear wall, her arms crossed, her eyes a deep emerald etching streaks of green lightning at me.

"Good morning, Eva," I said, trying to fake it.

"You just missed your little girlfriend from Jasper," she taunted.

It was a bad opening gambit, I realized as I cleared my throat. "I don't have a girlfriend in Jasper."

"Don't play games with me, Paul. You don't like to play games, *remember?*"

At least she wasn't calling me *Mr. Henry.* "Eva—"

"Why didn't you tell me about her?"

"There was nothing to—"

"She's cute."

"She's just someone I—"

"She's quite enamored with you. You must be a real charmer back in Jasper."

"Eva, please, let me explain—"

"Don't bother! She did a good job of that herself."

"I don't want to fight with you about—"

"Then don't!"

"Will you let me finish?"

"You *are* finished!"

"Can I have some coffee? I didn't get a chance to—"

Eva Marie jammed a cup in front of me, grabbed the pot, sloshed coffee over the rim of the cup onto the counter, slammed the pot back on the burner, and leaned back against the coolers with her arms recrossed, making no move to clean up the mess.

I took napkins from the dispenser and sopped up the spill as she glared at me. "I didn't come here to fight or play games, Eva. Barbara is a girl I dated a few times, that's all. I meant it when I asked you to be my girl last night."

"You're a cad, Paul."

"What's a cad?"

"An *asshole!*"

"Eva, please listen to me—"

"Where is she now?"

"On her way back to Jasper, I hope."

"Why didn't you tell me about her?"

"There was nothing to tell. Honest."

"Oh really? You were skinny-dipping with her in the moonlight at some place called Rocky Fjord just two nights ago, you liar!"

Oh, shit! "That was before you and I—"

"You and I were *last night*, Paul, the *day after* you and *her*. You move fast, Romeo!"

"That's not fair! You weren't even speaking to me two days ago!"

"What's not fair is that you almost had me believing your bullshit! Please leave! The coffee's on the house."

"You're not being fair about this, Eva," I pleaded.

"When were you going to spring the Chinese love-making tricks on me, Paul?"

Oh, shit!

"I understand they're quite sensual. How many are there? Over a hundred, I believe?"

"I can't believe you women even *talk* about stuff like that!" I blustered.

"You're a pervert, Paul. *Goodbye!*" She stalked through a swinging door at the end of the counter and disappeared into a back room.

"I've never even *met* a Chinese woman!" I shouted after her.

Greeted with silence, I tossed a quarter onto the counter beside my coffee cup and slunk away, my heart heavy. Women were a lot of trouble. And they cheated like hell in a fight; a man couldn't even get a word in edgewise when they were mad. They were all emotion and had no ability to rationalize a situation. Everything had to be their way, period. It just wasn't fair. Who the hell needed them anyway? Just love 'em and leave 'em, that's the only way to deal with them. I was so despondent I almost bumped into J. R. Henry standing just inside the door of the drugstore wearing an amused grin.

"Women trouble?"

I glowered. "Nothing I can't handle."

"I wonder if we could have a word together?"

I locked eyes with him. "We seem to be having one now."

His features hardened. "It's amazing how much like your father you are."

"Leave my father out of this!"

"Perhaps we could meet at my attorney's office early this afternoon? I have a proposition for you. A business offering that I think will save us both a lot of aggravation and expense."

"*My* lawyer's office is two doors down. I'll listen to your proposition there."

He nodded. "My attorney and I will meet you there at, say, one o'clock?"

I shoved past him out the door.

* * *

I stopped by Jason Jackson's office. He wasn't in, but Miss Gladys assured me his calendar was clear for the afternoon and that he would be available for the meeting with J. R. and his attorney. I walked back to my Cobra and paused at the drugstore window to look in at Eva Marie as she served the old geezer from before who slurped coffee from his spoon. I was certain she was aware of me standing on the sidewalk, but she didn't glance in my direction. I drove to the Clayhill Feed and Seed on the outskirts of town in a funk.

A young George Hiller Jr. directed me to a small office in the rear of the massive, barnlike facility filled with sacks of grain and bales of sweet-smelling hay, where George Hiller Sr., a stout, gray-headed man in his mid-sixties with a weathered face, worked over a sheaf of papers at an ancient, battered roll-top desk. His faded, blue speculative eyes lifted to study me from under bushy white eyebrows as I introduced myself.

He stood and offered his hand. "Mr. Henry. Welcome back to Clayhill," he greeted in a voice that tended to boom.

I took his hand and felt my own pulverized in his grip. "Thank you, Sir. Please call me Paul. I wondered if I might have a moment of your time?"

He sat back down in his ancient wooden chair and indicated a stiff-backed chair beside the desk. "Certainly. How is your mother these days? She was a pretty little lass."

"She's just fine, Sir."

"Good, good. She comes from fine stock. I knew her daddy well. Good man, good man."

"Sir, I'd appreciate it if you could tell me what happened on the day my father was arrested here at your business, if it wouldn't be an imposition on you."

Mr. Hiller frowned. "Well, it was a long time ago, Paul. My mind is getting fuzzier every day. I'll do my best, but I can't guarantee I'll remember everything. I knew your daddy well. Thought the world of him. It was tragic, just tragic. Never understood it myself. Why are you interested in the events of that day, if I may be so impolite as to inquire?"

"I want to try to understand why my father ... died like that."

George Sr. reached for a pipe in an ashtray on the cluttered desk and tamped the bowl. "If you figure that one out, I'd appreciate your sharing it with me. As I said, I never understood it myself. What do you want to know about that day?" He struck a match on the leg of the desk and held it to the pipe as he puffed and expelled blue clouds of pungent smoke.

"Just the facts as they happened, as best you can remember them."

He tossed the match into the ashtray. "Come with me. It might help my memory if we go to where it happened." He led the way back through the store to the cement loading platform stretching across the front of the wide building. "Wait here," he directed. He descended the steps, crawled into an old gray pickup truck, backed it around until its rear end was up against the loading dock, and rejoined me on the platform, where he stood for a minute staring at the truck in concentration as he puffed on the pipe.

"I think that's about the place he was parked. That's the very truck he was driving that day, by the way. It sat right there after he was arrested because we didn't have the key to move it. When we heard what happened, we pushed it around back. Your mother agreed to sell it to me. I got it appraised and offered her the appraised price. It was almost new, so I didn't get a great bargain on it, but trucks were still hard to come by at the time. It was right after the war and the automobile factories were still struggling to convert back to a peacetime industry. I had to have the ignition replaced because she couldn't find the key. I even refunded the money for the sacks of feed that your daddy bought that were still in the back of the truck. I was careful not to take advantage of her."

George Hiller's memory was a lot better than he claimed. Goose bumps fleshed out on my arms as I stared at the actual truck that had belonged to my father on the day he died. "I've heard you are an honest man, Sir."

He beamed. "Good, good. A man's name is all he comes in this world with and all he takes with him when he leaves it. Now where was I? As I recall, John had just bought some oats and loaded them into the back of the truck. Now, I was standing right here almost in this same spot I'm standing in now, talking to him as he was getting ready to leave, asking about his wife and all, just being sociable, which I take care to do with all my customers. I can't seem to teach that to my son. Customers are more than people you provide a service to. You've got to be their friend. Look out for them. The younger generation is getting away from that basic principle, it seems to me. Everything is all business now. Why, I'd wager that my son George couldn't tell you the first names of half of our customers today. But I know them all. I make it a point to." I fought my growing impatience as Mr. Hiller collected himself. "Sorry, I tend to ramble at times. I'm getting old. Where was I?

"That's right; I was standing right here talking to John, when this black Ford comes screeching up and stops in front of John's truck there, squealing the brakes and sliding the tires and all, sort of blocking him in. J. R. jumps out and starts cussing and threatening John about some legal papers that had been served on him. They both started yelling and cussing and pointing their fingers at each other and such, creating quite a commotion, as I recall. Along about that time the sheriff came driving up and jumped in the middle of things, which just added to the confusion, if you ask me. Anyway, John lunged at J. R., and the two men with J. R. jumped in and grabbed John's arms. The sheriff grabbed J. R. to sort of keep them apart and all, and J. R. and the sheriff got tangled up with each other and fell over, cracking J. R.'s head on the bumper of John's truck in the process, almost knocking him out. There weren't too much fight left in him afterward, as far as I could tell. The sheriff put handcuffs on John and put him in the patrol car and drove him off. Later that evening I heard John had … well, you know …"

"Mr. Hiller, didn't you call the sheriff that morning when they first started arguing?" I prodded gently.

"No. I stood right here the whole time," he replied without hesitation. "The thing didn't last more than a minute or two from start to finish. There wasn't time to call the sheriff, and he was already here anyway."

I tried to quell my growing excitement. "You said there were two men who came with J. R. that restrained my father. Do you know who they were?"

"Well, let me see." He crossed one arm over his chest to support the other arm as he placed his hand under his chin and studied the ground. "I didn't know them well, 'cause they weren't customers of mine. I know they both worked for J. R. at the brickyard and I saw them on occasion. Neither one of them went to church. Both of them were roustabouts and no great pride to our community. No, I'm sorry; I can't remember their names now. Just too many years."

"Was anyone else involved in the scuffle?"

He shook his head. "No, just John, J. R., the sheriff, and the two ruffians that came along with J. R. It all happened so fast there wasn't time for anyone else to get involved."

"Were there any actual punches thrown?"

He shook his head again. "No. John and J. R. just lunged at each other, and everyone grabbed them to keep them apart. The only injury was to J. R. when he fell over the sheriff and cracked his head on the bumper of John's truck there."

"And you're certain no one called the sheriff, to the best of your knowledge?"

"Nope, no time for that, he got here almost at the same time as J. R. did."

"Why do you think my father was arrested, Mr. Hiller?"

He smiled cagily. "Your daddy could be a handful when he was riled up, Paul, and he was plenty irate at the time. He was kicking at J. R.'s men who were holding him back and cussing at the sheriff and all. I guess the sheriff arrested him to give him a chance to calm down a bit before he did anything foolish. Like I said, he could be a handful."

"Are you certain that no blows were struck during the scuffle, Mr. Hiller?"

"As certain as I know how to be. Nobody got at anybody to hit them."

I held out my hand. "Thank you for your time, Mr. Hiller."

He crushed my hand in his. "Anytime. Good to see you back home. It seems like all our young people are moving off to the cities and leaving us old folks behind these days."

I nodded at the gray truck. "Someday I might want to buy that old truck back from you. I can't believe you still have it after twenty years."

He nodded. "It's been a good one. I've kept it up, had the engine rebuilt a couple of times and such, but it's been a good one. The day comes, we'll sit down and bargain on it."

"Thank you, Mr. Hiller." I drove off as he stood on the platform puffing his pipe.

There was still an hour before my meeting with J. R. I considered Pearle's for lunch but knew that was a copout. I parked in front of the drugstore instead, thinking maybe Eva Marie had calmed down a bit and would be more reasonable. An older, heavy-set woman stood behind the counter catering to half a dozen people as I slid onto a stool and waited until she worked her way down to me, order pad in hand.

"Cheeseburger and strawberry malt, please. Is Eva Marie here?"

She wrote on the pad. "She took sick today. Do you want that all the way?"

* * *

An uncharacteristically severe Miss Gladys showed me in promptly without going through the customary pleasantries, where J. R. and another man in a dark suit waited with Jason Jackson in his office. Though Mr. Jackson showed no outward signs, I sensed his underlying dislike for the two men as the man in the dark suit stood and offered his hand.

"Daniel Coonan, Esquire, representing Mr. Henry here. Glad to meet you."

I shook hands with the short, thick-set, middle-aged man standing arrogant and exuding an air of self-importance, which I found annoying, but then again, I wouldn't have liked him if he had been wearing a priest's collar since he represented J. R. Henry.

"Perhaps we would be more comfortable in my conference room," Mr. Jackson suggested. "I've asked Gladys to prepare a fresh pot of coffee."

We followed him across the reception area to a door on the opposite side and into a moderate room filled floor to ceiling with bookcases containing dusty law books. A long mahogany conference table ran down the center surrounded by plush brown leather chairs, where J. R. and his mouthpiece arranged themselves on one side as Mr. Jackson and I settled in across from them. Miss Gladys followed us in with cups of coffee and then seated herself discreetly at the far end of the table, notepad in hand.

Mr. Jackson cleared his throat. "Gentlemen, I'm somewhat at a loss as to what this conference is about."

"J. R. asked to have a word with me," I replied.

Mr. Coonan puffed out his chest, snapped some glasses on the bridge of his nose, and opened a notepad. "It is my client's intent to reach an understanding concerning the outrageous legal position taken by your client in regard to my client's estate. He desires to reach an equitable solution outside the court that is agreeable to all parties."

Mr. Jackson did not change expression. "It is not necessary to use inflammatory expressions such as 'outrageous' here, Daniel. We're not before a judge and jury yet. Let us hear your proposal."

Daniel Coonan flushed at the rebuke. "Need I remind you that some twenty years have passed since the assets of the estate were acquired by my client, and that in any case, a quitclaim deed was signed by Mrs. Susan Henry forfeiting all rights and interests in the estate for a very generous monetary consideration?"

Jason Jackson nodded, unperturbed. "Need I remind you that the estate never went through probate, Daniel, as you well know, and that any assets from the estate that Mr. J. R. Henry may have controlled during the intervening period may be subject to reinstatement by the court once the estate is properly probated? As an aside, Mrs. Susan Henry may have signed a quitclaim deed, but that document deals only with her secular interest in the estate, if any, and is not binding on my client. What is your proposal?"

Coonan's face darkened. "Case law has been established which would clearly indicate—"

142

Jason Jackson held up his hand. "Please, Daniel, save that for the court and your closing arguments. We're gathered here to hear a proposal from your client to my client, not to argue the merits of the case. Do you have a specific proposition in mind you wish him to consider?"

My admiration for Jason Jackson grew as I watched him scrimmage with J. R.'s attorney, thinking I had definitely chosen the right man to represent me. Or rather, my father had.

Coonan calmed himself. "My client has been greatly inconvenienced by the restrictions placed upon his current ability to handle the estate's affairs pending the outcome of this frivolous legal claim on your client's behalf. Based on that, my client is willing to make certain concessions in the interest of time, and to concede certain monetary assets to your client, in order to satisfy all parties so that the proper operations of the estate can resume."

Mr. Jackson nodded. "I realize that it is an imposition for your client to have to seek court approval to transact affairs of the estate, Daniel, but that is the proper arrangement which protects all parties with claims to the estate until the appropriate distribution of the estate's assets is complete under probate. As I stated, my understanding for this meeting was to hear what your client is offering to lessen both the time and discomfort of the restraints of the probate period. Please proceed."

Coonan's lips thinned. "Based on the fact that a legal action of this type could take months, or in some cases years, to settle, and due to the fact that your client has in fact no valid claim on—"

"Do you have a specific proposal?" Jason Jackson's voice held an edge. "If so, what is it, Mr. Coonan?"

Coonan smirked. "Fifteen thousand dollars, payment to be made upon the signing of—"

Mr. Jackson smiled as I stood and started for the door. "I believe my client has given you his response to your proposal, Mr. Coonan."

"I had hoped we could enter into a discussion here," Coonan retorted. "If you feel my client's offer is unreasonable, we would entertain your thoughts on a settlement—"

"Fifty thousand dollars," J. R. stated, his features complacent.

Coonan bristled. "J. R., under the circumstances, I feel that is far beyond—"

I paused at the door and turned to J. R. "Do the names Jarvis Holderman and Malcolm Grant mean anything to you?"

J. R. flinched, his face darkening as his eyes narrowed. "Should they?"

"They worked for you at the brickyard."

"Several hundred people worked at the brickyard," J. R. replied.

"I don't possibly see what—" Coonan began.

"Five million," I said.

Coonan's eyes bulged. "Five million dollars? Are you serious? That's absurd!"

I nodded. "You're right. I spoke in haste. I do that at times. Fifty million."

Coonan flushed. "It's quite obvious that we're wasting our time here, gentlemen." He directed his attention to Mr. Jackson. "Perhaps we can reconvene when you've had time to confer with your client and entice him to be reasonable in this matter."

"What do you consider to be a reasonable settlement for my father's life, Mr. Coonan?" I asked in a soft, cold voice.

"What does your father have to do with this?" Coonan demanded.

I smiled evilly. "Your client understands."

"Paul," Mr. Jackson interrupted, "please wait in my office."

J. R.'s face transformed to a splotchy blue-black as his eyes grew hard and acquired a deadly glint.

I walked out and closed the door behind me, crossed over to Jason Jackson's office, and breathed deeply as the cold grip of a terrible desire for revenge rose in me. J. R. could keep the estate for all I cared, *but the little pig-eyed son of a bitch was going to pay for what he did to my father!*

It was some time before the commotion in the reception area announced the departure of J. R. and his lawyer.

Mr. Jackson entered his office and tossed a pad on his desk. "You came dangerously close to saying too much in there, Paul."

"J. R. knows exactly where I'm coming from."

"That's not always a positive thing. Their bottom line is $150,000 for you to forfeit any claim you may have to the Henry estate and leave Clayhill."

"That's very generous of that murdering bastard, considering that he stole well over a million twenty years ago that's probably worth two or three times that today."

"I caution you to give serious consideration before applying labels, Paul. Murder is a serious accusation. Still, they've made an offer you need to consider."

I started for the door. "It's not about the money, Mr. Jackson. It never was!"

ELEVEN

I parked the Cobra under a shade tree, made my way up to the porch, and knocked at the Sherrills' door. Mrs. Sherrill opened it to look out through the screen at me with troubled eyes.

"Ma'am, is Eva Marie in?"

"She's not receiving visitors this afternoon, Paul. She's not feeling well, I'm afraid."

"I was hoping to speak to her, Ma'am."

"I don't like to pry, but have you two had a disagreement of some sort?"

"We've had a misunderstanding. I'd like to set things right with her, if I can."

She hesitated. "I'll see if she'll agree to see you."

Several moments later Eva Marie stepped out onto the porch. Though her makeup had been reapplied, her hostile eyes were still puffy. "I made my position clear this morning, Paul. Why are you here?"

"I just came by to ... say I'm sorry ..."

"Let's walk," she directed, leading the way off the porch.

"Eva, I want to work this thing out between us."

"Do you deny any of the things I was told this morning?"

"Some of them are misconstrued."

She led me along a narrow path into the woods, where she paused under a shade tree to sit on a low-hanging limb. "Okay, Paul, I'm listening. But I warn you, don't take me for a fool or play me for one."

I sat on a branch of the sprawling tree across from her, our knees almost touching. "First off, in many ways I'm not worthy of a woman like you—"

"That's not what this is about, Paul."

"Please try to hear me out, Eva. I've rehearsed this speech twenty times. If you keep interrupting me, I'll end up saying it all wrong."

"Continue." She began diddling in the dirt at her feet with a twig.

"Eva, what few social graces my poor mother managed to instill in me while I was growing up, I seem to have lost in the jungles of Vietnam. I haven't been around a decent woman in so long I don't know how to act anymore. What I'm trying to say is, I know I've got a long way to go before I'm worthy of someone like you, but I want you to know that I'm going to try real hard in the future to measure up to those things you expect of me."

She tossed her twig aside. "This is about your girlfriend, Paul, not your lack of social graces."

"Barbara was a girl I went out with a couple of times. I never made any commitment to her or asked her to make one to me. I didn't expect her or Elaine to drive to Clayhill, and I wasn't pleased about it when they did. I would not have been happy to see her even if you and I hadn't gotten together. She's nothing to me but someone I dated because I was bored."

"Are you sleeping with her?"

"I have no intention of seeing her again."

"That's not what she says. She says you're teaching her over a hundred erotic Chinese—"

"*That's not true*! I don't know anything about Chinese women. I don't even know how that got started."

She lowered her eyes. "Why didn't you tell me about her?"

"I didn't think there was anything to tell. Barbara was the furthest thing from my mind when I was with you."

She bit her lip. "Is sex such a casual thing to you, Paul? Does it have any meaning at all?"

"I've only been with one girl in my whole life that meant anything to me."

"What happened to her?"

"We were engaged, but she got pregnant by my best friend while I was in Nam."

Her posture softened. "I'm sorry. That must have hurt you a lot."

"It did at the time, but now I know she could never measure up to someone like you, so I count myself lucky."

"I find it hard to believe you've never cared about *any* of the girls you've been with but her."

"Why? You've admitted you've never cared about anyone but the guy you fell in love with two years ago."

"That's different, Paul, Jonathan was the only boy I've ever been with."

"Look, Eva, I admit I'd never take the other girls I've known home to meet my mother, but I'd take you home to meet her, and she'd be proud of me. It's been a long time since I've given her a reason to be proud of me for anything. I've given her lots of grief in my life."

She smiled. "I can imagine. Have you been with a lot of women you didn't care about?"

"Not a lot, but I can't undo that now. If I had known someone like you was out there I might have been more ..."

A thin smile tugged at her lips. "Discriminating? I told you I'm not a casual love kind of girl, Paul. To me, sex is a physical fulfillment of an emotional, spiritual union between two people who are committed to a long-term relationship. I know that sounds old-fashioned, maybe even prudish. I'm not a prude, but I am sort of old-fashioned, I guess."

"I understand that concept, even if I haven't practiced it. In my defense, I backed off the other night on the raft in the middle of that lake when I saw you weren't into casual sex. I respected you for that. I wasn't prepared to make a commitment at the time, just like you told Hal. It scared me to death, just like you said. But after I had time to think about it, I realized you're different from any girl I've ever known. I decided I do want to make a commitment to you. I meant it when I asked you to be my girl. I'd like to take you out to dinner and start all over."

A smile teased her lips. "That would be the third time we've had to start over."

"I may be a slow learner, Eva, but please don't give up on me."

"Let's have dinner with my family instead. I'm not ready to be alone with you just yet."

"That's good by me, since I'm more afraid of you than you are of me."

She lifted her head and laughed, sending shivers of relief through me as she stood and offered her hand. I took it and turned to lead her back up the trail to her house, but she yanked me back around, slid into my arms, and meshed her lips to mine.

"I'm definitely not ready to be alone with you yet," she swore, breathless, when we parted.

She led me back up the trail as the cold emptiness within me began to fill with soothing warmth.

* * *

Mr. Sherrill and I sat on the front porch talking about the heat and farming while the women busied themselves in the kitchen. Eva Marie served us lemonade there and paused at the door to look back at us in appreciative amusement. Conversation over dinner was pleasant and the home-cooked meal delicious. We avoided the subject of the Henry feud or of the quarrel Eva Marie and I had suffered. Mrs. Sherrill seemed approving of our renewed courtship and the fact that I had two helpings of everything. Mr. Sherrill and I retired to the parlor for dessert while the women cleaned the kitchen. Afterward, Eva Marie and I sat on the front-porch swing and talked about the millions of stars overhead and far-off places we wanted to visit someday. She walked me to the car and stood swaying in my arms in a lingering kiss good-night.

On the drive back to Hal's place, I decided I liked this old-fashioned dating thing. I parked beside Elaine's car in a mellow mood and got out, humming to myself as I made for the porch. Pounding hooves behind me snapped me out of my romantic reverie as I leapt for my life.

From the safety of the porch I spun around, my heart thudding. "You damned old goat!" I yelled, shaking my fist at Old Billy pawing the ground and snorting at me. "I've got bullets now. You keep that in mind, you old fool!"

Hal and Elaine opened the door amid peals of laughter. "Daydreaming, weren't you?" Hal chided. "How was dinner with Princess Eva Marie and her folks, Sport?"

I elbowed past him. "I see the grapevine in this damned burg's been buzzing, as usual. I'm gonna shoot that cantankerous old goat of yours first thing in the morning, Hal, I swear it!"

"You can't harm that sweet little guy," Elaine defended, still laughing. "You need to win him over like I did."

"I'd rather shoot him. How did things go with you two today?"

Hal rolled his eyes. "It was a long trip back to Jasper, Sport. I'd rather face the Henrys than that scene again. I'm glad you and Eva Marie are all lovey-dovey and that J. R. hasn't shot you yet."

"I'm sorry about asking Barbara to come with me, Paul," Elaine apologized. "That was presumptuous on my part. Are you still angry with me?"

"I hate that things turned out the way they did. I never meant to upset her, but I've never given her any reason to think we had anything permanent going on between us." I sank down in the easy chair as Hal and Elaine sat together on the couch and told them of the meetings with George Hiller and J. R. Henry.

"I'm certain my father's arrest was a setup," I finished. "I need to talk to a couple of guys named Holderman and Grant, who the sheriff's report said were with J. R. when my father was arrested. Do you know where I can find them?"

Hal shook his head. "I've never heard of either one of them. If they were still around Clayhill, I'd know them. Maybe Sheriff Tate can help."

"Hal told me some of the history of your family, Paul," Elaine said. "If this J. R. guy is willing to pay you such a large settlement, he probably paid those other two men off to get them out of town."

Hal nodded. "That makes sense."

I nodded grimly. "Finding them could bust this whole case wide open, *if* they're willing to talk."

* * *

I had a quick breakfast with a glowing Hal and Elaine, agreed to meet them for lunch at the drugstore, skirted around Old Billy, and headed for Clayhill. After parking I went to the phone booth on the corner to place a long distance call to my mother.

"Paul, is anything wrong, dear?"

"I didn't mean to alarm you, Momma; I just have a few questions to ask you."

"Please come home. I'm so worried about you."

"I wish you wouldn't worry so much. Do you remember George Hiller over at the Clayhill Feed and Seed?"

"Yes. Why?"

"Did you ever hear his story of how my father got arrested?"

"He and I never spoke of that day. Why do you ask?"

"Old Man Hiller claims his memory is bad, so I was hoping you could corroborate what he told me about how the arrest went down since his story differs from Sheriff Allston's report."

"Why does that matter after all this time?"

"I'm trying to get the investigation into my father's death reopened. I'm convinced he was murdered and that J. R. and Sheriff Allston were involved in it somehow."

"You're going to give me a nervous breakdown before this is over."

I grimaced, suffering pangs of guilt for her anxiety. "Did you know he still has that old truck of my father's you sold him?"

"He paid me a fair price for it."

"He told me he had to get the ignition changed because you couldn't find the key."

"I told him to do whatever he needed to do to fix it and that I would reimburse him for it, but he never billed me."

"The key was in my father's pocket when he was arrested. Didn't you see it when they returned his stuff to you?"

"No one ever returned any of your father's belongings to me."

"That's odd."

"Paul, please come home and forget this foolishness."

"I've got to go now, Momma."

"Paul, please ..."

"Hey, I almost forgot, I've met this girl."

"Girl?"

"You'll like her."

"You've never mentioned a girl to me before, even when you were seeing Linda. Tell me about her."

I grinned, pleased to hear her voice lighter now, tinged with anticipation. "Her name is Eva Marie Sherrill. She's a real baby doll, a little green-eyed vixen."

"Paul Allison, you mind your manners now! The Sherrills are good people. Don't you be doing anything with their daughter that will bring shame on me, do you hear me?"

"Why, Momma, I'm just *shocked* you would think such!"

"I mean it, young man!"

"I love you, Momma. Gotta go now." I hung up while she was still flustered. I was one smooth operator when it came to my mother. I'd had her number for years and could charm her to no end when the occasion called for it—as it often had when I was growing up and frequently at odds with her strong sense of morality and propriety. I fought off a brief attack of remorse for all the misery I'd given her over the years as I crossed the street to the jail.

Sheriff Tate looked up from his desk when I entered. He poured us a cup of coffee as I relayed the nuts and bolts of the meetings with George Hiller and J. R. "The key to this might be those two men who were with J. R. when my father was arrested, Holderman and Grant," I concluded. "Old Man Hiller is certain no one called Sheriff Allston that morning, which is at odds with his arrest report. Have you heard of them?"

He nodded. "Knew both of them. I arrested Grant a couple of times on drunk-and-disorderly charges. Holderman was a suspect in several petty larceny cases around here, but I never got enough evidence to charge him with anything." He frowned. "I did get the impression on a couple of occasions that Sheriff Allston favored them in some way, but it was nothing blatant. He just seemed to give them a tad more benefit of the doubt than most. You might have something there, but it's still speculative at best."

"Do you know where either of them are now?"

Sheriff Tate sipped his coffee. "Know where both of them are. Holderman is dead. Killed over in Louisiana; Shreveport, as I recall. Somebody carved him up in an alleyway. Don't recall that they ever caught who did it. His widow still lives here in Clayhill. She remarried Todd Vernon, who's about as bad as Holderman was. Some women never get a break."

"What about Grant?"

"He's serving a life sentence for homicide up in the state prison in Huntsville. Killed a man over in Orange in a barroom brawl. I arrested him here in Clayhill after I received an outstanding fugitive warrant on him and turned him over to the police up there. His wife divorced him after his conviction and moved on. I don't know where."

"Would it be possible for me to talk to him in prison?"

"If he's willing to add you to his visitor list."

"If he refuses to talk to me, could you talk to him on my behalf as sheriff?"

"I could, if I was conducting an official investigation, but you still haven't given me enough to go on to reopen the case. We have a limited budget here in the police department, and the town elders are particular about how I spend their money. I'll be glad to call the prison officials on your behalf to see if Grant is willing to meet with you, if you'd like."

"I'd appreciate that, Sheriff. How about Allston? I'd like to talk to him as well."

"I doubt it would do you any good. He retired for health reasons—he's in the early stages of Alzheimer's. His mind drifts in and out, and he gets worse as time goes on. Even if he did tell you anything, you couldn't rely on it."

"What about the coroner? Greene?"

"Died six years ago. He was in his sixties when this came down. But I don't think he could have shed any light on the case. He was only here a few minutes before I arrived."

"The matter of the severe bruises on my father's head, back, and shoulders concerns me. According to Hiller, there's no way they could have gotten there during the scuffle with J. R. because no punches were thrown. The only injury was to J. R., who tripped over Sheriff Allston and hit his head on the bumper of my father's truck. Where did those bruises come from and why? The wrists and heels can be explained by the cuffs and the cell bars, but not the ones on his head, back, and shoulders. My theory is that he was beaten into submission before he was hung, probably by J. R. and his two ruffians."

Sheriff Tate sat forward thoughtfully. "There's something I just remembered that was odd at the time. When I talked to your father in his cell he was still handcuffed. I was going to remove the cuffs, but Sheriff Allston forbade it. He said to let him cool down first. I remember thinking at the time it was strange. We've had a lot of rowdy people in jail over the years, and your father was certainly one of them, but I've never seen Sheriff Allston do that except for one other time a couple of years after your father died."

I leaned forward. "Tell me about it."

Sheriff Tate averted his eyes. "It's an incident I'm not particularly proud of. I came in from patrol late one night and found Sheriff Allston beating a handcuffed black man in a cell. He had his blackjack out and had the man down on the floor beating him something awful. If I hadn't pulled him off, he might have beat him to death. He said the man was an 'uppity nigger' from the North who had back-talked him."

"My father and Sheriff Allston argued that day when my mother visited. Allston was furious because my father called him J. R.'s puppet. It could account for the unexplained bruises on my father's upper body. If he was unconscious at the time, it would also explain how he was hung from the crossbar. In the picture afterward the handcuffs had been removed and his arms were hanging by his side."

Sheriff Tate sat back, frowning. "I don't know, Paul, it's plausible I guess, but I can't work off of unsupported speculation, only facts."

I drained my coffee. "I appreciate that, but you have to admit that there are some curious aspects to this case." I started for the door. "I'll keep you informed, and thanks for the offer to contact the prison officials to see if Grant will talk to me. By the way, there was an inventory list of my father's personal possessions in his file, but my mother said she never received them. What happened to his things?"

Sheriff Tate shrugged. "Beats me; I always assumed they had been returned to her."

* * *

It was too early to meet Hal and Elaine for lunch, but I decided to have a cup of coffee with Eva Marie anyway. As I walked past the phone booth I turned into it on a hunch and called my mother again.

"Momma, what time did you visit my father in jail that day?"

"I don't remember exactly, Paul. It was after lunch. I had to wait for a ride from my next-door neighbor."

"Give me a good guess."

"I'd say between one thirty and two."

"How long were you there?"

"Not more than half an hour."

"Was my father handcuffed in his cell?"

"He was furious because they wouldn't remove the handcuffs. When are you bringing the Sherrills' daughter to meet me, Paul?"

"Uh, to meet you?"

"Kathy and I'll fix Sunday dinner for you two."

"*Aw*, does *Aunt Kathy* have to be there?"

"If you brought a girl home and didn't invite her, she would pinch your ears off, and you know it."

I flinched, remembering Aunt Kathy's sharp, painful pinches when I acted up as a child. I rarely got away with anything around the old battle-ax. I'd have to find some way to neutralize the situation. There was no way I was going to allow Eva Marie into that lion's den to watch Aunt Kathy eat me alive without a diversionary tactic.

I sighed. "Okay, Momma, Sunday it is. Love ya, bye."

* * *

I slid onto a stool in the drugstore. "You're really going to be mad at me."

Eva Marie hurried over with the coffeepot, looked around to ensure no one was watching, and leaned forward to give me a quick peck on the lips. "I didn't sleep all night for thinking of you." She filled my cup. "What have you done now? Not another old girlfriend, I hope?"

"Nope, worse than that," I warned as she set the pot back on the burner. "I'm taking you to Jasper Sunday to have dinner with my mother and the old crone she hangs out with who masquerades as my aunt. They're a lovely pair."

Her eyes widened. "Your mother? Sunday? Dinner? What should I wear? My hair's a mess! What if she doesn't like me? I'm going to kill you!"

"Yes, my mother, on Sunday, for dinner. Wear anything you want to, your hair is perfect, she'll love you, and please don't kill me, J. R. would be annoyed if you beat him to it."

She frowned. "Don't kid around about J. R., Paul. He's dangerous."

I grinned. "So am I. As I recall, that's one of the things that attracts you to me—*stimulates* you, I believe?"

She blushed. "You're a jerk!"

"I thought I was a cad."

"That too! Really, I don't know what to expect. I've never been invited to meet a guy's mother before."

"My mother is a real down-to-earth person, much like your mother. She's all prim and proper and lives in terror of what other people think of me or of what I might do next. In fact, she's already threatened me because she says the Sherrills are decent people and I better not embarrass her while I'm around them or do anything disgraceful with their daughter."

Eva Marie grinned. "I like her already."

"The real problem will be the witch that'll be there with her. She answers to Aunt Kathy, but don't let that fool you: I'm fairly certain she once served as an iron maiden to Satan himself. She's devoted her life to ensuring I don't have any fun and believes that I ought to be kept in a cage and let out only on the end of a short leash."

Eva Marie laughed. "I like her too. This could be fun."

I scowled. "I can see where this is heading."

She leaned forward and kissed me longingly before jerking around in alarm as the little bells tinkled on the front door announcing someone's entry.

Sheriff Tate ambled down to us grinning. "Sorry to disturb you youngsters, but I had some information for Paul here and saw his car still parked outside. Would you prefer I come back at a more convenient time?"

"Please do, Sheriff. We were just getting warmed up," I teased.

Eva Marie turned a deep scarlet. "*No!* Paul and I were just … do you want some coffee?" She placed a cup before him and scurried to the end of the counter to fiddle with a display.

Sheriff Tate looked at his empty cup with an amused grin. "I found your father's personal effects, Paul. They're stored in the evidence room in the basement of the courthouse. If you want to walk over there with me and sign for them, I'll release them to you."

I slid a quarter onto the counter for my coffee. "That was quick work."

"They were logged in on the property register. It was a simple matter of looking it up."

"I'll be back for lunch," I called to Eva Marie. "Hal and Elaine are coming as well. If they get here before I do, make me a cheeseburger, please."

"Yes, Sir," Eva Marie replied, and then blushed again as the sheriff chuckled.

We crossed the street to the courthouse. "That's a fine girl," Sheriff Tate advised.

"I hope you're not going to threaten me too."

"Threaten you?"

"My mother promised me bodily harm by slow dismemberment if I do her wrong."

"Susan was always a very perceptive woman."

* * *

We entered the courthouse and took the stairs down to the basement, where an older woman sat at a desk talking on the telephone. She hung up as we approached, took the receipt the sheriff presented to her, excused herself, and entered the large, steel mesh cage behind her filled with filing cabinets, boxes, and other assorted trappings of stale government paraphernalia. She reemerged with a small, aged cardboard box sealed with tape and handed it to the sheriff. He signed a receipt before leading the way back up the stairs and across to the jail. There he pulled the file on my father and removed the inventory sheet, used his pocketknife to cut the seals, and opened the box. He extracted the items from the box one by one, checked them off on the sheet, and then had me sign the receipt acknowledging the items were all accounted for.

I opened my father's wallet with trembling fingers. It contained his driver's license, without a picture; a faded photo of my mother, who appeared much younger and was very pretty in an old-fashioned way; a photo of two men in army uniforms sitting at a table with bottles of beer before them; and another photo of one of the men and my mother standing together with their arms around each other. A chill passed through me. I was looking at my father for the first time outside of the photograph of him hanging in his cell with his face distorted.

The similarity in our features was striking. He was grinning, the devil dancing in his eye, as my mother smiled demurely. A lump formed in my throat threatening to choke me.

"I'd forgotten how much you favor him," Sheriff Tate observed. "He was a real lady's man, like you."

I stiffened. "I don't consider myself a lady's man, Sheriff."

He smirked. "Winning little Eva Marie's favor has been more than any man has done since I've known her, and I've known her all her life."

I thought of the farm boy who had won her heart two years ago as I placed the paper money into the billfold, stuck it in my pocket, and picked up the wide leather belt. I studied the large, time-tarnished silver buckle depicting a man riding a bronco and slipped it around my waist, surprised to find that it cinched in the third, much worn, notch where my father had worn it. I slipped the coins into my pocket after pausing to study the silver dollar, which was a well-worn, almost unrecognizable tarnished disk with blurred engravings. I opened the pocketknife with the yellow bone handle and found the humidity had left a light coat of rust on the blades. I pocketed it, wound the wristwatch, and placed it next to my ear to listen to it ticking. I tossed the stale, crumpled pack of cigarettes in the trash, pocketed the Zippo lighter, and studied the metal ring with three keys. One had a Ford emblem stamped on it. Another was to a deadbolt lock, my father's old house key, I suspected. The third key was flat with notches cut at irregular intervals on the end unlike any key I had ever seen before with the numbers 0001 stamped on the side.

"That goes to a bank safety deposit box," Sheriff Tate offered. He reached into his pocket, pulled out his key ring, and held up one of his keys beside it. They were identical, except his had the number 0067 stamped on the side. "I think you should consult with Jason Jackson before you open that vault box. There could be some legal complications that might affect the estate. In fact, you may not even be authorized to open the box until the court has determined ownership of the contents."

"Would you accompany me over to see him?"

"I'd be glad to."

* * *

Miss Gladys insisted on going through the pleasantries with both Sheriff Tate and me before ushering us into Jason Jackson's office, where I briefed Mr. Jackson on the sequence of events that led up to my possession of the key to the safety deposit box.

Mr. Jackson sat forward in his chair. "Sheriff, I'd like a certified copy of the inventory of John Henry's personal effects, as well as the receipt you signed with the county records division where they were stored. I'd also like to have a certified copy of the joint inventory of the personal effects signed by you and Paul."

Sheriff Tate stood. "I'll be back in fifteen minutes."

Jason Jackson pulled a law book from the shelf behind him and paged through it as we waited. He consulted two other law books and then studied the receipts when Sheriff Tate returned with the certified copies. He then called Miss Gladys in to type up a sworn affidavit for Sheriff Tate to sign that specified the chain of custody of the personal items from the date of my father's incarceration to the release of the items to me. When he had once again reviewed every document and an additional law book, he sat back in satisfaction.

"Gentlemen, the contents of John Henry's personal effects are not part of the Henry family estate as such. That is not to say that any legal documents that may be in that box are not part of the estate. That would be situational dependant. However, at this point the key and the contents of that box are legally the property of John Henry's heirs—in this case his lawful wife, Susan Henry, and his son, Paul Henry. Barring any objections by Susan, there is no legal reason Paul cannot open that box and take possession of the contents."

I leaned forward. "May I borrow your phone? I'll call her now." When she answered, I told her of the events of the morning and of the key to the deposit box. "What do you want me to do, Momma?"

"Well, I guess you should open it, if that's what Jason thinks you should do."

"Do you want to be present when I do?"

"Heavens no! It would take more than a bunch of worthless old legal documents to get me back to Clayhill. Put Jason on the phone and I'll give my permission for you to open the box without my being present."

I handed the phone to Mr. Jackson, who spoke with her and confirmed her wishes. When he'd finished, he handed the phone back to me.

"Your Aunt Kathy and I are having a nervous fit about what to prepare for dinner Sunday, Paul. Is there anything special Miss Sherrill likes that we should make for her? Oh, and Paul, please give Nelson Tate my regards. He seemed quite concerned about you when he called."

A bolt of true, inspirational genius struck me. "Gee, I don't know, Momma, but he just happens to be sitting right here. Let me ask him." I turned to Sheriff Tate. "My mother sends her regards and wonders if you're available to join me, Eva Marie, and one of her funky old spinster friends for dinner on Sunday? She says she would love to see you again after all these years."

Sheriff Tate shifted in surprise. "Uh, sure, I'd be delighted to come to dinner on Sunday. I appreciate her offering."

I put the phone back to my ear. "Momma, Sheriff Tate says he would be pleased to join us on Sunday, and thanks you for asking. Whatever you and Aunt Kathy want to fix will suit Eva Marie and him just fine. Okay?"

"Oh my *gracious goodness*, Paul, *I'm going to kill you!*"

"Yes, I'm sure you two will have a lot to talk about."

"Paul Allison Henry, you are *intolerable*! You wait until I tell your Aunt Kathy what you just did to me!"

"Momma, I've got to go now. We'll see you Sunday about noon. Bye now."

I hung up the phone with a smug smile. The enemy force was now neutralized. My mother would be preoccupied with Sheriff Nelson Tate's presence, and old Batty-Kathy would be so engrossed with him and Eva Marie she couldn't cause me any mischief.

Necessity had made the devil and I close allies over the years.

TWELVE

Jason Jackson and Sheriff Tate accompanied me across the courthouse square to the Clayhill City Bank. After conferring with the bank president and authenticating that I was the legal heir of John Allison Henry, I was escorted by a clerk down into the vault to a wall filled with green metal deposit boxes. The assistant inserted his key into the top lock of box 0001 and pulled an eight-inch-high, twelve-inch-wide, thirty-six-inch-long container from its slot. I followed him back out of the vault into a small room with a table in it. The assistant set the container on the table, told me to push the button on the wall when I was ready to return the box to the vault, and departed, closing the door behind him. I inserted the key into the remaining lock and the top opened an eighth of an inch. I lifted the lid and sucked in my breath. Almost the entire box contained neat, bound stacks of one-hundred-dollar bills.

A pack of aged, ribbon-bound legal documents rested inside the front portion, along with a ring holding five additional safety deposit box keys. The keys were numbered 0002 through 0006. I put them in my pocket, picked up the packet of legal documents, closed the box, and pushed the button. I accompanied the attendant back into the vault to replace box 0001 and hurried back up the steps to where Mr. Jackson and Sheriff Tate waited. I gave the legal documents to Mr. Jackson and showed them the remaining five keys.

"The box is slam-full of stacks of one-hundred bills," I whispered. "There must be thousands in there!"

"Check the remaining five deposit boxes," Mr. Jackson advised.

I again descended into the vault with the attendant, where he placed the five containers on a metal gurney and pushed them into the small room. After the attendant departed, I picked up container 0002, placed it on the table, and inserted the key.

It was filled with bound stacks of one-hundred-dollar bills as well. With pounding heart, I relocked it and opened the remaining four boxes. Each was stuffed with hundred-dollar bills. I replaced the containers on the gurney, rang the buzzer, assisted the attendant in returning the boxes to their slots, and hurried back up to Jason Jackson and Sheriff Tate. Wordlessly, I led the way out of the bank and back to Mr. Jackson's office.

"Each box is full of one-hundred-dollar bills," I advised when we were seated in Mr. Jackson's office. "Where did my father get that kind of money?"

Mr. Jackson smiled. "I think you've found old Robert Henry's hidden hoard from his bootlegging days."

I swallowed. "The loot everyone has been searching for all these years? What do I do with it?"

Sheriff Tate shrugged. "The statute of limitations ran out years ago. It's not a police matter as far as I'm concerned."

I looked to Jason Jackson. "What does that mean?"

Mr. Jackson's eyes glinted. "It means the government is going to get a handful of money when you declare it. Congratulations, Paul, you and Susan have just hit the jackpot."

"What about the estate having a claim on the money?"

"None whatsoever," Jason Jackson replied. "It was never an asset of the estate because it was never declared, most probably because it was illegally gained, even if no one can prove that for sure. Even if they could, as the sheriff said, the statute of limitations on the crime has already passed. The money was in your father's possession when he died. It's legally yours and Susan's after taxes. I'd estimate there's at least half a million, gauging by the size of the boxes."

Sheriff Tate looked strained. "Do you think Susan will still cook Sunday dinner for us?"

I laughed. "Momma's pretty set in her ways. Do you mind if I call her again?"

Mr. Jackson shifted the phone to the corner of his desk. "I recommend you hire a tax consultant to figure out how much the government is entitled to. You can make the tax payment through the bank. From that point on, you will be free to do with the remainder as you please."

"Wow!" I said as I dialed. "What were the legal documents in the first box?"

Mr. Jackson picked up the documents before him. "This s a copy of Robert Henry's will, of which I have the original. These are stock certificates from insurance companies, which may or may not still have some value. This is your parents' original marriage certificate, a copy of the marriage certificate of Robert Henry and your stepgrandmother, a copy of the marriage certificate of her later marriage to J. R., and oddly, a copy of a death certificate for a Deborah Ann Henry in Little Rock, Arkansas. This last sheet of paper has a series of letters with plus and minus signs of some sort that I can't make out."

"Hello?" my mother's voice responded on the phone.

"Hi, Momma, guess what?" I gushed.

"Oh, Paul, I'm so glad you called. Do you think it would be too passé to serve southern fried chicken, mashed potatoes with brown gravy, sweet peas, fried okra, and cornbread, with some sliced tomatoes and cucumbers on the side? For dessert your Aunt Kathy is planning your favorite banana pudding. We're so excited!"

"We're rich, Momma!"

"What?"

"The safety deposit box held a bunch of old documents and keys to five other safety deposit boxes. They were all stuffed full of cash!"

"Are you playing a joke on me?"

"I'm not kidding. Would you like to speak to Mr. Jackson to confirm it?"

"Your father never had that kind of money. There's been some sort of a mistake. Don't you dare touch that money until we find out who it belongs to!"

"We think it's the money my grandfather earned bootlegging, Momma."

"Then if it's illegally gained it should be turned over to the authorities."

"No, Momma, it's ours, even if it was earned illegally. The statute of limitations ran out on it years ago. We're free to spend it as we see fit after we pay taxes on it."

"Then it's the devil's money. Ill-gotten gains bring ill-gotten pains. It would be better to give it to the church so they can help the poor people of the world."

"Give it to the church! *We're* poor people, Momma! Why should we give it to some sharp-tongued, self-serving, panhandling hypocrite eaten up with his own self-appreciating bullshit piousness!"

"*Paul Allison Henry!* You just be glad you're not standing here before me right this minute, young man! Let me talk to Jason. I'll not continue this dialogue with you if you're going to spout blasphemy and speak ill of the church."

I handed the phone to Mr. Jackson, whose eyes were crinkled in mirth.

"Susan?" he inquired. I fidgeted through a series of "Uh huh's, okay's, I understand, yes, that's possible, that won't be a problem," before Mr. Jackson handed back the phone.

"Have you got your attitude adjusted, young man?"

"Yes, Ma'am."

"Good. Your Aunt Kathy and I are going to do the fried chicken. She says for you to mind your manners on Sunday when Nelson and your young lady friend are here."

"Love you, Momma. Bye." I hung up and turned to Sheriff Tate. "The Sunday dinner is still on. I might have to stand in the corner during the meal, though."

Sheriff Tate grinned. "That's great! Dinner, I mean—not you having to stand in the corner. What did she say about the money?"

Jason Jackson laughed. "She refuses to touch a dime of it because it was earned dishonestly. She said Paul could do whatever he wanted to with the money, and that her only hope is that she's raised him properly to be generous to those less fortunate."

"Momma's real old-fashioned," I apologized.

"Salt of the earth," Jason Jackson praised.

"She was always independent-minded," Sheriff Tate allowed. "She used to scare me to death when we were in school together. She was so cheeky I would get tongue-tied around her."

164

I chuckled. "She hasn't changed much." I turned to Mr. Jackson. "Do you know a good tax consultant?"

"I'll have one meet you at the bank if you'd like."

I looked at my watch. "I'm late for lunch. Please have him meet us there around one thirty."

"I think we need to keep this confidential for now," Mr. Jackson suggested.

"It would serve no purpose to make it public," Sheriff Tate agreed, rising.

* * *

I waved at Eva Marie, who was busy serving the small lunch crowd, and slid into the booth with Hal and Elaine. "Sorry I'm late. I've had a busy morning."

"We've already ordered," Elaine advised.

"You look like the fabled Cheshire cat who just ate the canary," Hal accused.

I grinned. "I found my father's personal things still in the evidence room over at the courthouse." I pulled out my father's billfold to show them the pictures.

"Look at that glint in his eye," Hal observed. "He looks just like you with that shit-eating grin."

"I think he looks dashing and handsome," Elaine added.

I profiled. "I get it honest."

Hal grimaced. "*Barf!*"

"Hal, I need a word with you outside." He followed me out.

I pulled out my wallet and handed him a hundred dollars.

"Are you crazy?" he sputtered.

"Take it," I insisted. "You can't even afford to buy Elaine's lunch right now."

"True, but I'd feel more comfortable with twenty."

"I can't have Elaine going hungry," I teased.

"It's a bit much, Sport, and I haven't done anything to earn it. Why are you doing this?"

"My mother raised me to be generous to those less fortunate."

Hal's eyes narrowed. "There's something you're not telling me."

"Suffice it to say I won't be hurting for money for a while."

"I hope like hell you screwed J. R. over somehow. Let's go eat lunch. I'm buying!" We returned to the booth. "So did you get a lead on those two hombres you wanted to talk to?" he asked as we settled in.

"Yep, one's dead and one's in prison for life. Sheriff Tate is going to ask the one in prison, Malcolm Grant, if he'll agree to talk to me."

Eva Marie placed our burgers before us, dashed off to fetch our drinks, and gave me a quick smile before hurrying off to cater to her lunch crowd.

"You know, you ought to take that little princess out of all this," Hal observed as he bit into his burger.

"Do you know a Todd Vernon?" I asked evasively.

He swallowed. "Yep, he's a drunk. What does Todd have to do with anything?"

"I want to talk to his wife."

"Mary? Why do you want to talk to her?"

"She was married to Jarvis Holderman before he got himself killed over in Shreveport."

"Ah, now I see the connection." He wiped his mouth. "We can stop by Todd's place after lunch. I suggest we bring along a jug of rotgut to distract him while you talk to her."

"You and Elaine run by Maybell's and get some. I've got an appointment at one thirty. I'll meet you back at your place."

Eva Marie hurried over to our booth and handed me the ticket for our lunch. "Don't overtip now," she warned.

I handed the bill to Hal. "Tell him; he's buying. What are you doing after work?"

She thrust her hip out and placed her palm on it in a good imitation of a truck-stop floozy. "Depends on what you've got in mind, big boy."

"I thought I might grill you a steak."

"Are Elaine and I invited?" Hal asked.

"No."

"You don't have a grill," Hal advised.

I scowled. "I'll buy one."

"You don't have any charcoal."

"I'll get some."

"You don't have any steaks."

"You're starting to piss me off."

"Who's gonna tie up Old Billy while you grill the steaks?"

"Okay, you're invited."

Hal beamed. "I'll pick up all the stuff when I get the rotgut for Todd."

"We'll get some salad mix and baking potatoes too," Elaine offered.

Eva Marie laughed. "I need to go home and freshen up first. Pick me up around seven."

I squeezed her hand. "See you then."

"Have you ever grilled a steak before?" Hal demanded as we departed.

"No, but I've seen it done."

"It's an art, Sport. You don't just throw a hunk of meat on a flame and burn it."

"You're free to make dining arrangements elsewhere, pal."

"You better let me handle things. I know what I'm doing. We'd probably end up eating sandwiches with an amateur like you trying to play chef."

* * *

I met the accountant and Mr. Jackson in the office of the president of the bank. Mr. Jackson stressed this was to be kept in the closest of confidences and told them what he wanted done. The banker set up a table outside the vault with an electric money counter and two clerks to recount under the supervision of the accountant. At the end of the process I deposited $312,400 into my new savings account after paying taxes. Not a bad haul, even if my mother did think it was the devil's money.

I drove to Hal's place afterwards, where, due to the Cobra's small backseat, Elaine chauffeured us to Todd and Mary Vernon's home in her Pontiac. When she parked in front of their shack, I soberly viewed the pitiful squalor they lived in, thinking the tiny, sagging tin-roofed hovel made Hal's place look like a palace. After exchanging small talk about coon dogs, Hal lured Todd out to the car for a shot of whisky as

Elaine and I settled in on the porch with Mrs. Vernon, a prematurely aged, work-stooped woman in her fifties with washed-out blue eyes that held no joy or hope in her deeply lined face filled with sunspots and blemishes. She sat silently, dressed in filthy, worn-out rags and men's shoes without laces in them.

"Ma'am, I need to ask you some questions about your late husband, if I may?" I requested, easing into the subject.

Her eyes darted out to her husband at the car. "What you wantin' to know?" she asked in a frail, low voice as if he would find fault with her speaking.

"Jarvis Holderman was involved in the arrest of a man named John Allison Henry some twenty years ago. Did he ever talk to you about that?"

She wrung her hands. "No," she whispered. "He don't speak to me about such."

"You weren't aware that he was involved in the arrest of John Henry?"

Her eyes darted away. "Maybe I hear him talk about it once."

"Would you mind sharing the things you overheard him say, Ma'am?"

She cut her eyes at her current husband. "He say he help arrest one of them high-and-mighty Henrys. Say he set for life. Say he never have to work again. Say he just sit back and drink whisky and hunt and fish all day. He be bragging with his friend, old dirty Malcolm, one night in the dark on the porch."

"Malcolm Grant?"

"He have a bad smell to him."

"What else did they say, Ma'am?"

Her hands twisted in her lap. "He don't say much more for me to hear. I don't want to hear more if it be bad things they be talkin' about."

"What bad things were they talking about, Ma'am?" I pressed. She dropped her eyes and remained mute. "Do you know if he came into any large sum of money during that time?"

"He come home with five hundred dollars. Say there plenty more where that come from. But when they find his dead body, he don't have no money on him."

"What else did he say to his friend that night on the porch, Ma'am?"

She looked away. "My man going to be mean with that whisky your friend giving him. He get mean on whisky. He start drinking the whisky, he don't like to stop. I have to sleep in the corncrib tonight until he go to sleep. I going to get me forty dollars someday. I going to my sister's house in Dallas. She done say come to live with her. I get me forty dollars for the bus, I go and don't never come back to here again."

I pulled out my wallet and held out sixty dollars. "I'd be willing to pay you to help me, Ma'am. It's very important to me. Please tell me everything they said that night on your porch."

She snatched the money and jammed it into her bosom. "They say they kill that Henry man," she whispered. "Say they hung him by the neck 'til he dead. That what they say that night when they drunk on the porch in the dark. I go to my sister's house in Dallas now. You be a good man for helping me do that."

My heart pounded. "Did they say who else was there when they did that, Ma'am?"

"They just say what they do. They say they set for life."

"Is there anything else you can tell me that they said, Ma'am?"

She shook her head and darted her wrinkled hand into her raggedy old blouse to insure the currency was safe. "That be all I hear."

I leaned near her. "Did they say why they hung him?" She shook her head. "Would you be willing to tell Sheriff Tate what you overheard them say?"

"Don't like to talk to no sheriff," she whispered, fearful now. "I go to my sister's house in Dallas. She done said come on to live with her. I never come back to this place no more."

Elaine put her hand on my arm. "Paul, please, you're scaring her. She's told you everything she knows."

I stood. "Thank you, Ma'am. I'm sorry about the whisky."

She nodded. "Maybe he drink enough to sleep now. I catch him sleepin', I be gone."

I considered her one of the saddest creatures I'd ever seen, and I'd seen a lot of sad people in Nam. I led Elaine off the porch, sincerely hoping Mary Vernon would find a better life in Dallas with her sister.

"You ready?" I asked as we approached Hal and Mary's disheveled husband where they stood at the back of Elaine's car.

"'Ont a snort?" The old man offered me the bottle and grinned from a toothless mouth.

"Keep the bottle. Enjoy it," I replied, fighting the urge to pummel him, hoping the old scoundrel would get drunk and pass out so the old woman could make her escape.

I briefed Hal on the way back. Elaine distracted Old Billy for me to make it to the Cobra to pick up Eva Marie as Hal began assembling the new grill for the steaks.

* * *

Mrs. Sherrill ushered me into the parlor. "Eva Marie is dressing. Frank is still in the fields," she apologized as she served me coffee. "I'll send Susan a basket of pears and some fresh squash and vine-ripened tomatoes on Sunday. I'm sure fresh fruit and vegetables are hard to come by in the city."

"I'm sure Momma will appreciate them," I acknowledged.

"Bring her to visit with us soon. We haven't seen each other in ages."

Eva Marie swept into the room, alluring in a pair of white slacks with a brown silk blouse that highlighted her slim, athletic build. Long, dangling gold earrings framed her cheeks from beneath her dark, swept-back black hair and glowing green eyes. If there was a more attractive woman on earth, I'd certainly never seen her.

"I'll be home late tonight, Mother, so don't wait up for me." She tucked her arm through mine, gave her mother a quick peck on the cheek, and led me out.

"You look breathtaking," I complimented after I settled her in the Cobra and pulled away.

"Pull over," she commanded as we rounded the bend from her house. She slid into my arms across the console and gave me a searing kiss. "I've needed that all day," she said huskily as she slid back into her seat.

"Glad to be of service to a lady in distress," I gasped.

"Do you have any reservations about us, Paul?"

"None," I assured her, knowing that to be the most truthful statement I'd ever made. I could never have my fill of this strange woman. "I want you and to hell with the harsh, unjust consequences."

Her eyes narrowed. "What harsh, unjust consequences?"

"You know, the loss of individual liberty, giving up all the other beautiful women in the world, being fitted for a nose ring—the usual trappings of a doomed man."

She punched me in the ribs. "You're doomed all right, but not in the way you imagine."

We were still laughing when I turned off the highway onto the dirt road leading to Hal's place and saw the boiling smoke and glowing red haze above the trees in the evening twilight.

"What the hell?"

"Something's on fire!" she exclaimed.

"That damn Hal's probably burnt the house down trying to cook those steaks," I swore, speeding up as much as I dared on the washed-out lane. We pulled into the yard to find Elaine's small figure, dressed in a bathrobe, struggling to pull Hal's large prone body through the grass away from the house, backlit by a towering inferno of flames engulfing the structure. I jumped out of the car and almost tripped over Old Billy lying off to the side covered in blood. Two of Hal's hounds lay stiffly close by in pools of blood. I shielded my face from the intense heat and fanned at the roiling smoke as I ran to help Elaine.

"What happened?" I yelled, taking in the blood covering Hal's face and chest and his scorched clothes smoldered in places.

She turned her smudged, tear-streaked face to me in anguish. "*They've killed him, Paul! Oh my God, they've killed him!*" She collapsed against me in wracking hysteria, exhausted from her efforts to pull Hal from the flames, her hair and robe singed in places with red burn spots marring her hands and arms.

Eva Marie drew up short of us, her hand going to her mouth in shock. I shoved Elaine to her and turned back to the unconscious Hal. A series of small holes marred his chest and face. From the pattern of the wounds, I knew them to be from a shotgun blast. He breathed in ragged, choking gasps, his facial color an unhealthy pale. From my Vietnam experience, I knew at least one lung, if not both, were punctured. I grabbed him under his arms and pulled him away from the swirling flames.

"Elaine! Do you have the keys to your car?" I yelled. "We've got to get him to a hospital!" She stared at me, uncomprehending. "Do you have your keys, damn it?" She looked at the burning house in confusion. I surmised the keys were still in there and that there was no hope of recovering them since portions of the roof were already falling in. "Help me! Take his legs and help me get him in the car!"

Eva Marie and Elaine each took a leg and helped me drag Hal to the Cobra. I opened the door on the passenger side and pushed the seat forward. We managed to pull Hal's limp body into the back with me tugging from inside and the girls pushing from the outside.

"Get in here with him, Elaine!" I ordered as I ripped my shirt off and thrust it at her. "I need your help. Can you understand me? If you don't get yourself together, he's going to die! Hold this shirt over these holes in his chest. He can't breathe. His lungs are punctured. See these bubbles? That's air! You've got to hold this over these wounds so he can breathe. Can you do that? Keep it tight now." I scrambled in behind the wheel as Eva Marie climbed in beside me and leaned through the bucket seats to help Elaine.

I spun the tires in a tight circle and sped off down the rutted lane. "What happened?" I shouted over my shoulder, fighting the steering wheel to keep the skidding Cobra out of a ditch.

"*Some men shot him! Some men came to the house and shot him!*" Elaine screeched. "*Oh my God, I can't believe they just shot him like that!*"

"What men? Who shot him? Get yourself together! Tell me what happened!"

She drew a shuddering breath. "I don't know who they were. They were in a blue truck. I've never seen them before. Hal made me stay in the house."

"How many were there?"

"Three, I think. Oh my God, he's going to die!"

"He's not going to die!" I swept onto the highway with the tires squealing and hit the throttle with the Cobra fishtailing as it leapt forward. "What did Hal say when they pulled up, Elaine?" I yelled back to her as I raced for the clinic in Clayhill, knowing Hal needed more than a clinic, but that the nearest hospital was in Jasper, forty miles away, and that Hal would never make that trip without stabilizing his wounds first.

"He … he was on the front porch … he had just lit the grill to get the coals ready for the steaks. I heard a car drive up out front. H-Hal came into the bedroom and said, 'Oh shit, this ain't good,' and … and got his rifle. He leaned it against the wall just inside the living room and … and told me to get back into the bedroom. I had just finished taking a shower. I asked him what was wrong. He said, 'Nothing I can't handle.' He went outside to talk to them. I went into the bedroom to get dressed. I heard gunshots. I looked out the window and … and saw a big man with a gun in his hands. I grabbed my robe and ran into the living room. The grill was turned over … fire was spreading everywhere … blocking the door. I ran out the back door and around to the front. Hal was lying on the porch covered in blood with flames all around him. I saw the blue truck driving down the road. I tried to get him away from the house before he burned up."

I went through the city limits of Clayhill at better than a hundred miles an hour and downshifted as I slung the Cobra into a power slide to navigate the turn onto the street leading to the clinic, downshifted again, locked up the brakes, and slid up to the front door.

"Eva, get us some help!" I yelled as I jumped out.

Eva Marie ran for the front door of the facility and returned with two nurses pushing a hospital gurney. Between the five of us, we wrestled Hal out of the backseat and up onto the bed of the device.

"Get him into the emergency room! I'll call the doctor!" one of the nurses yelled to the other as we pushed Hal to the double doors.

I turned to Eva Marie, who had blood on her pants, blouse, cheeks, and hands, with one gold earring missing. "Take Elaine into the waiting room. Try to calm her down. Call the sheriff. I'll help the nurse until the doctor gets here."

Eva Marie took Elaine by the shoulders and guided her toward the waiting room as I turned to help the nurse cut Hal's bloody shirt off him.

"The doctor's on his way," the other nurse informed us as she rushed back in.

"Get the donor book and type him, Shirley," the first nurse ordered as she applied thin plastic strips to the holes bubbling blood from Hal's chest. "Call a few of our volunteers with his blood type. He's going to need a transfusion. Mr. Henry can help me here."

Shirley hurried out as the first nurse placed my hands over the plastic strips on Hal's chest to hold them in place. I was relieved to see his labored breathing was steadying now that his sucking chest wounds were sealed. An elderly man rushed into the emergency room, pushed me aside to examine Hal, and began barking rapid orders at the nurse I was assisting. With my help no longer needed, I stumbled out to the waiting room, where Sheriff Tate and Deputy Miller were attempting to question a still-hysterical Elaine. Both paused to stare at my bare-chested, blood-covered torso.

"Are you hurt?" Sheriff Tate demanded.

"No, I'm fine. Eva, call your parents to come pick you up. This could take a while."

"We'll take Elaine home with us tonight," she reassured me.

I turned back to the sheriff. "Have you been able to get anything out of Elaine other than a blue truck with a big man and one or two other men in it?"

Sheriff Tate shook his head. "She claims she never got a good look at them."

"How many big men are there in Clayhill who drive blue pickups, Sheriff?" I demanded.

"This is a police matter, Paul!"

I turned back to the emergency room, where I found the second nurse taking blood from the first volunteer who had arrived. The doctor and the other nurse were still working to stabilize Hal, who now had tubes down his nose and mouth as they worked on his face to extract the lead pellets. I thought of the many gunshot and worse wounds I had seen in Nam as a lump formed in my throat above a hard knot in my stomach, knowing this was one hundred percent my fault.

"Is he going to make it, Doc?" I asked as I hovered at the end of the table.

"We're going to have to transport him to Beaumont by ambulance. He's going to require surgery. We've done about all we can for him here with our limited facilities."

"I'll go with him," I said grimly.

"He's not likely to regain consciousnesses until sometime tomorrow or the day after. You would do better to get yourself cleaned up and get some rest."

I went back to the waiting room, where Mrs. Sherrill now worked with Eva Marie trying to calm Elaine, who appeared to be slipping into a state of shock. Mrs. Sherrill rushed over to me when she saw my bloody appearance.

"I'm fine," I assured her. "Thanks for coming." I turned to the nurse taking blood from the volunteer. "Can you check Elaine's burns and give her a tranquilizer when you finish there?"

Feeling useless, I turned to the bathroom to clean the blood off me as best I could. When I came out, the nurse held out a green hospital shirt to me. As I slipped it on, she put salve on Elaine's burns. The doctor hurried out a short time later and quickly prescribed some pills to calm her and then rushed back to the emergency room. I helped Eva Marie settle Elaine into the back of the Sherrills' car and then returned to watch them load Hal into the back of the ambulance for the two-hour trip to Beaumont.

Sheriff Tate moved up beside me. "The volunteer fire department said there wasn't anything they could do once they got there. The place was too far gone. Paul, I *will* find the bastards who did this. Don't do anything foolish that will set you and me at cross-purposes. I need your word you'll stay out of this."

"I told you in the beginning that if the Henrys crossed the line, I would respond in kind," I reminded him grimly.

"If you go outside the law in this matter, I'll do what I have to do as sheriff. It's not worth it on your part. Let me handle this."

Waves of guilt consumed me. "It was me they came looking for, not him."

The nurse came out with a pan and towels. "Mr. Henry, I'll clean up the blood in the back of your car before it sets up in your upholstery. It's such a pretty car, I'd hate to see it ruined."

"I'm much obliged for your assistance, Ma'am. I'll help you."

"You finish your business with the sheriff. There's not enough room in the back for the both of us anyway."

175

I stared hard at Sheriff Tate. "I met with Mary Vernon this afternoon just before all of this came down. She says that twenty years ago she heard Jarvis Holderman and Malcolm Grant bragging about hanging my father and being set for life."

"Did she say who else was present when it happened?"

"No. That's all she overheard."

"I'll speak to her."

"She's probably halfway to Dallas by now. I gave her some money to run away from her husband."

"Why?'

"I felt sorry for her."

He shrugged. "It's hearsay on her part and not admissible in court as evidence anyway."

"It's enough that I know the truth of what happened to my father, and we both know it should be me in the back of that ambulance, not Hal."

Sheriff Tate met my stare. "I have a job to do, Paul. Don't hinder me in doing it."

"You do what you've got to do, Sheriff. I'll do the same."

"I placed that call to the officials in Huntsville. I should get an answer any day now. I'll go up there with you on my own dime if you'd like, assuming he's willing to meet with you."

"Whatever. Talking to Malcolm Grant just doesn't seem as important to me anymore."

"I can find an excuse to lock you up for a few days, if I need to."

"Goodnight, Sheriff."

"Good night, Paul." Sheriff Tate turned away with some trepidation.

I watched him walk off. I had come to respect the man more than most and hoped we wouldn't become at odds with each other in the future.

* * *

When the nurse finished cleaning the back of my car, I offered to pay her, but she refused any compensation for her labors. I drove to the

Pine View Inn, checked in, showered, and fell into bed in exhaustion. Almost immediately the phone rang.

"I wanted to check on you," Eva Marie whispered.

"How's Elaine?"

"The tranquilizers knocked her out. I've never been so terrified in my life."

"I'm sorry about tonight, Eva. None of this would have happened if it wasn't for me."

"You're not responsible for what other people do. Good night, Paul."

THIRTEEN

I dressed in my blood-caked pants and clean hospital shirt, stopped by the bank to draw some money from my grandfather's bootleg fund, and drove to the Sherrills'.

Mrs. Sherrill ushered me into the kitchen. "I called the hospital in Beaumont for Elaine this morning," she informed me as she poured us coffee. "Hal is in the intensive care ward. They said the surgery went well."

"Thank you, Ma'am, I appreciate that."

"Eva Marie has taken the day off to be with Elaine." Mrs. Sherrill hesitated. "Paul, please don't take this wrong. Eva Marie is our only child. If anything should happen to her, I don't know if I could survive it. What I'm trying to say is, I think you're a fine young man and all, but under the circumstances ..."

"I understand, Ma'am. Everyone in Clayhill has tried to tell me that this stupid feud with the Henrys is dangerous, but I refused to take it seriously until yesterday. I would never want Eva Marie to be in danger because of me."

"I'm so grateful you understand." She reached across the table to pat my hand. "I appreciate you being so noble about it."

"Oh, he's noble all right, a regular knight in shining armor," Eva Marie retorted as she stormed into the kitchen. "Unfortunately, he's also dumber than a rock." She whirled on me, her dark green eyes flashing fire. "Just who do you think you are? You're naive and presumptuous if you think you can make decisions for me without consulting me beforehand! How dare you!" She whirled to her mother. "And I don't appreciate you meddling in my personal affairs, Mother!"

I stood. "Eva, your mother and I just think—"

She turned on me. "You stay out of this! This is between Mother and me!"

Mrs. Sherrill reached for her arm. "Dear, I was only trying to—"

She jerked back from her mother's hand. "I agreed to live at home as long as you didn't meddle in my personal life, Mother! I won't be treated like a baby! If I need to move out to have a life of my own, I'll do so!"

"Paul and I are only concerned for your safety, dear," she soothed. "This thing with the Henrys is becoming violent and ..."

Eva Marie placed her fists on her hips and glared at her. "So I'm supposed to abandon the man I love because he's facing personal danger? I'm supposed to run and hide and tell him when he's weathered the storm alone to come back for me? I don't think so, Mother! Whatever he faces, I'll face with him, and I'll thank you to mind your own business in the future." She turned to me. "Elaine and I will be out in a minute. Finish your coffee so we can go."

"Eva, I really think it would be better if we—"

"Don't say it, Paul! If you try to dump me over some stupid, misguided notion of male chivalry, you can just keep on walking. I mean that." She stalked out and slammed her bedroom door.

I sighed. "I agree with your position on this, Mrs. Sherrill. I'll talk to her when she's calmed down a bit."

She gave me a tight, rueful smile. "Save yourself the effort, Paul. Eva Marie is unfortunately a very strong-willed, self-sufficient woman who will never relinquish one ounce of her independence."

I nodded grimly. "Next to her, dealing with the Henrys is a piece of cake."

"Take care of my little girl as best you can, and as she will allow you to. That's all I ask."

"I'll do my best, Ma'am." My assurance did nothing to quell my own apprehensions. If I allowed anything to happen to Eva Marie like it did to Hal, I knew *I* could never survive it.

Eva Marie stomped out of her room with Elaine in tow, now dressed in some of Eva Marie's clothes, which were too large for her tiny frame.

"Let's go, Paul. I'll call you later, Mother."

"Good-bye, Ma'am. Thank you for your kindness and for taking me in," Elaine called as Eva Marie tugged her out after her.

"Thanks for the coffee, Ma'am." I hurried out after them and fired up the Cobra as Eva Marie sat stoically beside me with her arms crossed.

"Well?" she demanded.

I glanced at her as I pulled out. "Well, what?"

"Apologize first, and then stop at our spot and kiss me, you fool."

"Yes, Ma'am." I pulled over at our spot around the bend from her house and turned to her. "I sure am sorry for being such a dumb-as-a-rock fool of a noble knight, and for being so naive and presumptuous as to think I could make a decision without consulting you beforehand."

She slid across the console into my arms. "Don't let it happen again," she murmured as her lips smothered mine in delicious swirls.

When she'd moved back into her seat, I drove off, my senses reeling. "You know, you used the 'L' word back there when you were yelling at your mother. You admitted you're in love with me."

She crossed her arms again, which I was beginning to gauge was not a promising sign. "Before you get too carried away with yourself, Paul, *dear*, what I *said* was that you were the man I *love*. That's a long way from being *in love* with you."

"That doesn't make sense," I argued as Elaine snickered from the backseat. "You can't love someone and not be in love with them."

"You don't know the first thing about love."

"Give me an example then."

"Okay, I love Paul Newman, but I'm not in love with him."

"Paul Newman's pretty good company to be in, I guess, but he can't kiss as good as me."

"You're so full of yourself!"

"I'm serious. He's got thin lips. One on one, I'd beat him hands down every time ..."

I drove into Clayhill, parked at the only clothing store in town, and thrust three hundred dollars into Eva Marie's hand. "Take Elaine into the women's department. Get her a full wardrobe with all the accessories. Make up for everything she lost."

"I can't allow that, Paul," Elaine protested. "I'll just borrow enough to buy one outfit."

"Hal's insurance will take care of it. He can turn in the bill and get me reimbursed. Go on, splurge."

"Are you sure?"

"Absolutely; don't worry about it."

Elaine and Eva Marie turned into the women's section as I headed for the men's department to purchase a new wardrobe for myself as well.

* * *

Afterward I stopped at a garage to arrange for a mechanic to follow us out to Hal's place to change the ignition on Elaine's car. As the mechanic worked, the girls followed me around the smoldering ruins. Nothing had been salvaged from the charred remains. Three new mounds out back marked the final resting place of Old Billy and the two hounds. I was surprised by the lump in my throat for the strange old goat as I stood over the graves. When the mechanic finished, the girls followed me back in Elaine's car to Pearle's for an early lunch.

"I'm glad Hal had insurance," Elaine mused after we placed our orders. "He would have lost everything he owned. Why did they just drive away like that with his house on fire all around him and him unconscious?"

"I assume they thought they had killed him and were trying to cover up the crime," I speculated.

"I want to go to Beaumont to be with him."

"I'll get you a room in the Pine View Inn for tonight, and we'll go there first thing in the morning. He won't regain consciousness until then. I'm anxious to find out who did this to him. Do you think you'd recognize any of them if you saw them again?"

"I only got a glimpse of them. I don't have a clear image in my mind. I'm sorry."

We finished our meal as the regular lunch crowd began to drift in. As they waited at the door for me to pay the tab, Elaine gave a startled gasp. I turned to her and followed her stare to the parking lot, where Garland Sanders was unloading his bulk from the driver's compartment of a blue pickup truck. Two other men got out on the passenger side. Jimmy Henry I recognized, the other I had never seen before.

I eased over to Elaine. "Is that them, Elaine?"

She trembled. "The big guy was the man standing in the yard with the gun."

Darkness descended over me. "Eva, take Elaine and get back out of the way. Call Sheriff Tate. Tell him to get over here on the double."

Eva Marie grabbed my arm. "What are you going to do?"

I pushed her away. "Go call the sheriff, damn it!"

The trio paused to stare at my Cobra. Garland Sanders said something that elicited laughter from the other two as they continued on to the restaurant door. I pulled a chair away from a table occupied by two men behind me and positioned it as the group walked in, still laughing.

I stepped forward. "Garland Sanders, I'm placing you under a citizen's arrest for attempted murder."

Garland drew up in surprise. "Do *what*? You ain't doing diddly-squat with me, you little asshole!" He placed his hand on my chest and shoved.

I stumbled back from his 250 pounds of quivering indignation. "I was hoping you'd say something like that." I grasped the chair with both hands and swung.

Garland threw up his left arm to block the blow. The wooden chair shattered into pieces as he yelped in pain. Staggering back into Jimmy, he dropped to his knees, grimacing as he clutched his left arm with his right hand. I picked up one of the broken chair legs and cracked Jimmy across the bridge of his nose. He stumbled back out through the doorway clasping his face in his hands as blood gushed through his fingers. I caught the second man across the forehead with a resounding whack that spun him into a table beside him, upsetting the table and sending the occupants scrambling in the chaos.

I turned to Garland and hefted the chair leg. "This is for Hal, you tub of pig shit!" I slammed the club across Garland's right ear, and he collapsed onto the floor. I beat at his head with a flurry of savage blows as he attempted to ward off the attack with his right hand, hammering at him without mercy, the blows making meaty thumps against his body. He rolled away in panic and jutted his head under a table to get away from me as the surprised occupants at the table shoved their chairs back to get out of the way. I flipped the table over and continued to club at his squirming body. Someone jumped on my back and locked their arms around my throat. I spun, attempting to shake them loose.

"*Paul!*" Eva Marie shrieked as she clung to me. "*That's enough! You're going to kill him! Stop, Paul! Please stop before you kill him!*"

I collapsed onto my knees, dropped the chair leg, and pried her arms from my throat, gasping for breath, my senses slowly stabilizing. In the distance, a siren closed in on us. Eva Marie sank down beside me on the floor in the debris with tears streaking the mascara down her cheeks. Elaine hurried over to hug her as I looked around at the carnage.

People backed away from me, some with food still in their mouths, staring at me as if I were a lunatic. Tables and chairs were strewn about amid spilled food and broken dishes littering the floor. Garland lay curled in a fetal position under the table moaning. Jimmy sat outside the door, his hands cupping his face with blood running down his arms in rivulets and dripping off his elbows to form a puddle on the pavement beside him. The other man lay unconscious in the wreckage of a table with splattered food all over him.

The siren wailed to a stop outside as I turned to Eva Marie sobbing on the floor beside me. "Are you okay?"

"*My God, Paul,*" she wailed. "*You were just crazy. I thought you were going to kill him.*"

"I'm sorry," I soothed, consumed with guilt as I pulled her into my arms. "Please don't cry. It's over now."

Sheriff Tate rushed in with Deputy Miller trailing after him and stopped to survey the destruction grimly. "Somebody call an ambulance," he ordered as he hooked a hand under my arm and jerked me out of Eva Marie's arms up onto my feet. "Paul Henry, you are under arrest. You have the right to remain silent. Anything you say or do can be held against you in a court of law—"

"Elaine identified Garland Sanders as the man who shot Hal!" I argued as he turned me around, jerked my hands behind my back, and closed cuffs around my wrists.

"You have the right to an attorney—"

"I tried to make a citizen's arrest! I was going to hold him until you got here. He resisted arrest. He gave me no choice!"

"... if you cannot afford an attorney, one will be appointed—"

"Will you *listen* to me, Sheriff? He *resisted* arrest!"

"*Aw, crap*! Put him in the car, Joe," Sheriff Tate directed, giving up the effort to read me my rights.

"Are you listening to me? Elaine identified Garland Sanders as the man who shot Hal!" I yelled as Deputy Miller pulled me outside, where Jimmy Henry still sat on the ground cupping his face with bloody hands. He stared up at me through puffy, terrified eyes, the swelling from his broken nose beginning to distort his features, as Deputy Miller led me past him to the patrol car.

"Deputy, would you take the keys to my car out of my right pocket and give them to Eva Marie for me?"

"Sure, Mr. Henry."

He extracted the keys from my pocket, helped me into the back of the cruiser, and went back into the restaurant. A crowd formed outside the building to peer through the window at the wreckage and gawk at me in the back of the patrol car, talking low and shaking their heads in wonder. An ambulance pulled up. The attendants ran around to the rear, pulled out a gurney, and rushed inside. A few minutes later they rolled it back out with a moaning Garland Sanders draped on it. They placed the gurney into the back of the ambulance and then helped Jimmy and the now-conscious but still dazed third man into the back before driving off.

Deputy Miller and Elaine ushered Eva Marie out between them. She paused to stare at me in the back of the police cruiser, her eyes confused and fearful as they met mine, the look suggesting she found me morbidly fascinating—a look one might give a caged tiger. Her bewildered stare sent a cold shiver chasing through me. She lowered her head, got into my car, and drove off with Elaine following in her car. The deputy slid in behind the wheel of the cruiser.

"What's going on, Deputy?"

"You sure made a mess in there, Mr. Henry."

"Will you tell Pearle, or whoever owns that joint, I'll pay for the damages?"

"I'm sure she'll appreciate that, Mr. Henry. They say old Garland's got a broken arm, some busted ribs, and a concussion. One old-timer in there said you were as wild as your daddy. It sure don't pay to get on your bad side."

"Have you heard any news on Hal?"

"Sheriff Tate's driving up there tomorrow evening to get a statement from him. Hal can be an aggravating son of a gun, but I like him a lot. Can you keep a secret and not get my butt chewed out by the sheriff if I go and tell you something?"

"Sure."

"Garland is the one who vandalized your daddy's grave. Sheriff Tate's got him nailed on that. But act like you don't know about it when he tells you, okay? Well, here we are." He helped me out of the backseat. "Do you want to go back in your daddy's old cell again?"

I sighed despondently. "Why not?"

The deputy led me inside, inventoried my personal possessions, stood me against the scale on the wall, took a Polaroid of me, led me down the corridor, placed me in the cell on the end, and locked the door.

"Can I get you anything, Mr. Henry?"

"You can get me the hell outta here, Deputy."

He waddled off. "You sure do make things exciting around here."

I sank down onto the thin cotton mattress and stared up at the corner where my father had hung. "Well, Dad, I'm back again. Just a chip off the old block, I guess."

I flopped back on the mattress in dismay.

* * *

Three hours later I paced around my cell in tight, angry circles. The worst thing about jail was that there was nothing to do, especially when you had the whole cell block to yourself. There was no one to talk to, nothing to read or listen to, and nowhere to go. I could pace in a circle for a while and then end the monotony by circling in the opposite direction for a time. Either way I got nowhere and accomplished nothing. Thanks to an obliging deputy, I could have an occasional cup of horrid coffee that would gag a horse, which I didn't dare criticize for fear of losing even that questionable treat. The minutes grew longer, resembling the pace of glaciers in the ice age.

That last, uncomprehending look from Eva Marie haunted me. The memory of her sprawled in a disillusioned, disheveled heap on the floor in the rubble tore at my conscience. She probably thought I was crazy, like some of the others who had witnessed the event. She didn't understand that I had been trained to strike hard and without mercy when faced with combat, that when you had the enemy down, you kept him down. As a civilian, she couldn't relate to the concept of battle. I needed to explain it to her so she could comprehend my actions and not think so poorly of me.

"Hey, Deputy!" I called. "Can I trouble you for some more coffee?" I hastened to pour the previous untouched cup down the drain as the deputy lumbered in to pour me a fresh slug of mud.

I extended my cup through the bars. "Has Sheriff Tate come back yet?"

"No, Mr. Henry, not yet. You asked me that not more than five minutes ago."

"What do you think is taking him so long?"

"There were a lot of witnesses to talk to."

"Was he pissed?"

"Oh, yeah, Mr. Henry, he was definitely pissed." The deputy waddled back into his office and closed the door.

* * *

In the late afternoon Sheriff Tate returned. After nearly four hours in jail I was frantic. I hurried to the bars as he paused outside my cell.

"You're a damned hard-headed fool, Paul," he greeted.

"He attacked me first. I informed him that he was under a citizen's arrest and he—"

"Spare me the sordid details. I've got a headache. The damage to Pearle's comes to $230. Deputy Miller says you offered to make restitution?"

"Get my checkbook and I'll write Pearle a check. When are you going to let me out of here? You've got no reason to lock me up without charging me with something."

"Joe, bring Mr. Henry's checkbook to him," Sheriff Tate called over his shoulder. "I can hold you for seventy-two hours on suspicion alone."

"What would that accomplish?"

"I'd know you're not running around half-cocked trying to do my job for me. You're a pain in the ass, do you know that?"

"Are you going to charge me with anything?"

"I haven't decided what I'm going to do yet."

The deputy hurried in with my checkbook, which I propped against the bars to write the check for the damages. "Let me out of here, Sheriff. I've got to talk to Rufus Washington."

"What does Rufus have to do with this mess?"

"I want to contract with him to rebuild Hal's house. He's got no place to live now."

The sheriff tipped his hat back with his thumb. "You're a man of contradiction, Paul. On the one hand, you've got a heart of gold. On the other, you're a borderline lunatic. You're real lucky you didn't kill Garland Sanders today."

"He put his hands on me first. Ask anybody who was there."

"Oh, I admit you set him up like a clay pigeon, but there is such a thing as 'necessary force' and 'measured response' to consider."

"If you were facing a gorilla like him, I'm sure you'd have a different take on things."

"I'm smart enough to call for backup and not play the Lone Ranger. What am I going to do with you?"

"What have I got to do to get out of here?"

"Convince me you're not a menace to society."

"How?"

"In view of your record, damned if I know."

"Come on, Sheriff, let me out of here! I did nothing wrong. I attempted a citizen's arrest, as is any citizen's right, and he attacked me. I was in a self-defense situation. Even if you charge me with assault, I'll beat the rap."

"I can still keep you locked up for three days."

"That won't solve anything."

"It'll help me sleep better at night."

"Don't I have the right to post bail?"

"You can't post bail until I charge you with something."

"Well, charge me with something, damn it, so I can post bail and get the hell outta here!"

"I don't have to charge you with anything for seventy-two hours."

"That's not fair, Sheriff."

"Nope, it ain't. *So?*"

"So ... I promise you I won't do anything stupid."

"You've promised me that before, but you went and done something stupid anyway. You have a real credibility problem with me."

"Yeah, but—"

"No *yeah, buts*, Paul; I want your solemn word this time. Your promises suck."

"My word?"

"*Solemn* word."

"On what, exactly?"

"You're hedging. This is nonnegotiable."

"You don't have to be such a hard ass. We're on the same team, remember?"

He turned back to his office. "Since when?"

"Wait! Let's talk this thing out!"

"You're starting to bore me. I missed lunch because of your antics. I think I'll mosey on over to the drugstore and get me a burger." He closed the door behind him.

I paced in circles for another half hour before the deputy came in. "You've got a visitor, Mr. Henry." He ushered Elaine in and closed the door.

I moved up to the bars. "Is Eva okay?"

She edged down the corridor. "She's pretty upset. You scared the hell out of us."

"I'm sorry. All I could think about is what he did to Hal."

"You going to prison for murder wouldn't have helped Hal. What were you thinking?"

I shrugged sheepishly. "I guess I wasn't thinking. Why didn't Eva come with you?"

"I'm on my way to Beaumont to see Hal." She ducked her head. "I hate to ask you, but what little money I had was lost in the fire. Can I borrow ten dollars for some gas?"

"You'll need more than ten dollars. You need to eat, and you may need a room or something. I'm officially hiring you to go to Beaumont and look after my buddy since I can't go myself. *Hey, Deputy!*"

"You're very generous, Paul."

The deputy opened the door.

"Would you please get a hundred dollars out of my billfold in the safe?"

"You'll have to sign a receipt, Mr. Henry."

"No problem, Deputy." I clutched the bars. "What did Eva say? Is she still upset with me? What can I do to make it up to her?"

"Be patient with her, Paul. Give her some time. Her nerves are all jangled up right now."

The deputy entered, handed me a receipt, which I signed, and then took a hundred dollars in twenty-dollar bills from my billfold and handed the money to Elaine.

"Take care of Hal until I can get this mess sorted out, okay?"

"Thanks, Paul." She leaned forward on her toes to give me a quick peck on the cheek. The deputy followed her out, leaving me in isolation again to pace in endless circles.

The deputy brought me a stale, soggy hamburger from the drugstore and a warm Coke for dinner in late evening.

"Where's the sheriff?"

"He's gone on home for the day, Mr. Henry."

I spent a long, miserable night in that cell. I lay on the soiled bunk tossing and turning, unable to sleep, my emotions ranging from bitter anger at the indignity and injustice of it all, to slothful self-pity for being so unappreciated and misunderstood.

Foremost in my thoughts was Eva Marie and that last, lingering, frightened look she gave me while I sat handcuffed in the back of Deputy Miller's patrol car.

FOURTEEN

At seven the next morning the deputy served me a cold fried egg sandwich and a lukewarm cup of coffee. I washed my face in the stainless steel sink and air-dried. And then I waited. At ten o'clock the deputy came in and unlocked my cell door.

"Sheriff Tate's waiting for you in the office, Mr. Henry."

Sheriff Tate sat at his desk. "Want some coffee?"

"Who made it?"

He smiled. "I did." He waited for me to pour myself a cup and settle into a chair in front of his desk. "Have you had time to do some serious thinking?"

"Are you playing mind games with me, Sheriff?"

"I'm trying to get your attention."

"Are you going to charge me with something?"

"Will you give me your solemn word that you will let me handle this matter?"

"Are you going to charge Garland Sanders with attempted murder?"

"That will depend on the statement I get from Hal in Beaumont this afternoon."

"Am I free to go now? I'd like to wash your jailhouse lice off me."

"Your solemn word?"

"Sheriff ..."

"It's nonnegotiable, Paul."

"*Yes*, damn it."

"Say it."

"I give you my word—"

"Your *solemn* word!"

"… my *solemn* word … that I will let you do your job."

Sheriff Tate tossed me a brown envelope containing my personal effects and slid an inventory sheet in front of me to sign. "Eva Marie is waiting outside."

* * *

Eva Marie sat in my Cobra in front of the jail.

I climbed into the passenger seat and studied her drawn features as she stared straight ahead. "Are you okay, Eva?"

She backed the Cobra out without answering, drove to the Pine View Inn, and parked in front of my room. She waited as I got my new clothes out of the trunk and then followed me in. When I attempted to take her in my arms, she pulled back.

"Take a shower, Paul. You smell bad."

I scrubbed myself half-raw under the steaming water, shampooed my hair, and brushed my teeth. When I walked out of the bathroom with a towel wrapped around my waist, I found the blinds closed and the light turned off. Eva Marie lay in bed in the semidarkness with the sheet pulled up to her chin, her clothes neatly folded on the chair beside the bed with the old air conditioner cranked up on high.

I sat on the side of the bed and leaned down to kiss her. "Eva, I'm so sorry about yesterday—"

She pressed a finger to my lips and folded the sheet back. I dropped the towel and slid under the sheet with her, her warm, nude body tantalizing against my dampness. She rolled on top of me, her hungry lips quickly fanning my desire to a passionate glow.

Afterward she lay exhausted, her trembling weight heavy on my body, her damp hair pasted to her forehead, her warm breath ragged against my throat.

"I love you, Paul Allison Henry," she whispered.

I fought to regain my wits. "More than Paul Newman?"

She pressed her tremulous lips to mine. I clung to her as I lay in the tangled, damp sheets with no strength to move. No woman had ever filled me with such throbbing intensity. Spent emotionally, exhausted physically, and supremely content, I did not have the stamina to evade the easy, comfortable darkness that tugged me down into a safe, bottomless pit. As I slipped away, I knew I was inextricably in love with this strange, bewitching woman. The thought of any other in my arms was repugnant to me. In the short time I had known her, she had stolen my heart, conquered my soul, and now ravaged my body. And I wanted more. I slept with her molded to me as one, her heart thumping solidly against my chest, strong and vibrant.

* * *

I awoke to find her staring down at me with liquid green eyes filled with anxiety.

I kissed her. "Why such heavy thoughts?"

Tears welled up. "You're going to break my heart a hundred times over and bring me nothing but pain and sorrow."

"I'll take good care of your heart, and I promise never to hurt you."

"You don't know how to do either of those things. You're too bold and reckless and insensitive and stubborn …"

"Remind me not to use you as a character reference."

"That's part of why I love you, but I hate those things about you too."

"I can see we're going to have an interesting life together."

Her eyes searched mine. "*Are* we going to have a life together?"

"You're more woman than I've ever known. You keep me off balance. It's an odd sensation. I don't quite know what to make of you."

"That's something short of a proposal."

"I'm working up to it."

Her eyes danced mischievously. "Oh really now? We've only known each other for a little over a week, and this is only our fifth date. You don't know anything about me, and I don't like half of what I know about you."

"You'll learn to like me in time."

"Don't count on it. Being in love with you doesn't mean I have to like you."

"That's quixotic—is that another one of those Paul Newman things?"

"You've got a lot of catching up to do where he's concerned."

"Oh I do, do I?" She squealed as I attacked her under the sheet and then draped over her, pinning her to the mattress as I stared into her eyes. "So, what do you think?"

"About what?" she whispered, apprehensive.

"About us ... doing it?"

Her eyes turned mischievous. "I thought we just did *do it*."

"Not that ... I mean ... *that* ..."

A vein in her neck pulsed in rhythm with her heart as her eyes grew fearful. "Don't tease me like this about something like that, Paul."

"I'm not teasing."

"Then ask me the right way, you cad!"

Ice water surged through my veins. "Eva, will you marry me?"

Her eyes widened and then narrowed playfully. "Not *that* way, Paul. You have to ask my father first and then go down on bended knee for me. You're impossible!"

"I'm serious, Eva."

The giddiness vanished. "Are you?"

I swallowed the rising panic. "Yes."

She searched my eyes. "You're scaring me, Paul."

"I'm scaring myself."

"Do you know what you're saying?"

"Yes."

"You would really ask my father for me?"

"I thought your mother made the decisions."

"She likes for Daddy to think he has a say in things." She smiled impishly. "I'll give you the same courtesy after we're hitched."

"Will you, now?" I attacked her under the sheets again as she squealed in delight. A discreet knock at the door froze us.

"I'll be the scandal of Clayhill if anyone sees us like this!" she whispered.

"Get in the bathroom! I'll see who it is."

She grabbed my damp towel off the floor, wrapped it around her, ran into the bathroom, and closed the door. I pulled on a pair of trousers and opened the door to find Rufus Washington standing on the stoop, hat in hand.

"Mr. Henry, Suh, the sheriff, he say you need to see me?"

I sighed in relief. "Yes, Sir, Mr. Washington, I want to build Hal Sutton a new house. I'd like it to be as close to the original floor plan as possible, but I want it totally modern and upgraded. Are you interested in overseeing the project?"

His eyes widened. "Yes, Suh, Mr. Henry, yes, Suh, I'd be delighted for the work. When you want me to start, Suh?"

"I'll write you a check for five thousand dollars right now and set up a draw at the bank for the remainder. I don't want you to spare any of the details. I want it built out of the best materials around, and you're to use the best craftsmen you can find."

"Yes, Suh, Mr. Henry. Work is mighty hard to come by these days. You'll get my best efforts, and I'll work for twenty percent under the going rate."

"How long will it take you to complete the job?"

"'Bout seven, eight weeks, Suh, I reckon."

I wrote out a check for the advance and handed it to him. "I'll make a deal with you, Mr. Washington: finish the house in four or five weeks and I'll pay you and your crew time and a half at the full going rate. How does that sound?"

"Yes, Suh, that sound good, Mr. Henry. It sure good to have you back, Suh. Things gonna change 'round here, old Aunt Elsie say. She got the magic eye. Uh, lookie here, Mr. Henry, Suh, you need to get on by there and see her."

I paused, unsure of how to respond, reluctant to admit to him that I didn't believe in fortune tellers in the face of his own obvious faith in them. "Uh, sure, I'll try to do that, Mr. Washington."

"She live just beyond my place, Mr. Henry. She say she been expecting you. She say to bring something of your daddy's with you."

"Well ... I'll try to get by to see her soon ..."

"Yes, Suh, thank you. I get started right away on Mr. Sutton's house. Good day to you, Mr. Henry, Suh."

"Good day to you, Mr. Washington. I appreciate your assistance."

"It be my pleasure, Suh."

As I watched him hurry off, Eva Marie stepped out of the bathroom with the towel wrapped around her. I closed the door, pointed at the towel, and flicked my fingers. She hesitated, and then let the towel slip to the floor, blushing as I walked to her, my eyes roaming over her boldly.

"To be such a scoundrel, there's no end to your kindness," she whispered as I took her in my arms.

"The pleasure's all mine," I mouthed against her neck as she quivered. "I'm delighted to be of assistance to such a beautiful lady in her time of need."

She giggled. "I was speaking of the house you're building for Hal, you jackass!"

"Oh."

* * *

I awoke in a sluggish pall to the jarring ring of the telephone beside my head and fumbled it off the hook in the darkened room. "Hello?"

"Paul?" Sheriff Tate boomed. "Pack a change of clothes. We need to be on the road in half an hour."

"Do what?"

"Are you asleep?"

I yawned as Eva Marie stirred beside me in drowsy lassitude. "I was, damn it."

"What are you doing in bed in the middle of the day?"

"I couldn't get my beauty sleep in the roach palace you run."

"Who is it, darling?" Eva Marie asked groggily, her eyes still closed.

"Is that Eva Marie?" Sheriff Tate asked.

"Where are we going and why do I need a change of clothes?"

"We're driving to Beaumont to get Hal's statement and then on to Huntsville tonight. Malcolm Grant has agreed to meet with you. We need to be there by ten in the morning. By the way, that part of the trip is on your dime. Are you going to be here on time or not?"

I sat up. "I'll jump in the shower and be right there."

"Tell Eva Marie I said hello." The line went dead.

Eva Marie dropped me off at the jail, where Sheriff Tate waited beside his cruiser impatiently. I kissed Eva Marie bye and strolled over to slump in the passenger seat of the cruiser as he slid in behind the wheel.

He glanced at me as he backed out. "Tough day, huh? You look beat."

"I'm getting to where I really don't like you very much, Sheriff."

I closed my eyes as he chuckled and tuned the radio to a country and western station.

* * *

Elaine met us outside Hal's room and hugged me. "He's been asking for you. He's afraid you're hurt or dead or something and that I'm not telling him."

"How is he?"

"He regained consciousness about ten this morning."

"Has he said anything about the incident?" Sheriff Tate asked.

"I haven't pressed him. He's very weak. I haven't told him about his house burning down, or about Paul's run-in with Garland. The doctor said not to upset him."

"Don't tell him about any of that," I urged. "I'm having a new house built for him. We can surprise him with it."

She studied me. "You were lying about the insurance, weren't you?"

"Let's go in," I suggested.

Hal lay in an elevated hospital bed with bandages covering his face and chest surrounded by discolored flesh. When we paused at his bedside, his eyes slit open and he tried to smile below the tubes running up his nose.

"Hi ... Sport ..."

"You look like shit," I appraised, "which is actually somewhat of an improvement."

His lips twitched. "Good ... to see ... you, too."

"Can you tell us what happened?"

He licked his lips. "Garland ... Jimmy ... Dale ... came to the house. Wanted to talk to you. Told them you weren't there. We had words. Told him he was trespassing ... to get off my land. He got out to argue with me. Old Billy ... almost knocked him down. He pulled his shotgun out of the truck ... and shot him. I grabbed ... my rifle. Don't ... remember ... anything else."

Sheriff Tate leaned forward. "Did you point your rifle at him or threaten him?"

Hal swallowed and tried to focus on him. "Intended to just scare him ... to shoot his truck for shooting ... Old Billy."

Sheriff Tate nodded. "But you did order him off your land, right?"

"He refused to leave ... until he talked to Paul." Elaine held a glass of water with a straw for him to sip and then rubbed ice on his chapped lips. "Sorry ... tired," he sighed as he closed his eyes, his labored breathing growing deeper.

Sheriff Tate turned to the door. "I think we'd better go now and let him rest."

I pulled out my wallet and handed Elaine another two hundred dollars. "Stay with him. If you need anything, call the sheriff's department in Clayhill. They'll get word to me."

Elaine took the money. "Thank you, Paul. This is way more than I need."

"Keep it just in case."

"Are you still under arrest?"

"Hell, I never know around this crazy damned lawman!"

Sheriff Tate chuckled as she hugged me.

"Well, what do you think?" I asked as Sheriff Tate and I rode the elevator down.

"I'm not the prosecutor, so I can't say for sure what he's going to do, but I'm fairly certain Garland is going to plead self-defense when I charge him with attempted murder. The case may never come to trial."

"You've got to be kidding me!"

"What would you have done if someone pointed a gun at you?"

"It still doesn't make what happened right."

"No, it doesn't, but there's only a slim chance he'll be prosecuted, even though he was warned off for trespassing. The problem is, it's Hal's word against the three of them. I predict that the prosecutor will drop the charge of attempted murder and choose not to prosecute on the charge of trespassing. He'll offer to plea-bargain on the charges of malicious injury to the three animals and arson for burning his house. We'll be lucky if Sanders gets five years and serves more than one."

"What about Jimmy Henry and that Dale jerk?"

"I'll agree not to press charges on them as accessories if they'll agree not to press charges on you for assault."

"Damn! Can I go arrest the son's a bitches one more time for you?"

"Not unless your word is meaningless."

"My *solemn* word, as I recall. You really know how to hamstring a guy."

"I've learned with you to look for that extra bit of an edge."

"I'm *really* getting to where I don't like you, Sheriff."

"Are you going to curl up and sleep all the way to Huntsville like a contented tomcat, or have you recharged your batteries enough to stay awake and keep me company now?"

"It depends on whether you're going to play that God-awful country and western crap or not. And since we're on my dime now, let's find a good steak house on the way. I'm starved."

* * *

If getting out of prison was more difficult than getting in, I could understand how there were few escapes. We went through a number of check stations, fences, locked corridors, steel doors, and narrow-eyed guards before being ushered into a small room containing a metal table and chairs. As a courtesy to Sheriff Tate, we were allowed to meet with Malcolm Grant in one of the rooms normally reserved for convicts to meet with their attorneys and not be restricted on time.

Malcolm sat handcuffed to a steel ring on the floor by a second chain, which allowed him to sit with his hands in his lap but restricted his lateral movement and prevented him from standing. He was a short, squat man somewhere past middle age with close-cropped, graying hair, a thick nose that protruded below bushy eyebrows, and cold, calculating brown eyes. A mole on his nose and another on his chin sprouted tufts of coarse black hair. Tattoos festooned his arms above calloused, scarred fingers and knuckles. His broad lips curled into a semblance of a smile, albeit one of contempt, as he looked at me for a brief moment before focusing his full attention on Sheriff Tate.

"Well, Deputy, long time no see."

"Actually, it's Sheriff now," Sheriff Tate replied.

"I guess if you lick enough boots and kiss enough ass, it eventually pays off."

"I appreciate your agreeing to meet with us," Sheriff Tate replied, unperturbed.

"Oh hell, I'm just dying of curiosity. I asked myself, now, *Self,* why in hell would Deputy Tate and Paul Mister-Big-Shot Henry want to meet with poor little old nobody me? Couldn't for the life of me figure that one out, no sir, so curiosity got the best of me. Besides, it's boring in this joint. I ain't seen my ex–old lady in eight years or my son in five. The little bastard wants to go to college. Can you believe that shit? Got a letter from him just last month. Wants to be a educated little son of a bitch. Says maybe he'll go to law school and get me out of this joint someday. I was framed, you know. They claimed I killed that man in that juke-joint in Orange. Weren't me, though, but the lying bastards swore it was in court."

"Paul would like to ask you some questions concerning your involvement in the arrest of his father twenty years ago."

"So this pecker-head really is John Henry's little crumb snatcher? Well I'll be damned all to hell. Done growed up to be might-near a man now. Looks a lot like his daddy, too, don't he? Bet he's a real lady's man, like his paw was. Know what we do to pretty boys like you here in the pen, Paulie? We—"

"You've got diarrhea of the mouth," I observed. "Has your asshole been punched all the way up into your throat in here?"

Malcolm glared at me for a hard moment and then relaxed and sneered. "Be nice to me now, Paulie boy. You're here at my invitation, remember? It don't take a rocket scientist to know you want something from me. I know you do or you wouldn't even be bothering with trash like me, you bein' one of those high-and-mighty Henrys that are always so full of themselves. So you mind your tongue now, boy, and indulge me. I don't agree to talk to people like you everyday."

"What do you want?" I asked.

Malcolm's eyes narrowed. "What do *I* want? You're the one that asked to see me, Paulie boy. What do *you* want from old Malcolm here?"

"I want to cut to the chase. I don't have the gift for gab you do, nor the patience to sit here listening to your nonsensical bullshit all day. You knew what I wanted before you agreed to see me. You expect something in return, or you wouldn't have agreed to meet with me. So let's dispense with the crap. What's your deal?"

Malcolm sneered. "Twenty-five thousand, all cash. I want to help my boy. He's got a low draft number. He says if he can get in college he can beat the system. Says he don't want to have to go over there and serve next to all them baby-killing rapists. He wants to be somebody and not have to eat shit from little pricks like you who've been given a free ride all their life while they walk around trying not to choke on the silver spoon they got stuck in their mouth."

"What do I get in return?"

"You get the skinny on how your pappy died, Paulie boy. Ain't that why you're here? You pay my boy his education money, and I'll give you the real honest-to-God scoop on the way things went down way back then."

"You'll admit that you helped murder my father?"

Malcolm snorted. "Were you born in a turnip patch, Paulie boy? I was just at the point where I was thinking you was as smart as you are pretty. Don't you know there ain't no statute of limitations on murder, pretty boy? Are you dumb enough to think I'd put my own ass in the 'lectric chair? No siree, Bob, I ain't murdered nobody, not even the asshole they framed me for when they put me in this shit-hole. But I might know who did. And then again, I might not. Get my drift, pretty boy?"

"Who were the other people involved?"

Malcolm giggled. "You buying the package or not, Paulie boy?"

Sheriff Tate cleared his throat. "It will be necessary for you to testify to anything you tell us concerning the events of that day."

"Testify my ass! I ain't no snitch. You can forget that shit!"

"There is a possibility we can give you some form of limited personal immunity if you are willing to turn state's evidence and offer testimony against the other parties involved," Sheriff Tate reassured him.

Malcolm shook his head. "Ain't testifying against nobody. Ain't no courtroom rat, for you or nobody else. My boy gets his college money, you get the sordid facts—off the record. Take it or leave it."

"And what will these facts reveal?" I asked.

"Who killed your daddy, that's what we been talkin' about, ain't it?"

"Your story would be of no value to us without your testimony," Sheriff Tate argued.

"Ain't my problem, Deputy. The boy here wants to know who did his daddy in, I'll tell him for a price. Ain't my problem what he does with the information after that."

"No deal." I stood. "I know who killed my father. Proving it is what I'm after. If you can't help me do that, your little pussy of a boy can get him a job and work his way through college, assuming he doesn't get drafted and sent to Nam to get his nuts shot off first."

"Oh yeah, big shot?" Malcolm snarled. "What's your draft number? I bet you're already in college so you don't have to worry about it!"

"I've already been there." I raised my shirt and exposed the scars. "I don't think you want anything like this to happen to delicate little draft-dodging Malcolm Jr., do you, asshole?"

Malcolm looked at the purple blotches and sneered. "You rich shits don't have to do no real fightin'. How'd you get those? Drop your own hand grenade on yourself in basic training?"

I pulled my shirt down and leaned on the table. "Let me clear the air here, you sick-minded piece of shit. Thanks to you and your degenerate buddy Jarvis Holderman, I never had a father to give me a free ride. And thanks to the slimy bastard who hired you two to murder my father so he could steal my inheritance, I wasn't born with a silver spoon in my mouth. The fact is, I've never had a dime to my name other than what my widowed mother and I earned on our own accord. As for the war, you puke-faced pimple on a real man's ass, I spent my time over there in that green jungle hell, and when I wasn't too preoccupied with killing babies and raping innocent young women, I managed to get my ass shot off three different times so worthless pieces of shit like you and your son can lie around whining about how unjust the world is. Now you take your information and jam it up your ragged ass sideways." I turned to the door and knocked on it to call the guard.

"Hey, hold on now, boy! We got off on the wrong foot is all. Come on back here and sit down now."

I turned as the guard opened the door. "Here's the real deal, you fruitcake. One, I'll escrow twenty-five thousand dollars with a signed letter of agreement that will release it to your son upon the arrest and conviction of all parties involved in the murder of my father in which you are instrumental in providing testimony against. Two, I don't personally give a damn if you provide any of that information or not. I'm only doing this within the limits of the law because I happen to like and respect this man here." I indicated Sheriff Tate. "Based on that, I'll give his judicial system its best shot. But if that fails, I'll seek justice on its own merit for those involved. And that will include you locked up here in this prison facility. Twenty-five thousand dollars will buy me a lot of friends inside this place."

Malcolm tried to stand, but the constraining chain on his cuffs held him to a half stoop. "You—you're threatening me! You can't threaten me, boy. Did you hear that, Sheriff? You're my witness, he threatened me!"

"Actually, Malcolm, it's a promise," I replied as I turned and walked out into the corridor.

"Did you hear him threaten me, Sheriff? Did you hear that, Guard? He threatened me!"

"I didn't hear any threat," the guard replied. "All I heard him say was that he could buy himself a lot of friends in here for twenty-five thousand dollars. I might want to be his friend myself for that kind of money." He grinned evilly at Malcolm Grant.

Sheriff Tate rose. "You know the terms and how to contact me." He followed me into the corridor.

When we reached the parking lot, Sheriff Tate cranked his cruiser and sat idling as the air conditioner worked to cool off the superheated interior, his face grim.

I sighed. "Okay, Sheriff, spit it out. I've pissed you off again, right?"

He turned to me. "First of all, I had no idea you had been injured that badly in Vietnam. I've gained another degree of respect for you for having faced what you have."

"Aw shucks, you're embarrassing me, Sheriff."

"Second, you scare the living hell out of me. I know that was no idle threat back there. I want you to look me in the eye, Paul, and listen carefully to what I say. I *am* the law, and if you cross the line, I *will* bust you for it. Do you understand me?"

"Can we go now?"

"Paul ... *do you understand me?*"

"Yes, damn it, I understand you, and I think you understand me, so let's get the hell back to Clayhill. You're beginning to rub on my nerves!"

FIFTEEN

The ride back to Clayhill was joyless. Sheriff Tate and I spoke in sparse spurts and restricted our comments to the traffic and the heat until he dropped me at the motel.

He cleared his throat fretfully as I got out. "Am I still invited for dinner tomorrow?"

I shrugged petulantly. "Why wouldn't you be?"

"I don't want you to feel uncomfortable with me tagging along."

"Just because you're the most aggravating lawman I've ever known doesn't mean we can't be sociable, I guess."

"Well, if you can live with that, I guess I can live with the fact that you're the most stubborn, pig-headed, arrogant young man I've ever known."

"Well okay then."

He nodded. "Okay then."

"Eva and I'll meet you at the jail at eleven."

"We can take my car. We'll have more room."

"Whatever jingles your bells," I offered callously as I hurried in to call Eva Marie.

"Hey, doll baby. Miss me?"

"Tons! How was Hal?"

"Weak. Sheriff Tate doesn't think Garland will be prosecuted for shooting him. He thinks he'll plead self-defense and that we'll be lucky if he spends more than a year in jail for arson."

"You're not going to do anything foolish, are you?"

"Me? Never. Look, I'm going to hop in the shower. Why don't you come on over and meet me in bed?"

"I thought you might come to dinner tonight and speak to my father … unless you've changed you mind?"

My stomach sank. "Uh, no, of course I'e haven't changed my mind. Hey, uh, why don't we … you know … just elope? We could be in Louisiana in—"

"No way. I want the whole old-fashioned, bended-knee shebang, and if you're really serious about this, we need to pick a date."

My stomach sank further. "Date? Um, what date do you like?"

"I've always liked June."

My spirits rose; that was almost a year away! "I like June, except it's *so* far away." I grinned. *Damn*, I was *good*!

"There's a lot to do. You just don't realize that, but we can make it April if it suits you better."

My stomach sank again. April wasn't *nearly* as far away as June. "Oh, no, no, June is fine! I don't want you to feel rushed." Sometimes I wasn't nearly as good as I thought I was.

"Oh really?" she teased. "What if we can't be together again until we're married?"

"Um, April would *definitely* be better."

She giggled. "Does April fifteenth suit you?"

"April fifteenth suits me fine," I acknowledged glumly.

"Rehearse your speech to Daddy. I'll pick you up at six."

"Speech? Um, what do I say?"

"You ask for his permission to marry me, Paul, what do you think you say?"

"I don't know … I've never done this before. What if he says no?"

"He won't say no."

"He might. He might think, uh … you can do a lot better."

She heaved a sigh. "Then I suggest you be convincing."

"How?"

"You've got three hours to figure it out. I love you."

"Uh, me too," I mumbled.

"Then say it."

"I … love you too, Eva."

"That's better. You didn't forget the ring, did you?"

"Ring?"

"My engagement ring?"

"Oh, no, I didn't forget."

"With you I'm never sure."

"I'm not a complete dummy, you know."

"I didn't mean to doubt you, sweetie. See you at six. Love you."

"Uh, me too."

After she hung up, I dialed the police department. When Sheriff Tate came on the line, I took a deep breath. "Are you still pissed at me?"

"I just dropped you off not more than five minutes ago. Has anything changed in any significant manner since then?"

"I need your help."

"I *knew* I should have kept you locked up!"

"No, no, it's nothing like that. It's even worse."

"Worse?"

"I need you to help me, uh, buy a ring …"

"A ring? What kind of ring?"

"Uh, an engagement kind of ring."

"*What!*"

"I've got to have it by six tonight. Can you come pick me up?"

"This is the sheriff's department, not a damn taxi service."

"Eva Marie still has my car. If it's too much trouble, I'll figure something else out."

"Oh hell no! I think too much of Eva Marie to leave this solely in your hands!" He hung up.

Sheriff Tate drove me to the only jewelry store in Clayhill, where a distinguished-looking older gentleman surveyed us as we entered.

"Good afternoon, Sheriff," the man greeted.

"Mr. Dickerson, this is Paul Henry. He's interested in making a purchase."

The man arched his eyebrows. "And how may I help you, Mr. Henry?"

"You can start by calling me Paul. I'd like to see your best engagement ring."

The man laughed. "You sound like your father twenty-one years ago. He walked in and said almost the same thing when he proposed to your mother. Give me a moment." He turned to a large safe standing against the rear wall. "I won't waste time showing you what I've got in the display case. The *very* best I keep here in the vault." He placed a black velvet case on the counter. "This is a complete wedding ensemble consisting of a two-caret solitary diamond of flawless perfection and a one-and-a-half-caret matching wedding band." He opened the velvet box. The stones sizzled in a stunning display of brilliance.

"This is your very best?" I demanded.

"This, Sir, is the best you will find anywhere. I personally guarantee it."

I held the engagement ring up as it shimmered. "I'll take it."

"What the hell did you need me for?" Sheriff Tate demanded.

The man nodded. "Will you require terms?"

"Probably so; are they something that normally goes with an engagement ring?"

He chuckled. "I meant *credit* terms, Mr. Henry."

"Oh, no, I'll pay cash."

His smile thinned. "This particular set runs $12,500, before tax, Sir …"

"I need it now. Do you accept checks?"

He looked distraught. "I … normally verify the availability of the funds with the bank for such an amount, Sir. That might be difficult under the circumstances since it's Saturday …"

"I'll vouch for the funds, Mr. Dickerson," Sheriff Tate injected. "Or, if you prefer, we can call the bank manager at home."

Mr. Dickerson waved his hand. "No, no, Sheriff, your verification is all I need." He rang it up, and I wrote the check.

"Do you know the size of the lucky lady's finger, Mr. Henry?"

"Uh, no, I didn't think to ask."

"If she's local, I can probably tell you her size. I know most everyone in Clayhill."

"Eva Marie Sherrill," I said.

Mr. Dickerson clapped his hands together. "What a beautiful girl for such a beautiful ring! You've chosen well on both counts. I have her size in my book. It'll take about an hour to get it fitted."

"We'll grab some coffee and be back in an hour," Sheriff Tate replied.

The jeweler hurried into the rear of the store as we departed.

Over coffee at Pearle's, Sheriff Tate tipped back his hat. "Congratulations! She's a fine young woman. Why all the hurry?"

"I've got to ask her father tonight."

"I wish you two every happiness."

"Does this mean you're not pissed at me anymore?"

"I'm sure you'll spoil that before long."

* * *

Eva Marie picked me and my bundle of raw nerves up promptly at six in my Cobra.

"How do I do this, Eva?"

"Wait until after dinner to approach Daddy. Mother and I will fix coffee and dessert in the kitchen while you and my father talk in the parlor."

"We could be in Louisiana in less than—"

"*Paul!*"

* * *

Dinner was a disaster. I had no clue what they served. I dropped my fork on the floor, and then my knife, and damned near toppled my glass of tea over on the table as well. Mrs. Sherrill looked at me with some anxiety on more than one occasion as she or Mr. Sherrill spoke to me and I failed to acknowledge them. An hour later I panicked when the women began clearing the table. Eva Marie gave me a meaningful look as Mr. Sherrill and I were ushered into the parlor to await dessert. Mr. Sherrill sat in his easy chair and I took the sofa, my mind whirling in circles trying to come up with a smooth opening.

"So, Paul, have you given any thought to your future now that you've got your service obligation behind you?" Mr. Sherrill asked.

I swallowed and rubbed my damp palms on my trousers. *I'm going to die right here and now. That should take care of my future. Okay, on three. One, two—*

Mr. Sherrill frowned. "Paul?"

I took a deep breath. *On three, damn it! One, two—*

"Here we go—fresh perked coffee to go with the apple pie I baked just this morning," Mrs. Sherrill announced as she swooped in, set a tray on the coffee table, and passed cups to Mr. Sherrill and me before seating herself in the other easy chair.

My throat constricted. *I can't do this with her sitting here!*

Eva Marie appeared in the doorway. "Mother, would you please give me a hand with the pie?" She locked eyes with me and inclined her head at her father.

"Are you feeling alright, Paul?" Mrs. Sherrill asked as she rose to help with the dessert. "You look ill."

I swiped at the beads of sweat on my forehead. *I'm fine, I'm just scared shitless, is all.*

"Paul?" Mrs. Sherrill paused to stare at me.

"Uh, no, I'm … just, uh …"

"Mother?" Eva Marie called from the kitchen.

Mrs. Sherrill turned to the kitchen. "Eva Marie, darling, I don't think Paul is feeling well. He looks puckish to me, and he hardly touched his dinner."

Okay, on three. One, two, three! I sprang up, set my coffee on the table, hurried around to Mr. Sherrill's chair, and fell to my knees on the floor before him as he lurched back in surprise, sloshing coffee over the rim of his cup.

"Mr. Sherrill, can I please have Eva's hand?" I begged.

Mrs. Sherrill entered the parlor carrying two saucers of pie. "*What in the world?*"

Mr. Sherrill gaped at me in alarm. "W-What …?"

"Can Eva marry me?" I gulped. "In April. The fifteenth. I think. I mean, can I marry Eva? Your daughter? I mean, *may I?*"

"*Oh, my God!*" Mrs. Sherrill gasped as the blood drained from her face.

Eva Marie peered around her mother. "Paul? Why are you on your knees?"

"Y-You *said* I had to ask on b-bended k-knee," I stammered.

Eva Marie collapsed against the doorjamb in a fit of laughter. "No, silly!" she gasped. "You ask *me* on bended knee, not my father!"

"I told you I've never done this before!" I argued as I knee-walked around to face her. "Eva, will you marry me?" I dug the velvet box from my pocket and extended it to her.

Her mirth faded and her eyes widened as I opened the box. Mrs. Sherrill rushed to admire the ring, and both women broke out in tears as they hugged each other. Eva Marie turned back to me, still kneeling on the floor, knelt, and wrapped her arms around my neck.

"I love you, Paul Allison Henry! I love you so much! Only you could do something like this!"

This wasn't going as envisioned ... I still didn't have an answer. What was the deal here anyway? "So ... will you?"

"Of course I will, you fool!" she gasped, laughing through her tears.

"Will your father let you?" I asked apprehensively, glancing at him over my shoulder.

Mr. Sherrill wiped at his eyes. "I would be proud to call you my son, Paul!"

Mrs. Sherrill knelt and hugged us both amid her tears. *"I'm so happy!"*

I sighed. *That seems to pretty much settle the matter. I'm going to love Eva Marie forever, because I sure as hell ain't ever going through this shit again!*

* * *

I picked Eva Marie up the next morning, and we met Sheriff Tate at his office to switch to his car for the drive to Jasper. All decked out in a new tie and sports coat, he appeared nervous and out of sorts but dutifully admired Eva Marie's ring as though he had never seen it before. He had a good laugh at my expense as she described me falling on my knees before her father to beg for her hand. The drive to Jasper was otherwise pleasant, other than arriving all too soon for my comfort.

Aunt Kathy and my mother met us on the front porch dressed in their Sunday best. My mother shook Sheriff Tate's hand and welcomed him cordially as I congratulated myself on my stroke of genius in inviting him along as a diversion and introduced Eva Marie.

Aunt Kathy immediately grabbed her hand and held it up to admire the ring. "Oh my Lord—is this what I *think* it is?"

Eva Marie's green eyes danced as much as the diamond on her hand. "Paul proposed to me last night."

My mother and Aunt Kathy embraced Eva Marie in a rush of squealing excitement. In an instant the three of them dissolved into a bawling, laughing mishmash of jumbled emotions as Sheriff Tate and I stood watching. They then turned and stumbled into the living room so caught up in each other and the moment that they left us standing on the porch, forgotten.

He grinned. "I think they approve. The poor souls have probably been conditioned to expect the worst from you over the years."

"Very funny," I sneered. "Come on in, I'm sure there's fresh tea made." I led him past the women still clustered together on the couch admiring Eva Marie's ring to the kitchen and took two glasses from the cabinet.

Aunt Kathy rushed in and elbowed me aside. "You continue to amaze me, Pooh," she gushed as she filled the glasses with ice. "Eva Marie is just *precious*!"

"*Pooh?*" Sheriff Tate asked, a gleam in his eye.

Aunt Kathy laughed. "That's my pet name for him. When he was just a baby he couldn't say *Paul*, he would say—"

"We're *not* going to do the baby stories, Aunt Kathy!" I growled.

My mother hurried into the kitchen and hugged me. "Paul, you should have *told* me! What a wonderful surprise!" She essentially sounded more amazed than surprised.

"Everyone out of the kitchen now," Aunt Kathy ordered. "Scoot on back into the living room. I'll serve the tea in there. You can visit while I finish dinner."

We clumped back to the living room. Eva Marie sat beside me on the sofa and reached for my hand as Sheriff Tate and my mother settled into easy chairs across from each other.

"Nelson, you look the same as you did twenty years ago. Why hasn't some woman caught you up by now?" my mother teased as he blushed.

"Momma, here are my father's things." I handed her the billfold, key ring, pocketknife, wristwatch, Zippo, and coins as Aunt Kathy rushed in with a tray and dispensed glasses of tea around.

My mother studied the smooth round disk of worn silver. "This was the silver dollar your father always carried. His father gave it to him when he was ten years old. He told your father to always keep it in his pocket and he would never be broke. Your great-grandfather gave it to your grandfather on his tenth birthday. I'd forgotten about it. I suppose your father would have given it to you on your ..." She glanced up at me and then quickly handed the items back. "You keep these things, Paul. I'm sure he would prefer you have them."

I took the items back. "In the safety deposit box there were also stock certificates, marriage licenses, an old list of some kind, and a death certificate for somebody named Deborah Ann Henry in Little Rock, Arkansas. Did you know her?"

"No, but I'm sure she was one of our distant relatives. I can't imagine why your father would have her death certificate. He went to Arkansas a week before his death and seemed excited when he returned, but he never spoke of the trip to me." She turned to Sheriff Tate. "Thank you for your concern for Paul, Nelson. I hope he hasn't been a bother to you with this issue of his father's death. He's prone to be rash at times."

Sheriff Tate squirmed. "We've ... managed admirably, Susan. He can be a bit headstrong at times, but you know where he gets that from." They laughed as though sharing some intimate joke.

I smiled thinly. *He's a phony, Momma. Ask him about locking your baby boy up twice now in his nice little jail.*

She stood. "Come with me, Eva Marie, and you too, Nelson. Let me show you some of Paul's mementos."

"*Momma, please!*" I begged.

Eva Marie stood. "I'd love that."

I drifted into the kitchen as they followed her into my bedroom.

Aunt Kathy glanced at me. "Your mother doing the tour bit, Pooh?"

I sighed. "Why does she *always* have to do that?"

"She's proud of you, Pooh."

"Aunt Kathy, please don't call me Pooh in front of Eva Marie."

"Oh my goodness, you make the biggest fuss over nothing. Did you notice I made banana pudding for you?"

"Did you put lots of vanilla wafers and bananas in it?"

She clucked her tongue. "I've been making this pudding for you for twenty years now, and suddenly you're worried that I don't know what I'm doing? Where did you find such a fine young lady? It appears you've risen far above your normal standards with that one."

"I'm sorry if I've been such a disappointment to you," I said sourly.

She hugged me. "Oh, Pooh, you've been a delight to me for the most part, but you were born rebellious and were all-boy all the time. Your daddy's genes, I suppose, and the fact that you've never had anyone but women in your life to teach you. God knows your mother and I've done our best under the circumstances. I think for the most part we knocked all the rough edges off, and unless I miss my guess, that bright young lady in there will put the finishing touches on you and you'll turn out to be a fine young man in spite of yourself."

"She likes me just fine the way I am."

"Nelson seems like a nice fellow. This is the first time I've ever saw your mother show interest in a man. Maybe now that you're practically grown she can find a place in her heart for someone else. God knows she's still an attractive woman."

My stomach knotted. "S-She's *interested* in *Sheriff Tate*? As-as-as a *man*?"

Aunt Kathy turned to me in gleeful disbelief. "You're jealous! You've had her all to yourself so long you can't bear the thought of sharing her with anyone else."

"But ... but *Sheriff Tate*!" I gasped. *Why in hell did I ever invite him to Sunday dinner*!

"And why not Nelson Tate?" she asked as she went back to creaming the potatoes. "He's handsome, well mannered, successful, and single. That's a hard combination to find in a man these days."

"*Sheriff Tate*?" I demanded, the thought of the two of them, well ... *kissing* ... filling me with revulsion!

She paused in the middle of preparing the mashed potatoes. "Pooh, your mother loves you with all her heart. There's never been room for anyone else in her life. But it's time she lives a little for herself now, don't you think?"

Hell no! Sheriff Tate?

She turned back to the counter. "The tour's over, so get your finger out of the pudding and go on back in the living room with them and mind your manners or else."

"Why do you always have to threaten me?"

"Force of habit, Pooh. You've instilled vigilance into me over the years. Now skedaddle on out of here so I can get dinner ready!"

I went back into the living room newly sensitized to Sheriff Tate and my mother, where they were indeed acting strange toward each other, with her talking too much and laughing in nervous titters as he politely hung off every word she uttered while staring at her like a devoted, dopey little puppy. I'd made a huge miscalculation with this diversion thing.

Eva Marie slid over and slipped her arm through mine. "Your team won the State Football Championship and you were the most valuable player in the game?"

I scowled. "That was years ago."

"And you never said anything about being a hero in Vietnam."

"Eva, *please* …"

"You're *modest*! That's so sweet! I … assume the picture on your nightstand is your ex-fiancée and your best friend. She's really pretty."

"Would you like some more tea?" I picked up her glass and headed for the kitchen.

Dinner was mostly a success, mainly because my mother and Aunt Kathy stayed so focused on Sheriff Tate and Eva Marie I was all but ignored. The only discomforting part was the fawning attention showered on the sheriff by my mother and his own trumped-up, exaggerated compliments on everything she said or did in return. When the dinner ordeal itself was over, I had to endure coffee and dessert in the living room before we could finally leave. Hugs and kisses were again distributed around to Eva Marie and me, and my mother gave a warm handshake to Sheriff Tate, who appeared to be in a state of near euphoria, before we made our escape.

Eva Marie snuggled against me in the car, her eyes filled with mischief. "You're lucky to have a mother and aunt who love you so much, *Pooh*."

* * *

Eva Marie kissed my cheek as we pulled away from the sheriff's department in my Cobra. "I've got a surprise for you, Paul."

"A surprise?" Surprises were fast becoming my bane where this woman was concerned.

"A special place called Little Rapids on the backside of our farm. It's the most beautiful spot in the world. I go there sometimes to be alone and think. We can get to it by a back road that runs around our property."

I followed her directions and parked at the end of a little-traveled lane that led through the woods. We walked hand in hand down to a shallow creek and then followed it to a small waterfall where the creek narrowed into a tossing, tumbling rush of water over smooth rocks before widening back out into a pool feeding the slower-moving creek bed.

Eva Marie slid into my arms. "I had a wonderful day."

"It wasn't as bad as I thought it might be," I admitted. "This is beautiful, Eva. Thank you for sharing it with me."

"Come on." She took my hand. "Let's go swimming."

She peeled off her blouse and skirt as I shucked my clothes. We waded naked hand in hand into the pool of cool water, which was just short of chest deep, where she turned and slipped into my arms.

"I want you, Paul, here and now."

I pushed her to a smooth, flat rock still warm from the setting sun. As I explored the wonders of her body, I found myself distracted by a subliminal transmission tugging at me, pulling my senses to a distant, unheard voice nagging at my subconsciousness, seemingly compelling me to come closer. I pushed the lingering perception away irritably and forced my attention back to Eva Marie's welcoming arms. Afterward we slipped into the water and clung together as darkness settled around us.

"You seem troubled, Paul. Are things moving too fast for you? Are you having second thoughts about us?"

"Are you?"

"You're the one who was afraid of commitments."

"I made the commitment with the full knowledge of what I was doing."

"Then what's troubling you?"

"Do you remember Mr. Washington telling me Aunt Elsie was expecting me?"

"Yes. He encouraged you to go see her. Why?"

"According to Hal, she's some sort of fortune-teller or something."

"They say she can see the future as well as the past."

"Do you believe in that sort of thing?"

"A lot of people swear by her. Is that what's bothering you?"

"Just now, when we were making love, I felt ... strange. It was almost as if she, or at least *someone,* was calling out to me. I know it sounds crazy, but it was as if she was reaching out to me somehow."

Eva Marie shivered in my arms. "You're spooking me, Paul."

"It's probably only my imagination."

"Maybe you should go see her. I'll go with you if you like. I've always been curious about her."

"How about tonight? It'll be interesting to hear what she's got to say."

She kissed me. "Let's get dressed and go then. You've got me all content for the moment."

We drove past Rufus Washington's house and pulled up in front of a squalid shack with a dirt yard. Coffee cans filled with flowers decorated the front porch. A dim light lit a curtained window. Eva Marie took my hand as we walked up the rickety steps. Before I could knock, a firm voice called to us from inside the house.

"You kids come on in out of that night air."

I opened the screen door and led Eva Marie into the dim interior, where the only light came from a kerosene lamp on a table near the back of the room. There an ancient black woman sat in a cane-bottomed chair behind a small card table. A brightly colored scarf covered her head above her wrinkled face. A black shawl hung around her shoulders. She stared unseeing at us from one light blue crystal-clear eye and one eye that appeared to be black with a misty film covering the pupil.

"Welcome to my humble home, Mr. Henry, and you as well, Miss Sherrill," Aunt Elsie greeted in a well-modulated tone. "Best wishes to you on your betrothal. Love is a wondrous thing when you're young. Please have a seat. Would you share some hot tea with me?"

"I'd love a cup," Eva Marie replied. "I'll serve if you'll allow me to."

"You are a dear, sweet girl. The kettle is on the stove, if you would be so kind. I take mine with one spoon of sugar, if you please." Eva Marie went into the kitchen to prepare the cups of tea. "Don't mind my eyes, Mr. Henry. You see, I'm blind as you know vision to be. The one is glass and the other filled with cataracts, which rob me of sight. How is your mother, child? You had dinner with her today, I believe?"

I smiled, no longer surprised by everyone in Clayhill knowing my every move. "She's fine, Ma'am. Thank you for inquiring. Do you know her?"

"We've never formally met, but I knew of her as a child before she moved away. She was a beauty, I understand, much like the one you've chosen to be your life-mate. They tell me your Eva Marie has the most compelling green eyes. I would love to view them firsthand."

She paused as Eva Marie returned with cups of tea and placed one in front of Aunt Elsie before seating herself beside me.

"Yes, Ma'am, her eyes are very unique," I agreed. "I think I fell in love with her the first time I saw them."

"She sends out powerful psychic signals, which indicates strong values and a forceful character. She will counterbalance what I perceive to be your own inclination for rash actions."

I laughed. "Yes, Ma'am, I'm discovering that."

Aunt Elsie nodded as a smile played across her lips. "Most women are smarter than their men. It's a wisdom born of pain through centuries of male dominance and repression. We have learned to survive by our wits instead of our brawn."

"Ma'am, if you're blind, how did you know it was us when we arrived here tonight?"

"Old age has robbed me of earthly sight, Mr. Henry, but not of insight and perception. I have been expecting you for some time, even finding myself becoming impatient with you for waiting so long to visit with me. I used my psyche to search you out earlier this evening. I sensed you and Eva Marie on a warm flat rock near a swift-running stream cleaving together in youthful enthusiasm. I summoned you to me."

Aunt Elsie reached across to pat Eva Marie's hand as she blushed. "There child, don't be embarrassed. When you give yourself to the one you love, it's a beautiful experience that gives your affection depth and meaning."

I collected myself. "Why did you feel it necessary to summon me?"

Aunt Elsie sipped her tea with a troubled frown. "A great storm is building around Clayhill, Mr. Henry. You seem to be the focus of the disturbance. I wanted better insight into the coming troubles."

I glanced at Eva Marie. "And now that I'm here, what does your insight tell you?"

She sat for a moment as if in a trance. "You have an object on you. It is sending out intense signals. May I hold it in my hand?"

"What object is it, Ma'am?"

"Empty your pockets. Put the contents on the table before me."

I emptied my pockets and placed the contents before her. She held her hands palm down over the items, picked up the silver dollar, and clutched it in her hand. She trembled and then cried out as she rocked to and fro. Sweat beaded her forehead as her eyes stared unseeing. She opened her fist and the silver dollar dropped onto the table. Smoke drifted from a circular burn the size of the coin on her palm. The smell of charred flesh filled the air as she sagged, gasping.

Eva Marie rose from her chair. "Your hand is burned!"

"There's some salve on the shelf behind you there," Aunt Elsie rasped. "Thank you, child, that's very soothing," she murmured as Eva Marie spread the salve over her burn. "If it's not too much to trouble you with, I would appreciate another cup of tea. I feel faint at the moment."

Eva Marie hurried into the kitchen, poured her a cup of tea, and rushed back. "We should take you to the clinic to get your burn treated."

Aunt Elsie sipped at her tea. "No, child, I'm fine now. It will heal itself in time."

"What just happened?" I asked, still shaken.

"It's called an extrasensory phenomenon, Mr. Henry. One of the strongest I've ever experienced. The object was charged with energy that needed to be released. It startled me with its force. The burn comes from the intensity of the signal I released."

"What did you see?"

She took a trembling sip of her tea. "I saw many things, all jumbled together. I saw a woman in a casket. A man grieved over her, distraught, while a small girl child cried nearby. I next saw the child in a small coffin and the man grieved yet again, his soul full of remorse. I saw this man later with a young woman in the throes of passion. He called her *Carrie Ann.* Soon afterward the man placed the young woman on a train. This woman was with child, which the man rejected as not being of their union. He denounced her for this as she pleaded with him and offered him reassurances, which he did not want to hear because he felt them to be false. She swore vengeance against him.

"There was a second man, one not the same as the first. He was filled with laughter and stood with a young woman holding a male child. Then he was older and distressed as he stood before a coffin with the woman inside. There was a third man, again young, very young. The second man gave him the coin I held in my hand.

"This third young man was surrounded by explosions and fallen bodies. Then he was with a woman who filled his heart with longing and soothed his troubled soul. They were in a field with beautiful flowers and sunshine, bounded by happiness. Then a terrible darkness descended around him as he screamed out at the injustice of some terrible fate besetting him. Those are the images I saw."

"What do they mean?" I asked.

"I do not know the answer to that. I can only reveal the images to you as I saw them. Give me your hands." She stretched out her hands palms up. I placed my hands on top of hers. She sat for some time, twitching. "You have many troubles ahead of you. There are those who do not wish you well, who even now plot against you in evil ways. You must be very careful, for the future holds great danger to you." She hesitated. "Perhaps it would be better if we spoke alone?"

Eva Marie stiffened. "I would prefer to stay. I've sworn my life to Paul. If I'm to stand with him through his troubles, I need to prepare myself as much as he."

"Very well, child. Mr. Henry, you are destined to travel a path your father sought many years ago. You will face great physical and emotional pain along this journey before your troubles end. Ultimately, an appalling anger will blind and consume you as it propels you into a tunnel of dark sorrow from which it will be difficult to escape. You must tread this course with care or you may become lost and never find the path of light again. Bless you, child, for you will be tested far beyond what most in life must bear. But if you prevail in this terrible trial, your rewards will be richer and more satisfying than most ever hope to achieve. I fear for you in what is to come, but many will envy you and benefit from your endeavors in this most trying time. You must go now, for I am tired and weak. I can tell you no more beyond this."

I stood. "Ma'am, how much do I owe you for your services?"

"Recompense comes from the heart, Mr. Henry, not from a stipulated fee," she replied.

I placed ten dollars on the table, scooped up the loose change and the silver dollar, which was still warm to the touch, took Eva Marie's hand, and turned to leave.

"Mr. Henry," she called. "There is one favor you can do for me, if I may impose?"

"What would that be, Ma'am?"

"You may keep the money you placed on the table if you will give me the whisky in the glove compartment of your car. I am in need of a calming toddy tonight."

I was startled, having forgotten the half pint of Maybell's imported finest in my glove compartment. "I'll get it for you, Ma'am, and you may still keep the money."

When I returned from the car, Eva Marie sat at the table with her hands in Aunt Elsie's hands. She stood quickly and hurried out wiping at her tears as I set the whisky on the table.

"Go now, and offer her comfort," Aunt Elsie advised gravely.

"What happened while I was gone, Eva?" I asked as we drove away.

"She gave me a brief read of my future. She was tired, but I insisted."

"Was it as bad as mine?"

"We made a mistake coming here tonight."

"Why do you say that?"

"There are some things better left unknown. I … need some time alone. Please take me home now, Paul. I'm so tired …"

SIXTEEN

I spent a lonely, restless night in my motel room as a thunderstorm raged outside sending streaks of lightning and torrents of rain crashing down around me in the darkness. I dreamed of caskets with bodies in them, the faces hidden, and of people grieving as I moved among them unseen. I awoke exhausted late the next morning to the telephone ringing.

"Mr. Henry, this is Gladys. I hope I haven't disturbed your rest too early?"

"No, Ma'am, I'm awake."

"Mr. Jackson wonders if it would be convenient for you to meet with him this morning?"

"Yes, Ma'am, I can be there in half an hour."

"That would be fine, Sir. I'll make a fresh pot of coffee."

Miss Gladys squealed in delight and ran to congratulate me on my engagement to Eva Marie when I entered. She then ushered me in to Mr. Jackson, who stood to greet me with a broad grin.

"Congratulations, Paul! You've shown excellent taste in women!"

"Thank you, Sir. I'm a fortunate man."

He settled in behind his desk. "How is Hal?"

"He's recovering, but still weak."

He nodded and picked up some papers. "I appreciate your coming on such short notice. There are a number of things we need to discuss, but I'm having a hard time making sense of most of them. Let me begin by saying that the two stock certificates are quite valuable. Your grandfather bought five thousand shares in a small company called Texas Mutual. A few months later he bought an additional five thousand shares in the same company. He paid a dollar a share, for a total investment of ten thousand dollars. My inquiries reveal that over the years Texas Mutual grew and split its initial offering of stock three separate times. Five years ago Liberty Life Insurance Company absorbed Texas Mutual on a two-to-one exchange of existing stock. Liberty has since split its stock twice and absorbed two other insurance companies. At their current market value these certificates are worth roughly $10,560,000."

I gaped. "Ten million dollars!"

"Unfortunately … these certificates are legally part of the Henry family estate."

I sank back in my chair. "Why the stocks but not the money?"

"There's no way to prove original source of the funds in the safety deposit boxes. In essence, your father, through indeterminable means, could have legitimately acquired the money on his own accord. But the certificates are clearly the property of your grandfather Robert and, as such, subject to the proper right of inheritance as established by probate."

I stood and paced. "Which means that J. R. could end up with all the money if we fail to establish a legitimate claim to the estate?"

"That is correct. I have no choice but to report this to the probate court and have it included in the assets of the estate."

I took a deep breath and exhaled slowly. "The stakes in this venture just went right up through the stratosphere!"

"It appears so. On another note, I'm still puzzled by the list of letters and signs on this document, and the significance of the marriage certificates, as well as by the death certificate of Deborah Ann Henry. Your father obviously put some value on these documents prior to his death, but I can't make sense of it. I think the key may lie in Arkansas."

I sank back down in my chair. "Why do you say that?"

"Shortly after filing suit against the Henry estate, your father went to Arkansas. When he returned, he was very excited. He called me and said he had discovered some very important information. Unfortunately, I was going out of town for a few days on an urgent personal matter. When I returned, your father had died. I never discovered what he learned in Arkansas. But this death certificate seems to be tied into it in some way, along with the marriage certificates."

I picked up the bundle of papers and studied each of the documents. "I can't make sense of them either. This one document seems to be written in some sort of code."

"I've got a friend whose son runs a detective agency in Dallas. With the stakes as high as they are now, you may want to consider engaging him to do some research on this matter. I don't think he would charge more than a few hundred dollars, if you agree."

"While he's at it, have him see if he can find my two lost aunts. He can start with the one who moved to Tyler."

"I'll get him started right away."

I stood. "Thank you, Mr. Jackson. I'll see myself out."

I crossed over the courthouse square to the bank to set up the draw to complete the construction on Hal's house. Afterward I drove to Hal's place to check on Mr. Washington and his crew of workers, where I found a beehive of activity. A dozer had cleared the rubble and buried it in the pasture. Now teams of carpenters hammered and sawed in a confusion of noise as a skeleton of a house rose from the bare earth. I reviewed the floor plans with Mr. Washington and added a two-car attached garage on one end and a wrap-around porch on the other end to tie in with the front and back porches. Mr. Washington recommended the roof overhead be increased to provide additional shade, all of which was relatively easy to do and would not hinder the completion date. I left him to his work and drove to the drugstore to have coffee with Eva Marie.

She leaned over the counter to kiss me. "Paul, how do you feel about children?"

My knees buckled as my insides turned to jelly. "A-Are you pregnant?"

She laughed. "No, silly. At least I don't think so."

I heaved a sigh of relief. "Oh, well, kids are okay, I guess. Can I have a cup of coffee?"

"I want to get pregnant the next time we make love."

My heart pounded. "Are you talking about us waiting until April before we …?"

"Do you truly love me, Paul?"

My insides melted under the intensity of her stare. "Of course I do, Eva!"

"Then I want to carry your child in me as soon as possible. We can elope like you said instead of waiting until April."

"Eva! Slow down! What happened to the old-fashioned way of doing things? I thought we were rushing things by waiting until April! Elope? Get pregnant! Your mother and father will kill us!"

"I'll call Gail in to relieve me. Let's go somewhere private to discuss this."

* * *

Eva Marie led me down to the small pool at the bottom of Little Rapids and slid into my arms. "Make love to me, Paul. I need you so."

"Let's talk first."

"Don't you want me?"

"What's got you in such a tizzy all of a sudden with this eloping and baby business?"

"We may not have much time, Paul. We need to make the most of it."

I took her by the shoulders. "Eva, you're not making sense. We have a whole lifetime together. What's going on?"

She clung to me. "Aunt Elsie said … I should cherish every precious moment I have with you, for our time together may be short. Oh, Paul, I can't bear the thought of life without you! You said we could be in Louisiana in no time! Make me your wife today!"

I held her at arm's length. "Eva, you're letting a bunch of psychotic babble get to you! You heard Aunt Elsie say she doesn't know what her visions mean. You're misinterpreting what she said."

"Oh, Paul, please take me away from Clayhill! Let's don't ever come back to this awful place again!"

"Is that what you're thinking, that if we marry we'll leave Clayhill?"

"We could start a new life together. Please, let's just leave, Paul!"

"I can't do that, Eva. There are some new developments with the estate that make it virtually impossible for me to leave Clayhill right now."

"We don't need the Henry land and money. Let J. R. have it. Something terrible will happen to you if you stay here, I just know it!"

I pulled her to me. "Don't talk foolishness! I've faced a lot tougher people than J. R., and I'm still around."

"Why do you always have to be so damned stubborn?" She pushed free of me. "I want to go home now."

"I thought you wanted to make love."

She wiped at her cheeks. "I'm not in the mood anymore."

"Eva, please, you're not being rational!"

She shuddered. "I can't believe I made such a fool of myself begging you to marry me like this! Go do whatever you want to do!"

I pulled her to me, her anxiety melting my core, knowing I loved this woman more than life itself. Why was I hesitating? To wait even one more day to make her mine would be a sin: to hell with my petty fears and insecurities of being worthy of her. "You're the most obstinate woman I've ever known," I breathed against her hair. "If you really want to elope, we will. But it's going to hurt your parents, and my mother, and cause a lot of malicious speculation with every gossip in Clayhill."

She lifted her tear-smudged eyes to me beseechingly. "Our parents will get over it, and I don't give a damn what anybody else thinks!"

"Do you understand this is not your ticket out of Clayhill?"

"If you keep on, you can't get me pregnant tonight because you won't be in my bed."

"That's a *horrible* way to start a marriage!"

* * *

Two hours later we exchanged vows before a minister in an obscure parish in Louisiana that did not require a waiting period before obtaining a marriage license.

"Now what, Mrs. Henry?" I asked as we climbed back into the Cobra.

She leaned over and kissed me. "You've made me the happiest woman in the world, Mr. Henry. Now find us a bed and plant your seed in me!"

I found a motel and checked in. When I came out of the office, Eva Marie was in a telephone booth. She came out drying her eyes.

"Mother says she's going to kill us," she said, laughing through her tears. "Now it's your turn."

I placed a collect call. "Hi, Momma, how are you?"

"What's wrong, Paul?"

"Nothing's wrong. In fact, everything is right."

"Why are you calling me from Louisiana? What have you done now?"

"Eva and I eloped. You now have a daughter-in-law."

"Paul Allison Henry, I'll kill you!"

"You'll have to beat Mr. and Mrs. Sherrill to it."

"Are you serious, Paul?"

"I'm serious, Momma. Eva and I got married half an hour ago. Now she wants me to carry her inside a seedy motel and knock her up."

"Paul Alli—"

"Duty calls! I love you, Momma. Bye now!"

We spent a glorious week in New Orleans on our honeymoon. Part of it was to take the time to get to know one another. The other part was to allow things to settle down with our parents back in Jasper and Clayhill.

During that magic week I realized I had found a rare treasure in Eva Marie. She was full of mystery and filled with laughter as we explored the fabled city by night and day. We ate in the finest restaurants, shopped for clothes in the most expensive stores, and lived in a world full of extraordinarily newfound love. I sensed that though we had known one another only a brief time, we were truly soul mates. Staring into her bewitching green eyes filled me with wonder; feeling her warmth at night, a soothing balm; tasting her lips, a heady tonic not unlike the finest wine; devouring her eager body, a potpourri of physical and emotional fulfillment. I never imagined love could bring such poignant depths of genuine pleasure, or the overwhelming possessiveness I felt when with her. The thought of our lovemaking producing a child, *our child*, filled me with tender anticipation incomparable to anything I had ever experienced.

I knew this to be the highest personal plateau I would ever attain and marveled when her adoring eyes rested on me, leaving me humbled with the dancing happiness flashing there. I knew no other woman could ever affect me in such a compelling manner with the hint of a smile, the flash of amusement in a glance, the glint of teeth as she threw back her head and laughed. This woman categorically owned my body and soul and would control my heart forever.

We called home several times during that magnificent week. When the other party could talk to us without wailing, we judged the honeymoon over and set sail for Clayhill in a warm cocoon of sated bliss.

When we pulled into the Sherrills' drive late on the afternoon of the eighth day, Eva Marie reached over and squeezed my hand. "Any regrets?"

I grinned weakly. "Only that we've got to face the firing squad now. Want a blindfold?"

She kissed me as her mother came out onto the porch. I went around to Eva Marie's door to help her out, and we walked hand in hand up to the porch as Mrs. Sherrill stared down at us. When we paused at the bottom of the steps, she came down in a rush to hug us.

"I'm so glad you children are home! That was so foolish of you, but what's done is done. Welcome to our family, Paul!"

Mr. Sherrill came out onto the porch grinning. "I had a feeling you kids wouldn't make it until April!" He shook my hand and hugged Eva Marie. "Wish we'd had the courage to do that back when we got hitched. It would have saved me a lot of misery!"

"Oh, you hush now," Mrs. Sherrill scolded him, laughing as she dried her eyes. "Come on inside. I've got supper almost ready. I assume you two will be staying with us until you find a home of your own. Paul, Mr. Jackson has been calling almost every day. When I told him you were on your way back, he said it was imperative that he meet with you at ten in the morning. Lord, I can't believe my daughter is married and that I have a son now!"

* * *

When I entered Jason Jackson's office the next morning, Miss Gladys hugged me and then scolded me for eloping as she ushered me into the conference room, where Mr. Jackson, Sheriff Tate, and another man waited.

Mr. Jackson beamed at me. "Congratulations, Paul! You'll be a long time living this down around here. Did you know your father and Susan eloped as well?"

"No, my mother never told me," I replied in surprise.

"You're certainly your father's son, no doubt about it."

"I concur." Sheriff Tate shook my hand as he grinned. "And you may have cheated us out of a wedding, but we still expect a party."

Mr. Jackson cleared his throat. "Paul, this is Harry Bradshaw, the detective from Dallas you had me hire on your behalf."

I shook hands with Mr. Bradshaw, a slim man in his late thirties dressed in a tweed sports coat and gray slacks, with neatly parted brown hair and inquisitive eyes.

"While you were busy with your honeymoon, Harry has been in Arkansas. He's got some rather interesting information for us. I took the liberty of asking Sheriff Tate to attend this meeting because there are certain legal repercussions that I feel will follow. Harry, please proceed."

Harry opened a file in front of him. "First of all, I appreciate you selecting me and am happy to be of service to you.

"Mr. Jackson directed me to research Deborah Ann Henry, who died on December 5, 1946, in Little Rock, Arkansas. This case got interesting from the very beginning. It seems that Deborah Henry was murdered in her home by a single gunshot wound to her right temple. No suspect was ever charged, but there were strong indications that the murder was committed by a man named Jarvis Holderman, whose last known address was here in Clayhill. I won't bore you with all the details, but suffice it to say that a warrant was in the works for Mr. Holderman's arrest prior to his own untimely demise in Shreveport, Louisiana, after succumbing to numerous knife wounds in a dark alley, the apparent victim of a robbery.

"When I reported these facts to Mr. Jackson, he asked me to gather additional information on Deborah Henry. In my continuing investigation, I found that she was formerly Deborah Ann Duboise, born in Little Rock, Arkansas, on September 10, 1910.

"Miss Duboise attended school in Little Rock and lived with her parents until October 1, 1929, when she married James Robert Henry, also of Little Rock, Arkansas. They had two daughters in this marriage,

Patricia, born September 12, 1930, and Kathryn, born two months premature, on July 11, 1931."

"Is this James Robert Henry our current J. R. Henry?" I asked.

"Oh, yes indeed, it is," Mr. Jackson affirmed.

"How is this information of any use to us?"

Jason Jackson beamed. "Consider the salient facts here. J. R. married Deborah Duboise Henry on October 1, 1929. He married your stepgrandmother, Cathie Fields Henry, on November 2, 1946, a month before Deborah Henry was murdered."

"Is this leading to where I think it is?" Sheriff Tate asked.

Jason Jackson smiled. "Please continue, Harry."

Harry sat forward in his chair. "J. R. filed for divorce six months before Deborah Henry was murdered, but she was contesting it and it was never ratified. He was still legally married to her when she was murdered."

"Then he *did* commit bigamy!" Sheriff Tate vowed grimly.

"That is correct, Sheriff," Jason Jackson affirmed. "He apparently abandoned Deborah and his daughters when he moved from Little Rock to Clayhill. I surmise one could also infer he hired Mr. Holderman to murder his wife after his marriage to Cathie to get her out of the way since she was contesting the divorce. In any case, since there was no divorce, his marriage to Cathie is legally invalid, and as such, he has no lawful claim to the Henry estate. It also means he committed perjury and fraud in claiming the marriage to be valid and laying claim to the estate. Mr. J. R. Henry is in a bit of a legal mess, not to mention the possible connections to his wife's suspected murderer, who was employed by him here in Clayhill."

I sat stunned. "So what happens next?"

Mr. Jackson pulled a series of papers from his folder. "I'm meeting with the probate judge at one o'clock to present this evidence and Mr. Bradshaw's testimony. Based on that, I'm certain all assets of J. R. Henry will be seized and frozen. I then suspect that Sheriff Tate will arrest J. R. on one or more of these crimes. Within thirty days I expect the court to rule to probate your grandfather's estate in accordance with the will. Congratulations, Mr. Henry, you seem to have won."

I stared at him in astonishment. "Just like that?"

"Just like that," Mr. Jackson agreed.

"Incredible. And my father figured all this out before he died?"

"Apparently so, since he had all of the documentation in his safety deposit box."

"Which might be *why* he died," Sheriff Tate added.

"So I should inherit the entire Henry estate now?"

"I expect that Jerry Henry could, and quite possibly will, file suit as a legitimate son and rightful heir of your grandfather Robert and his mother Cathie," Mr. Jackson replied. "As such, in the worst case scenario, he would be entitled to half of the estate along with your father."

"What is Jerry Henry like?" I asked.

"He's by far the brightest of the bunch, next to J. R.," Sheriff Tate replied. "He's never been in trouble with the law and keeps a low profile."

"I agree," Mr. Jackson added. "He's an unknown factor in this issue. We'll have to wait and see if he files claim against the estate. Even if he does, we still have a strong argument that the will should have been probated as written before his birth, which means your father should have received the estate."

"I have no desire to cheat him out of his rightful inheritance," I vowed. "He's never done anything to warrant my animosity, and he is legally my father's half brother, right? I think we should meet with him as soon as possible, give him the facts, and work with him to settle the estate as quickly as possible. What about my two aunts?"

"I'll be going back to Tyler this evening to follow up on a couple of promising leads," Harry replied.

"I find your position concerning Jerry Henry admirable," Mr. Jackson continued. "After the sheriff fulfills his legal obligations, I will contact Jerry to see if he's willing to meet with you. Lastly, I know this document has some bearing on this case because it was with the other documents in your father's safety deposit box, but I can't decipher its meaning." He handed me the hand-printed sheet that seemed to be some sort of code.

I stared at the scrawled letters penned by my father twenty years ago, which read:

$$m + f = c$$
$$b + o = b / o *$$

1. *(ja - b + rm - o) = ra - b* *
2. *(ja - b + ca - o) = jr - a* X
3. *(ra - b + oj - o) = ja - b* *
4. *(ra - b + k - o) = jr - a* X
5. *(jr - a + k - o) = jr - a* *

I looked at Mr. Jackson, perplexed. "It doesn't make sense to me either. I'll copy it and study it. You keep the original here with you." I made a copy and passed the original to Sheriff Tate, who professed bafflement as well.

When I got back to the Sherrills', I sat Eva Marie and her parents down at the dining room table and told them of the startling developments concerning the Henry estate.

Eva Marie sat in shock. "What are you going to do with all that money, Paul?"

"I don't know. What do you want us to do with it?"

She sat for a moment composing her thoughts. "I want to restore the old Henry mansion. I've driven by it a million times. It's so grand, and I've heard so many stories about it. Could we make it our home?"

I stared at her, dubious. "I don't know. I've never even considered it. It's been boarded up since my grandfather was killed." I laughed hesitantly. "Hal even says it's haunted. Maybe my crusty old grandfather's ghost scared J. R. off. In any case, I thought you wanted to leave Clayhill. That was your dream when we first met. After all the legal stuff is finished, we can do that now if you wish."

She leaned forward and kissed me. "That was because there was nothing here for me before. Now that you've given me the whole world, I want to stay near my family."

"It's a big house, Eva. What would we do with all that space?"

"Our children would love a big place like that to romp around in."

"If you have plans of making us grandparents anytime soon, you *better* stay close," Mrs. Sherrill threatened.

"I'm already pregnant," Eva Marie declared with smug confidence as she hugged her mother. "I just know I am! Can we make the Henry mansion our home, Paul?"

I sighed. "I'll call Mr. Jackson and see what he says."

I went into the hall and called Mr. Jackson, who agreed to approach the probate court with the issue that afternoon when he presented the documents and testimony of the private investigator. I agreed to meet him back at his office at two o'clock. When I returned to the dining room, Eva Marie slipped onto my lap and wound her arms around my neck.

"I think you should invest some of the money back into Clayhill as well, Paul. This town was built around the Henrys. It's almost dead now because J. R. killed the business this place thrived on and sucked the life out of it. I strongly feel this is your true heritage, and always has been."

I hugged her to my chest. "Spoken like a true heiress to the Henry legacy, Mrs. Eva Marie Sherrill Henry—you are a rare and beautiful woman!"

SEVENTEEN

I escorted Eva Marie to Jason Jackson's office promptly at two that afternoon, where Miss Gladys squealed in delight and ran to embrace her. After exchanging the pleasantries, she ushered us into the conference room, where we found Sheriff Tate, Mr. Jackson, J. R.'s attorney Daniel Coonan, and one other man waiting.

Mr. Jackson took Eva Marie's hands. "Congratulations, Mrs. Henry. I'm delighted for you and Paul."

"Thank you," Eva Marie replied as he pulled a chair out for her at the table. "It was an impulsive thing, but it's proving to be the happiest experience of my life."

"Mr. Henry, you know Mr. Coonan. Allow me to introduce Mr. Jerry Robert Henry."

I extended my hand across the table to Jerry. "I appreciate your coming. It's a pleasure to meet a member of my family."

Jerry, black headed, dark complexioned, with a thin, muscular build, sat immobile ignoring my outstretched hand, his dark brown eyes boring into mine like a cold drill. "We don't need to pretend to be sociable. Two members of *your family* are still recovering from their injuries, and a third is in jail. All of our assets are frozen and our whole lives disrupted. I'm here out of curiosity to see what your next move might be."

I withdrew my hand and sat down. "Fair enough. I came here to visit my father's grave. The unpleasantness that followed has been forced on me. I'd like to see it come to an end by resolving our differences, if possible."

"Your attempt to steal my family's assets is not an acceptable condition for an amicable resolution of our differences."

"Jerry, your *half* brother Bruce picked a fight with me on his own accord. Your *half* brother Jimmy was involved in the attempted murder of my best friend. Your piece-of-shit *step*father murdered my father, who was your half brother, twenty years ago and stole *his* and *your* inheritance, along with the endowments to your two half sisters, by committing bigamy with your *mother*. I'd like to end this stupid feud by offering not to contest your position as a rightful heir along with my father in the probate of the Henry estate. If that's not acceptable to you, then you can go to hell."

Jerry stood, trembling. "I swear you'll regret ever coming back to Clayhill."

I stood as well. "I'm sorry we couldn't work things out."

"There is one other legal matter we need to address," Mr. Jackson said in an even tone. "My client has petitioned the court to take control of the old Henry mansion. The court has directed an appraisal of the property and for its value to be factored into any future divisions of the estate in the final probate proceedings. We can each get our own appraisal of its value, or we can reach an agreement on its current worth and agree to an offset that suits both parties, should the estate be divided."

"One hundred thousand dollars," Jerry snapped without hesitation.

"Agreed," I answered.

"Good day." Jerry turned to the door.

"Good day," I replied and sat back down.

Mr. Coonan stood. "Draw up the agreement and send it over to me this afternoon."

"I'll have it delivered to you within the hour, Daniel," Mr. Jackson replied as Mr. Coonan followed his client out.

"That was interesting," Sheriff Tate observed after the door closed.

"Paul, I've warned you about making accusations in the matter of your father's death," Mr. Jackson lectured. "I urge you to keep these suspicions to yourself unless you have evidence to the contrary."

"Everybody in this whole damned town knows it's true but hasn't got the guts to come out and say it."

"I'll escort you out to the Henry mansion to take possession," Sheriff Tate offered in the strained silence. "We'll probably need the locksmith to get us in. I'll stop by the jail and call him from there."

I stood. "Thanks, Sheriff."

* * *

I slid into the Cobra and glanced at Eva Marie's perturbed expression as we pulled away. "What's on your mind?"

"Maybe it would be best if we did leave Clayhill, Paul."

"I'm *not* going to be run out of town, Eva. I'd hoped that Jerry and I could bury the hatchet since he's one half of the old Henrys, but I guess that was wishful thinking."

"I just want to live our lives without all this conflict surrounding us."

"I warned you about that before we eloped. If trouble comes my way, it won't be because I invited it."

"If this continues, I'm afraid you'll do something you'll regret for the rest of your life."

I turned onto the lane leading to the old Henry mansion and stopped before the massive white brick house, once the pride of the mighty Henry clan. We stood together in front of the Cobra looking up at the sweeping wrap-around cement porches and big columned balconies on the two upper levels and then turned to view the once-superb grounds now choked with weeds and vines with the three discolored fountains down the center bordered by the tangled flowerbeds.

"I hope we haven't bought a pig in a poke," I joked in the hush.

Eva Marie hugged me. "I can't believe Jerry put such a small value on it."

"I'm sure it's in pretty bad shape after sitting empty for twenty years. I probably allowed him to overvalue it." I followed her around the huge structure, feeling somewhat intimidated by its size and disrepair, and paused to stare at the dilapidated bathhouse, swimming pool, double tennis court, and stable with attached harness room.

"I've heard so many stories about this place," Eva Marie whispered in awe. "It's the oddest sensation, but I almost feel as though it's willing me to breathe life back into it."

I took her in my arms. "Well, you're officially the new mistress of the place now, so do with it as you please."

"You've made all my dreams come true, Paul. Please don't let this thing with your family spoil it for us."

"That mostly rests in my family's hands, Eva."

"Let's go see the inside," she urged as the locksmith's van turned into the drive.

We greeted the heavyset old man as he climbed out and followed him up onto the front porch, where he studied the lock on the front door and began picking through a large ring of keys.

"I installed these locks thirty years ago," he informed us with pride as he opened one of the double doors. "There you go. What else can I do for you?"

"Please ensure all of the doors inside are open before you go," I requested as I followed Eva Marie inside. "And change the locks."

"These are quality locks made to last a lifetime, Mr. Henry. I can rekey them for a fraction of the cost of new locks. I'll get started on it now." He turned back to his van for the materials.

We paused in a huge main room housing a massive old crystal chandelier coated with a thick layer of dust, inhaling dank, fetid air emanating from the vast interior. A black marble scripted *H* was inset on the white marble floor in the center. A huge marble fireplace took up most of the back wall. Two sweeping stairways covered in faded red carpet on each side of the room curved up to a wrap-around balcony on the second floor. A scattering of antique tables and chairs was spaced oddly about as if abandoned. Faded gold-gilded framed paintings adorned the walls in numerous locations. A large piano and other dated musical instruments stood abandoned in the first room on the right, along with a couple of ragged, dust-covered chairs and sofas.

I followed Eva Marie as she drifted into the next room on the right, which featured a marble fireplace, with several old musty sofas, easy chairs, and small game tables strewn about in disarray. The last room on the right held an extended dining table with two dozen matching, moldy chairs. More faded paintings hung on the discolored, peeling rose-papered walls. Matching carved wood serving tables stood along the interior wall facing rows of draped windows on the outside wall. Eva Marie opened one of the drawers in a serving table and exposed rows of discolored red satin, which had once held silver utensils. A faint, moisture-streaked scene of a foxhunt with galloping horses and chasing dogs decorated the ceiling above three large crystal chandeliers.

We drifted back into the great room and across to the left side of the mansion. Behind the first door we found a wood-paneled study with a large wooden desk, bookshelves lined with dusty leather-bound books, a set of faded red leather chairs, and yet another marble fireplace. A floor-to-ceiling library with row upon row of dusty books occupied the room next to the study, with a sliding ladder fitted into slots in the floor connected to the front of the bookcase. Carved wood tables and chairs with reading lamps dotted the moldy green carpet, and large windows on the exterior wall provided ample reading light between marble fireplaces accenting each end of the room. The last set of double doors on the left fed into a ballroom with a music dais on the far end rising above the white marble floor. The room held very little furniture other than a couple of ornate, aged chairs spaced along the wall.

Back out in the great room the doors on each side of the fireplace led back into a connecting hallway behind the fireplace, which in turn opened into a large kitchen containing antiquated stoves, ovens, and refrigerators covered in grime. Large sinks, cutting tables, food bins, and a round kitchen table with matching wood chairs cluttered the room. Beyond the kitchen was a spacious, dirty glass-walled sunroom overlooking the pool and tennis courts with several discarded, decrepit lounge chairs scattered about.

"Hello! Anyone here?" Sheriff Tate called from the front of the house. We went back into the great room and found him looking around in wonder. "This place is huge!"

"It's a wreck," I complained.

"The furniture here is priceless," Eva Marie swooned. "It'll be so much fun getting it restored. Let's go upstairs!"

Sheriff Tate and I followed her up the stairs into the master bedroom to find a raised bed under a draped, tattered cloth covering and a marble fireplace with an old sofa and table arrayed before it. Heavy gold curtains mildewed with age and discolored from the sun laced the windows. Dual bathrooms, one blue marble with attached dressing room, the other a soft pink with sunken tub and an even larger dressing area with a lighted built-in dressing table, bordered the room on each side. The fixtures in each were antiquated brass crusted with age. We found five other bedrooms with private bathrooms on the second floor, each once elaborately decorated but now in disrepair. The third floor contained a large common room with a brick fireplace and an additional four bedrooms, each with its own small private bath.

"It's almost as if someone locked the door and walked away," Eva Marie marveled as she led us back down to the main floor.

"It appears that *someone* looted all the good stuff and left the junk," I scoffed.

Sheriff Tate tipped back his hat. "I think you got a bargain at a hundred grand."

"I think I bought a money pit," I grated.

"When can we start putting it back together?" Eva Marie asked, eyes dancing as she turned in a circle of eager anticipation. "I'm so excited!"

The locksmith handed me a ring of keys, each labeled, and bid us good day.

* * *

Back at the Sherrills' that evening I had a message to call Elaine in Beaumont. "How is Hal?" I asked as soon as she came on the line.

"Much better! They're releasing him tomorrow."

"Great!"

"Congratulations, you ass; I can't believe you conned Eva Marie into eloping."

"Actually, it was her idea," I retorted happily. "It seems she couldn't wait a whole year for me."

"She has all of my sympathies."

"You haven't told Hal about the house have you?"

"I haven't said a word."

"What time will you arrive here?"

"Around noon."

"Eva and I'll meet you at the Pine View Inn."

"Hal wants to talk to you."

"*Hey, Sport! I knew that little green-eyed gal had your number! You didn't have a chance. Another good man bites the dust! Ouch!*" he whined as Elaine popped him in the background.

"It'll take me a week to bring you up to speed when you get back home," I said.

"*I can't wait to get back!*"

"See you around noon then."

* * *

Eva Marie and I stopped by Hal's place the next morning to find Rufus Washington's workers scurrying about hammering at the walls and roof like an army of industrious ants.

"Mr. Washington, can you handle two projects at once?" I asked as he assured us they were ahead of schedule.

"What you need doin', Mr. Henry, Suh?"

"Follow us," I instructed. When we arrived at the mansion, I unlocked the door.

He hesitated, his eyes darting about as he peeped inside. "They say your granddaddy still be here, Mr. Henry," he whispered. "They say that why the new Henrys don't live here no more. That what folks say."

"If he is, I feel as though he's welcoming us," Eva Marie replied solemnly.

He looked at her with some apprehension. "Yes'm, I sure hopes so."

"This place needs a complete renovation," I instructed impatiently. "I want to hire a team of contractors for you to supervise. Mrs. Henry will make all decisions as to colors and materials. Is this something you can oversee?"

Mr. Washington nodded hesitantly. "Yes Suh, Mr. Henry. It gonna take some time, but it something I can handle."

"Good, I want to get started immediately, and I want everything first class."

He turned to Eva Marie. "Mrs. Henry, Ma'am, you tell me what you want and I give it to you. If I do something you don't like, you just tell me and I redo it 'til you happy."

"Thank you, Mr. Washington. I look forward to working with you."

I wandered around behind them as they walked the rooms with Eva Marie describing in detail what she wanted.

* * *

Elaine pulled her old brown Pontiac into the Pine View Inn shortly after noon. Hal, pale and weak, moving with a slight hunch favoring his still-healing chest, hugged Eva Marie gingerly.

"Married life agrees with you, darlin'; you're prettier than ever." He grasped my hand, his grin infectious. "I've about worried myself to death laid up there in that hospital certain you'd end up dead or in jail without me here to watch over you. Why are you staying here instead of out at my place?"

"Actually, you're staying here while I have some renovations done to your place."

"That old place ain't worth the expense, Paul. I hope you're not pissing away more of your money for nothing."

"Let's drive out so you can judge for yourself."

When we pulled up, he got out and stared at the hustling workers as his pack of mangy hounds swarmed around his feet in a clamorous welcome. "What the hell?"

"Your place burned down after Garland shot you," I explained. "Apparently the charcoal grill was knocked over either accidentally or deliberately and set the place on fire. Elaine pulled you out of the fire and saved your life. I'm having the place rebuilt. It'll be finished in a couple of weeks, if you'll stay out of Mr. Washington's way. I've also provided a budget for furnishings."

"How in hell am I supposed to repay you for all of this?"

"It's the least I can do since you almost got killed because of me."

"That's bullshit, Paul. I got shot because I was dumb enough to pull my rifle on Garland for shooting Old Billy."

"Whatever. Oh, and as of now you're promoted to my personal assistant. How does $150 a week and expenses sound?"

"Like it's about three times above scale and a good ways beyond any stupid guilt you may feel about me and my house."

"Good, then I'll expect you to work three times as hard."

"Thanks, Sport, but I can't accept all this. It smells like charity. I knew the risks better than you when I hired on."

"This is not charity. I need your help. I'm thinking about investing in the future of Clayhill."

He cocked his head. "Do you want to elaborate on that?"

"J. R. was already married when he married my stepgrandmother. His first wife was murdered a month or so afterward. The prime suspect was Jarvis Holderman, who was murdered in Louisiana before he could be arrested and brought to trial. The DA is filing charges on J. R. for bigamy. His marriage to my stepgrandmother is invalid; therefore, he has no claim on the Henry estate. He'll probably be charged with fraud in that respect as well."

Hal whistled. "When did all this come down?"

"A couple of days ago. But the important thing is, it seems that the estate is now going to be probated according to my grandfather's will, or at worst, divided between Jerry and me."

"So you've won, Sport. What now?"

"The first thing I want to do is renovate the old Henry mansion," I said as I took his elbow and eased him under the shade of a maple tree where Eva Marie and Elaine waited.

"So exactly how do I fit into that?"

I hugged Eva Marie to me. "For starters, I want you to take charge of getting this place finished so Eva and I can concentrate on our own place."

"You're really going to live in the old Henry mansion?"

"That's what Eva wants."

Hal studied Eva Marie pensively. "Do tell ... what about all the rumors about your grandfather haunting the old place?"

"He's welcome to stay as long as he doesn't become annoying," I allowed expansively.

"Poor guy," Hal sympathized, still watching Eva Marie in an odd fashion. "Why do you want to live in a big old place like that, darlin'? It's more house than five families can use."

Eva Marie hesitated. "I just feel ... drawn to it ... like I'm meant to be there."

Hal nodded, troubled. "Maybe you are, darlin', maybe you are." He turned back to me. "So, Sport, what did you mean about investing in the future of Clayhill?"

"Damned if I know. My little green-eyed queen here wants me to do something to help Clayhill. I'm not sure how yet, but I'm beginning to understand what my family once meant to this community. This place was built around the old Henrys, and right now, thanks to J. R. and his clan, it's almost dead. I'd like to find a way to change that somehow."

He grinned smugly. "The Baron of Clayhill …"

I scowled. "Not royalty, just a solid business investment of some sort!"

"You don't need my help to figure that one out, Sport. Start with the brickyard. Bring it back. That's a good business investment. You've got the natural resources right here in the soil, and it will provide a great employment opportunity for this place, which will also bring back the businesses around the courthouse square where you own almost all of the buildings anyway. And lease out some of your land to farmers instead of letting it sit fallow. Get involved in the local politics. Most of the people holding office today have been put there by J. R., which is almost always at odds with what's best for the locals."

"I'll have Mr. Jackson make some inquiries concerning the brickyard. I don't know the first thing about that business, but I guess I can learn. In any case, I'd like you to be part of whatever I decide to do."

"I'd like to be a part of things too, Paul, but $150 a week is still a trifle high, don't you think?"

"And expenses," I reminded him. "That's just for starters. As we build, we'll adjust as necessary." I offered my hand.

He grinned as we shook. "Okay, Sport, I guess I'm officially your gopher now. Can I have a week off in about two months or so?"

"For what?"

He draped his arm around Elaine's shoulders. "As soon as I get all healed up, I'd like to go on a honeymoon."

"You're kidding, right?" I scoffed. "I take it you're assuming you can find some poor, unfortunate girl somewhere dumb enough to have you in the first place?"

Tears of happiness welled up in Elaine's eyes. "That poor, unfortunate dumb girl would be me, Paul."

I hugged her to my chest. "Bless you, child, for you know not what you do!"

"We'll have the wedding at the mansion!" Eva Marie declared joyfully.

* * *

The following weeks became a blur as I painstakingly hired an army of workers and independent contractors under Eva Marie's exacting specifications. Crews cleaned out the old Henry mansion from top to bottom and carted off the residual furniture for restoration. Others stripped wallpaper from the walls and hauled off truckloads of demolition refuse. Electricians and plumbers ripped out the old wiring and plumbing systems in preparation for the new. Technicians designed a new state-of-the-art heating and cooling system. Landscapers dug up the fountains on the front lawn for pressure washing and resetting, plowed up and reshaped the flower gardens and rosebeds, trimmed the hedges, installed a sprinkler system, and reseeded the lawn. Independent contractors cleaned and resurfaced the pool and tennis courts, reroofed the main house, stables, bathhouse, and barn. Specialists ripped out the kitchen and redesigned it, renovated the bathrooms, and even added a new one downstairs in a former storage room off the corridor by the kitchen. On any given day upwards of a hundred workers busied themselves on various tasks as Rufus Washington supervised the whole operation.

Eva Marie spent countless hours with the upholstery contractors picking fabrics, with the painters choosing colors, with the wall-covering vendors selecting wallpaper, and with the kitchen contractors choosing appliances and refining the design for the new kitchen. By the third week the place looked like a total wreck with gaping holes in the walls, wires hanging from the ceilings, pipes stacked on the floors, carpet ripped up, paint scrapings cluttering the area, and men shouting and almost coming to blows as they hustled about tripping over each other. I mostly stayed the hell out of the way, as Rufus ran roughshod over them and Eva Marie charmed them in the ensuing chaos.

Hal's house was finished the second week he was home from the hospital. He and Elaine furnished it with the allowance I provided.

Hal then assisted Rufus Washington on our home, taking on the most troubling or vexing jobs to get the problems straightened out.

Eva Marie took over the old study and filled it with drawings, catalogs, paint and fabric samples, and architectural plans. She soon drafted her mother and Elaine as assistants, and between the three of them they kept the workers hopping and ahead of schedule. I bought Eva Marie a light blue Cadillac to ferry them to Beaumont, Houston, and Dallas to select window treatments and visit trade shows featuring the latest new home marvels.

Sunday afternoons became a family affair with catered food served amongst the wreckage for my mother, Aunt Kathy, Mr. and Mrs. Sherrill, Sheriff Tate, and Hal and Elaine, so that all could inspect the previous week's progress. Constant streams of locals stopped by to see the renovation firsthand and stood around in groups gawking at the maze of workers. Eva Marie kept coffee, Cokes, and doughnuts available for them and proudly escorted them on tours to view the reconstruction. I was sure the place would never be habitable again, but dared not voice my reservations in the face of her untiring efforts.

* * *

I spent a considerable amount of my time with Jason Jackson and a hired accounting firm getting a handle on the Henry estate assets, reviewing contracts on the house, writing checks to subcontractors, and overseeing the heavy construction phase of the remodeling. On one of my visits to Mr. Jackson's office, I was ushered into the conference room by Miss Gladys to find the county prosecutor sitting at the table with my attorney.

"Come in, Paul," Mr. Jackson greeted. "I believe you know Mr. Jordan."

I seated myself at the table. "The last time we met he was trying to put me in jail for sixty days on a trumped-up thirty-day charge."

Jordan's lips twitched. "No hard feelings, I hope. I was just doing my job."

"One you took great pride in, if it met with J. R.'s approval, it seemed," I countered.

"Mr. Jordan asked to meet with us today," Mr. Jackson injected as Jordan's face settled into a scowl.

"Why?"

Jordan adjusted his tie and opened a file lying on the table before him. "Part of my job is to save taxpayer money by holding down court costs as much as possible. Based on that, there are times when justice is better served by reaching certain settlements with the accused. As such, I have been negotiating with Mr. Coonan concerning charges that have been brought against individuals he represents. As a courtesy, I wanted to discuss those agreements with you and your legal representative."

"I can't wait to see how much tax money you're saving the good citizens of Clayhill," I responded dryly.

Jordan cleared his throat. "Garland Sanders has agreed to plead guilty to arson for the burning of Mr. Sutton's house and for the vandalism of your father's headstone at the cemetery in return for a sentence not to exceed three years in prison."

"When will he be eligible for parole?" I asked.

"He could be eligible for parole in something less than twelve months."

"What about restitution for Mr. Sutton's home and Paul's father's headstone?" Mr. Jackson asked.

Jordan shifted. "Umm, that would be a civil matter, not a criminal action."

I glowered. "He takes a *sledgehammer* to my father's tombstone, *drives* over the fence with his truck, *shits* on my father's grave, and then *shoots* Hal Sutton with a shotgun, kills *three* of his valuable animals, sets his *house* on fire, with *Hal* on the porch *unconscious*, and destroys *everything* the man owns while leaving him with over six thousand dollars of medical bills, and *you're* saying he only needs to spend something less than *twelve* months in jail?"

"There were mitigating circumstances—"

"That's bullshit! You're J. R.'s man, and everyone in this town knows it. Count your days in office, Mr. Jordan; you're going to be my first priority in the next election."

"I warn you, Sir, I will not sit here and be threatened—"

"Please continue, Mr. Jordan," Mr. Jackson interrupted, laying his hand on my arm.

Jordan drew a deep breath. "Jimmy Henry and Dale Colliers have agreed to drop assault charges against you in return for Mr. Sutton dropping the charges against them as accessories to arson. As you can see, this process works *both* ways."

"How convenient," I retorted as Mr. Jackson squeezed my arm again.

"Lastly, J. R. Henry has agreed to plead guilty to the bigamy charge in return for the dismissal of the fraud charge. He will serve a sentence of eleven months and twenty-nine days in a minimum-security facility near Houston, without parole."

"That's mighty agreeable of him, considering he should get ten to fifteen years of hard time," I pointed out acidly.

"Not necessarily," Jordan argued. "One is presumed innocent in this country until proven guilty, need I remind you?"

"Need I remind you that I spent *my* money to get the evidence that I turned over to you, which is in the form of irrefutable written documentation?" I demanded. "If *you* can't get a conviction on those terms, *you* shouldn't be the county prosecutor."

"And what of my client?" Mr. Jackson asked in the strained silence. "What plea-bargain agreement are you offering him on the remaining charge of assault and battery against Mr. Bruce Henry?"

Jordan drew himself up. "I would be prepared to offer Mr. Henry a twenty-one-day sentence and a $100 fine for an admission of guilt."

"That's a reduction of less than one third of the maximum sentence of thirty days and a $150 fine," Mr. Jackson protested.

"Also, he would have to agree to pay all medical costs to Bruce Henry. I'm told that those medical bills are somewhere in the neighborhood of $3,600."

I stood. "We'll see you in court."

"Actually, Mr. Henry, I think you would be wise to consider my offer," Jordan urged. "I believe—"

"Would you excuse us? My attorney and I have personal business to discuss. I've listened to all the bullshit I want to hear in one day."

Jordan closed his file firmly and stood. "Judge Ferguson has rescheduled the trial date for October 15. Until then, good day, gentlemen." He hurried out.

Mr. Jackson sighed. "Paul, you must learn to exercise a little tact and diplomacy."

"I prefer direct and to the point—there's less room for misinterpretation."

"There's one other bit of bad news," Mr. Jackson continued. "Jerry Henry has laid claim to the entire Henry estate as the sole surviving son of Robert Allison Henry."

"*What?* That greedy bastard! What does that mean?"

"It will delay the probate of the Henry estate by several months, possibly even a year. Neither of you can touch the assets of the estate without court order during this period, and then only to benefit the estate or to maintain the estate's assets."

"If that's the way he wants to play the game, then I want to contest it all the way!"

"I presumed as much," Mr. Jackson replied. "Unfortunately, he has also petitioned the court to require you to post a $100,000 bond for the purchase of the Henry mansion in the event he wins his action and the court awards you no assets."

"That bastard!" I gritted.

"It's either that or you must stop your reconstruction efforts, because if he should win, all of the monies you have invested in the mansion would be unrecoverable."

"I'll post the bond. I can't disappoint Eva Marie by stopping her in mid-swing."

"Now the good news. Harry Bradshaw has located one of your aunts, Rose Olivia Henry Davidson, in Tyler, and through her, your other aunt, Alice Jane Henry, currently living in Las Vegas. They have agreed to meet with you here in Clayhill on October 10th at my office."

I shoved my chair back and stalked to the door. "I'm glad to hear *something* is going right!"

EIGHTEEN

I met with my two aunts, Rose and Alice, at Mr. Jackson's office. Rose, in her mid-forties with fading blonde hair, quiet blue eyes, and a slim frame, was accompanied by her husband, Bernie, in his early fifties, thickset, with a balding head buttressed by gray wingtips. From the investigators report, I knew both were schoolteachers in Tyler and had no children. Alice, a year older than Rose, was a platinum blonde with brittle blue eyes, heavy makeup, a trim figure, and a suspicious attitude. Mr. Bradshaw reported she was a former dancer in Las Vegas who had never married. The weathered texture of her skin bespoke a fondness for alcohol, and it was apparent that her career as a dancer had long since passed. Her attorney, who introduced himself briskly as "Joel Small, Esquire," accompanied her. Mr. Jackson gave them a quick overview on the legal ramifications of my claim to the Henry estate and the counterclaim by Jerry Henry as the sole surviving son of Robert Henry.

"How does this concern us?" Rose asked.

"It doesn't at this point," I answered. "I wanted to meet you. I've never had the opportunity to get to know my father's side of the family. I also wanted to reassure you that if I'm successful with my claim against the estate, I'll ensure you get what you're entitled to."

"And what do you think we're entitled to?" Alice demanded.

"I've never actually read the will, but Mr. Jackson can give you the details."

Mr. Jackson picked up the document. "Your father, Robert, anticipated that you would receive an endowment of some two hundred thousand dollars each upon your marrying. Until that event, you were to have a home in the Henry homestead for as long as you had need of it and an unspecified monthly stipend for living expenses. There were also some provisions for land, some ten acres each I believe, if you cared to build a home."

"How much will Paul get from all of this?" Alice asked.

"That will depend upon how the assets are evaluated," Mr. Jackson evaded. "There's also a chance the will may be invalidated and the estate divided between Paul and your half brother Jerry, at which time you would have no entitlements."

"I would like a copy of the will," Mr. Small requested.

"I have taken the liberty of making a copy for each of you." Mr. Jackson handed a copy of the will to Rose and Alice. Alice handed hers to her lawyer, who began studying it. Rose folded her copy and put it in her purse.

"You said upon our marriage? What if we never marry?" Alice asked.

"There are unfortunately no provisions in the will for that contingency," Mr. Jackson replied. "It would be up to Paul's discretion in that unforeseen event."

Alice fixed her hard blue eyes on me. "And if I never marry, Paul?"

I shrugged. "As far as I'm concerned, the money is yours as soon as it's released to me, whether you're married or not."

"That's mighty damned charitable of you. I'll bet you're getting five times that much. Why would you be so generous to us? You don't even know us. I think you're trying to hide something."

I fixed her with a steady stare. "I'm trying to do the right thing, as I'm sure my father would have done if he had lived."

"Nobody gives away four hundred thousand dollars unless they have to. My attorney will get to the bottom of this before it's all said and done," Alice threatened.

"Your attorney is holding the document that controls that, Miss Henry," Jason Jackson pointed out. "That's assuming the will is probated as written. If the will is rejected, there are no provisions for either of you."

"I'll withhold my opinion until I've had adequate time to study this situation," Mr. Small injected. "At that time, I'll render my opinion and advise my client on how to proceed."

"How is Susan, Paul?" Rose asked in the silence that followed.

"She's fine, Ma'am. She lives in Jasper now. I was hoping I could gain some insight from you on my father."

Rose smiled. "He was a good man who lived life with gusto. It's a shame you never had the opportunity to know him. You favor him a lot."

Alice shifted impatiently. "He was as wild as the hills and couldn't do anything wrong in Daddy's eyes. What the hell difference does it make now anyway?"

"You say you're going to give us two hundred thousand dollars if you gain control of the estate, Mr. Henry," Bernie injected. "Are you willing to give us a written guarantee of that?"

"My grandfather gave his daughters that money," I corrected. "Not me."

"You didn't answer the question," Alice snipped. "Are you willing to put it in writing?"

"I believe it's already in writing in the will," I pointed out irritably.

"That's assuming the will is probated as written," Mr. Jackson added. "As I said, there are no guarantees if the court should reject the will."

Mr. Small cleared his throat and looked to Mr. Jackson. "It would seem to me that if the will in fact is rejected, my client would have as much claim to the estate as your client or Jerry Henry. She is an heir as much, if not more so, than your client, is she not?"

"I'm not in a position to render legal advice to your client," Mr. Jackson replied.

"I'm beginning to get the picture now," Alice accused. "You want us to just sit idly by while you grab the lion's share for yourself! Be good and well behaved now, girls, and I'll throw you some crumbs.' Well, let me tell you one thing: that was our Daddy's money! If anybody is entitled to it, it's us, not you. You weren't even born when our father died. How could you be entitled to a damn thing?"

"The will provides that John Allison should inherit the estate," Mr. Jackson replied calmly. "By extension, since John died intestate, Paul is the legal heir of his assets."

Alice glared at me. "Something is fishy about all this, and I intend to get to the bottom of it. You can count on that."

I stood. "It's good to finally meet you, Ma'am. I'm going to leave now before you really piss me off."

"Now hold on here, young man," Mr. Small insisted. "We're not through with this matter yet. It would seem to me—"

"Yes, we're through, jerk-off," I replied. "I've heard all of the insults from your client I'm going to listen to." I turned to Rose. "Ma'am, I plan to do the right thing if I'm successful in this legal action. If you want that in writing, my attorney will be glad to draft up something to give you that reassurance."

I stalked out of the conference room. *So much for kinfolks ...*

* * *

I went before Circuit Judge Ferguson, a tall, taciturn, distinguished man in his mid-sixties with penetrating blue eyes, five days later for my trial on assault and battery against Bruce Henry. Bruce provided his account of the attack, after which Mr. Jordan, the prosecutor, called ten witnesses. Jason Jackson performed a masterful job of cross-examining each witness, even getting seven of them to admit that Bruce had provoked me. I refused to allow Eva Marie to testify, to Mr. Jackson's dismay, and took the stand to give my version of the incident. Under heavy cross-examination from Mr. Jordan, there was no getting around the fact that I had struck the first—and only—blows in the altercation. I was judged guilty on the lesser charge of simple assault and sentenced to serve ten days in jail minus time served, which was one day. The court also required me to pay a one-hundred-dollar fine and reimburse Bruce Henry half his medical costs, some eighteen hundred dollars. Anxious to get the incident behind me, I refused to appeal and turned myself over to the custody of Sheriff Tate the same day to serve the sentence.

Sheriff Tate walked me over to the jail, booked me in, and escorted me back to cell number three, where I found a new mattress installed on the bunk, the whole cell block cleaned and disinfected, and a new card table with two chairs installed.

"I'm placing you on trustee status," Sheriff Tate advised. "I will lock your cell door only at night. During the day I'll allow you unlimited

visitor access to conduct business with your workers and use of the
phone in my office to make local calls as needed. Eva Marie can bring
you dinner every night and share it with you if she wishes. That's the best
I can do. Judge Ferguson could have made it a lot harder on you."

"I appreciate the new mattress and your having the place cleaned,
Sheriff."

My mother and Aunt Kathy took my incarceration in stride. Sheriff
Tate set up a table in his office for our customary Sunday dinner together,
where it was obvious he and my mother were fast becoming something
more than just friends. I was undecided on how I felt about the issue.
Eva Marie had dinner catered in each evening from Pearle's. Hal and
Elaine joined us in my cell, where the three of them kept me up to date
on the renovation progress at the mansion.

Near the end of my incarceration, Alice Jane Henry filed a new
lawsuit against Jerry, Rose, and me for twenty-five percent of the assets
of the Henry estate. A couple of days later, Mr. Jackson received a letter
from Alice's lawyer, Mr. Small, offering to settle out of court for five
hundred thousand dollars cash. I directed him to ignore the offer.

On the ninth day Sheriff Tate released me after I paid my fine and
the medical judgment to the clerk of court. Eva Marie drove me to the
mansion in her Cadillac, and there I found the demolition complete, the
debris hauled off, and the house filled with painters finishing the walls.
I walked around admiring the refinished wood and the new carpet
covering the floors. The kitchen was a masterpiece of ultra-modern
design and the baths superbly refurbished and updated. Outside the
roofs shone with new tile, the fountains flowed, the pool reflected
blue water, and flowers bloomed in pristine beds amid a sea of green,
manicured grass. An eighteen-wheel truck parked at the rear held the
new and remodeled furniture.

A week later scores of laborers set the furniture in place as others
hung draperies and replaced the paintings on the walls. A day later
new silver glistened, chandeliers sparkled, and marble floors reflected
waxed perfection. After ten weeks and sixty-eight thousand dollars, the
mansion stood beautifully restored. Eva Marie ushered me into my new
study to show off the brown leather high-backed chairs, the refinished
massive desk on a new blue oriental rug, and the inviting fire crackling
in the marble fireplace.

As I admired it all, she moved into my arms. "I needed a moment with you before our guests arrive. I'm pregnant."

My heart hammered. "Are you sure?"

"I'm due the middle of April. Are you happy?"

"I'm scared to death!"

We walked out of the study to find my mother, Aunt Kathy, Sheriff Tate, Hal, Elaine, the Sherrills, Mr. Jackson, Miss Gladys, Rufus Washington, and his wife Agnes all waiting expectantly to welcome us into our new home.

"*I'm going to have a baby!*" I shouted as I pushed a mortified Eva Marie to the forefront.

The women rushed to hug her, and the men clustered around to slap my back. Hal then presented me with a house-warming present—a large, glass-framed picture of Eva Marie in the black bikini she had worn at the lake reclining in a sulky, sexy pose on the hood of my Cobra, which he had conned her into posing for while I was in jail. As Eva Marie blushed amid the men's whistles and catcalls, I placed it above the mantel in my new study. Life was indeed good.

* * *

We settled into a comfortable routine, with me devoting myself to matters of the estate and poring over plans for the reopening of the brickyard as Eva Marie continued to supervise the workers in the mansion putting the finishing touches on the place. She hired Sara, a live-in cook, and Angelina, a live-in maid, who moved into rooms on the third floor with their husbands, Ike and Zeke, whom she hired as full-time gardeners and handymen.

On November 14th Eva Marie threw a surprise birthday party for me. She escorted me out to the newly paved driveway of the mansion and presented me with the keys to my father's old truck, which, with Hal's help, she had purchased from Mr. Hiller and had restored. I choked up as I admired it, thinking it the grandest present I had ever received.

After the other guests left, Hal and I ambled into the old music room, now a comfortable den containing a large TV, a stereo, and a pool table. We racked up the balls as Eva Marie and Elaine retired to the sitting room next door to review the plans for Hal and Elaine's impending wedding. Hal ran the table and ended by slamming the eight ball into the corner pocket.

He smirked and held out his palm as I scowled and placed a quarter in it. "You're a pool shark, Hal. That was a nice touch on my father's truck."

He racked the balls. "It's tough getting something for a man who has everything. Mr. Hiller gave us a good deal on it. I ferried it to Beaumont for the restoration. Double or nothing?"

"I prize it as much as your friendship," I said sincerely.

"Aw shucks, you're not gonna get all melancholy on me, are you? What's the latest on the brickyard?"

"Mr. Jackson says the people who bought J. R. out have gone out of business now, but he's located the son of the former owner, who's agreed to sell the land for fifty-two thousand dollars."

"I thought his daddy bought it for over half a million?"

"It was a working business then. They only bought it to shut it down and lower the competition. I've got a group coming in to see what it'll take to get it going again."

"Just wait until the word gets out. The folks around here will be delirious." Hal fired the cue ball and scattered the rack.

"We've still got a lot of obstacles to overcome yet," I cautioned as I eyed my shot. "Not the least of which is getting the court to authorize the expenditure of money to purchase the land and approve the funds to get it going. Jerry is opposing it, naturally." I missed my shot.

Hal walked around the table checking angles for his shot. "I think that jackass has got more Arkansas Henry in him than Texas Henry." He sank two balls before missing the third.

I lined up my shot. "I wish Jerry and I could work together." I missed again.

Hal leaned his tall frame over the table to line up his next ball. "Look, Sport, I don't mean to sound like a disgruntled employee, but you haven't given me anything to do in the last two weeks to justify this ridiculous salary you're paying me." He made the shot.

"Things will pick up soon enough."

He sank two balls in rapid succession before missing. I missed, and he ran the table. I dug a quarter out of my pocket and flipped it to him as a loud, muffled boom reverberated through the mansion, causing him to miss the catch. As the quarter rolled across the floor, we hurried to the next room where the girls, who had been sitting with their heads together looking at bridal gowns, stared up at us in alarm.

"What was that?" Eva Marie asked.

"I thought one of you broke something," I replied, looking around.

Elaine pointed. "I think it came from across the great room."

We hurried across to the study and switched on the lights. A sheet of paper lay in the center of the leather pad on my otherwise clean desk.

"What is it, Sport?" Hal asked as I picked up the sheet and stared at it.

"It's the strange code of some sort my father left in his safety deposit box that I copied in Mr. Jackson's office. I took it out of my billfold a couple of days ago to try to figure it out and put it here in my desk drawer afterward." I opened the top right-hand drawer to be sure it was empty and glanced at Eva Marie standing in the doorway with Elaine. "Did you put it back on my desk?"

She took the paper, glanced at it, and handed it back. "I've never seen it before, and in any case, I don't prowl around in your desk. Are you sure you put it in the drawer?"

"I'm certain of it. I was working at my desk just this morning and would have noticed if I hadn't."

"So how did it get on your desk?"

"I haven't a clue," I replied, mystified.

"Do you think it has anything to do with the noise we just heard?" Elaine demanded.

"There doesn't seem to be anything else out of place in here," I said, looking around uneasily.

"Let's look through the rest of the house," Hal suggested. "It sounded like something heavy fell onto the floor."

When we came out of the study, Angelina and Zeke stood at the bottom of the stairs with Sara while Ike peered down at us from the third floor.

"What was that noise, Misses?" Angelina asked.

"I don't know," Eva Marie replied. "We're going through the rest of the house to have a look."

"That was a shotgun blast, I think," Zeke advised fearfully as he stared about wide-eyed.

We searched every room in the house but found nothing amiss. After we got the staff settled down and back in their quarters, we returned to the study, where I immediately noticed the sheet was missing from my desk.

"The paper is gone," I announced as I checked the floor around the desk.

"What the hell, Sport?" Hal retorted. "I saw you put it right there on the blotter before we left to search the rest of the house!"

"No one could have come in here without us knowing it," Eva Marie insisted.

I opened the drawer and extracted the sheet of paper. "Okay—tell me I'm not losing my mind here, folks!"

"I think that noise sounded like a gunshot too, not like something falling," Elaine said as she shivered visibly. "Should we call Sheriff Tate?"

I laughed. "And tell him what? That we've got a ghost running around playing games with things on my desk and making loud noises?"

"Maybe the old place really is haunted," Hal mused. "Hell, I know I'm sort of spooked by all this!"

"Well, if it is a ghost, it appears he's trying to tell us something," I replied skeptically.

"Like what?" Hal demanded.

Chills chased up and down my spine. "Damned if I know."

* * *

Early the next morning Eva Marie, her mother, and Elaine departed on an overnight jaunt to Beaumont to outfit the new nursery, leaving Hal and me to fend for ourselves. I drove over to Hal's place for breakfast. The hounds interrupted the harmony of the morning with their excited yowling as I watched Hal cook pancakes for us. I went to the front door and found Sheriff Tate climbing out of his patrol car.

He set his Stetson on his head and ambled toward the porch, his manner somewhat skittish. "Morning, Paul. Angelina said I'd find you here."

"Morning, Sheriff. What brings you out this way?"

He removed his Stetson nervously and clutched it to his chest. "I was hoping to have a word with you."

"Come on in. Hal's got a pot of what passes for coffee brewing."

He kicked at the ground with the toe of his boot. "Could we speak privately?"

"Sure, but I swear I didn't do it. Where Hal's concerned, I'd require an iron-clad alibi."

He grinned and ducked his head. "Aw, this isn't an official visit."

I eyed him carefully as a sense of foreboding settled over me. "It isn't?"

He blushed. "Well, uh, you see, Susan is a right fine woman. Why, any man would be lucky to draw her eye."

My stomach fluttered. *Yee gads!*

"Hey, Sheriff!" Hal appeared in the doorway behind me. "Come on in. The coffee just got done brewing."

Sheriff Tate toed the ground again and cleared his throat. "I don't want to impose on you boys. I just came by to have a quick word with Paul."

"Whatever Paul did, I wasn't a part of it. Hell, I probably even tried to talk him out of it."

"He wants to court my mother," I advised weakly, attempting to quell my alarm. Aunt Kathy was right: my mother deserved a life of her own. I needed to be a man about this and learn to live with it. I did admire him more than most men. In retrospect, she could do a lot worse than him. But she was my *mother*, for Christ's sake!

Hal grinned. "You aiming to be Paul's daddy someday, Sheriff?"

Yee gads! I hadn't even *imagined* something as ghastly as *that*!

Sheriff Tate flushed a deep scarlet. "Uh, I'll come back another time."

"You ain't gettin' off the hook that easy," Hal chortled. "We need to know your true intentions before we can give our blessings—*and* we need to lay down a few ground rules."

Sheriff Tate sighed. "You boys are going to make this real hard on me, aren't you? It'd mean a lot to me knowing you approve, Paul."

"She could do a lot worse, I reckon," I said soberly.

"Do we each get one get-out-of-jail-free card?" Hal bargained. "Come on in and have some coffee and pancakes while we negotiate the terms of this."

Sheriff Tate laughed. "Thanks, but I need to start my rounds. You boys stay out of trouble, now." He turned to his car with a lighter step and then turned back to me. "Oh, I almost forgot; Mr. Jackson wants you to come by and see him this morning."

"Why?"

"He didn't say. And Susan mentioned something about fixing dinner for us on Sunday."

"I'm sure that will be fine with Eva. Tell her Hal and Elaine will join us."

Hal turned to me as the sheriff drove off amidst the howling hounds chasing him down the lane. "So how do you *really* feel about him courting your mother?"

I elbowed him aside and turned to the door. "If it makes her happy, so be it."

"He's a good man," he insisted.

Yeah, but she's my mother, you idiot!

A new red Ford pickup turned onto the lane followed by a sedan and pulled to a stop. The driver of the truck got out smiling.

"Hi, Mr. Henderson," Hal greeted. "That sure is a mighty fine truck you got there."

Mr. Henderson held out the key to him. "I'm glad you like it, Mr. Sutton. Mr. Henry ordered it a week ago."

Hal turned to me. "What's the deal, Sport?"

"We need a company truck."

"We do?"

"Yep."

"Why?"

"You've got an old Jon boat out back we need to haul around so you can teach me how to fish. Besides, it beats Elaine driving you everywhere you go. That's bad for my image."

Hal walked around the truck admiring it. "It's a beauty!"

Mr. Henderson pulled out a folder with the paperwork inside. "If you'll sign these two documents right here, Mr. Sutton, I'll get the paperwork completed for you."

"Me sign? I thought it was a company truck."

"Actually, it's a bonus," I replied. "But I'll expect it to be used on company business when the situation calls for such."

"Paul, I can't accept—"

"For Pete's sake, would you quit whining and sign the damned papers before you bore me to death!"

Hal beamed like a kid at Christmas. "Okay, Sport! There's an old black pond down behind the Henry mansion I've wanted to try for years. But I ain't baiting your hook or taking them off the line for you. And you have to clean what you catch, too."

"Let's go see Mr. Jackson and then we'll load up and go fishing," I agreed.

* * *

As usual, Miss Gladys insisted we do the pleasantries, offering her opinion on names for the baby before ushering us into Mr. Jackson's office, where he greeted us in a subdued manner.

He cleared his throat as Hal and I settled into chairs. "Paul, I regret to inform you that J. R. has filed claim on the estate as the illegitimate son of your great-grandfather."

"As my great-grandfather's *illegitimate* son?" I demanded, stunned. "Now where in hell did that come from?"

Mr. Jackson sat down and formed a pyramid with his fingers. "This is a serious challenge to the estate by J. R. If it holds up in court, he could legitimately claim the estate as the sole surviving son of your great-grandfather, preempting claims by you, Alice, and Jerry. At best, we could hope to reduce the estate to half between him and your grandfather. In that instance you three could end up splitting the remaining half if Jerry and Alice are successful with their claims."

I sighed despondently. "So I could get all, half, a sixth, or none of the estate at this stage?"

"That is correct," Jason Jackson replied.

"What is J. R.'s basis for claiming he is the illegitimate son of my great-grandfather?"

"He claims he is a child born out of wedlock to a certain Carrie Rhodes, formerly of Clayhill, and your great-grandfather."

"*Carrie Ann* Rhodes?" I asked, startled, recalling Aunt Elsie using that name for the crying woman put on a train by one of the three men in her vision.

"He claims his mother, Miss Carrie Ann Rhodes, was the teenage mistress of your great-grandfather, James Allison Henry. He claims that when she became pregnant, James Henry shipped her off to his kinfolks in Little Rock to avoid a scandal. She was sixteen at the time, and he was a widower twice her age at thirty-three. Supposedly, he was to later marry her and claim the illegitimate child, but that never happened. Miss Rhodes gave the child the surname of Henry in spite of this and raised him on her own. In the disposition, Miss Rhodes seems quite bitter about the events of that era."

"Let me get this straight. My great-grandfather, who was widowed at the time, got a sixteen-year-old girl pregnant and sent her to live with his relatives in Arkansas. She bore a son, named him Henry, and that man is J. R.?"

"That is what the sworn statement of Miss Rhodes claims."

"And J. R. married Deborah Ann Duboise, fathered two daughters by her, and later committed bigamy when he married my stepgrandmother?" I sat back, bewildered. "So J. R. is my father's illegitimate uncle and my grandfather's half brother?"

"In view of the affidavit, that would appear to be the case."

"Why did the son of a bitch wait all these years to stake his claim?"

"Technically, it wasn't necessary after he married your stepgrandmother. He already had everything until the marriage was invalidated."

"He probably didn't want people to know he was a bastard by birth," Hal retorted. "Well, Sport, let's go teach you how to fish. You might need a way to feed your family before long, the way things are shaping up."

* * *

Late that evening we loaded the Jon boat into the rear of the truck and set the cooler of fish inside as dusk settled around us in a purple glow.

"I can't believe you caught more than I did," Hal grumped as he slid behind the wheel of his new truck and pulled off.

I snickered. "Mine were bigger too."

"Beginner's luck … *what the hell!*" He slammed on the brakes as we approached the rear of the mansion, throwing me against the dash.

I looked to where he pointed and saw the outline of a man staring down at us from a second-story window. "What the hell is he doing in my bedroom?"

"Let's go ask him!" Hal lurched forward again.

When I opened the locked front door, the security system beeped its warning. "That's strange," I observed as I reset it. "How could someone have gotten in here with the alarm on? Where's our staff? *Hello? Anybody here?*" When I received no answer, I hurried up the stairs to the bedroom with Hal following close behind. It was empty.

"Where did the son of a bitch go?" Hal asked, checking the closets.

We walked through the house, finding no one. We checked the windows and doors. All were locked. As we searched the third floor, a loud bang similar to the noise we heard before reverberated through the mansion. We rushed down the stairs to the great room in the eerie silence. Without a word we moved to the study. Hal pointed at the marble fireplace. A large square on the top left corner was separated from the others by several inches. I pulled at it. The marble square swung outward on hidden hinges. Behind the block was a two-foot by two-foot steel safe with a combination dial in the center. I swung the block closed. It fit back into its groove, matching the other blocks. I tugged. It again swung open.

"Well, I'll be damned," Hal swore. "I think this damned place *is* haunted. Do you remember when we thought we saw a man standing in that same window once before?"

"Don't be silly, Hal," I chided uneasily.

"I'm not trying to be silly, Sport! This time I *know* that noise was the blast of a shotgun. That's what killed him, remember? I think he's trying to signal you for some reason."

I studied the hidden safe, unnerved. "I wonder what's inside this thing."

Hal examined it. "We couldn't blow this thing open with a keg of dynamite, but I'm certain he showed it to you for a reason."

"Maybe the locksmith can open it."

"Are you sure you want to continue living here, Sport?"

"If it's haunted, he seems to be on my side," I allowed.

Hal looked around anxiously. "I sure hope he understands I'm your best friend."

"Mister Henry?" Sara called, causing us both to jump.

"In here, Sara," I called back.

Sara came to the door of the study. "I been out getting some fresh vittles. Will Mr. Sutton be joining you for dinner?"

"I'll be having dinner at his place. Where is Angelina?"

"She and Zeke gone to check on her mother. She got the rheumatism bad. She be back in 'bout two hours. Do you need something, Suh?"

"No, that's fine. Let's go, Hal."

I led him back out to the truck, and we drove to his place and cleaned the fish. He set about frying potatoes, hush puppies, and golden brown bass as I used his new telephone to call Sheriff Tate. He agreed to join us for dinner after he heard the menu and the tale of the curious intruder at the mansion. I then called the locksmith and arranged for him to come by the next morning to check the safe.

* * *

"You boys aren't pulling my leg on this now, are you?" Sheriff Tate demanded as he speared another piece of bass. "I've never held much stock with ghosts."

"We're not exaggerating," I assured him. "I don't believe in such either, but you do have to admit the goings-on are strange."

"It downright gives me the creeps," Hal swore as he munched on a hush puppy.

"The locksmith seemed to remember his daddy installing a safe in the old mansion over forty years ago," I advised. "He said he'd research his files to see what he could find concerning it. He agreed to drop by in the morning to take a look at it."

"I reckon I'll mosey on out there with him then," Sheriff Tate allowed.

NINETEEN

The next morning I opened the door for Hal, Sheriff Tate, and the locksmith, who handed me a thin file yellowed with age. I escorted them into the study, where the locksmith examined the safe while I opened the file, which contained two sheets of paper. The first outlined the specifications of the safe. The second was a purchase order signed by my great-grandfather.

"It says here the combination is preset before shipment," I observed. "The combination can't be changed without replacing the locking mechanism."

"I could open it with a torch, but it would probably destroy everything inside," the locksmith informed me.

"Would the company that sold it have the combination on file?" Sheriff Tate asked.

"That company has been out of business for twenty-five years," the locksmith answered.

"If it was preset before shipment, then your great-grandfather probably used a combination he could remember," Hal suggested. "Maybe his birthday or something?"

"It's worth a try," I agreed. "The brochure says the combination is two turns left, one turn right, and then back left." I turned the dial twice left to 4, once right to 14, and then left to 75 and turned the handle. It didn't budge. I wrote down my great-grandmother's birth date and tried those numbers. No luck. I then tried my grandfather's and grandmother's birth dates, to no avail.

"Try little Rose Marie's birthday," Hal suggested. "The one that died so young."

I tried both her birth date and the date she died. "Any other suggestions?"

"What other date would be important to him?" Sheriff Tate asked.

I looked back at the file. "Hal, try 2 twice to the left, 7 once to the right, and then back left to 18."

Hal spun the dial and pulled down on the handle. A soft click rewarded his efforts and the door swung open. "I'll be damned. Where did you get those numbers from?"

"It was the date he signed the contract," I answered.

Hal stood back as I looked inside and pulled out three bundled stacks of money and handed them to Sheriff Tate. "I suspect Mr. Jackson will say this belongs to the estate."

Sheriff Tate looked at the bands on the bills. "There appears to be about six thousand dollars here." He turned to the locksmith. "Roy, would you observe my verification of the amount as a disinterested party?" The locksmith watched Sheriff Tate count the stacks and then signed a sheet of paper to verify the amount of fifty-six hundred dollars present. Sheriff Tate placed the money on the desk and turned back to me. "Okay, what's next?"

I extracted a gold pocket watch with a trailing waist chain and opened the front cover to reveal a faded photograph of a whiskered man in a black frockcoat and a small woman in a dark dress with her hair done up in a bun. The back of the watch held the inscription *James, my beloved son, choose your course with care and stray not from your set path.*

I handed the watch around to the others. "I think the picture is of my great-great-grandfather and grandmother. They probably gave it to my great-grandfather before he left Arkansas to seek his fortune." I reached back into the safe and withdrew a stack of forms bound by a faded red ribbon. The packet contained a series of deeds to land, notes from people who owed the Henrys money, and a ledger of old bank accounts. I handed the items to Sheriff Tate, reached back in, and withdrew a single sheet of yellowing paper with a series of handwritten letters on it, which read:

$m \quad f \quad os$

$b + o = b/o$

$$(ja - b + rm - o) = ra - b \; correct$$
$$(ja - b + ca - o) = jr - a \; wrong$$

I handed it to Hal. "This is real similar to the paper my dad left in his deposit box and we found on my desk the first time we heard the bang."

"Good grief!" Hal exclaimed as he studied it before handing it to Sheriff Tate.

I pulled the sheet of paper from my desk drawer that I had copied from the document in Jason Jackson's office and handed it to Sheriff Tate. "It's a close duplicate of the paper in my father's bank vault, but the handwriting is different. This copy appears to match my great-grandfather's signature on the contract for the safe. The one in Mr. Jackson's office matches my father's handwriting on the inventory list in your office."

Sheriff Tate studied the two documents closely. "But why did your father add more equations to the bottom part of it?"

I reached for the sheet to inspect it. "*Ouch!*" I swore as blood ebbed from a small paper cut on my finger.

"Sorry," Sheriff Tate apologized, handing me his handkerchief to blot the blood. "I must have had a spasm or something."

"It's nothing," I said as I wrapped my finger in his handkerchief and studied the two handwritten sheets.

"Nothing, hell," Hal argued. "It's another signal from your grandfather's ghost, if you ask me. But why would he make you cut your finger on it if he wanted you to have it?"

The locksmith edged toward the door as he looked around uneasily. "Mr. Henry, do you have any further use for me?"

"Thank you for your assistance," I replied absently. "Send the bill to Mr. Jackson's office, if you don't mind."

"And *I* need to get this stuff over to Mr. Jackson," Sheriff Tate added, scooping up the documents and the money.

"I'll go with you," Hal offered. "And draw your pistol until we get out of here, if you don't mind."

"I can't shoot a ghost," Sheriff Tate argued as they made for the door together, laughing.

* * *

The next morning I awoke to find my finger red and swollen. I drove to Hal's place for breakfast.

"You've got an infection, Sport," he advised, eyeing my finger as I held my fork gingerly. "I hope that's not a bad omen of some kind."

We spent the day at the old brickyard with a group of consultants putting together an estimate to modernize the old mill and get it operational. When we returned to Hal's place that evening the girls were waiting filled with excitement from their shopping spree. Eva Marie leafed through a stack of catalogs showing me what she had picked out, while Elaine helped Hal grill steaks for us. While we ate, Hal told the girls about the man in the window of the old mansion and of the discovery in the safe.

"Look at the cut on Paul's finger," he instructed them. "I'm telling you, it's an omen or something. See how it's all infected?"

Eva Marie took my hand and examined the cut. "It *is* infected, Paul." She turned to Elaine. "Do you have any alcohol?"

"I've got a small first-aid kit."

Eva Marie cleansed the wound with iodine and wrapped a Band-Aid around it.

* * *

I awoke the next morning with a low-grade fever and an inflamed hand.

"You're going to the infirmary," Eva Marie ordered.

She drove me to the clinic as I fought nausea and dizziness. The doctor lanced the swollen finger, cleaned it, and wrapped it in a bandage. As we were leaving, the nurse approached us with a worn, clothbound ledger in her hand.

"Mr. Henry, since you're a member of our community now, I'd be proud to enter you in our blood donor book."

"Thank you, Ma'am, but I'm kind of shy about needles," I hedged.

"Oh, don't be a baby," Eva Marie scolded.

"This book goes back for years," the nurse explained. "It contains practically everyone who has ever lived in Clayhill. All of your relatives are in it. It's our way of handling emergencies when they arise, such as with your friend Mr. Sutton. If it weren't for the volunteers on our donor list, he would have died that day."

"Yes, Ma'am, but …"

She opened the book. "Here's your great-grandfather, your grandfather, and your father under the B blood type. Over here are your great-grandmother, your grandmother, and your mother under the O blood type. It's a family tradition." She held out the book for my inspection. It was almost three inches thick, with labels jutting out from the sides of the pages at intervals marked O, A, B, AB. I took the book from her hands.

"Are all of the Henrys in here?" I asked, examining the book, a nagging thought nibbling at my subconscious.

"Certainly," she assured me.

I flipped the pages under the O's and scanned the names. "I don't see J. R. and his clan."

"They're in the 'A' section." She took the book and turned to the *A* section.

I frowned, the nagging thought suddenly coming to the forefront. "Ma'am, what determines the blood type of an individual?"

"The parents of a child determine the blood type of their offspring, Mr. Henry. Why do you ask?"

"I'd like to talk to the doctor, if he's available. I'd be glad to enter my name in here if he'll explain this to me!"

"Are you concerned about what blood type our child will be?" Eva Marie asked as the nurse hurried off to find the doctor.

"I think it's odd that the old Henrys and the new Henrys have different blood types. I'd like to know why. Take this book and go through it while I talk to the doctor. List the blood types of all the old and new Henrys and their wives for me. Look for the blood type of Carrie Ann Rhodes as well."

I turned to meet the doctor. "Hi, Doc. Sorry to bother you, but I need to understand how blood types work, if you've got a minute."

"I understand you're bribing Janice here to get your name added to our donor list. What do you need to know, specifically?"

"How do the blood types of the parents affect the blood type of the child?"

"That's easy," he said, turning to a pad on the counter of the nurse's station. "The blood type of the offspring is determined by this chart." He began sketching a series of letters across and adding columns under it. My heart pounded as I watched. He handed the sheet to me. "Is there anything else I can help you with, Mr. Henry?"

"No, Doc, that gives me all the information I need. I think you just solved a mystery."

"Glad to be of service. Now, if you'll excuse me, I've got to check on a patient." He walked away as Eva Marie brought the book back to Nurse Janice, who supervised me as I added my name, address, and telephone number to the bottom of the B list.

"Did you get all the information?" I asked Eva Marie as we departed.

"Yes. Why are you so excited?"

"Let's get Sheriff Tate to join us in Mr. Jackson's office. I think we've just hit the jackpot!"

* * *

After we'd seated ourselves around the conference table, I pulled out my father's and great-grandfather's lists and placed them beside the notations the doctor had written out for me.

"I think I've solved the riddle of these coded messages. This sheet was prepared by the doctor. It's a chart for determining the blood type of a couple's offspring. Taking my great-grandfather's sheet and applying initials to the code, you can interpret it as follows:

In the first line, *m f os, m* means male, *f* means female, and *os* stands for offspring. The next line reads *b + o = b/o*, which means that a blood type of B in one parent and a blood type of O in the other parent will produce a child with a B or O blood type. The third line, which reads *(ja - b + rm - o) = ra - b correct* means that James Allison, my great-grandfather, with blood type B, and Rosemary, my great-grandmother, with blood type O, sired Robert Allison, my grandfather, who had blood type B, which is correct. The fourth line reads *(ja - b + ca - o) = jr - a wrong,* means that James Allison, my great-grandfather, who had blood type B, and Carrie Ann, blood type O, could not have sired James Robert, or J. R. as we know him, with a blood type of A, so there is no way J. R. was his illegitimate son. That would explain why he never married Miss Rhodes or accepted J. R. as his son.

"Next, if you apply my father's note, which is an extension of my great-grandfather's sheet, you will see that the first two lines of $m + f$ $= c$ and $b + o = b/o$ mean the same thing: male, female, and child; and blood types of B and O must produce a child with a B or O blood type between them. The next line, *1. (ja - b + rm - o) = ra - b* *, says exactly the same thing as my great-grandfather's code, that James Allison and Rosemary produced Robert Allison with blood type B, which is correct, symbolized by the asterisk placed beside it. The next line, *2. (ja - b + ca - o) = jr - a X*, means that James Allison's blood type of B mixing with Carrie Ann's blood type of O to produce J. R.'s blood type of A is wrong, symbolized by the X placed beside it. The next line, *3. (ra - b + oj - o) = ja - b* *, means that my grandfather Robert Allison's B blood type mixing with my grandmother Olivia Jane's blood type of O to produce my father, John Allison, with blood type B is correct, symbolized by the asterisk. Line four reads *4. (ra - b + c - o) = jr - a X* and means that Robert Allison with blood type B, plus Cathie Fields, my stepgrandmother, with blood type O could not have produced Jerry Robert with a blood type of A, symbolized by the X placed beside it. In other words, Jerry Henry is *not* my grandfather's son. In fact, he is most likely J. R.'s son, which was what my father was so excited about, indicated by the last line, which reads *5. (jr - a + c - o) = jr - a* * and means that J. R., with a blood type of A, plus my stepgrandmother Cathie, with a blood type of O, could have, and most probably did, produce Jerry Robert, who has blood type A. As such, neither J. R. nor Jerry is actually a *Henry*."

They studied the sheets, matching the letters with the doctor's blood type sheet.

"In other words, Carrie Rhodes was pregnant by someone else and your great-grandfather knew it," Mr. Jackson mused. "That would explain why she never came forward with a claim on behalf of J. R. as his son until recently."

"It also means that J. R. was probably having an affair with your stepgrandmother Cathie when she was married to your grandfather, and that J. R. got her pregnant with Jerry," Sheriff Tate added. "A logical extension of that line of reasoning is that your grandfather confronted

J. R. and Cathie and that your grandfather was likely killed to keep them from being exposed."

Mr. Jackson nodded. "That would explain why they got married within such a sociably unacceptable short period of time after your grandfather's death. If true, this means that Paul is the *only* heir to the Henry estate!"

"It might even mean that Cathie herself was murdered by J. R. a few years later due to the blow to her head that caused an aneurism to her brain," Sheriff Tate continued. "This thing has all kinds of implications."

I scowled. "I *know* the son of a bitch killed my father, and I suspected he probably had his wife back in Arkansas killed. Now it looks like he may have killed my grandfather and possibly even my stepgrandmother as well. Hell, we probably should look at my great-grandfather's death in a new light too. It seems odd that a lot of the Henrys died within a very short time for J. R. to have ended up with everything."

Mr. Jackson cleared his throat. "The important point here, Paul, is that you're obviously born of the true Henry lineage as verified by the blood types of the two different factions of your family, and that J. R. and Jerry are not. I suggest we get a second medical opinion to confirm what the infirmary doctor says, and that this be kept quiet until it's confirmed since it has such explosive potential …"

* * *

I immersed myself in the complexities of reopening the brickyard, where Hal and I spent sixteen-hour days going over blueprints, running cost analyses, meeting with contractors, and overseeing the modernization of the old facility.

Sheriff Tate conducted a thorough investigation of the Henry blood line. Jason Jackson filed a series of affidavits, sworn statements, and expert medical opinions to support the contention that both J. R. and Jerry were in fact not of the Henry lineage. Mr. Jackson further petitioned the court for use of funds to purchase the land and for the revamping of the brickyard. The court approved the request in view of the growing invalidity of J. R.'s and Jerry's claims on the estate and the looming economic impact these acts would have on the job-starved local community, as well as the enhanced value they would bring to the estate.

Thanksgiving was a big affair at the Henry mansion. All of the Sherrills attended, which I discovered included a large, extended family of aunts, uncles, cousins, and nephews. The smaller Henry clan consisted of my mother, Aunt Kathy, Rose Olivia, her husband Bernie, and me. Alice Jane declined to attend. Special friends included Sheriff Tate; Hal and Elaine; Elaine's parents, younger sister, and grandparents; the Washingtons, including eight of their assorted children and grandchildren; and even Deputy Miller and his widowed mother. It was a gala affair, with mounds of food and goodwill served in the main dining room.

The Henry mansion became the talk of Clayhill at Christmas. Droves of cars passed each evening in a slow procession to view the elaborate decorations and nativity scene adorning the grounds. Electric candles lit each window. White lights covered the trees bordering the driveway. The great room held a fifteen-foot Christmas tree. Soft theme music piped out from hidden speakers in the wall. Eva Marie hosted an open house the week before Christmas for the local community, which attracted an endless stream of curious visitors. Over three hundred people dropped by to sip eggnog and eat finger sandwiches as they milled about in the great room with its lights, music, and blazing fireplace to speak fondly of the olden days when the Henry clan hosted such shindigs.

New Year's Eve worked its way into a black-tie affair held in the great ballroom. The free flowing party poured out onto the lawn at midnight to stare up at the fireworks Eva Marie had arranged to ring in the new year. Happy couples kissed and cheered with their glasses of champagne to the orchestra's striking rendition of *Auld Lang Sine*.

Easter brought a massive egg hunt, where kids ten and under searched for the hundreds of brightly colored eggs hidden in the grass behind the mansion. Each child received a decorative basket containing candy and fruits as the adults watched the scramble in amusement. Afterward everyone helped themselves to abundant food from tables set up around the pool and enjoyed four separate church choirs singing religious hymns for their entertainment.

Eva Marie grew larger with each passing month. By April she resembled a windup toy woman who had swallowed a basketball and waddled around like a penguin as she attended to every detail of the estate. On the fifteenth of April, our former wedding day, she delivered a six-pound, eleven-ounce baby boy into my petrified arms. I lay beside my exhausted wife as I held the tiny infant and stared down into its red, wrinkled face in wonder while Eva Marie smiled at us in satisfaction, her emerald eyes filled with love.

The mansion filled with well-wishers bearing baby gifts as all of Clayhill celebrated with us. Mrs. Sherrill, my mother, and Aunt Kathy rushed in to help Eva Marie tend to our newborn son, each fussing over him and awaiting her turn to smother him with love. Hal was selected as official godfather and Elaine as godmother of the infant. Eva Marie insisted on naming him John Allison Henry in honor of my father.

May brought the biggest wedding Clayhill had seen in ages as Hal and Elaine exchanged vows under the new gazebo beside the pool on the mansion grounds. Every surface was adorned with mounds of flowers and strings of colorful ribbons. A reception with a live band was held in the ballroom. Tables laden with food stood among guests raising their glasses in toast prior to the couple departing on their honeymoon to the Bahamas.

July 4th renewed the Henry tradition of inviting every citizen of Clayhill to an outdoor bash. Cauldrons of baked beans simmered in great iron pots surrounded by tubs of iced soft drinks. Barbeque roasted over glowing beds of hickory coals, the tantalizing smell making mouths water in anticipation. Over seven hundred people attended the event, in effect every able-bodied man, woman, and child in the town. Platforms built for dancing were crowded below stages holding two live bands. All had a great time with kids running wild and splashing in the pool, while adults frolicked together in a contented tide of newfound goodwill. The climax of the social event left all weeping with pride as a gigantic fireworks display lit the night sky and patriotic theme music floated over the hushed crowd in celebration of our nation's birthday.

Two weeks later I escorted Eva Marie back to New Orleans for our anniversary. There we spent a glorious week rediscovering each other and reaffirming our love. My mother, Aunt Kathy, and Mrs. Sherrill tried to outdo each other spoiling Little John, as our son was by now called, in our absence.

Throughout these times the citizens of Clayhill watched the brickyard progress steadily, awaiting the expected employment opportunities and economic turnaround it would bring. Hiring started the first week of August. By the end of the month the plant was operating at full capacity with a two-month backlog of orders for our product. The empty buildings around the courthouse square blossomed with new stores and shops. Even finding a parking spot was a problem. New houses were under construction, and old ones were being refurbished to meet the demands of the swollen workforce. Pearle's bustled under a complete renovation in spite of two new restaurants that opened, and Eva Marie headed a community drive to upgrade the clinic to a small hospital.

In the dizzy swirl of events, no one paid any attention to the small paragraph in the newly opened *Clayhill Gazette* that ran on September 22 reporting J. R.'s release from prison after serving eleven months and twenty-nine days for bigamy, his former dark domination of the town having slipped into little more than an unpleasant memory from the past. Three weeks later Garland Sanders's parole from prison after serving thirteen months for arson attracted even less notice.

Eva Marie hosted a costume ball at the Henry mansion for Halloween, where two hundred guests dressed in their most outlandish outfits attempted to win door prizes for the most original costume. The younger children reveled in their own party in the pool house, while the teenagers enjoyed a rollicking costumed barn dance in the old stable house, each festooned with green-faced witches, robed wizards, evil blood-sucking Draculas, and sinister horned devils. The party lasted until long after midnight with all present swearing it was the finest event they had ever attended.

* * *

The first week of November brought the joyful news that Eva Marie was again pregnant, and less than a week later Elaine and Hal made their own happy announcement that she was with child. Late in the evening of November 13, with Little John put to bed and attended to by his new nanny, Constance, Hal and I shot pool in the game room while Eva Marie and Elaine huddled over catalogs in the sitting room looking at nursery furnishings.

I leaned across the table to make an improbable shot. "So what's Eva got planned for me tomorrow?"

Hal snickered when I missed and chalked his stick. "I don't follow you, Sport. What's tomorrow?"

"Don't pretend you don't know it's my birthday. What's she up to?"

He tapped in his ball and switched ends of the table. "Sorry, Sport, don't know what you're talking about." He missed and scowled.

"It's us against the women," I warned as I lined up my shot. "You remember who your friends are when it counts." I slammed the ball into the corner pocket with authority.

"You couldn't make that again in five tries," he complained.

"Don't change the subject. What am I walking into tomorrow? A surprise birthday party with five hundred guests or some sort of trip disguised as a vacation to get me away from the brickyard for a week or two?" I rolled my next ball in and walked around eyeing the table.

"You could use a few days off. Damn if you ain't grouchier than a wet she-dog with half a dozen starving pups hanging off her tits these days. You've been working too hard. We could all use a break from you, if the truth be known."

"So it's to be a trip, is it? Where to?" I missed and grimaced.

"I ain't said nothin' about no trip," he argued as he sank his last ball and followed the cue ball with his eyes as it banked off the rim.

"You're a crook, Hal. You always let me get a glimpse of victory and then run the damned table on me. If you didn't say it was a surprise vacation, what did you say?"

"I didn't say anything about a surprise anything. Besides, beating you is easy when you get all your balls outta the way for me. I'm calling the eight in the side pocket."

"That's too easy. Double or nothing says you can't put it in the corner pocket."

He eyed the angle. "You're on, Sport."

"So what are you saying, then? What does she have planned for me?"

"Do I look like Eva Marie's social secretary? What makes you think she confides in me about such trivia?"

"You're a lying dog, Hal. I'd tell you."

"Sure you would, Sport, just like you did when Elaine dragged me off to Vegas for four days on *my* birthday." He cut the eight ball and it dropped in the corner pocket in a slow roll as he grinned and held out his palm.

"You're a sorry excuse for a friend," I swore as I dug in my pocket.

He reached for the rack and flinched as a loud, muffled boom reverberated through the mansion. "*What the hell?*"

I followed as he hurried out to the great room, where the girls appeared at almost the same instant.

"It sounded like that ghost again," Elaine exclaimed, her face ashen.

"Mrs. Henry, what that loud noise was?" Sara called from the banister on the third floor. Zeke, Ike, and Angelina hovered just behind her wide-eyed. Constance appeared out of the nursery on the second floor with Little John on her shoulder.

"It was nothing," Eva Marie reassured them. "Please go back to bed."

They turned back to their rooms, expressions doubtful as I led the way across to the study and switched on the lights.

"It's like a deep-freeze in here," Hal swore, shivering in the frigid air.

I surveyed the scattered ledgers and papers lying about on my desk. "I don't see anything out of place."

Elaine rubbed her arms against the cold. "It was definitely the same noise."

Eva Marie pointed. "Look at the fireplace."

We turned to observe a wisp of smoke hanging in the air.

I walked over to the fireplace to peer inside. "There hasn't been a fire in here since last March. It was cleaned in the spring and hasn't been used since."

Hal moved over to inspect it for himself, leaning closer to stare into the blackened interior. "Then where did the smoke come from?"

"Look!" Elaine gestured to the photograph above the fireplace of my Shelby Cobra with the sultry, bikini-clad Eva Marie reposing on the hood. "The glass is broken."

Hal stared at the picture intently. "I've heard of sharp sounds breaking glass before."

"It's trying to tell us something again," Elaine insisted.

"Don't call my grandfather an *It*," I admonished, trying for humor but missing the mark.

"So what is *he* trying to tell us this time?" Hal demanded.

"Relax, he's a friendly ghost, remember?" I argued.

Eva Marie rubbed her arms. "Paul, I'm frightened."

"Of my grandfather? You said yourself you felt like he wanted you to come here and breathe new life into this place."

"No, of course I'm not afraid of him; I'm afraid of what he's trying to tell us."

Elaine turned to Hal. "I think we need to go home now."

"You can't leave now; Hal's got all my money," I protested.

Elaine hugged Eva Marie. "It's after eleven and this thing has got me spooked."

"I'll pick you up at seven thirty in the morning," Eva Marie promised as she guided Elaine out of the room. "We need to get an early start to visit those nursery stores in Beaumont."

"They're lying," I whispered to Hal as we followed the women into the great room. "Eva Marie's got her helping spring my surprise birthday party on me."

Hal smirked. "The surprise might be that she forgot it *is* your birthday, Sport."

"Remember who you aligned your loyalties with," I warned. "What goes around ..."

"I swear I don't know *nothin'* about *nothin'*, Sport."

"People go to hell for lying," I insisted as I opened the front door.

"I'm innocent, I tell you!" he protested. "I'll pick you up around seven in the morning. We've got an early meeting in Mr. Jackson's office to meet with some new vendors coming in."

I leered at him. "Now I get it: your job is to keep tabs on me and keep me out from under foot until the trap is sprung, right? You don't know nothin' about nothin', my foot!"

Hal followed the girls out onto the porch. "You've got a suspicious mind! I'm your buddy, remember?"

I smirked. "Oh, I remember, and so will *you* when the time comes!"

TWENTY

I sat across from Eva Marie holding Little John in my lap as I fed him his morning bottle while Constance looked on anxiously.

"Constance, please fix a travel bag for John," Eva Marie instructed as Sara placed dry toast and orange juice before her.

"You need more than toast if you're going to be *shopping* all day," I admonished with a secretive smirk. "You're too thin as it is. You need some meat on your bones."

"Missus Eva, Ma'am, Little John, he be balky all night," Constance argued. "He might be coming down with the fever. It be better if you leave him here with me."

"I'll be putting on weight soon enough," Eva Marie teased. "John is fine, Constance. He'll have a good time with Elaine and me today."

"Yes'm, if you says so, but I don't know that for sure," Constance fussed.

"You just scoot on 'long now and do what the Missus tell you to do, and quit being so opinionated," Sara scolded. "Missus can take care of her child. You ain't the only one who can look after him."

"Yes'm, if you says so," Constance pouted as she left the kitchen.

Eva Marie laughed as she leaned forward to tickle Little John's chin. "You're a lucky little fellow to have so many people who love you. Do you know that, handsome fellow?"

"Mister Paul, you gonna make the Missus eat proper before she go out today?" Sara begged. "Lordy, I can't do nothin' with her. She eat like a little bird. Don't knows why I even bothers to cook. It mostly goes to waste, and with all them people starving over there in China. I swear, it just not right." She shook her head, distraught.

"I can't do anything with her either, Sara," I replied as Eva Marie narrowed her eyes at me in mock anger. "She's more stubborn than any mule I've ever seen. She's going to just dry up and blow away one of these days in a gust of wind and I'll have to go to the trouble of finding you a new mistress."

"Well, I don't knows about all that, Mister Paul, I just knows she don't eat enough to sustain herself. She gonna get ill if she don't eat right, I here to tell you that much."

"So what are Hal's instructions for today?" I inquired solicitously.

Eva Marie arched her eyebrows. "What do you mean? He works for you, not me. I'd imagine you'll have him doing the most distasteful job around, as usual."

"I only ask so I can spend the day making him miserable and worrying him half to death," I explained. "Is there anyplace in particular he's not supposed to let me go, or a specific time he's supposed to have me somewhere?"

Eva Marie feigned puzzlement. "I swear you talk in riddles sometimes. You're free to go wherever you want, as far as I'm concerned. I've got enough to worry about without trying to keep up with your and Hal's unpredictable wanderings and mischief-making."

"Here Little John's bag, Missus." Constance said, setting it on the table by Eva Marie. "He be better off here with me today, that what I think. I take him now, Mister Paul. I s'pect he need burping and a change of diaper about now." She took the baby from my arms and propped him on her shoulder as she left the room.

Sara slid a plate of eggs, toast, and sausage before me. "I wish you'd make the Missus eat proper, that what I wish," she scolded.

Constance brought Little John back down to Eva Marie as I finished breakfast.

"I better get going." Eva Marie rose. "I told Elaine I'd pick her up by seven thirty. Since you're riding with Hal, do you mind if we take your car today? The dealership is scheduled to pick mine up this morning for servicing."

"Help yourself. I'll walk you out." I grabbed the baby bag, smugly aware that it was another of her ploys to keep me under Hal's supervision for the day while they prepared my birthday surprise. "I'll take the car seat out of your Caddy and put it in the Cobra."

"I do that for the Missus, Mister Paul," Constance offered as she followed us out the back door to the car. Eva Marie opened the door and worked the seat forward so Constance could put Little John's car seat in the back. When she sat him in the seat he began wailing, his tantrum growing in volume as she strapped him in.

Hal drove up and climbed out of his truck, grinning. "That's a Henry, alright. I could hear him raising Cain all the way down the lane."

"Missus, he do better to stay here with me today," Constance pleaded. "He balky, I tell you. Might be comin' down with the fever or somethin'."

"I think she's right, Eva," I advised. "You and Elaine can't get any *shopping* done if he's going to be fussing like that all day. Constance can care for him better here at home."

Eva Marie sighed. "You're probably right. I just hate not seeing him all day. We'll be late this evening getting back from Beaumont."

"He'll be fine," I assured her. "Hal and I'll look in on him at lunch."

Eva Marie unstrapped Little John and held him up in the air in front of her. "Mommy is going to miss you, sweetheart," she cooed as he stopped crying and reached out to touch her face. "You be a good boy now. I love you, sweetness." She handed him to me and kissed me, squashing him between us as he squealed in delight. "And I love you too, Paul."

I patted her stomach. "You and Elaine drive careful now. We don't need either of you getting into an accident in your condition."

"We'll probably be late, so don't worry about us." She kissed me again.

Hal and I turned toward the porch.

"I take the child now, Mister Paul," Constance insisted, reaching for Little John.

A brutal force slammed into my back, propelling me forward. I instinctively jerked Little John back into my chest as I hit the ground, trying to protect the child with my arms as searing heat washed over me. Little John's face twisted around his open mouth, but the ringing in my ears prevented me from hearing his screams. I looked around, dazed. Constance lay on the ground near me, her face contorted in pain. Hal was stretched out on the ground behind me. Beyond him the Cobra was a twisted, wrinkled mass of flames, with its hood missing. Eva Marie slumped behind the wheel virtually consumed by the blaze.

I ran to the car, igniting my clothes as I clawed through the inferno to pull her from the wreckage. I stumbled away and collapsed across her, covering her body with mine to smother the flames, hugging her to me. I drew back to find most of her clothes burnt off and the hair on her head singed down to the scalp above great red streaks and black splotches clotting her face and arms. I sensed rather than heard the guttural, heartrending scream and realized it was coming from me.

* * *

I fought against my reeling wits, dimly aware of my own pain-filled body, and stood on shaky legs beside Eva Marie's still-smoldering form as the heat from the blazing car seared my flesh. Hal moaned and stirred, attempted to rise, and then collapsed back onto the ground. Constance crawled toward Little John, whom I could hear wailing now, though my ears still felt as if they were stuffed with cotton. I stumbled around to look back down at Eva Marie's unmoving body, her emerald green eyes staring unseeing up at the sky. Angelina, Zeke, and Ike ran toward us, their eyes filled with terror. Beyond them a figure slipped through the woods toward a blue pickup truck parked on the side of the road. A terrible rage grew within me as I recognized Garland Sanders.

I stumbled to Hal's truck, jerked the 12-gauge shotgun from the gun rack behind the seat, and turned back before realizing the distance was too great. I jumped in the cab, fired up the engine, and stomped the throttle as I cut the wheel, digging up clumps of grass as the tires searched for traction across the backyard and Angelina, Zeke, and Ike leapt out of my path. Garland looked back over his shoulder as I roared toward him, jumped into his blue truck and pulled off with his tires kicking up gravel.

I bounced across the field and hit the ditch on the side of the road, leapt precariously into the air, and came back down hard, swerving from side to side as I gained the asphalt, the tires fighting for a grip. The distance between us closed rapidly as I held the throttle to the floor and rammed the back of Garland's truck. Metal crumpled, and I fought to maintain control as he swerved to keep me behind him. I again closed the distance and rammed him at better than ninety miles an hour as we sped down the highway. He slid sideways into a ditch, bounced, and skidded back across the road into the opposite ditch as my own vehicle lost traction. I fought the wheel as my truck spun around in a dizzying circle, threatening to overturn. Garland's truck came out of the second ditch with the tires spinning mud in long trails behind it and regained the road, speeding by me. I spun the wheel and stomped the throttle, boiling blue smoke from the tires as I set out after him again. I again slammed into his rear, sending him fishtailing almost out of control. I jerked the steering wheel left, surged up beside him, and slammed into his side in an attempt to force him off the road. An old Dodge sedan suddenly appeared ahead of us in my lane. I locked up the brakes and turned in behind Garland's truck seconds before I hit the Dodge head on, which swerved into the ditch to avoid me. I glanced in the rearview mirror to see the Dodge bounce through the ditch and career back onto the road. Garland had fifty yards on me as I pushed the throttle to the floor. He locked up his brakes and slid onto a side road. I tore into the turn and chased him down the lane. He jolted to a stop in front of a large two-story house and jumped out of the cab with a rifle in his hands. I bore down on him as the muzzle sprouted orange and splinters of glass flew into my face from the shattered windshield. His eyes widened as he attempted to fling himself out of the path of my onrushing vehicle just before the fender caught him, cartwheeling his body across the front of the manicured lawn.

I slid to a stop as the right window of my truck crumpled amid the report of a rifle. I tumbled out of the driver's side, pulling Hal's shotgun after me, ran to the end of the truck, and peeped around the tailgate as J. R. fired again. My 12-gauge recoiled against my shoulder, knocking him backward into a rosebush as Jerry ran out the front door and fired point-blank at me. The sharp sting of pellets strung my upper body as I returned fire and fell backwards with Jerry crumpling as well.

I looked down at the spreading plumes of blood on my chest and back up to see Jerry crawling toward his gun. I staggered up and limped over to him.

"Don't do it, Jerry!" I gasped as he swung the muzzle in my direction. The impact from my shotgun threw him back in a shower of blood. I limped over to J. R., gasping for breath. "You son of a bitch! I'm going to enjoy killing you!"

"Drop the gun, Paul!" Bruce yelled from the door of the house as he pointed a rifle at me. "I don't want to shoot anybody!"

"Shoot the son of a bitch!" J. R. gasped, his features twisted in pain, his face and arms covered with blood. "Shoot the son of a bitch, Bruce!"

The rifle wavered in his hands. "I can't let you shoot my Daddy, Paul! Please drop the gun!"

"Shoot the bastard, goddamn you! *Shoot him!*" J. R. yelled, still on his hands and knees.

"It's too late, Bruce," I gasped, leveling my shotgun at his midsection. The twin explosions came almost as one. Something slapped my left shoulder as Bruce flew back into the open doorway behind him. I turned back to J. R. as he rolled onto his side and cowered.

"Don't— don't, Paul."

"This is for my father and Eva Marie, you son of a bitch!" I pulled the trigger and got a small *click* in return. I tossed the empty gun aside, staggered to Jerry's prostrate body, picked up his shotgun, and turned back to J. R. as a police cruiser turned into the drive with its siren wailing.

"No! Please don't! Wait!" J. R. pleaded.

The screech of brakes behind me mingled with the roar of the shotgun as J. R.'s head exploded in a gory mass of blood and pink matter.

"Paul! Drop the gun!" Sheriff Tate screamed from behind me. I shuffled around with the shotgun held at my waist as he hurried to me pulling his pistol from its holster. "Don't do this to me, Paul," he begged grimly as I faced him. "Think of Susan!"

I let the shotgun slip to the ground muzzle-first and collapsed onto my knees, my energy fading fast, unable to work my arms to catch myself as I fell forward onto my face to embrace the welcoming blackness.

* * *

When I opened my eyes, I was in a white bed in a white room. I tried to shift but could only lift my head a few inches off the pillow.

Elaine's face appeared above me, her eyes anxious. "Paul?"

I tried to answer but could not move my lips to speak.

"Paul, if you can hear me, blink your eyes."

I blinked.

"You're in the burn unit in Galveston. You've got bandages all over your body. You're tied down so you can't move. Do you understand?"

I blinked.

Tears slid down Elaine's cheeks. "Hal went to the cafeteria to get a sandwich. He'll be back any minute now. Do you understand me?"

I grunted, trying to speak. *What about Eva Marie and Little John!*

"You can't talk. You've got bandages on your face. You were burnt badly in the fire, and you've been shot. Do you understand me?"

I blinked once, and then blinked several times.

"I don't know what you want me to do. Do you need me to get a nurse?"

I forced my head to loll left and right.

"No? Do you want me to get Hal for you?"

I blinked.

"I brought you a tuna sandwich and a soda ... is he awake?" Hal's face appeared over me. "Paul?"

"He hears us," Elaine sobbed. "But I don't know what he wants."

I blinked in rapid succession, locking eyes with him.

His eyes shifted away from mine. "You want to know about Eva Marie and Little John, don't you, Sport?"

I blinked once.

"Little John is fine. Constance and Mrs. Sherrill are taking care of him."

I blinked once and waited.

Elaine wept in the background as Hal's eyes again shifted away. "Eva Marie ... I'm so sorry, Sport ..."

My heart clutched so tight it threatened to stop beating, and I surrendered to the blackness as my soul slipped into a deep, cold void.

I awoke to searing pain. Two nurses worked over me, scrubbing me with wire brushes, removing seared flesh from my arms. The darkness came again. I resisted it, welcoming the pain, wanting it to match the boundless ache eating at my soul, but could not force it back.

I awoke for short periods over the next week, relishing the intense, numbing pain of the nurses working over me. I lay immobile as Aunt Kathy sat beside me talking. I looked away as my mother sat beside me in stoic silence. I ignored Elaine fussing over me, adjusting my bed, fluffing my pillow. At some point I saw Mrs. Sherrill standing by my bed holding Little John.

I grew weary of my mother's silent grief, Aunt Kathy's endless chatter, and Elaine's constant efforts to make me comfortable. I wanted to be alone. I willed them to go away, but one or the other was always there. I refused to look them in the eye or to blink when they tried to communicate with me. I refused to think, for when I did, the grief inside me filled my body with bitter, choking bile.

At the end of two weeks, they removed my facial bandages. I could talk now but chose not to, turning my head to the wall when they tried to converse with me. The numbness inside me matched the mass of unbearable agony outside. I sought the relief of darkness, wanting to stay there forever.

Hal's voice pulled me from the blackness: "... so everything is fine there. Mr. Jackson expects a hearing in the next few weeks to settle the estate. He says it's just a formality at this point. Hey, Sport, I know you can talk now, and that you're just being stubborn. Why do you want to be such a jackass?"

I turned my head and locked eyes with him. "You ... need to ... tell me everything."

He sighed. "Oh sure, you always give me the shit details." His hopeful smile melted when I continued to stare. "Okay, Sport. I guess it's my place since we're best friends.

"There was a gasoline bomb wired to your car. Garland Sanders has admitted to setting it. It was supposed to be his and J. R.'s birthday present to you. Garland's still in the hospital in Beaumont. He has more broken bones and internal injuries than I can name. You busted him up pretty good with my truck, which is a wreck itself now. J. R. and Jerry are dead. Bruce is alive but has lost most of his stomach. They say he'll be a cripple for the rest of his life. We were lucky you two decided to leave Little John at home. You got some pretty bad burns when you ran back to pull Eva Marie out of the flames. It's a wonder you didn't get killed in the fire too, or in the gunfight that followed. You were shot in the face and chest with a shotgun and have a rifle wound to your left shoulder. You've been in the hospital four weeks now. They're talking about letting you go home in a few weeks. Your son needs you, Sport. We all need you."

"Tell me … about the funeral."

He lowered his head. "It was a closed casket. Everyone in Clayhill was there. Everybody loved that little girl, Sport."

"Where did … they put her?"

"In the old Henry plot, next to your father. Mr. Farr is waiting for you to pick out the headstone. People come by every day and leave flowers on her grave." He paused to wipe his eyes, unable to meet my stare. "We all loved her, Sport, and that's a fact." He reached for a Kleenex on the table beside my bed and blew his nose. "Sheriff Tate says he doesn't see any charges being brought against you. They reconstructed the crime scene and said it looked like you chased Garland into J. R.'s yard. Even Bruce admits his father shot at you first. He swears he didn't know J. R. and Garland were planning to bomb your car. They say he was grief-stricken when he learned they killed Eva Marie instead of you."

I turned my eyes to the ceiling as the salt from my tears aggravated the wounds on my face.

"Don't think that way, Sport," Hal pleaded. "This wasn't your fault. It just happened that way through some crazy chance of circumstance. I know I can count on you to be reasonable and think this thing through, right?"

I closed my eyes and slipped back into the welcoming void.

Christmas and New Year's came and went in the hospital. I ignored their half-hearted attempts at cheer and goodwill. At some point I awoke to find Mrs. Sherrill in my room with Little John in her arms. The child looked at my wrinkled, scarred face and began screaming.

"Take him home," I whispered. "Don't bring him back again."

They transported me back to Clayhill in an ambulance the third week of January, after almost eleven weeks in the hospital. I lay on the stretcher in back looking listlessly out the side window at both sides of the old country road leading to the mansion crowded with parked cars. When the ambulance pulled into the drive, hundreds of people stood in front of the house holding banners welcoming me home. When the rear doors opened and they lifted me out, the people began cheering and applauding. The medical technicians wheeled me up to the main doors as two television crews followed, training their cameras on us. Inside my mother, Aunt Kathy, the Sherrills, Sheriff Tate, and Elaine engulfed me as Hal watched from the fringes. After the technicians settled me into my bed, I pleaded exhaustion to get everyone to leave me in peace.

Near midnight, I worked myself off the bed and staggered over to the window to look out, unable to sleep. I was startled to see a dark figure with a rifle drift through the shadows beyond the pool. I stumbled over and clawed the phone off the bedside table.

"*Hello?*" Hal's sleepy voice responded.

"Hal, bring me a gun! Somebody's prowling around out back!"

"*What? Are you sure?*"

"I just saw them. Bring me a gun!"

"*I'm on my way!*"

Minutes later Hal's old partially wrecked truck tore into the drive followed by Sheriff Tate's cruiser. Hal, Sheriff Tate, and Deputy Miller spilled out armed with rifles as I watched from the window. They lowered their guns and turned out their headlights. A few minutes later Hal and Sheriff Tate knocked at my bedroom door and entered as an anxious Angelina hovered behind them.

"Well, Sport, we almost got into a shooting match with Rufus Washington and his crew," Hal reported. "For a minute there we each thought the other bunch were the bad guys. Things were mighty tense."

"Rufus Washington?" I asked.

"Yep, he and a few of his pals decided they'd stake this place out at night for a while."

"Rufus Washington has got armed men guarding my house?"

Sheriff Tate grinned. "About ten of them working in shifts the night through. Said they plan on being here as long as they're needed. I took a minute to swear them in as honoree deputies in case they feel the need to kill somebody. That'll save the city a bundle, but I don't think the city council would argue it wasn't money well spent if I'd put them on the payroll."

"Why are they guarding my house?"

"They want to make sure this thing is over."

I worked my throat as tears slid down my cheeks. "It's ... over ..."

"For you and Bruce, maybe, but some say Jimmy's still swearing vengeance against you. We'll be back tomorrow. Sleep well."

Sheriff Tate led them out as I tumbled back into bed.

Somehow I had to end all of this craziness.

And I had to get away from here. I could not bear the misery of a place that reminded me so strongly of Eva Marie ...

* * *

I recovered in seclusion, refusing to see anyone outside of the daily visits from the clinical staff who came to treat my injuries, keeping myself sequestered in my study or my bedroom. Constance and Mrs. Sherrill took care of Little John, whom I refused to allow near me in my disfigured state. The last week of February the probate court, after almost twenty-two years, released all Henry estate assets exclusively to Paul Allison Henry. The total came to over sixteen million dollars in liquid assets and land, including the brickyard. The next day, I summoned Jason Jackson to my study and spent the better part of a day with him behind closed doors.

On a Friday in the first week of March, I drove myself in my father's old gray truck to the Clayhill Cemetery and stood with bowed head as a crane lowered the new huge white headstone for my father's grave and an emerald green, ten-foot-tall marble sphere for Eva Marie's grave into place. As was the way of Clayhill word spread and half the population rushed out to watch from a discreet distance. Afterward I climbed back into my father's truck and drove through the assembled crowd looking neither right nor left as they called out greetings to me. I stopped at the new Henry plot and walked to the fence to stare at the two new graves beside my stepgrandmother Cathie Fields Henry's headstone. J. R.'s and Jerry's sites had only flat markers on the ground, as once adorned my father's grave, with grass encroaching over the small slabs and weeds choking the earth over the untended mounds.

On Saturday morning Jason Jackson announced I had left Clayhill for an undisclosed destination to undergo a series of skin grafts to my face and body.

On Monday, Mr. Jackson summoned Hal to his office and handed him power-of-attorney papers giving him full operating authority in the running of the brickyard and all other Henry-owned commercial properties. His salary was set at one thousand dollars a week and included a quarterly bonus program based on the profit margin of the enterprise. He also received the deed to the thirty-seven acres his mother had left him that J. R. had taken from him, and the keys to a new, bright red truck.

Later that afternoon, Jason Jackson summoned my mother, Mr. and Mrs. Sherrill, and Sheriff Tate to inform them they were court-appointed trustees to govern the Henry liquid assets comprising a fund of almost eleven million dollars. Each was to receive a fee of twenty-five thousand dollars a year for their services, plus a percentage of profits earned from their collective investment of the funds.

On Tuesday, Mr. Jackson called the Washingtons, Jacobs, and Jeffersons to his office. Each was deeded ten acres of Henry land surrounding their homes. Mr. Jacobs and Mr. Jefferson each received a fifty-thousand-dollar bonus for their loyal support and service to the Henry family over the years. Mr. Washington received one hundred thousand dollars.

On Wednesday, Rose and Alice met with Mr. Jackson at his request. Each received an award of one million dollars. Alice was distraught when she learned she was obligated to give thirty percent of her money to her attorney, Joel Small, as per their contract, and was threatening civil litigation action against him when they departed.

On Thursday morning Mr. and Mrs. Sherrill met with Mr. Jackson in his office and received temporary joint custody of Little John. Under the terms, they were required to move into the Henry mansion to supervise his daily care, for which each would receive fifty thousand dollars a year in personal compensation, and jointly control a one-hundred-thousand-dollar-a-year discretionary fund for household staff and operating expenses.

That afternoon Mr. Dickerson summoned Sheriff Tate to the jewelry store to select an engagement ring, with instructions to present it to whomever he might choose.

On Friday morning Daniel Coonan accompanied Bruce and Jimmy Henry to Jason Jackson's office. Jimmy accepted the house he formerly lived in and five acres of land, and Bruce accepted J. R.'s house and five surrounding acres, both of which properties had reverted back by court order to the Henry estate, along with twenty-five thousand dollars each, in return for their agreement to change their names from Henry to their grandmother's maiden name of Rhodes.

Lastly, Mr. Jackson set up an exclusive account of one million dollars in the name of Paul Allison Henry.

* * *

So now, after all these extensive months of painful physical reincarnation, I held the jubilant telegram in my hands stating my mother and her newly betrothed, Nelson Tate, would pick me up on this, my scheduled discharge date, to transport me back to Clayhill, where the noble populace who had settled into their newfound prosperity were eagerly awaiting my return.

I rose as the nurse approached my door with the requisite wheelchair to convey me to the hospital doors, where I had arranged for my father's old truck to be waiting. I handed her a note to give to my mother upon their arrival expressing my preference that the good citizens of Clayhill await their new Crown Prince and heir apparent to the Henry Empire, Little John, to come of age, as they had so patiently awaited my own return for over twenty years.

I then settled back in the driver's seat to embark on the fearsome journey to redeem my miscreant soul ...

... as so forbiddingly forecast by Aunt Elsie via her magic eye seemingly eons ago.

LaVergne, TN USA
18 November 2009
164556LV00003B/74/P